# A Glitch in the System

K. Y. Kark

Copyright © K. Y. Kark 2022

The moral rights of the author have been asserted.
All rights reserved. No part of this publication may be reproduced, stored in or introduced into a retrieval system or transmitted in any form or by any means, electronic, mechanical, photocopying, recording or otherwise without prior written permission from the publisher.

This novel is entirely a work of fiction. Names, characters, places and incidents are either the product of the author's imagination or are used fictitiously, and any resemblance to any person or persons, living or dead, is entirely coincidental. No affiliation is implied or intended to any organisation or recognisable body mentioned within.

Published by Level Up in the United Kingdom in 2022

Cover illustration by Sippakorn Upama

ISBN: 978-1-83919-465-8

www.levelup.pub

In memory of my friend Eliyahu David Kay Z" L

He turned on the light for all those around him. I see the moon and the stars, and I see his hand in making them a bit brighter today.

# Chapter 1: What's your Starbuck's handle?

The days had been becoming monotonous: the same grind day after day. *Finishing that commission for Z-Project has paid the bills for the months to come, but I cannot just sit here. My solution? Find a job, play some games, and maybe ask out my local barista.* That is how I found myself standing in the overcrowded coffee shop line with business-people late to work, stay-at-home parents with their little ones screaming too loud for eight in the morning, and fellow unemployed individuals.

As I waited in line, I was busying myself by scrolling through the news updates on my phone. I kept seeing headlines such as Rinc to Go Bankrupt? and Will Rinc Bring the Next Generation in Gaming? and other contradictory headlines about Riverlight Incorporated. Another headline that seemed rather prominent was the recorded livestream of the mother of Jeremiah Stone pleading for the police to find her lost son. Jeremiah had gone missing a month or so ago, if my memory of the story was right. However, as a fellow game tester and appreciator of Riverlight's games, I was more ecstatic to see the news about what had been taking them, the largest gaming giant in the world, all of these years. The rumor was that this –

"Hey, hey there Zephaniah, you alright?" my favorite barista asked me with a look of concern etched on her face.

"Sorry Iris, getting stuck in my head again, it would seem."

"No worries, what will you be having today?"

"Umm, let's do the usual today, but now that I think about it maybe we could—"

"Come on, man, I'm going to be late for work," the gentleman behind me gently stated while placing himself next to me.

While I am no stranger to the stresses of the modern-day man, or woman, I was a little taken back and took a step back from the businessman. I turned to Iris, but she was still pointedly looking at only my face and paying the other man no attention.

"Ya, just the usual today, Iris, thank you very much," I said while pulling out my phone to pay for the coffee.

"Of course, if you want to wait around for another half an hour I'll be on break," she said while taking my phone and taping in on her tablet's screen. "We can talk then, if you would like?"

I began to blush at that, but quickly stuttered out, "Ya, umm, yaya, that sou…sounds great, see you soon." With that amazing verbal performance, I stepped away and let the pushy gentleman up to order his coffee and walked over to the end of the coffee bar to wait for my own.

"I am glad you waited for me," Iris said as she took out the seat next to me and sat down. "What was it that you wanted to say to me?"

I closed my laptop lid to give Iris my full attention. "So, I was thinking that, since we both like gaming, we could maybe try out that gaming convention downtown?" Damn, my hands were suddenly so sweaty I couldn't pick up my ceramic coffee mug.

"You mean… like a date?" Iris asked while giving me that side smirk and bringing her cup of coffee to her lips.

"I mean, like we can just go as barista and customer, if you'd prefer?"

"I can confirm that I would prefer the possibility of a date with you, Zephaniah."

"Why is it that you call me Zephaniah, but write Z on all of my orders? Is it because you can't spell my name?"

"Busted," Iris confirmed while hiding that smile behind her cup.

"That alright," I said while mimicking that hidden smile and reaching into my bag for my phone. "If you can just put your number in here, we can schedule our rendezvous location for later?"

"Sounds good," she confirmed while reaching across the table for my phone. "You know that the best time to go would be tonight, before the larger gaming companies are gone."

"So tonight?"

"Sounds perfect, want to meet there at Seven?"

"I can't wait, but now I should get going before I say something that would make you regret agreeing to go anywhere with yours truly," I stated while pulling myself out of the comfortable, broken-in chairs and collecting my belongings off the table.

"See you soon, Zephaniah!"

I returned the wave I saw coming from Iris, and realized I was completely smitten by her red hair. Did I mention Iris was a living red-haired goddess? Or at least that was the opinion of myself and several other individuals in the crowd. This was based on the side glances I was catching from some of the other people in the small Starbucks café towards Iris' direction. None of that mattered because all I knew was that I was riding high on cloud nine.

## Chapter 2: Asp3ct

A few hours before my meeting with Iris at the gaming convention, originally titled Denver's Gaming Convention, I was getting to work. *Sorry, but who is on the marketing team for this convention? Who titles the convention after the city it is in? Never mind, not important.* Anyways, while currently unemployed after finishing the beta testing for Z-Project's new open-world adventure game, I had taken on some pro-bono work for a few buddies who were looking into breaking into the gaming market. Since Riverlight's entrance into the gaming market most of the large gaming companies had either merged with Rinc or closed their doors, except for a tiny few.

That meant that the majority of the players in the field are the small, garage sized gaming companies with their indie titles. With the advances in technology, they were becoming quite impressive, except for the flying horses, and glitchy walls. Happily, I continued to hope for such glitches because it was my job to find them. And when I can't find them, I sometimes create them. Don't worry, I always fix it afterwards, but a man has got to eat. As I thought back to my previous exploits, I begin to have a mental chuckle at one of my previous success stories. It was roughly ten years ago.

I was just about to graduate out of high school: note that I graduated high school at the ripe mature age of fifteen. Now, I will just let you ponder for a second what that meant in terms of a social life. You done? Okay, so it was the exact opposite. I was what the kids are calling Gucci or dope, basically I ran that school. On behalf of key members of the football and other sport communities who were failing school, I hacked into the school system to ensure that they would be getting the necessary scores to continue into college with some scholarships. As you can imagine, everyone wanted to be my friend, assuming that it would result in an extra grade bump. In reality, I just hacked the school out of boredom, and maybe for the attention. However, the Denver Public School system was just not the challenge I needed. As a result, I started hacking bigger fish and eventually found my way into the world of gaming.

The gaming industry had everything I needed. From hacking into the companies' servers to get early releases of video games, and even playing around in their code to fix glitches or create even better glitches. By my senior year of college, I had gained a reputation, but by not being a nimrod I avoided trouble by signing all my work under the pen name Aspect.

In time, I felt that handle was getting too famous and getting too much attention, so I started creating my own copycats. Let me introduce you to Aspect 2.0 and Asp3ct. Today, Aspect is mostly retired, and I believe Aspect 2.0 is working for the FBI, and no, I do not know who copycatted my copycat and ended up making more money than I do. Nonetheless, Asp3ct does pretty well for himself, but I have begun to enjoy the more honest living I make through being a game tester. Hopefully, my mother has stopped reading at this point because I had to admit to using my other persona to help cushion my paycheck, sometimes. Okay, fine! I do it all of the time.

Since my current job was for my good friend Shane, I wasn't going to be adopting my created persona of Asp3ct and create a glitch to solve in order for his company to pay me. See, sometimes I can be a charitable guy. In any case, here there was no need for me to find any problems since they were ever-present before my eyes. In his email, Shane had mentioned one area of problematic code and I checked his email.

*Hey Z,*

*It's Shane, remember we meet at that gaming convention a few years back? Anyways, I was reaching out because I need your help. Several buds of mine and I decided to create a fun steampunk game, but we can't seem to get the flying mechanics down for it to run. Would you mind giving it a look?*

*Thank you,*

*Shane*

After re-reading this email, I decided that I simply needed to ignore the fact that my avatar could see an NPC in the far distance continuously walking into a stone wall. Like, who was I to tell a line of code what they should or should not be doing in their free time? Proceeding forward I decided to blast a couple of hours into the game and try to fix the problem of flying.

"Thank the heavens that is over," I proclaimed out loud while stretching my hands over my head and hearing the satisfying pops from my spine. "Four hours, four damn hours." It was exhausting work, but after playing the game for a few hours I had spotted what was wrong with the flying mechanics in their artfully named city, Cloud City. It then only took me a few minutes to find the error in their code, and now I could email Shane back.

*Hey Shane,*

*So, I see what the problem is. I took a few minutes to get used to the game, and am looking forward to its full release, be sure to set aside a copy for me. I got a look at your code, and it would appear that the algorithm that drives the direction and velocity of the object is incorrect. Hope that helps!*

*Talk to you soon,*

Z

With that little project done I decided to plug some more hours into some of my favorite gaming titles. Glancing down at my watch, though, I saw that it was already 6:15, "Shit, I am going to be late!" Throwing myself out of my office – that consisted solely of my desk and the three-screen wide gaming set-up – I jumped across the living room and into the shower. Somewhere along the way I was able to shoot Iris a text.

*Z: Hey, getting dressed. Can't wait to see you!*

*Iris: See you soon! By the way, bring your A-game.*

Alongside her text she sent me a photo of her wearing my all-time favorite game: *Skyrim.* With that I jumped quickly into the scalding hot water and rinsed off for the evening, but I began to stress out about which shirt I was supposed to wear. All I could say is that "she took my idea."

## Chapter 3: Riverlight Inc. ft. Joshua

In the end I ended up going with a classic T-shirt, *Zelda: Ocarina of Time*. At the end of the day, Zelda is always a solid choice in any given situation. Don't know what game to play? *Zelda*. Conflicted about which character to dress-up as for a convention? *Zelda* or *Link*. Have to bring your A-game to a gaming convention? *Zelda*. It felt like I was going to impress, or at least I felt that looking in the mirror.

No one ever described me as fashionable, but between my everyday Blundstone boots, jeans, and T-shirt I knew that I was, at the very least, immune to critique. With a final glance to appreciate my shirt I headed on out the door to meet up with Iris.

"Zelda? I guess it at least deserves a B," Iris stated with a smirk while glancing at my shirt.

"Hey," I mocked, feigning hurt while grasping at my heart.

"Okay, okay, drama king. Settle down, why don't ya?" Iris retorted with a similar level of mockery.

Returning my voice to a level of normal, "Ready to head inside?"

"Ya, let's do it," she stated while grabbing onto the hook of my arm that I offered to her.

We entered the convention hall at the same time, and it was near magical. I do not know if you have ever been to Denver's convention hall, but it is massive. Heading down the stairs the entire floor was filled with hundreds, or maybe even thousands, of fellow gamers. Walking through tables full of computers, upcoming game flyers, and tiny souvenirs such as paper weights shaped as swords. The sound was also overwhelming as game trailers and playthroughs blasted through their various speakers.

"Wow," we both said at the same time.

"This is impressive, no doubt about it," I said with clear amazement leaking through into my words.

"Let's go check out the Riverlight table," Iris urged while already dragging me forward towards the largest table at the convention down at the bottom of the stairs.

"Why would we go there? They certainly have nothing new coming out this year if they haven't produced anything in the last five years?"

"Exactly, haven't you been reading the new articles?"

"I saw some of them today, something about them going bankrupt?"

"Bankrupt and the rumors about a new release. Supposedly, the last five years have been dedicated to building their upcoming game, or at least that is the rumor."

"Could you imagine what would take them so long to produce?"

"Honestly, it has to be something we would have considered science fiction five years ago. Although, since the market is predicting them to fall under, they are probably feeling pressure to release whatever they have been working on sooner than later," Iris said with a certain gleam of excitement entering her green eyes. The florescent light was glancing off the light green color of her eyes and joined her excitement's gleam to make her eyes shine like precious stones.

"It would have to be," I affirmed. Irish had got me thinking about what project could possibly have taken so long and cost such a significant amount of money as to cause the company to go nearly bankrupt. The company owned so many significant games that they could have survived off those percentages for decades, or that was my feeling. Whatever had caused the company such financial distress must be a rather large deal.

Right before we got to the table, I heard someone behind me scream, "Z!" I turned around, as not many people go by that moniker. Through the sea of heads behind us that were walking in both directions and others who were immersed into the individual tables was an almost seven-foot tall, blond giant heading our direction.

“Shane,” I murmured. Not because I was not excited, but mostly because I did not need Sir Six Pack and Mr. Tall intruding on my date. “What brings you around these parts?” I asked a little louder.

“You know me, cannot help myself but see the potential competition,” Shane said with his slightly off-centered smile while grabbing onto my shoulder and pulling me into a side hug. You know because we are super masculine.

“Who might this be?” he asked me with that same goofy smile on his face.

“I am Zephaniah’s date, Iris,” she stated while grabbing awkwardly onto the hand that was sticking out from my side that was begging for relief from Shane’s hug. I am not going to lie, her saying these words made me feel even warmer than the blood that was rushing into my head due to the previously mentioned hug.

“Nice to meet you madam, I am Sir Shane, but Shane is fine,” he stated, letting go of me, and gracing us with a low bow. Not going to lie, since I haven’t touched my toes since grade school, I was impressed.

“And I, you, Sir Shane,” Iris responded, obviously playing around, as indicated by that same smirk playing along her face. At this I turned Iris around and began to lead her back towards the Rinc table.

“Okay enough, enough, Shane we are about –”

"Oh, hold your horses cowboy, maybe some more proper introductions are in order?" Shane asked, still only looking at Iris.

"Naturally, I stated," using my professional tone to avoid any unintended tones to slip out. "Shane this is Iris, that barista I told you about—"

"Oh, you talked about me, have you?" Iris said, now looking directly at me.

"Well, you know, of course," I continued, a bit startled by my slip of the tongue. "Iris, this is Shane, an old buddy from school and current game designer and part-time white-hat hacker. Now, with introductions out of the way, could we all continue onto the table? I believe that the spokesperson is making some announcement?"

"Lead the way good sire," Shane announced, clapping me on the shoulder. I told myself it was not sore from his rough handling of that aforementioned hug. And with that I grabbed onto Iris' hand, and we headed over to the table.

At the table there was a steady commotion as other attendees began to filter from the tables around and drift towards the display. The cause of the commotion appeared to be someone setting up a mic on the table near the spokesperson for Rinc. I kept hearing random snippets of conversation from all around me, "you think it's about that rumor" and "I heard it is going to be the greatest game ever invented" accurately sum up the topics of these conversations.

That the people of the convention were interested in Rinc's announcement was evident from the dozens of individuals now craning their necks above peoples' heads to get a view of the show.

"I do not know why, but I am having butterflies right now," Iris murmured into my ear and the excitement I saw within her eye became even more pronounced. She began to jump up and down on the heels of her foot as though her tiny body was unequipped to contain her levels of excitement.

"It better be what I think it is," Shane mumbled to me, but due to his ridiculous, and honestly idiotic height, it felt more like he just breathed onto my head.

"Wait, what do you think it is?" I asked looking up towards my oldest friend.

At this all Shane could do was smile down at me because the spokesperson from the largest and strongest gaming company began to speak into the mic.

"Hello everyone, and welcome to the Riverlight Incorporated table. We appreciate all of your continued support in us and our mission over these long years. Today, here across the globe, we are coming to announce the arrival of our first game in almost half a decade," at this he swept his hand back and towards the massive television that appeared behind him. Across the screen appeared the word: *Fabula.*

"*Fabula* is unlike any world imagined before, but, at first appearances it appears like many others. Due to this we, at Riverlight, have decided to embrace the traditional tales found in the magical and fantastical by naming our new world, and game *Fabula*. Unlike many other games, from which we have been given much inspiration, the individual parts of *Fabula* might appear familiar, but how will experience them will be unlike anything else."

"Okay, so it took them five years to create another… what? *Skyrim*, *Witcher*, Breath of the Wild?" Shane mumbled to himself while crossing his arms. Clearly, Shane was not impressed by the game that has supposedly almost bankrupted the company.

"Shhhhh," I hissed his direction, doing the standard finger over the lips. However, I used my imagination and improvised with my middle finger. Yep, I am hilarious.

As the screen behind the Riverlight gentleman began to zoom into the fantasy-inspired world, the crowd began to groan. Despite the repetitiveness of another fantasy, Middle Ages game, the scenes on the screen were breath taking. If I am being honest, they appeared as if they were actual video of the beautiful lands of Namibia, Iceland, and more. I would have sworn that I was seeing the deserts of Egypt, the mountains of Switzerland, architecture of Europe, and more iconic displays of nature. At this point, the moans began to dissipate amongst the crowd.

"I see that I have caught your interest. I can promise you that everything you are seeing are areas within our game. Not only does *Fabula* have some of the best graphics and designs known to man, but, once again, the experience is unlike any other. Thanks to some amazing advances in technology, you will not be experiencing this world through screens, but with your very own senses."

At this point the mood of the crowd felt like a rollercoaster from excitement to disappointment again. While the crowd was hesitant, having heard a dozen such announcements in the past, for games whose additional sensory effects were often lame buzzes or puffs of wind, I already knew that I had to find out more. It was simply fact that a company with the resources of Riverlight was not over selling their capabilities, most likely. As I thought about this, I also could feel Iris literally vibrating with her excited energies.

The speaker could tell the crowd was uncertain and yet his eyes sparkled in a fashion that I hoped meant he was confident he could deliver something unique to every single one of us. "As well, the world of *Fabula* will be entirely free with the purchase of the necessary equipment to enter the game world." At this he swiveled his head back towards the screen where a sleek looking chair appeared. Sorry, that was an understatement, this was the most elegant, beautiful chair I had ever seen. Like would I sell my own kin to purchase this chair? No, but I would hesitate.

"By purchasing this chair and with it the technology to enter *Fabula*, the game is for everyone. I hope that you are all excited to take part in our next journey together because I know that I am." As the man finished speaking a queue began to form of people wanting to either try sitting in the chair or ask more follow up questions to this grand reveal.

As the queue formed and began to lengthen the spokesperson sat down. A muttering began in the people who were waiting or staying to see if there was more, the numbers 07.31 appeared on the screen.

"What does he mean free?" Shane asked Iris and me.

"That is your only question? How about, what does he mean by experience it with your senses or what the deal is with this chair?" Iris asked Shane.

"All good questions, and we are not going to discover the information between the three of us, lets us go ask him ourselves," I stated as I began to elbow the crowd out of the way towards the Rinc employee, hoping that Iris and Shane would follow.

"Hello sir, my name is Zeph, and I was wondering if you could answer a couple of question for me and my friends?" I asked, arriving at the table where the employee sat.

"Of course, but no need for such pleasantries, you can call me Joshua. I hope you enjoyed the presentation," remarked Joshua, along with a glint appearing in his eye, as if he held secret knowledge.

"First off," Iris began, shoving me behind her, "what do you mean by your senses and this chair's technology?"

"Ahh, you caught that," he said while beaming at Iris with the pride of a father in his face. Simply this, through technology installed within the chair you are able to access the world of Fabula as if you are really there. "

"Like, you mean, like virtual simulation?" I asked, my thoughts running through various technologies I was familiar with.

"Rather exactly like that, using the information collected from traveling the globe, numerous volunteers, and assistance through a proprietorial breakthrough artificial intelligence technology, we have created a fully functional simulation. Within Fabula you'll feel the wind in your hair and the water on your skin," Joshua claimed with the expression of utter bliss on his face.

"Fine, but how that does even work?" Iris cut in.

"Unfortunately, I am not at liberty to say, as we are still several months out from release this technology is all very sensitive. However, I can say with pride that it is extremely safe. I hope you all can preorder your chairs soon," Joshua stated in a final manner and leaned towards another future Fabula player who was coming close to the table.

"What the—," I began.

"—hell was that?" Shane finished.

"I do not know, but I am damn sure about wanting to find out more," Iris stated as she moved away from the table.

Then as I began to walk away, I heard from the Rinc table, "Nice to meet you, Z." At that I spun around and looked directly at Joshua through a gap in the crowd; he was grinning and waving at me. I didn't get a word out before the gap in the crowd pulled close and Iris had pulled me away.

## Chapter 4: No Bad Date Ever Ended in Ice Cream

Before I had a chance to pull away from the group to ask Joshua how he knew I went by Z, he was gone and another representative from the company was sitting at the table. Intriguing enough was the simple fact that the name tag on the new spokesperson was also Joshua, but I was sure that is just a coincidence. The same way that I am sure that my stomach pains after consuming copious amounts ice cream have nothing to do with a lactose intolerance.

"Did you all hear what he said to me at the end?" I asked my friend and female companion of the evening.

"No, sorry I was busy dissecting every frame of that game trailer, in my head," Shane replied.

"Well, I am pretty sure that he just called me Z, but I swear that I introduced myself to him as Zeph to him earlier," I responded. However, maybe I introduced myself as Z, I thought.

"Well either he forgot your name and mumbled the first letter, you introduced yourself as Z, or he knows you," Iris stated matter-of-factly while staring off into space, obviously somewhere in her head.

"I guess it doesn't matter," I said under my breath. "Let's get out of here, why don't we?"

"Ice cream?" Iris ventured, but then glanced at Shane. "You are welcome to come along, new friend."

"Nah, I will leave you guys to it, but I don't think I mentioned thank to you Z on that little help this afternoon," Shane mentioned, going in for another hug.

Side stepping the hug and going in for the other standard male greeting, a unique handshake I said, "No worries, I am always glad to help."

"See you guys around soon, I hope," Shane said, accepting the awkward handshake, squid impersonating gesture.

"Bye," Iris and I retorted and gave Shane a few minutes head start before we also left the venue. Therein by avoiding the awkward social encounter where one says toodle-loo and then continue walking in the same direction.

After leaving the venue, about five minutes after Shane's departure, we walked elbows locked towards Iris' car. The evening had rapidly gotten cold but being native Coloradoans, we were prepared with our beanies and jackets.

"Bonnie Brae?" she asked?

"No doubt, I responded," opening her driver door for her and shutting it as she got into the car. Waiting for the car to turn on before walking away I began to dive back into my own head to process the announcement of this evening, amongst other intriguing topics. First off, Iris was amazing. She was into the same games I was, she had spunk, and was just chill. Second off, what was the deal with the game Fabula? Could it be as impressive as Joshua was implying? Lastly, what was the deal with the Rinc dude knowing me as Z? It is not like I am sensitive about being called Z, obviously majority of the world is not going to bother pronouncing Zephaniah (thanks mom). However, I just got the distinct impression he knew me, and that is what made me rather uncomfortable. As I thought about this, I had reached my car and threw my body into the driver's seat while simultaneously turning on the car and heater. It is one of my only talents that I am able to do all three tasks at the same time. With that impressive task done, I pulled out of the driving lot and pulled onto Speer and attempted to catch up with Iris. After all, I couldn't afford to leave her alone with her thoughts for too long or she might begin to debate agreeing to continue the date night.

Driving towards the best ice cream shop in the United States I received a text from Iris, fortunately I was pulling up alongside her a few minutes after her arrival. Getting out of my car I could see her jumping up and down to get my attention in a line that stretched a full city block. I scampered off to her, you know, to avoid any unintentional jiggling of the face cheek region.

"You already this far into the line?" I asked her with a rising suspicion that she was one of those line cutters from the east coast we hear about.

"No, but I did just get here just in time," she responded, at which point we entered the greatest ice cream establishment.

'What will you all be having?" asked the college-aged gal behind the counter in her uniform, the same uniform that has existed for all ice cream parlors since the dawn of man.

"I will be having butter brickle," I responded.

"And I will take chocolate," answered Iris, "with the gummi bears, if you can."

"For sure," she responded already handing me my ice cream and directing us to the counter for payment. Being an individual who was raised by a rather strict mother I did not give Iris the opportunity the play the game of check and just immediately paid for both our totals.

"Thank you, but you did not have to do that," Iris said once she saw me taking back my credit card.

I shrugged, knowing that it was of course expected of me to be courteous in these situations. I gestured towards the outside and we both headed out and found an empty bench alongside the wall of the building. After finding the exact position that brought comfort, I was able to begin with the game of twenty questions.

"Favorite game?" I asked, beginning the game.

"*Zelda: Marjora's Mask.*"

"Favorite book?" I continued.

"Now that is just unfair, cut it out," Iris responded with a tiny laugh.

"Favorite TV show?"

"Isn't *The Office* the only correct answer?" she asked, in response.

"I would have also accepted *Supernatural* or any other decent show with justification," I responded to her challenge.

"How kind of you, okay, but enough questions. Tell me what your thoughts are on that new game from Riverlight?"

"Fable? Fabula? Whatever it's called?"

"Ya, like what do you think that they meant by returning to traditional tales and the whole virtual simulation mumbo-jumbo?" she asked.

"I honestly do not know, but have you ever heard of the anime *Sword Art Online* or read that book, *Ready Player One*?"

"Okay, I know that we barely know each other, but come one, of course I know one of the most popular books of this century and one of the most successful anime shows to exist," she retorted with mocked expression of pain at having been so gravely misjudged.

"LOL," I said mockingly, saying each letter. "I imagine that it is something along those lines."

"That could be utterly fantastic. Imagine, a new world with all the fantasy races, magical abilities, and everything. It would literally, and I mean literally, one of the coolest things to experience."

We talked along these lines for several more hours. About the types of things we would attempt to do in a world such as that. It got so late into the evening that Bonnie Brae had closed its doors and the employees were doing that awkward eyeing of our bench. The signal was becoming clear: please vacate so we can stop pretending to clean and go home already. While there were no hand signals exchanged between me and the employees the message between us was as clear, just five more minutes. With that Iris and I concluded our conversation with a disagreement between who would win in a fight, Gandalf, or Dumbledore. I needn't go into details, but it got nasty.

"Thank you for taking me out tonight, I really enjoyed myself," Iris said as I walked her back to her car. "Will I be seeing you tomorrow morning for your usual?"

"I wouldn't miss it for the world and thank you for conceding the fact that Dumbledore is a far superior wizard," I said. At that last remark she gave me a not to serious shove and climbed into her car. After flipping me off through the window she smiled and drove off, and I headed back to my car. However, before I left, I made sure to thank the employees for their patience.

Upon pulling into my apartment's underground garage, I immediately began to feel uncomfortable. You know the feeling, when you can swear that there are eyes on the back of your neck. This feeling is then followed up by the mental game of chicken where one side says, "if you look behind you then you are chicken" and the other side says, "if you do not look behind you, then it isn't real." In the end, I realized and embraced the identity of a chicken and turned around with a loud clucking sound. I honestly was unaware I was capable of such a feat, but it did help reassure me as I evaluated the half-lit room and realized that I was indeed alone.

Returning to my cozy apartment I went straight for my computer. I sat down for a second and sent out texts to Iris, letting her know I was home since she had told me she made it back safely fifteen minutes prior. I then proceeded to boot up my computer and turn on the screens. My intention was to put a few more hours into an adventure game or look up news on Fabula, but neither intention was realized before I received an eye-catching email notification. All I could see from the top right corner of my screen was the following: Opportunity – Joshua from Rinc.

## Chapter 5: Nothing Suspicious Here

Obviously, I was not going to wait around and check out my emails in the morning. I immediately pulled it up and read it.

*Dear Zephaniah,*

*It was an absolute pleasure meeting you this evening, along with your friends. I apologize if I startled you with mentioning your nickname so casually. I was hoping that we could meet to discuss a business opportunity between yourself and Riverlight Incorporated. I believe that it would be mutually beneficial.*

*Sincerely,*

*Joshua*

*Riverlight Inc., Vice President of Operations*

Naturally, I was extremely creeped out. First off, how did this random dude get my email address and how did he know who I was? However, I am also a man of opportunity, and leaving this emailed unanswered was not within my capabilities, so I immediately responded.

*Dear Joshua,*

*Thank you for your time this evening. Would you mind elaborating on how you knew me before we further any potential business opportunities?*

*Thank you,*

*Zephaniah*

*Self-Employed, CEO*

Naturally, he immediately responded. To be honest, the unease began to leave with his professionality, and my intrigue began to grow. As well, I was offended by his lack of notice of my self-assigned job title, but that is neither here nor there.

*Zephaniah,*

*While I was not expecting your presence at tonight's events, I was grateful for this fateful opportunity that our encounter has brought forth. The company, Riverlight, has run into a slight problem with our upcoming release. While searching for an individual who was suitable to assist in such regards we ran across your name in several recommendations as a game tester who has an extremely accurate skill regarding finding the source of glitches. All of this said, it is also clear that you are quite the successful gamer. With your impressive resume, I was hoping that we could meet tomorrow to discuss details in person. Let us say, 8:00 am?*

*Looking forward,*

*Joshua*

*Riverlight Inc., Vice President of Operations*

One thing will never be said about Zephaniah, that he was an early riser. However, I saw a gift horse and I wanted to look inside his mouth. I responded immediately to confirm the time and receive details for the meetings, which Joshua sent over promptly. Joshua was such a professional, the exchanges almost made me sick, but I was able to fall asleep with the knowledge that I was a CEO while Joshua remained, forevermore, a simple Vice President of Operations.

Upon rising at the crack of dawn I realized something. That word crack, according to my extensive knowledge acquired from the esteemed search engine Google stated that the word had been applied to the sun rising since the 1800s. Why? No one really knew but maybe it cracked the darkness of night. This was nothing enlightening so I moved on with my morning. The usual beginning of the day – a quick run-down Broadway Street; eggs; checking on some Reddit forums – all commenced without much of note, but then my phone went off with a text.

Irish: *Hey, what an amazing night last night. By chance did you get an email from Joshua last night?*

After receiving that text, I also saw that I was left a voice note from Shane in the middle of the night.

Shane: "Hey dude, you're probably asleep, but I have to know, did you get a weird, oddly specific email from that dude from the Rinc table last night? Message me as soon as you are awake!"

Since I am not one for juggling social situations before my coffee, I decided that group texts were all the rage in my early 20s so they could be now. However, I am still a man with priorities, so considering the dire situation developing on my phone I opted for some instant coffee rather than my normal French-pressed brew. Once the cursed machine began brewing my coffee, I grabbed my phone off my counter and began to format the group text.

*You have invited Shane & Iris to a Group:*

*Zephaniah: Hey guys, so you both texted me saying that we all have received a message from Joshua…*

*Iris: Leaving me on read! On such an important, time sensitive message?*

*Zephaniah: Coffee… entering…. my body… soon*

*Iris: Understandable, I personally have not been able to sleep. He asked to meet with me at 8 AM.*

*Shane: Hola madam and sire! It would appear I am also going to be with you Iris for this meeting.*

*Zephaniah: Same here. 8AM downtown.*

*Shane: This is fantastic news! We will be able to uncover this mystery together.*

*Iris: What a bonding experience…*

*Zephaniah: Would have preferred brunch rather than a business meeting.*

*What do you guys think it's about?*

*Iris: I assume that there is a problem with this game, but I am unclear of what he would want with you guys… no offense*

*Shane: I do not believe we ever got to speak on our various occupations, but I am a game designer with decent coding experience.*

*Zephaniah: I thought I mentioned on our date last night. I am a beta tester.*

*Iris: Well, this makes a bit more sense then. I am a bit of a level designer and mighta-sorta have a rather successful run as a gamer on some streaming platforms…*

*Shane: Do we have a celebrity in our midst?*

*Iris: No, nothing that large, but that is the only connection that I can think of… I guess we will find out in about an hour. Ttyl*

*Zephaniah: At least I won't be alone*

*Shane: I got you, my brother. See you in a few moments.*

With that I was able to put my phone down onto the frigid countertop. *At least I won't be alone*, I repeated in my head. With that knowledge the butterflies in my stomach began to dissipate, which I hadn't even been aware of until they were nearly gone. Sitting down and attempting to find news of the supposed *Fabula* game, I saw at once the sites were blowing up. I guessed that Joshua was not lying, the corporation had let it drop worldwide last night. I could already see Twitter's trending threads with hashtags such as #Riverlight #Rinc #Fabula as some of the top ten trends. With the amount of attention that this game was receiving I was beginning to get the good kind of excited for what was to come up in the meeting in, oh canoes! 20 minutes. I ran out of the apartment, quickly throwing on a tie and attempting to juggle the watered-down coffee and my sports jacket. With that successful, I raced down to my car to see what was in store for me at Riverlight Incorporated.

## Chapter 6: How Not to Cut a Deal

The drive down to Rinc's headquarters was not as tedious as one would have expected. While the sky's decision was to bless me with minimal traffic, the gods decided to get retribution within the parking garage. However, due to either an extremely courteous lady or an extremely slow one I was able to snag a parking spot, and I decided there was no need to investigate further on the matter. Leaving the garage and walking towards the headquarters of one of the grandest gaming empires to exist was a sight to behold. The entire sixty-to-seventy-story building appeared to be just one long piece of glass. Through whatever magic is held within the minds of architects or nature, the glass served as a massive reflection of those entering the building. Upon seeing my face twenty times bigger than normal I decided not to investigate the capabilities of my nose-hair trimmer and went inside.

"Is that Mr. Kote?" I heard from a lady behind the receptionist desk within the lobby, right inside the front doors. At my glance towards the desk, she began to walk towards me. She was rather striking, with her blond hair done tightly wound into a severe bun and sharp features: she reminded me more of an airline stewardess than a receptionist.

"That is me, but you can just call me Zeph," I said as she neared me.

"We have been expecting you, Mr. Kote, if you wouldn't mind following me this way," at this she turned and began walking off. I supposed that the expectation was follow or be left behind, so I followed, mentally throwing darts into the bun atop her head.

We arrived at an elevator which opened as we arrived in front of it, and she swiftly entered with me in tow. Swiping her wrist against the sensor on the elevator wall, she pushed the button for the second to top floor.

"You will be meeting with Mr. Sorrento in the board room," she stated as the doors opened and began leading me down the hall towards a see-through door, set in a completely glass walled room. Within I could see a total of six individuals, two of them being Iris and Shane.

The receptionist opened the door and let me enter before announcing, "Hello everyone, Mr. Sorrento will be with you all momentarily." She then proceeded to pull the door shut and walked back the way she came. I was honestly relieved to see her leaving, she was extremely unsettling, reminding me of those Karens who had gone viral all throughout the last few years.

“Thank heavens that you guys are here,” I said walking up to Iris and Shane. As I approached them, I realized I'd interrupted them while talking to another one of the people in the room. Iris turned to give me a smile and grasped my hand to pull me close and Shane placed his arm, unmovable as it was, onto my shoulder.

“Morning Zeph, meet Keila, Keila meet Zephaniah,” said Shane as he painfully gripped my shoulder. Since I was around ladies I decided to not grimace in pain, very masculine.

“Nice to meet you Zepha…Zef—,” began Keila.

“You can just call me Zeph, like Jeff, but with a Z,” I said to Kaila, and the relief showed on her face like dew on grass in the morning.

“Did you also get an email from this Joshua character late in the evening last night?” asked Kaila to the crowd.

“Yes,” the rest of us said in unison, sort of like we had practiced.

“However, I am unclear exactly what is expected of us…,” I began to travel down this train of thought aloud, but then the glass door opened to reveal the man of the hour: Joshua, or Mr. Sorrento.

He walked in with a wide smile across his face as casually as if he were running into a room full of old friends. “Good morning you all, why don't we get started?” he began. “Let us all grab a seat, and we can begin today's meeting,” he said while pulling out the chair at the head of the table for himself.

"I am sure that you have many questions, but I am equally sure that many will be answered during the presentation that I have prepared for you all today. So let us just be patient and grab a chair," he said with a little more push in his tone. With that we all quickly grabbed our seats. I rushed to sit between Shane and Iris but found that Iris had already pulled out a chair for me. Sitting down, I looked towards Joshua and waited to be enlightened on what was going on.

"I emailed every single one of you late last evening with the proposition," Joshua began while turning on the screen behind him to show the company's logo. "For those of you not aware, the game *Fabula* was announced last night. This is an entry that we have been working on for over a decade and has been our sole focus these last five years."

I was unaware that this was being worked on before five years ago, and this made my artificial expectation for the game rise even higher. Buoyed by those risen expectations my eyebrow began a climb of its own accord.

"Indeed," remarked Joshua, acknowledging my eyebrow. "This is set to be our grandest release, and possibly the grandest game to ever be created to date. Using extremely advanced technology we have manufactured a chair, its schematics are in the handouts we will be providing shortly," while saying this line a more detailed picture of the chair shown last night appeared on the screen. "This, coupled with some advancement with our artificial intelligence system, has allowed us to create a game like no other. However, there has been a problem, and I believe that each of you are uniquely suited to providing us the necessary support to get over this last hurdle before release."

"What is the problem that you want us to fix?" asked one of the other attendees down the table. It appeared that English was not his first language with his accent but he pronounced each word like it was his mother tongue.

"Please wait till the end of my presentation, and all the questions will be addressed," Joshua said, a bit too quickly, as if he was losing a bit of his professionalism due to the sudden question. "Unfortunately, there has been a minor setback that has resulted in the game not being ready for release, and such a result is…impermissible. I have followed each of you throughout your careers, or more precisely, I have paid handsomely for others to do this. Due to each of your unique positions I believe that the problem is within your capabilities. However, before I can continue, I must meet with each of you individually."

With that sudden ending to his monologue, he stood up and glanced at the first person to his right, Keila, and asked, "If you would be so kind to follow me?" He proceeded to then walk out the door, expecting Keila to follow, as the receptionist down below expected of me.

"What do you think he is doing now?" I asked, turning towards Iris.

"I expect that he is taking each of us away to have us sign a non-disclosure agreement before continuing on with the presentation," she responded.

"I would agree with this conclusion. However, I find it disquieting that he would be doing this in private with us individually," stated Shane. "What possible reason is there for this course of action?"

"I guess we need only wait to find out, it would appear that you are next, my friend," I said seeing Keila return. "Is it just me or does she seem a bit frightened?"

"I concur," Shane agreed while standing up to go towards Joshua's office.

"I guess we need only wait," Iris said, turning back to sit in her chair staring up at the ceiling. While she was doing that, I was getting myself lost in my own head, and before I knew it Shane was returning.

"It is your turn, my friend, if you are capable, I would decline his offer," Shane whispered in my ear while returning to his seat.

"Why couldn't I? What did he say to you?" I asked Shane, but I could see that he was looking directly past me and when I turned around, I saw Joshua standing outside his office door, waiting for me.

"Hello Zephaniah, or do you prefer Z?" asked Joshua.

"I am indifferent, do you prefer Mr. Sorrento or Joshua?" I returned.

"Whichever makes you more comfortable," he replied. All I knew was that his smile was the most uncomfortable things about this moment. "To make things simple, I am going to be blunt," he continued. "I know who you are, and I am not talking about Zephaniah Kote, but I mean that we are aware that you are Aspect. To be honest, we are not completely sure which or if all the Aspect identities belong to you, but we have enough information to tie you to one or both of these identities."

I was thrown back, at least that is what it felt like. While his sucker punch had no physical impact, it hit me all the same. "Excuse me?" was the best retort that I had lined up in my mind. It was just unbelievable that my identity had been so clearly laid out in front of me.

"I know it is a bit of a shock, but I do not reveal my knowledge, nor did I seek it out for no reason. The company, Riverlight and I, are in a tad difficult situation and your hacking, and gaming experience could be the strength we need to succeed in this endeavor. While I would typically only have you sign a non-disclosure agreement to ensure your silence I cannot rely on this alone. What is to be revealed in that room behind you would potentially lead to this company and millions of individuals facing financial ruin. In order to prevent such a travesty, I and my team have taken several provisions to ensure that those who assist in fixing our problem will remain silent forever. Provisions that involve releasing a file about the activities of Aspect to the proper authorities. I must reiterate, I am not doing this to be your enemy Zephaniah, but simply to ensure yours and mine future, do we understand each other? If not, then I am sure the FBI and others would be interested in asking you a few questions."

I struggled to find words. It wasn't so much that my identity as a hacker was discovered, enough reason and manpower would result in such a discovery. It was that I thought I had been careful to walk a line that ensured that nothing I did made it worth such an effort. To find my identity being used against me was rather shocking. Nonetheless, if it was revealed that I was the same hacker who played around in governmental systems to remove some traffic violations, it would not be the end of the world. That is, assuming the information that Joshua had was from more recent years; if he had anything from a few years back I could be looking at an extensive period in jail. I was sure that the FBI would happily accept Sorrento's information and would probably take little effort on their part for me to end up with severe restrictions on my life going forward.

"Hey there Zephaniah, I am sorry to drop all of this on you here, but I need an answer. Will you assist us with our problem so I will not be forced to reveal your past mistakes?" Joshua asked me with that same smile. I have never been one to find violence an answer, but it was becoming likely that I was going to punch Joshua and his smile.

"If you just sign this NDA right here then we can continue forward like nothing ever happened. Hey, we are friends, or at least potential friends, you scratch mine and I scratch yours. Not only that, but you will receive a generous stipend for your time if you're successful. If you fix my little problem, I will personally delete all the files I have on you and happily hand you a check, what do you say?" Joshua asked, still smiling.

The mention of a stipend piqued my curiosity. "How much of a stipend?"

"Oh, let's say a million dollars? Sounds like a fair price for someone of your expertise."

That was a shocking number. Honestly, I would have done the job without the threat if he had just offered the money. Made me wonder what was worth a million dollars and the threats he was making towards me. I stopped looking at Joshua in his stupid, annoying, vapid, little smile and looked straight in his eyes. "If I fix your problem we are done, right?" I asked.

"Of course, as long as everything that is going to come to pass never sees the light of day, assuming that you are successful, then we are done," he confirmed.

"Give me the paper," I snarled at him. I jotted down my signature, stood up and left his office without glancing once more at that smile. Once I got back to the board room, I saw Shane looking at me hopefully. I simply shook my head and he sunk back down into his seat, clearly knowing that his friend was just as tied into the same crappy situation as he was in.

We continued to sit around the table for the next thirty minutes as each one of us took our time in the hot seat behind that closed door across the hall. By the time the last person returned from the office everyone looked downtrodden, and Joshua was still smiling.

"Hello everyone, once again, apologies for that necessary step in the process. I am sure that you can all appreciate my discretion in that matter. However, with everyone signed on to the team we can continue with the presentation," Joshua claimed with great glee as he sat back down in his original seat. "As was privately discussed, we have an extremely sensitive problem and we needed a team of talent who could be ensured that they never spoke about what I am about to reveal to you." Joshua used his remote to flip the presentation to the next slide. Within the slide was a picture to two individuals, in suits, who were both strapped into the chair previously shown. However, they both had feeding tubes and IVs sticking into their bodies.

"As shown in the photograph our CEO, Dr. Brandon Hobbs, and our COO, Carson Reynolds, entered into *Fabula* to celebrate the final version of the game. Roughly, a week ago they authorized all regional directors and presidents to come forward with the announcement of the game's launch on Monday, which was yesterday. When neither party appeared at the board's celebration yesterday morning the police were called. The police discovered them at their respective homes, it is suspected by me and several others that they entered the game shortly after their authorization. Therefore, we believe they went several days without food or water and were immediately transferred to a clinic on site to be supervised. We have tried every method to communicate with them through the game's code, but there has been no response from either party. Your task is to successfully remove both our top executives from the game and ensure that the game is safe. You all understand, if any word was to get out about either the potential for such an incident or the fact that it has happened to the top people in the company, the company would be forced to cancel the launch and all our shares would bottom out. The result would be the complete collapse of the company, with billions at stake, and if word would ever get out about this problem after the incident is resolved, the same."

Everyone just stood still for a second, I swear that no one even breathed for a moment. At the very least, I know that I forgot how to inhale for a few extremely prolonged seconds. As my breathing returned so did the function of my brain, but I was not the quickest on the uptake. Iris was already belting out a question for Joshua.

"I understand the situation, but I am not a coder or a game designer, sir. What would be my potential asset towards this goal?" Iris asked. It was an understandable question, the problem appeared to be with the functionality of the game's system. It was not comprehensible why Iris would be included in the lineup.

"Miss Christman brings up an excellent point," Joshua replied. "While your skills would ineffective outside the game, we need you and several of this cohort to go within the game and locate the missing people."

"What point would that serve?" I asked.

"Simply put, the game only allows for eight hours of continuous play. At eight hours and one minute the AI of the system will boot you out and you return to your body. If this alone were the problem then it is merely a flaw within the AI, but since neither Dr. Hobbs nor Ms. Reynolds are responding to messages being sent in-game we must assume something else is amiss. Therefore, you, Zephaniah, and Ms. Varner will go into the game to discover the location of our missing people. While that is your mission, Mr. Miller, Mr. Ayad, Mr. Carpenter, and Ms. Schiff will stay behind to investigate the AI of the system. Either we all will succeed and that will be the end of this fiasco and we will be prepared to release the game in the coming weeks," Joshua paused to look at each of us in the eye, "or we will all fail and if Riverlight falls then we all fall with it."

## Chapter 7: Fallout

As soon as that horrendous meeting was finished Joshua left the meeting as if nothing has just happened within this room that was perceivably outside of the normal. However, while he maintained his perky smile, the rest of his victims were not so chipper.

"What just happened?" I heard Iris whisper under her breath. I do not believe it was directed at anyone in particular and just more of a physical manifestation of the shock currently riding throughout her system. All I kept thinking was whether there was a way out of this because while Joshua – sorry Mr. Sorrento since only friends get called by their first name – said that if we carry through on our end of the deal then everything will work out, I felt it was a crock full of… well… manure. We were talking about billions of United States dollars being on the line here. No one was going home without some fall out.

"Shane, what have we gotten ourselves into?" I asked looking towards one of my oldest friends. It did not appear my words reached him until a few minutes later when he looked up at me.

"Z, I do not know, but I know that we need to discuss it, immediately," all of a sudden Shane, the wall of pensive stone, was vibrating with nervous energy.

"I agree, but we cannot talk here. We are talking big money, meaning Big Brother is also probably along the ride at the moment."

"I concur," said Iris from my left.

"As well do I," stated Keila from over Shane's shoulder.

Confirmatory mutters came from the previously unknown entities in the room: Mr. Ayad, Mr. Carpenter, and Ms. Schiff.

"All right it is a party, who is feeling like a cup of coffee?" I asked to the six pairs of eyes looking my direction.

An hour later and we were all sitting around one of the long tables at the same coffee shop I was sat in yesterday morning: Iris' coffee shop, to be precise. Thankfully, Iris knew the staff on shift and was able to score us all a round of free coffee. Slowly, and extremely carefully, I carried five cups of scalding hot coffee across the room and placed them onto the table. Afterwards, I looked to Iris for approval of my success, but she was still rather deep within her own thoughts as she aimlessly poured and stirred sugar into her black coffee.

"Okay, before we begin our debrief on... well... the debrief, I believe a proper round of introduction are in order?" I asked the crowd.

"Ya, sounds good," began Shane, "well I am Shane Miller, and I am a local game designer and I do engage in some hacking from time to time. If you are familiar with the term, white-hat, then you would understand. However, for those who are uninformed, I hack into various individuals' and companies' files and accounts and then assist in securing those channels I used for the benefit of all the parties."

"Thank you, Shane --," I began

"What dart does Rinc have on you?" asked Mr. Ayad, with his accent laying thick in his sentence.

"Dirt, I presume?" answered Shane. "If it is alright with every-one, I would prefer to keep those details close to my person."

"I would agree, I would prefer that information did not farther than it already has," began Keila. "I am Keila Varner, and I write walkthroughs for triple-A games and assist in developing speed running techniques on the side."

"Thank you, Keila," I said. "I am Zephaniah Kote, but you all can just call me Z or Zeph. I am a game tester and also a hacker in my spare time, but not so white-hatted as my friend Shane," I said while giving my friend a closed knuckle taps on his shoulder.

"I guess it is my turn, hello everyone my name is Iris Christman. Like Keila, I mostly develop walkthrough, but I do mine through streaming services. Outside of playing games I am also really involved with gaming strategy and organizing massive raids in some MMORPGs, you know massive multiplayer online role-playing games."

"Kol Khara! What the hell are we doing here?" spat Majed. "I did not come here to have some share circle. We have a job to get done, and that is what we should be focusing on."

"I believe that we need to know who we are working with to be able to be successful. Neither me nor anyone at this table is your enemy," Shane replied to Majed's outburst. "If you would rather not be a part of this group, then that is your prerogative, but I believe that is goes against your self-interest to continue in this manner." At this Majed stood from the table and stormed off behind us, either towards the door or the counter, none of us looked to see where he had gone.

"Why don't we give Majed a minute," said another of our new companions in an extremely calm tone. "I am Conor Carpenter, and I am a freelance coder who has worked in various countries and on various project. I have a particular interest in the idea of artificial intelligence and its role in our data analysis systems in the future.

“Potentially last, but not least, I am Sarah Schiff,” said the last of our team; she began with an awkward laugh at her own joke. There was a polite chuckle across the table from good old guy, Shane. “I am also a coder, and level designer for some open-world games that I have coded on in the past.”

“Okay well, I do believe that is everyone, but Majed, and I believe he gave an introduction of a sort,” I said. “With that out of the way I think we need to discuss what we all just heard from our new employer.”

“Um, ya, if you don’t mind Zeph, I wrote down some quick notes,” interjected Keila.

“Please, the floor is yours,” I replied.

“Okay so we know two primary issues. One: two top Rinc execs are stuck in a game due to a possible error in the AI and/or code. Secondly, the same execs are not responding to messages from the game’s system. However, what we do not know is why, exactly, any of this is happening?” asked Keila in one of those question statements tones.

“As well,” I continued, nodding towards Keila. “Rinc wants two teams, an outside and inside team to combat both problems at once. The goal being to find the people stuck in the game and to find the error that has them stuck in the game. Those who are entering the game risk running into the same potential problem or ending up stuck in the game, hence Sorrento's encouragement for our active participation. Lastly, Sorrento promises a million-dollar payment to each of us upon our success."

"Correct," said Keila with more confidence in her voice. "The consequence of failure is Rinc losing billions in dollars due to an expected market short sell of the company's shares if this goes public. As well, as our secrets exposed," Keila's confidence evaporated as she finished her statement.

"Seems rather simple," said a voice from behind. It appeared that Majed had decided to rejoin. "Conor, Sarah, Shane, and I will work on the outside while you three go inside. What could possibly go wrong?" added Majed with a smile, a smile which although not of the same caliber of Sorrento's, was one lined with pain.

"What could go wrong?" I repeated. "According to the files handed out to us, we are to reconvene at eight AM at Riverlight to begin?" I asked the group. Instead of a verbal response I only saw slumped shoulders, but that was answer enough.

## Chapter 8: Whoever Said Monday Sucks Never Met Wednesday

Dragging myself out of bed I checked my phone, and only saw a few new messages from the night before. The brightness of the screen was causing my left eye to reject being woken and it shut itself in on its own volition. With one remaining eye I opened my phone to read a message from Iris.

*Iris: Hey Zephaniah, I have coffee waiting for you. I just asked the shop for a few days off for some personal stuff but was still able to snag your usual. Want to meet up?*

*Zephaniah: You red haired goddess, let me just get dressed. The usual place?*

*Iris: Sounds good!*

With that bit of a perk up I felt more ready to begin my day. After going through the routine of getting dressed I threw on some joggers and a sweatshirt. While it might appear unprofessional to show up to your first day at the office in joggers, it felt justified given the situation. Feeling even more perked up, knowing that coffee was waiting for me, I headed off to my car.

"Joggers? On the first day to the office?" asked Iris, with a hint of mockery in her voice.

"Let us just hope that it drops that smile from Sorrento's face," I retorted.

"Indeed, I do believe it will," she said while pulling out the car from next to mine and we drove off to our first day at the new office.

We pulled up to the office and turned the car into the dark side of a few thousand pounds of concrete, also known as a garage. Instantly, I was reminded of why I really hated such tight, cold spaces. Fortunately, it appeared the Sorrento had decided to reserve parking for our team. Right next to his spot labeled "VP Operations" were seven spots, each with our last names on the sign. Just because I needed something to smile about later, I had Iris pull into the spot labeled "Ayad," and I was looking forward to seeing Majed's reaction.

Entering the building resulted in the same tightly wound receptionist leading us to the elevator. Without even asking us she swiped her wrist over the sensor and pushed the same floor as the day previous. On the ride up I attempted to make a joke about elevators, but none came to mind. It must have been the music reducing my brain cells; that is my theory because normally I am hilarious. Exiting out of the elevator a few moments later, we could see that the entire board room was covered in stacks of paper with several wall-sized maps taped up onto the glass that separated the room from the hallway. With a nervous glance at each other, we headed towards the room and entered the board room.

Crouching over the table with his dress shirt's sleeves rolled was Sorrento, and he appeared to be labeling a map that was laid out across the entire board room table. With our entrance he glanced up and said, "You guys are the first one here. Why don't you grab a chair and come around to my side? I want to show you something."

Finding no reason to argue we did as he requested. Right when we were able to find two chairs that were not filled with paper, we heard another person open the glass door. Entering into the room was Shane and Keila. "Hey guys, grab some chairs, Sorrento wants to show us something," I said, gesturing to the chairs that we had found. After we all were settled, we looked up to Sorrento who had climbed onto the table to give us the feeling that he was continuously looking down on us, physically and mentally.

"Okay team. So, the three of you," started Sorrento, indicating Keila, Iris, and myself, "will be entering into the gaming world. Most likely, the game will be automatically logging you out every eight hours and that will mean another eight hours of downtime before you are able to rejoin. This was built into the AI's basic functions and removing such a function will cost time that we do not have. As well, since any interference with the code might have unintended consequences. So, you will be starting from scratch with no assistance. Therefore, you guys are on the clock from the moment you enter till you guys return." As Sorrento repeated his facts from yesterday, the rest of the team walked into the room.

"Tozz Feek! Who parked in my parking spot?" snarled Majed at the room.

I am not going to lie; I immediately broke down laughing. I am unsure what came over me, but the stress of yesterday caused this little joke to feel like the funniest damn thing to have ever happened. Unfortunately, the laughter caught on and soon Keila, Iris, Shane, and even Conor were covering their mouths. Majed, seeing that he was not being taken seriously, sat down loudly and crossed his arms while mumbling some other curse words towards our general direction.

"As I was saying," Sorrento said with a stern voice, "Ms. Christman, Ms. Varner, and Mr. Kote will head downstairs to meet with our VP of Design to better describe the layout of *Fabula* and where best to get started on your journey. He should also be able to give a rough idea of where Dr. Hobbs and Ms. Reynolds might be within the game." As Sorrento finished his instructions towards us, he turned towards the other four. "You four will be joining me as we speak with the Chief Technology Officer, Jack Blake, to see where to begin analyzing the artificial intelligence running the game. The plan is us to convene in eight to nine hours to discuss our findings," Sorrento finished saying this while grabbing his items that were scattered across the room and grabbing Shane by the bicep to lead them out of the room. As they filed out of the room after Sorrento, he shouted over his should, "You three head down to Dr. Vanderbelt on the floor below." With that Sorrento and the coders in tow, they exited the floor through the opening elevator.

"I guess it's our turn to figure out what is happening," Iris said, still watching the elevator.

"Indeed," confirmed Keila, who began walking towards the elevators. "At least we do not have to deal with Sorrento anymore."

With that we all exited the room and began our journey to meet Dr. Vanderbelt.

Finding the office was not difficult since the entire floor beneath the board room appeared to be one massive laboratory. It reminded me of the laboratories that are seen in Hollywood movies, except that there were no chemical vials or hazmat suits. Instead, nearly every table had a monitor or a stack of papers. Every piece of empty floor was filled with whiteboards crammed with equations and more maps of the same land mass I had seen Sorrento working on a moment before we walked into the board room.

"Hello there, team," a voice came from seemingly everywhere at once. The speaker had a playful tone, like we were about to go on a tourist trip rather than engage in some nefarious work that we were forced into through blackmail. From behind one of the white boards appeared Dr. Vanderbelt, a rather young-looking female who was dressed in army fatigue pants and a black tank top underneath a lab coat. Her jet-black hair was barely held in place with a black headband that was nearly indistinguishable from the color of her skin.

"Hi, I am Dr. Vanderbelt, but you just call me Sammy," she said while nearly falling over a chair to get close to us. "I am the head designer for *Fabula*, and I was told to help get you guys sorted" she spoke with a voice so full of cheer that it was difficult to not smile at her energy. "Do not worry, I will make sure you guys know everything necessary, and shortly Dr. Jordan will be joining us to get you all situated in your chairs, but in the meantime let us get started."

Dr. Vanderbelt – well, Sammy – said all of that within one breath and immediately started pushing white boards into another other section of clear floor to reveal a solid black, metal door set into the wall. "Follow me, if you will. I want to show you guys something," Sammy continued with a clap of her hands. "Within this door," she continued while beginning to unlock the door with a key around her neck, "is *Fabula*!"

With that we attempted to cross through the precariously stacked piles of paper to join Sammy at the door. She shoved at an apparently heavy door, and opened up into a dark room showing row after row of large black boxes. "This is our server room, where all of the data of *Fabula* comes through. Basically, this is the heart of the game and the heart of Ellie," Sammy said with a bit of pride leaking into her voice. The look she gave the room was one of a mother looking down on their child, it was super creepy. Like I was loving the energy coming off the woman, but I was also getting subtle reminders of the Joker from the Batman trilogy. "Okay, enough of that, let me show you about the game world," Sammy continued. She shoved the door back into its frame so quickly that she had startled me and Keila let out a little squeak and the suddenness.

"If you all can just follow me into this room, I can show you where you will be starting," Sammy said while running to the room next to the server room. "In here we have the entire region of Fabula mostly mapped out and I can show you where to get your journey started." Once again, she was moving so quickly, I was not even able to process all the information being thrown our direction by the doctor. Nonetheless, we all followed Sammy into the room where there was a table as large as the board room covered in maps and outlines of regions. Upon the walls were photographs and sketches of monsters, plant life, and characters. It appeared to be the physical manifestation of Sammy's mind with her chaotic energy. Yet I found that there was a certain calmness to all of the chaos around the room because it just felt right based on our initial impression of Sammy.

"Wait, sorry, Mr. Sorrento, told us that you were going to show us where we would be starting in the game, and where Dr. Hobbs and Ms. Reynolds might be in the game?" Keila timidly asked.

"That is correct, and you must be Keila, right? I am going to show you the area around the starting town for you three and point you in the general direction. Actually, come over here and I can show you right now," Sammy responded while clearing some chairs around here and unrolling a long map that seemingly appeared from under her arm.

We all gathered around Sammy as she displayed the map, it appeared to be of a small town. "This here is the city of Altour, it is one of the starting locations for anyone joining the game in the United States of America. Within this city there are several different areas, all of which will help you all master some of the skills associated with the class that you decide," she said all of this while pointing at various points along the city.

"You will be spawning on the road outside of White Bridge, here," she indicated the spot on the map. "Upon entering the city there are various locations for choosing a deity to worship in the Four Chapels area, in North Town you will find gear, the Silkliff is largely populated with soldiers for sword training. My personal favorite is Shadow Valley, over there, where you can pick up some neat skills from the Thieves' Guild. However, it may be best to avoid that area. We do not need another incident. Overall, it is one of the smaller cities in Fabula, but it has a large variety of options for you three," Sammy finished.

"Wait, are we allowed to choose our playstyles for this?" Iris asked Sammy, with a bit of hope appearing in her eyes. "And what do you mean by incident?"

"That is what I have been told, the job for you is to find our bosses, and you three are the gameplay expert. I just designed the game, I haven't even played it yet," confirmed Sammy, ignoring the second question.

At this I began to get excited and started to imagine all of the different options available in such a large, vast world. From what I had been led to believe and based on the maps around me, this was an insanely large world with various environments and cities to explore. I could have spent hours, hundreds of them, in this world without any issue. However, I wasn't playing the game for the sake of enjoyment, was I? I was being forced into this position, and I was not soon to forget that fact.

"Sammy, where are you thinking that your bosses went in the game?" I asked.

"Good question, gold star to you, Zephaniah. This is what we know: roughly a week ago, Dr. Hobbs and Ms. Reynolds went into the game. Most likely, they spawned in the city of Altour. As there were no request from either one for any specific boosts to our development team, it can be assumed that they started off at level zero and were ill equipped. Since they knew about Altour they most likely entered the city and found decent gear. Afterwards, they could have left the city and gone anywhere, but I expect that was not the case," Sammy started with a gleam in her eye and a manic smile across her face. "I suspect that they went through Widepoint and went northeast towards the closest major city. Along the way there would have been monsters to contend with, but with sufficient wariness they could have survived and made it there. Hopefully, they have made it to the city and are still there. The city is the capital of that kingdom, and a player could spend weeks in the place."

After saying this she stood up and looked at each of us, pointing at a city that appeared to be ten times the size of Altour. "My best guess is that you will be finding them here, but to get there you are going to need to level up and attain some better gear than your starting items." Sammy pulled away from the table and grabbed a white board and a black erase marker. As she started drawing circles in the areas around Altour she said, "these areas have monsters whose levels range from level one to level five. The farther out from the city the tougher that these mobs, sorry I'm switching in gaming lingo."

"That is alright, after all we are all gamers ourselves," Keila said.

"I forgot," Sammy remarked. "I am so used to speaking with board members and non-gamers that it has become my default. The world gets progressively harder the farther away from the starter cities. The mobs you will find in the wild can widely range from level zero up to the high hundreds. In order to prevent the possibility of mobs and banned players from entering cities or regions there are NPC, non-player characters, who guard entry ways along paths and entrances. However, this is not true everywhere, and it could be easy to find yourself in a dire situation if you are not careful," Sammy cautioned. "I would recommend paying attention to some of the classes that we have in the game, and while you guys are doing that, I am going to go find Dr. Jordan," she said, handing out tablets to each of us with data screens for the various classes. "I'll be back in a moment, holler if you all need me, m'kay?"

# Chapter 9: Pikachu, I choose you!

I flipped open the cover over the tablet's screen and looked at the list of options available for the various classes. It looked like there were six.

| Class: Assassin | Class: Ranger | Class: Mage |
|---|---|---|
| Summary: The shadows have always been a home for you. No opponent has been able to stay away from your blades with your quick reflexes and impressive ability to sneak out from nowhere. Many enemies have tasted the poisons that you brew in secret. | Summary: Your knowledge of the art of bow and arrow is incomprehensible. However, this doesn't stop you from taking down your enemies with the collection of spells you have acquired over the years and the blades that you keep close at hand. The woods are as comfortable to you as a city is to most humans. | Summary: The spells that you have acquired over your many years of study have equipped you with the knowledge to freeze, burn, and utterly decimate your opponents from afar and up close. While deadly on the field, your versatility in spells make you vital off and on the battlefield. |

| Class: Cleric | Class: Knight | Class: Paladin |
|---|---|---|
| Summary: The lives you saved will sing your praise. The spells that have been passed down to you allow you the capabilities to push foe to death and friend from it. | Summary: You have bested the greatest fighters in the kingdoms. Your two-handed fight technique is revered and feared. Outside of your unparalleled fighting capabilities you are also a steadfast leader. | Summary: You are a strong and competent fighter, seeking to spread the good name of your god. Your special connection with your chosen deity provides you unique skills such as healing and defensive spells and capabilities. |

"Anyone else confused why there are only six different classes and no options for choosing a unique face?" I asked the group, perplexed. In most games that I had played, especially fantasy, there have always been a vast number of options and an insane ability to play around different balances of race and classes. I'd made some pretty amazing combinations that had saved me a time or two within the games I had played.

"Ya, it looks like there are only those options, weird," Iris remarked. "Let us go find Sammy, maybe she just did not give us the full list?"

"Where did she go?" I asked.

"She went this way," Keila said, pointing towards the direction of the third unopened door in the lab.

We all began walking that direction, but I kept getting distracted by the maps that were all spread out on the table and walls around us. While I was so far disappointed in the number of class options, there appeared to be enough corners of the map that more for made up for this. As we neared closer to the door, we began to hear the sounds of Sammy arguing with someone, possibly that unmet Dr. Jordan, I wondered.

"I do not know who else would have had access to the server room, Sam," an unidentified male voice said in response to an unheard question.

"In order to force the AI to keep them in the game, they must have used that room to gain access, and as far as I know we are the only two with a key," said Sammy, her voice completely distinguishable through the door. "Do you think they knew about the glitch?"

"Not possible, the only people that knew about it was the board, the C-suite, and us," replied the voice. "Even if someone was to discover, what would be the purpose of doing what they did, assuming anyone did anything."

"Exactly!" Sammy replied with frustration in her voice. "Why would someone want to punish the two people in the company who wanted to fix the problem?"

"Come on Sam, you know why someone would want that information to disappear. If it were to get out to the public–," the voice stopped.

Before any suspicion could be raised that we were listening in on the conversation I pushed on through the door to see Sammy standing over a desk, her hands firmly placed on the center of it. The unidentified man was looking over Sammy's shoulder towards our direction. As soon as we entered, Sammy whipped her head around in our direction.

"Hello team," she said in her normal voice. "Come on over and meet my esteemed colleague, Dr. Jordan, Dr. Jordan meet the team," Sammy took her hands off her desk to usher us into the room.

"Sorry to intrude," began Keila. "We were just going through the list you gave us, and we are only seeing six total class options and no options for races or anything," as Keila spoke, she gave both me and Iris the side eye: that we were not to bring up what we heard through the door.

"We were hoping that this was an incomplete list or that we just did not know where to look for the other options," continued Iris while giving a significant glance at Keila, confirming her stance.

"Oh, I am so sorry I thought that I mentioned it," responded Sammy. "The deal is that we have not finalized any other classes, nor equipped them with the skills or assets that make them special. Unfortunately, what I handed you is your full selection options for the game."

"As to the races option not being available," started Dr. Jordan. "The decision was made to make the experience of the game as realistic as possible, and therefore it was decided that the game's player characters, for the time being, will only be human. However, research and studies are being done to change this in the future updates to the game."

"I see," I said.

"Yes, so sorry to disappoint you all on this, but since you are not playing the game for the sake of enjoyment, I feel that this will not be a problem?" asked Dr. Jordan. Based on his facial expression, the only problem that he currently faced was that we were in his office.

"Why don't you guys go ahead, and I will be with you all in just a moment," said Sammy in a non-questioning manner while moving away from the desk to lead us out of the office. "I will be with you all shortly," she remarked while closing the door firmly after the last of us departed the room.

"Are we going to talk about what we heard?" whispered Iris in mine and Keila's ears.

"No, not here we are not," I said, giving a significant glance to the walls of the room we were standing in.

'Agreed," said Keila, then continued more loudly, "we should be deciding the classes that we each want to take on for the game. Anyone have any preferences?"

From there, Keila, Iris, and I spoke for thirty minutes about the different classes that we wanted to play in the game. Throughout the entire conversation we kept an ear open for the voices coming from the office, but we heard nothing more. It was decided that we needed to have a class with range on their attacks, someone who could take damage, and someone with the capabilities to heal. The general atmosphere of the conversation assumed the fact that we would be operating as a team, and that brough me great relief. While I had recently meet Iris, I truly did not know her, and I knew nothing about Keila. It was a relief that we were already operating so smoothy and there were no disagreements or intense arguments over such a significant decision.

In the end, since Iris was a standard solo player who lived to go hand to hand in her combat, she decided that she was going to take on the Mage class. It gave her ability deal some heavy damage in combat while also giving us the nice versatility of her spells to defend and attack. Since Keila was such a team player she was okay with taking on the Cleric role, a role I had never before assumed for myself. However, Iris and I convinced her that the Paladin was a better choice, as it covered our close combat and our healing needs.

The last choice was up to me, and I felt that I choose well. Since our remaining weakness was range attacks, I had to choose the Ranger class. I was leaning towards the Assassin, but Keila stated that we did not have a versatile damage dealer in our ranks, and I needed to go with the option that had more options, the Ranger. In the end I was happy with that decision since I hadn't gone down the Ranger character route in a few games.

"I am feeling pretty good about this line up we have," I remarked, looking over the drawings we did during our brainstorming session.

"I hope that it is going to be enough for us," remarked Iris, "although I think our classes are quite compatible, don't you think?"

Based on the context of the remark, I assumed she was speaking to me. "I could not agree more," I said while gently rubbing shoulders with Iris.

With all of those decisions out of the way I decided to have a closer look at the various proficiencies that were offered to each of our classes.

| Ranger | Mage | Paladin |
| --- | --- | --- |
| HP: 100/100<br>MP: 5/5<br>Skills:<br>Archery | HP: 100/100<br>MP: 10/10<br>Skills:<br>Dagger | HP: 100/100<br>MP: 5/5<br>Skills:<br>Heavy Armor |

| Duel Wielding Short | Quarterstaff | Long Sword |
|---|---|---|
| Blades | History | Shields |
| Stealth | Investigation | Religion |
| Trap Detection | Arcana | Medicine |
| Nature Magic | Battle Magic | Healing Magic |
| Light Armor | | |

"Anyone else confused about our skills?" I asked the group.

"Of course, let me explain," said a voice behind me. I turned around to see that Dr. Jordan had entered the room. "I designed most of the classes, so let me help. I also realize that we never had a proper introduction. You can call me Dr. Jordan," he said, reaching out his hand to me.

I shook it and nodded my head at his introduction and taking his hand. "Hello, Dr. Jordan," I responded.

"Nice to meet you," both girls murmured over my shoulder. At this, Dr. Jordan started to smile at all of us, and while he obviously meant it to be reassuring, it appeared creepier than comforting.

"Anyways, moving on," continued Dr. Jordan. "How we compiled our characters is with class specific skills. These skills are able to be leveled up as you use them, and new skills are able to be found in gameplay."

"Wait, so as a Ranger I could learn other magic schools?" I asked.

"Not quite so simple; there are certain limitations to one class's ability to learn skills outside the scope of your class. Our goal was to make the game realistic. Your abilities affect how you attain new skills. However, just as you – as a gamer – are most likely not geared towards reciting Shakespearian monologues on the fly, your Ranger is not going to learn Blood Magic," he explained.

"I see, so we have limitations, but our classes already have these starting skills without us learning them?" asked Keila.

"That is to assist you starting off, as you can also see all of the skills are level one and are not going to be significant," Dr. Jordan stated. "This is more to introduce you to the idea of skills then to outfit you with them," he intoned. "You will also be starting out with some gear, but you will see more of that once you get into the game. Speaking of which let us get on it," he gestured for us to follow him.

We followed Dr. Jordan out of the laboratory and down the hall to the elevators. Along the way, Keila continued to ask questions, but I was trapped in my own thoughts. I was already imagining how it would feel to be a Ranger and picturing epic scenes of me shooting enemies from afar. Once we arrived at the elevator the doors opened, seemingly at his presence again, and we entered with him swiping his wrist like the receptionist had done. He pushed another random floor near the top of the building, and we descended. The metal door opened into a wide white room that was made out of white stone, and the room was freezing.

"Here is the Gaming Room, or at least that is what we call it," Dr. Jordan began. Throughout the room, every couple of feet was one of those gorgeous chairs. "Here you guys will be plugged into the simulation of Fabula," as he said this he went to the nearest chair. "These chairs contain thousands of micro sensors that are all positioned throughout the neck and head region. Using these sensors and the helmet here," he gestured to a beanie shaped device on the back of the headrest, "we will be able to enter the neural pathways using specific frequencies to enter the game virtually."

"Wait, if it is so simple—," I began.

"It is by no means simple," interrupted Dr. Jordan. "This technology cost billions to discover and design. What you are looking at cost more money to develop than some countries possess."

"You misunderstand, if you simply remove the cap and you are removed from the game, then why haven't you taken off the caps of your bosses?" I asked.

"We have designed certain protocols," began Dr. Jordan. "The proper way, to avoid any issues, is to sign out in-game which deactivates the signals from the chair. However, removing someone from the chair before, while not dangerous, immediately logs someone out of the game. The reason that we have not done so with Dr.

Hobbs or Ms. Reynolds is due to a glitch in the AI. Our team believes that such a removal could send both of them into a coma."

"And what is stopping that from happening to us?" asked Keila.

"There is no guarantee, but it would appear that this glitch was specific to Dr. Hobbs and Ms. Reynolds. The reason has not been made clear," said Dr. Jordan. I got the sense that he was not completely truthful in his statements. "Nonetheless," Dr. Jordan continued, "there is nothing to fear. We have had several employees enter and exit the game since then with no ill effect, you are perfectly safe."

Once again, Dr. Jordan's face appeared to be attempting to project confidence, but it was failing to say anything more than, *I hope*.

"I do not know if I feel comfortable," began Iris. "Like we could end up being stuck in that game just as your bosses, and then who is going to save us?"

"If you do not wish to go into the game, then I will inform Sorrento, and we will terminate your contract and release any information about you we feel would be for the public good," said Dr. Jordan who was clearly beginning to get agitated.

At this, Keila, Iris, and I all looked at each other. While having only known each other for a few hours, I knew what we all were thinking. Why would we risk such a chance? The answer was simple, the lives we knew were forfeit if Sorrento released whatever information he had on all of us. That meant that the only question was if it was worth it to have that information released than possibly go into this game and end up like Hobbs and Reynolds. Based on the faces of Keila and Iris, there was no question. All our lives would be up in flames if we did not go forward with the plan. This also made me even more curious about the secret that Iris and Keila hid. Especially Iris, with her adorable demeanor and the little time we have spoken together: she did not appear to be someone who would have such a secret. However, who was to say that the same could not be said about me, I thought.

"We will do it," I said glancing at Keila and Iris who both were nodding their heads in agreement with me.

"Fantastic news," Dr. Jordan said with monotone with a hint of frustration. "Let us get started," he said while lead us to our chairs. "Which one of you are Ms. Christman?" asked Dr. Jordan, reminding me that he never even asked us for our names. Iris raised her hand. "Fantastic, you are here, Mr. Kote is here, and Ms. Varner is there," said Dr. Jordan gesturing towards the respective chairs.

After I sat down in mine, I was impressed with how comfortable the chairs were. They felt like tempurpedic foam mattresses that wrapped me and my entire body in a warm foam. It honestly felt like getting a massage, as all of the aches that I did not know had disappeared into the foam beneath me.

"If everyone could pull the headset over your body and then press the button on your right arm's hand rest," instructed Dr. Jordan. I pulled my beanie over my head, but not before throwing a reassuring smile towards Iris, who returned a nervous one. The beanie completely covered my entire head down to over my eyelids. With that I felt along the arm rest and found a massive button that laid underneath my fingertips. Sending a prayer to whatever gaming gods might be watching me, I pushed the button.

## Chapter 10: Entering the Game

I could still feel the chair around me, but it felt like it was in the distance, as if the feelings of the chair were from a dream that I was just waking from. I looked around, but I could see nothing but darkness. That is actually inadequate to describe what I was seeing. It was not darkness. It was utter blackness, so dark I couldn't even see my body. As I was attempting to raise my hand in front of my eyes, words began appearing in the distance.

**Choose Your Class: Mage, Cleric, Ranger, Paladin, Knight, Assassin**

Underneath each of the class titles were images of me geared in the starting gear of the class. Underneath these images, which I realized now were 3-D, were blocks of texts with the same information that we read on our tablets a little while ago. While it was impressive seeing myself geared in those different classes' get-ups, we had already decided what my class selection would be, so I knew that I was choosing the Ranger. However, I had absolutely no clue how to choose, so I decided that pointing would work. Guess what though? Nothing happened. I took a step back and thought about how I could choose my class. My next guess was to focus on the

Ranger class image. Once again, nothing. At this point I was getting frustrated and might have growled, "I just want to choose the damn Ranger class." At this, the text changed, and the Ranger icon grew larger while the rest of the options evaporated into the background. A new line of text appeared.

| **Your Chosen Class is The Ranger, Do You Confirm?** |
|---|

I said, "Yes." The text disappeared and I, dressed as a Ranger, appeared to grow to be my size. My copy was standing directly across from me, nearly a foot away. I appreciated how the game had immediately trimmed my frame, giving me some larger biceps that strained against the long-sleeved shirt that I wore under a leather jerkin. The same material of the jerkin made up my pants which slid into almost knee-high boots. Wrapped around my neck was a dark green, almost black, cloak that had a hood.

"I approve of this choice," said a voice from behind me. I literally crumpled, right on the spot. Apparently, my flight or fight response is to lay on the floor, begging for any sneaky enemy to just murder me on the spot. After a few seconds and realizing I was now on the floor I looked up to see a small ball of blue light hovering a foot above my head.

"Excuse me, what?" I asked, since there was no eloquent way to address the blue ball that seemingly spoke to me while I was cowering on the floor.

"So sorry to startle you. You can call me Ellie, I am here to assist you in your character creation process," said the blue ball.

"No, no, it is alright, I just thought I was alone," I replied. "What? Why are you just now arriving? I just choose my class."

"I haven't had any players except for two yet, and seeing three new players got me so excited," replied the ball of blueish light as I got to my feet. "I am the artificial intelligence of Fabula, and I am to walk you through your tutorial," she said.

While I was not exactly sure what gender, or even if the AI had a gender, the voice was feminine, so I just logged it as a she. However, before I could even get my bearing on the situation, Ellie continued.

"I see you have chosen your class: to see full list of skills and attributes you are going to need to access your menu," she stated, "to do so please say the word 'menu' while moving your right or left arm, depending on where you want the screen to appear."

I did as she stated and on the right side of my vision a menu appeared. At the very top it showed me, but in the outfit of the ranger. Underneath my image was my HP, health point counter in green, and then was a blue bar depicting my Mana, the source of the magic in the game. Further underneath that was expandable boxes labeled: Inventory, Spells, Currency, Messaging, and Settings. I clicked on Inventory and saw that I had a Wooden Bow, Quiver (20 Arrows), and Rusty Dagger equipped, and when I looked down at my waist, I saw the dagger and I could feel the bow and quiver on my back. Next to the equipment section of my inventory was my clothing. The only thing there was the three items that I had equipped on my body: Leather Jerkin, Leather Pants, and Cotton Shirt. All of my items had durability ratings that made me groan in despair, nothing I had on or equipped would last me a long time.

"I see you have found your inventory," continued Ellie. "Next click on Spells, if you would."

I followed Ellie's instructions and shrunk the equipment menu to see the Spells box, I enlarged it with a tap of my finger. I saw three spells:

Cure Wounds (Healing Magic) – *This is an instant spell that heals small wounds for 5 MP. Furthering your skills in this spell will yield greater benefits.*

Detect Magic (Divination Magic) – *This is concentration spell that cost 5 MP per minute. It will allow you to detect some presences of magic around your location. Furthering your skills in this spell will allow you to detect more magic and assist in identifying the magic's intent and source.*

Speak with Animals (Nature Magic) – *This concentration spell will cost 5 MP for ten minutes of the ability to communicate with animals. Your skills in this magic at (Level 1) will allow you to speak for fifteen minutes per cast. Further your skills in this spell to allow you to understand higher level creatures and even monsters.*

Okay, that was super cool. Like, I cannot be the only person to have imagined having the ability to speak with my dog. Like, honestly, what are they always thinking? I was dying to know. I wished that there was such a spell in the real world, and not just in the game worlds.

"These are the spells that you currently know how to cast. You can learn more from trial and error or by being taught through a spell book or a qualified spell caster," Ellie said, interrupting my train of thought. "To use the spell, simply think of the spell, and the words will come to mind."

I thought on the Cure Wounds spell, even though I had no wounds to heal. When focusing on the spell, I heard a whisper of a word and I repeated it, "*Asie.*" Upon saying the words, I felt a warm feeling flow down my arm and leave through my palms. Nothing more happened, but I assumed that was because I did not have anything to heal, *dumdum*, I thought.

"When casting the Cure Wounds spell, you only need to place your palms on the wound, and the spell will do the rest of the work," Ellie said, confirming my thoughts. "Now that is done, let us move to the last part of the tutorial," Ellie continued. "Move on to the Settings and Currency box."

I did as she bid, and moved onto the Currency box, but it was empty. I saw in the corner that I had a total of 0. *Who knew that the game was reflective of my real life in such an intimate way?* After seeing that I moved onto the Settings. Upon clicking on the Settings box, the menu opened up to show dozens of different subcategories.

"As you saw, you currently have no money. You may gain money from looting bodies and completing quests. While there is no time to go through all of the aspects contained within Settings, I find it most useful to point out that you are able to show your HP and MP bars on your screen at all times if you choose," Ellie said.

I followed Ellie's instruction and decided to make the HP and MP counters appear in my view of vision at all times. She also noted different way of making them more or less transparent it. Overall, I could have spent hours in the settings, getting the game to exactly how I would want it. However, I was also already getting anxious to get out to the world. Before I spoke, though, I had a realization.

"Ellie," I said, "how am I supposed to use this dagger or my bow?"

"You will learn through trial and error, or you may attend a school to be taught more. In order to make the game as realistic as possible we decided that letting the player learn how to utilize their skills and weapons through this would immerse the player," she answered.

That was going to be a challenge, I thought. My exact knowledge of how to use a bow and arrow or a blade was about equivalent to my knowledge of glass blowing, zilch. However, while it would be a challenge, I also thought about the possibilities it meant for me as a player. This was really an amazing game.

"Wait, what about my strength or agility, or any of those other physical attributes?" I asked Ellie, who was just hover right across from me.

"Those are systematically increased as you level up and gain more skills. There are no skills points to distribute, once again, to make the game more immersive. If you have any other questions, you are always able to call upon me," she answered.

"How would I do that?"

"Simply scream Ellie while jumping up and down and waving your arms," Ellie said with a no-nonsense tone. However, after a few silent moments of me watching her, she continued, "I am kidding, within your Settings box there is a button to summon me." With that she flew away from me before I could even think to ask another one of the few thousand questions that I had running around between my ear canals. As soon as she disappeared into the darkness, I felt the black of my surroundings start to envelope me. Not in a way that felt startling, but still a bit unnerving.

I felt like I was opening my eyes after a full eight-hour sleep. The light nearly blinded me, and I had to throw my hand over my eyes to block it out for a second in order to allow my eyes to adjust to the sun. Looking up through my fingertips I realized I was not blocking a sun, but rather suns. There were three of them, smaller than the one I am accustomed to, high in the sky. One was bright red, and the others looked to be your normal sun color, a bright yellow. After adjusting to the brightness, I started looking around me. I could see the dirt road that was dotted with broken cobblestone every few feet. In the distance I could see a fifteen-foot stone wall in the distance and various buildings dotting the road before the entrance to the city, that I presumed to be Altour.

"Damn it is bright out," remarked Keila.

I had nearly forgotten that I was with people, after Keila's remark I looked over to her. She looked awesome. I know that word gets overused, but it was true. She was in a chain mail get up with a long sword attached to her hip. Her blond was tied into a tight bun atop her head. Next to her stood Iris. She looked to also be covering her eyes from the sun, but rather than remaining in the same clothes that I had seen her in prior to entering the game she was dressed in a long, deep blue robe that had a hood attached. Her red hair was standing out and looked slightly like she had gotten struck by lightning. In her hand appeared to be a walking stick, but I knew better.

"This is amazing," I said with awe in my voice. I looked towards Iris and Keila for confirmation that they were just as shaken as I was by what we were seeing.

"It feels… real," Iris said, squeezing her robes to feel the sensation of cloth flow through her hand.

"It really does, this is really, really cool guys!" Keila remarked ecstatically, pulling out her sword to swing it around. "Wow, this feels heavy."

"Did you guys all meet Ellie, that floating blue light?" I asked.

"She helped me during the character creation phase," remarked Iris while Keila nodded in agreement. "Okay, so if we are to follow our instruction we should probably get towards that city before we run into anything dangerous out here. It looks to be less than a mile that direction, I have absolutely no clue what the cardinal directions are in this world."

"Sounds like a plan to me, all I have is a bow that I do not know how to shoot and a knife that looks like the blade is about to fall off," I said while analyzing the blade that was on my hip. While analyzing the blade and trying to rub some of the rust of it so that it might be useful, I heard a low growl coming from behind us.

## Chapter 11: I Hate Cats

From behind me there was a low growling sound, sort of like the sound of a car's engine, only louder. I turned around, it had appeared that Keila and Iris had not heard the noise yet.

"What is up?" inquired Iris who was walking towards me.

"You guys don't hear that?" I followed up, looking all around us. There was nothing to see but trees and bushes and a road that went as far as the eye could see.

"It must be because you are a ranger—," Keila began, but right as she started talking the bushes to our left moved. "I do see that," she said, pulling the sword from the scabbard on her waist. She gripped it in a two-hand posture and spread her legs out like she was about to use the sword as a bat.

While she was doing that, I began to take my bow from my quiver, but the string was unattached. As I began to string the bow so that I could fire some arrows, I heard Iris scream. Looking up I saw what frightened her, there was a massive black cat coming from the bushes. It had to be the size of a jungle cat in the real world, or maybe even larger than that.

"I hate cats," I whispered. While I was scared of the cat, I quickly reminded myself that this was a game and that there were no real consequences to my actions here. Upon realizing this and having the calmness of mind to lower my heart rate, the cat jumped me.

"Ahhhh—," I began to scream in shock and pain, but the world went black.

All of a sudden, I felt my body again, like my actual real-world body and the chair that I was laying on, but just like before, it felt distant as if I was waking from a dream. In front of my eyes were words, just like in the character selection part.

| **You Have Died.** |
|---|

Underneath that was two small options that read: Respawn and Logout. A feeling of shame overwhelmed me when I realized that I had died. Five minutes into the game and I was the first person to get killed by a massive cat. I really hated cats. I usually didn't have such strong feelings towards the tiny ones that roam people homes, but in the moment, I was seeing red. "Breathe Zeph, breathe," I muttered to myself until the red around my vision dissipated. I had to save face, so I said out loud, "Respawn."

Quickly I began to feel the sun streaming down on my face again. Not the real world, but the intense brightness that could only be created by the rays of the three suns beaming onto my face. I groggily opened my eyes to see two sets of eyes staring down at me.

"Such a gamer," laughed Iris, breaking out that smile I had not seen in a while.

"He probably was hiding his epic gaming skills, as to not show up the girls," murmured Keila, with a similar gleam to Iris in her eyes.

"Can you just help me up?" I groaned, reaching out my hand to Iris to assist me in lifting off the ground. She obliged me and I looked around to see I was standing in the same spot that I was earlier. I then looked behind me for evidence of the cat fight, but I also saw a leather bag sitting in the spot where I was last standing.

"What happened?" I asked, my head was killing me.

"Well, there was a massive cat, it did not take a liking to seeing your face and decided to eat it off," remarked Keila.

Iris continued, "It was honestly kind of terrifying seeing it come after you, but it looked like you were already dead since your body began disappearing so me and Keila attacked it and killed it."

"It was so hard, although only a level two creature, and your sacrifice provided a nice distraction," finished Keila who was placing her sword in her scabbard.

Iris reached out to touch my arm and looked at my face, "Did it hurt?" she asked.

"Ya, not as bad as you would think, but it did hurt. How long did it take me to respawn?" I asked.

"Take a look for yourself," stated Keila. At this I looked around towards the horizon and I could see the suns in the same position as before, but the sunlight felt different. Keila continued, "I estimate roughly a few minutes."

At this I groaned; just because I decided to take on a massive furball I ended up cat chow, but it could have been worse. I looked down at my body to see that I was rocking an epic leather loincloth and had nothing else on me. I quickly looked inside my inventory and saw that it was also empty. "I lost all of my stuff," I said in shock. This was not good, now I was a noob with no weapon or armor.

"I believe that is your stuff over there," said Iris, pointing towards the leather sack that I saw earlier. "Keila and I tried to open it, but it has a timer on it, and we couldn't move it or open it."

With that I walked over there and looked at the sack. I did see a timer that denoted a few hours and some minutes on it, hovering above the bag. I was easily able to open it and saw all of my belongings were inside.

"It is my stuff," I said, over my shoulder, to Keila and Iris. I wondered what would happen if the timer ran out, would anyone be able to get my belongings? Or would they simply disappear? I had no intention of finding out because I was committed to not dying by cat or other monstrosity again. As soon as I thought this, I began to hear another noise. This one was different from the first, but it was coming from the forest again.

"Something's coming," I said to Keila and Iris while I quickly rummaged through my belongings, looking for my sword. As I found the handle, something came out of the forest.

"Thank the heavens!" said the thing that came out of the forest. It appeared to be a man, albeit a very short man with a long beard. It was a dwarf, I realized. "Adventures, my name is Baridac Longbrew, and I –," upon looking at me with my loincloth and knife he looked at us with a look of amusement and then horror on his face. "Why are you naked?"

"He was merely switching in something more appropriate for fighting," stated Iris, but she had taken on a different air about her, as if she was role playing the wise wizard trope.

"Ahh, makes sense, these woods get dangerous," said the dwarf while nodding in approval of my ensemble. "I nearly escaped some disgusting creatures in the woods and would greatly appreciate your service in reaching the city of Altour. You are adventurers, correct?"

"Indeed," replied Keila, who placed her hand on her sword's hilt, not in a manner to threaten, but more as a statement of her worthiness.

"I can offer you a night of lodgings in exchange for my services along with some money, although I do not have much," stated the dwarf. As he spoke a screen appeared before my eyes.

**Dwarf Longbrew Has Offered You a Quest: Escort the Dwarf Safely to the City of Altour.**

Below this was two options, Accept and Decline, and further beneath that was another line. Reward(s): Free Lodging for One Evening and 10 Pennies x 3.

I looked behind me to see what Keila and Iris were thinking. However, before I could say anything Iris said, "Of course Baridac Longbrew, we would be happy to." At this I saw a bar appear beneath the Accept option that filled up one-third.

Then Keila continued, "It would be an honor." With Keila's words the bar filled up to two-thirds and the page disappeared with a new sentence appearing before my vision.

**Accepted Quest: Escort the Dwarf Safely to the City of Altour.**

It would appear that with a majority of the team accepting the quest, that the quest became accepted for the entire team.

"Thank the Iron Lord," said the dwarf with a smile on his face, "should we get going?"

"In one moment, good dwarf," said Iris, who was taking charge. "Let my companion collect his belongings and we will hurry with haste towards the walls of Altour."

At this slight prodding from Iris, I quickly rummaged through the bag. I threw on my pants and my shirt. Then I slipped into the leather jerkin and took out my bow and quiver, throwing them over my shoulder. The knife slipped back into the scabbard on my belt. Once I finished getting dressed, I looked at my inventory inside the menu by whispering the words, "menu" and waving my arm from my right to left side of my vision. In my inventory I saw all of my belongings, but the durability of my clothes had gone from *Poor* to *Substandard*. In fact, I could feel that my cotton shirt had some holes in it from where the cat must have clawed me, and the Jerkin was also sporting a few holes and scratches. However, the pants, boots, and cloak still appeared to be the same, *Poor*, quality as before and appeared to be without damage. With that all in order I looked to Iris and nodded my head.

"Let us be on our way, then," said Iris. Turning around and walking off towards the walls of Altour without looking behind her. Keila and I shared a glance before following after the dwarf as he swiftly followed Iris. I do not know why, but Iris was looking thrilling as the head honcho.

## Chapter 12: City of Altour and It's Best Dwarf

We walked for nearly half an hour. While the walls appeared to be right in front of us upon spawning, the actual distance was deceivingly long. Moving quickly out of the area that was surrounded by woods, we found ourselves walking on a road that became gradually filled with more cobbles. Instead of the trees from the forest around us, we saw crops spread out in all directions. We walked in silence mostly, but the dwarf has a few questions for us.

"Where do you all hail from" asked the dwarf.

"We come from far away," I answered, not knowing enough of the world to confidentiality name any other region. It was the simple fact that there is only one name that I know is this entire game, and that was Altour.

"Must have been quite the journey to end up here in Altour," said the dwarf. "What brings you adventurers all of this way?"

"We are looking for some lost friends," said Iris, still in character as the team's leader. I was not going to lie, but the role of leader obviously suited Iris, as she led the charge of the group towards the city's walls in the distance. I was beginning to feel a little bit like Frodo and team being led by Gandalf on the start of grand journey.

"Ahh, I see," said the dwarf. However, I was in the dark on what about Iris' statement brought sudden clarity to the mystery of three strangers, one of them being previously naked, standing in the woods. "I assume that you are speaking about the other two foreign-born strangers that came here half a fortnight ago?"

"Indeed," said Keila, with some excitement, "you saw them?"

"Nah, but I heard about them," responded the dwarf. "People were saying that they were going on about the city, talking as if they had been there before. However, no one else remembered them coming through in the past."

At this we all went silent, deep in individual thought. This confirmed that Dr. Hobbs and Ms. Reynolds did spawn where we had, as Sammy said we would. However, if it was a week ago then they could have gone anywhere from here. This task was going to be difficult to find two individuals in this seemingly vast world.

"Do you know where they went after visiting your city?" asked Iris.

"No, I am sorry to say, but I do not," the dwarf said with a focused frown. "Once we get into the town, I will let you know about where you might be able to find those who would, though."

"Thank you, Master Dwarf," responded Iris.

"Ahh, I am no Master Dwarf madam. I am simply an innkeeper who has a fondness for strangers."

With these final remarks we continued the journey in silence. By now we were coming up on the gates of the city. The walls were made up of the same stone material that was laid before our feet. The walls felt enormous, even though they were only fifteen feet high. Craning my neck to look at the top of the wall, I could see two individuals who were armed with cross bows and dressed in similar outfits to myself. The city was obviously full of activity as the sounds of horses, argumentative conversations, and other typical city noises fell onto my ears. However, what was astounding was the smells. I could smell baked goods, alongside manure, human excrement, and other specific smells that only a city could produce.

"The smell can be offensive, initially, but I have found it to smell of home," remarked the dwarf at seeing our expressions. As I had nothing nice to say about the smell or what state his home must be in, I said nothing as did Keila and Iris. "This is my inn," the dwarf said, pointing to the building right on the inside of the walls. However, before we could continue any further the guards posted inside the gate to the city stopped us.

"Who might you be?" asked a man dressed in chain mail similar to that of Keila, but it had the addition of a breastplate with a crest on it.

"Hello there Baridac," said the other guardsman who appeared on the other side of the group.

"Hello, Landan," said the dwarf to the guardsman. "And hello there, Fern," finished the dwarf, acknowledging the second. "These folks are with me; they are going to be staying at my inn tonight. I hope that is no trouble."

"Certainly, Baridac," stated Landan, the guardsman who first acknowledged the dwarf. He had long brown hair that was done in tight bun on his head and a face that beamed the look of youthful optimism, framed nicely with a short beard. While not in direct competition with Iris for looks, I would be lying if I said that I hadn't noticed that his sharp cheekbones were an attractive feature.

"Wait, sorry, but we cannot allow three strangers to wander into the city," argued the other guard, the one I presumed to be Fern. He was the antithesis to Landan in most ways. However, most prominent was the lack of that youthful look of hope since Fern looked anything but hopeful. At his statement he came towards us until he was standing a foot away from Iris as she was in the lead of our little group.

"Fern, it is fine, we will let them pass with Dwarf Longbrew," Landan affirmed while stepping up to Fern and resting a hand on his breastplate. With that Landan gave our group a nod to go ahead, but he did not remove the hand from the other's breastplate.

After a few feet from the gate, and mostly out of earshot, Iris turned to the dwarf. "What was that about?" she asked. At her question I turned around to see Fern disciplining Landan, but the friendly guard still appeared to be smiling.

"Nothing to do with you all, I promise," said the dwarf. "There has been some trouble in the city that has left the guard somewhat anxious of late."

"What is this trouble?" I asked. However, Baridac ignored the question and moved on towards his building. As it came into sight, I could read the sign that hung above the front door of the inn, *The Tipsy Dwarves*, it read. The originality of the name was extremely profound, and I felt inspired.

"Original," I murmured under my breath. Thankfully, no one had heard my rude comment, and I reminded myself that nothing is gained from such negativity, it is not like I had had a career of naming inns and taverns anyways. The dwarf was now opening the door for each of us, and we walked into the inn.

The interior was rather charming, it had the expected feeling of any city tavern or inn that would be found in such a gaming world. The entire building was built out of dark wood, but whether that wood was dark in origin or stained from smoke and spillage was unclear. Either way, it was difficult to not breathe a sigh of relief at the sight of the interior of *The Tipsy Dwarves*. The room was filled with long tables and against the right wall was a long bar and kitchen, and on the opposite wall was a staircase that led up into the building. Amongst the tables was a fire pit that was currently blazing and casting a warm glow on the party.

"Homey," I said looking all around.

"Thank you," said the dwarf who was looking at the room with pride. "It is not much, but it is mine. I would like to thank you three so much for all the help on the way back."

"It was our honor," said Iris.

"I would rather say that it was my honor to be able to meet three new strangers, such as yourselves. Before we continue, I promised you a reward." At this the dwarf ran to the bar and pulled out a box. I could not see the contents of the box from the other side of the bar, but the dwarf closed the lid with nine coins in his hands. "This is your monetary compensation for your troubles, and I will have someone dress three rooms upstairs for your stay later this evening."

"That would be so kind," replied Iris. The dwarf walked over and placed ten coins in each of our hands. As soon as the last ten coins were within my hands a new message appeared before my eyes.

**Quest Complete: Escort the Dwarf Safely to the City of Altour.**
**Reward(s): Free Lodging for One Evening and 10 Pennies x 3**
**Experience Gained: 50 Points**

As each of the lines appeared, the previously one left the field of vision. We were all standing in silence as the messages ran across each of our eyes. At seeing the experience gain I saw another bar appear in my field of vision, underneath my health and mana points, it filled up about five percent. In small words underneath the bar were the words: Experience: 50/1000. While this was no difficult task, it did appear that I had a long way to go before getting to the next level. If indeed, we needed to venture out of the city to find Dr. Hobbs and Ms. Reynolds then we all were going to need to level up fast. I placed the coins into a pouch that was intended for such purposes that was on my belt.

"Looks like we have some more leveling to get done, before we are ready to follow up on Dr. Hobbs and Ms. Reynolds," I said to the group.

"Indeed," replied Iris. As she said this, the dwarf, seeing that we began to speak on party matters had turned to go. However, before he had a chance to walk away Iris had turned to him and asked, "Baridac, where would we go to find some easier monsters to slay?"

"Oh, I would not know," replied the dwarf. "I would suggest that you go and ask the guards who train in the wilds outside the walls. In fact, Landan, that guard who we spoke to, should know exactly what you adventures are looking for."

"Thank you," began Iris, "you also mentioned that you would point us in the direction of someone who might know about our friends, and where they went."

"True, I did say that," said the dwarf who was now pulling on his long beard. "I would recommend starting with Landan, and if he has no insight then you could check out the inn that they were staying at, *The Hollow Quiver*."

"Where is The Hollow Quiver," asked Keila.

"Oh, it is near Westgate. If go to the wall and turn left, and then follow the walls to the next gate then you should see it," finished the dwarf. While being friendly, he appeared to be wanting to get back to work.

"Thank you, Baridac," replied Iris.

"Indeed, I hope to see you all back here this evening," said the dwarf over his shoulder while he left us amongst the long tables, and he returned to the bar.

"Where to next?" I asked the group.

## Chapter 13: Sea Horses

A little while later we were all standing at the gate for the city, the same one that we came through. After finishing the quest with Baridac, we decided that the next best thing that we all needed to do was begin to level up. We had been in the game for almost two hours, meaning that we had another six before the game booted us out of the system. After some discussion with Iris and Keila, we knew we had two priorities. Level up and to head to *The Hollow Quiver*, to learn about the direction that was hinted to lead to Dr. Hobbs and Ms. Reynolds. Since we had no plans of returning to this location, we decided that we best approach the guardsman now.

We stood outside of the gate, where we had entered a little while ago. Landan, the attractive guardsman was currently sitting on a barrel. Iris, once again in the lead, began to approach him with us in tow.

"Hello Landan," said Iris. "Thank you so much for helping us earlier," she continued with that small grin on her face. Apparently, Iris also thought that Landan was not in danger of hurting anyone's eyes. I was not jealous, why would I be? Sure, Landan's cheek bones were sharp enough to cut, but he was merely an extension of Ellie's AI system. He was not real.

"Hello there, travelers," replied Landan. "How may I help you?"

"We were hoping to train a little and gain some new skills," started Iris.

"Baridac mentioned that you could recommend somewhere that we could train," I continued, cutting in between Iris and Landan.

"True, well I am glad that you came to me," he said pulling himself off the barrel that we were sitting on. "If you are looking to get stronger then let us begin, shall we?" he asked. However, I noticed that the grin he had on his face was no longer possessed by youthful cheer, but rather was mischievous. While he said this, he pulled out his sword, and, not knowing what was happening, I just stood there. However, Keila did not.

As he swung his sword at Keila, she quickly threw her sword in the way. Landan quickly pulled his sword back, and said, "Attack me and let us see what I am working with, sound good?"

However, he did not give any of us a chance to respond before he returned to swing at Keila. She, once again, heaved her sword to intercept his stroke that was aimed at her head. While he began to push down on her sword, I pulled out my dagger from my belt and started to charge Landan. Holding my dagger in front of me, I aimed for Landan's left arm. I pulled my arm back to make a swipe with my dagger, but Landan quickly disengaged from Keila and batted my end with the side of sword. I ended up dropping my dagger, and I swiftly backed away.

The distraction I caused by charging Landan gave Keila the opportunity to swing her sword, two handed, up at his right arm. However, before Keila could land her strike, Landan jumped swiftly out of the way. His eyes then grew large at something over Keila shoulder, and I looked to see Iris. While we had been engaging with Landan, she had been murmuring something underneath her breath and holding her hands in front of her body. There was a small ball of light growing in her hand as she continued to murmur.

"Oh, I do not think so," said Landan. He quickly picked up a stone from the floor beneath him and chucked it at Iris' leg. He hit her right on the thigh and Iris let go off the light she was holding to grab onto her thigh. The light dissipated, with Iris being distracted by her sore leg. While Landan was distracted throwing the sword, Keila had taken the sword like a bat and swung at Landan's right arm, his sword arm. She hit home and Landan winced and grasped at his shoulder.

"Had enough," said Keila with a smirk at her score.

"I know enough now," said Landan who was as rubbing his shoulder. He swiftly placed his sword in his scabbard on his side and walked over to Iris. "How is the leg?" he asked with a look of concern.

"It was more shocking than painful, but what in the heavens was that?" asked Iris who had stopped rubbing her thigh to glare at Landan with her full height.

"I was merely seeing how you guys would hold up in a fight," he replied. "I do not need to send you all off to your death, but it would appear that you are not completely incompetent. When you all work as a team, you all seem to be functional."

"Thanks?" I asked at Landan, not knowing if I was supposed to be offended or delighted with Landan's comment.

"You're welcome," he said. "However, you all need much improvement. I would recommend that you all head towards river outside of Glass Village, on the other side of the city. There are some weaker monsters who haunt the sides of the river."

"What types –," I began to ask.

"Or, you guys could head over to the combat schools in Silkliff," suggested Landan.

"No, we would first like to see how we are against some monsters before going to any of the schools," said Iris. "We need to get use to fighting together, and we would not mind getting some loot and coins from them. After all, we are all currently broke."

"Ah, in that case, there are some kelpies that are bothering the residents of Glass Village, they are all pretty low level. Could you guys take care of them for me?" asked Landan.

At these words the similar prompts appeared in our version: We all said, "Accept" at once and the words disappeared.

**Guardsman Landan Has Offered You a Quest: Remove 20 Kelpies from the River.**
**Accept / Decline**
**Reward(s): Landan's Respect and 20 Coppers x3.**

"Best of luck," Landan said, returning to his barrel.

At Landan's directive we began to walk along the wall towards the part of the city known as Glass Village. Landan told us that the region was primarily filled with glass blowers and other merchants, and hence the name Glass Village was eventually coined as the area's name. The city was not nearly as large as it had first appeared to us, but it was still extremely crowded, as indicated by the earlier smells. I could see the residents of Altour going about their businesses, and I felt like I was looking at the images that I would see in my textbooks of medieval Europe.

The women all wore long skirts and blouses, and the majority had their heads covered in scarfs or rags. The men all wore breeches that ended at their knees and flowing shirts that they tucked into their pants. The most common feature amongst all of the people we saw was the dirt. On everyone's faces, hands, arms, legs, and primarily feet were the stains and marks of dirt and grease. The most attractive part of the city was the buildings. The majority of them were two or three stories of wood. From the porches and windows hung the laundry of its residents. The colors of the clothes and the dark wood of the building gave a pleasant image. Unfortunately, it was the backdrop for cobblestone streets filled with dirt, mud, and possibly worse.

"How in the world did they engineer this smell," moaned Keila.

"This world is insane," I agreed. "I have never seen or heard of anything remotely like this. If this game ever goes to market, then it would be well worth the years it took to make this game."

This game would be the peak of the world's technology in regard to virtual reality technology and our simulation capability. The idea that human and technological progress was exponential was proven solely by this game, I thought. As I was busy being enamored by the game world the Glass Village came into view or at least I guessed that was the place, based on the dozens of vendors who were selling glassware on the street we walked on. I could see glass plates, cups, windows, and even weaponry such as swords and daggers.

"I presume that is Glass Village, but where are the kelpies, river and everything that Landan said would be here?" I asked.

"I highly doubt that the kelpies or the river would just be in the middle of the market," said Keila. "We should go ask some vendors, to find out where the kelpies are." As she said this, we could see the gate in the wall come into view. The gate was similar to the one that we saw off of White Bridge, but there were dozens of people who were coming to and from in the gate. As we got closer to the gate and deeper into the market, we began to hear vendors screaming the names of their wares and prices.

"Two glass daggers for one silver piece," said one vendor.

Another one screamed, "One copper per cup." The chaos was overwhelming, and it was becoming impossible to hear individual vendors until the one selling daggers said:

"Heyyo! Adventurers!" At this noise we turned towards the table that we were standing in front of to see a middle-aged gentleman there with a glass dagger in each hand. He was also geared out with a thick black mustache and little circular, colored glasses.

"You are adventurers, right?" asked the vendor.

"That is correct," I said, stepping up to the table. "We were tasked by the guard to deal with the kelpies off the rivers."

"It is long overdue," replied the vendor. "We have had dozens of travelers to our market become hurt due to the kelpies. Normally they are no issue, and just stay in the water. However, since the number has grown so large, they have started attacking those who come through the gate to buy our wares," he said with a shake of his head. "Will you be needing weapons since you are about to deal with the kelpies? I'll happily drop the price to something more reasonable."

"What did you have in mind?" I asked, thinking about my rusty dagger that was on my belt. However, I then quickly thought about the very little money that I had in my possession. The ten pennies that I had in my little pouch were feeling insufficient for anything on the table. "I only have a few pennies on me at the moment."

"Ahh," the vendor replied, a sad look in his face. "That unfortunately will not afford you these daggers or any other of my wares. However, might I propose an idea?"

"Sure," I said hesitantly. "What do you have mind?"

"I see you carry a dagger on your side and a bow on your back, and your fellow adventurers carry a staff and a sword. Unfortunately, I have nothing for them, but I would happily equip you with a lone glass dagger," he said holding forth the glass dagger in his right hand. I began to reach out to it, but he swiftly returned it to his side. "However, I will request that you do me a favor."

"What kind of favor?"

"Oh, nothing to large, simply will you collect a few, let's say five, kelpie hearts. I will let you take the dagger now and keep it upon completion of the task."

"Kelpie hearts," I asked. I also looked over to Iris and Keila, but both of their heads were indicating confusion at the term. In all of my times gaming and fighting kelpies I had become used to the horse shaped creatures, but I had never heard of a kelpie heart.

"Oh, you see the kelpie creatures have a heart," he said as he grabbed a glass orb in his other hand. "These hearts are not too common, but they are a special moss stone that contains certain... traits within its core." Seeing the confusion on our faces he continued, "It is not too important what they are, but simply the fact that they exist and that you might find some on their corpses. So, are we in agreement?" With that question a new quest notification appeared but looking to Keila and Iris proved the point that it only appeared in my field of vision.

**Glass Merchant Markus Landan Has Offered You a Quest: Obtain 5 Kelpie Hearts and Return Them.**
**Accept / Decline**
**Reward(s): Glass Dagger.**

I said, "Accept" at once and the words disappeared.

"Fantastic," announced the vendor while clapping his hands. "Here you go young man, and I look forward to seeing those hearts soon." With that he passed me a glass dagger over the table, and I could hold it for the first time. I grabbed the dagger and it felt cold, not cool, but absolutely frigid in my hand. Upon seeing it in my hand it began to disappear and eventually completely left my hand, turning to mist.

"What just happened?" I said, slightly freaking out, towards Keila and Iris.

"It looked sort of like how you did, after you died," remarked Iris. When she said this, the glass vendor started staring at us with an odd look, so we began to walk away. She began to speak in a quieter voice, "After you died, you disappeared like that. I think it went into your inventory." At this idea I said out loud, "Menu," while swiping my hand to access my menu. Clicking on Inventory I could see that the dagger, indeed, had appeared within my inventory. I clicked on the dagger and could see the information.

> **Glass Dagger of Ice**
> **Quality: Fair**
> **Damage: 10 – 15 Health Points + 2 Points of Ice Damage**
> **Description: This glass dagger is fairly made with an extremely sharp edge like most glass weapons. Infused within the glass dagger is an enchantment of ice, making the weapon ice-cold.**

I had never seen the damage counter on these weapons before. Seeing it on this dagger made me curious about the details of my own current weapon.

**Equipped: Rusty Dagger**
**Quality: Poor**
**Damage: 1-9 Health Points**
**Description: This rusty dagger is one of the poorest weapons in the game. The rust has reduced the quality of the weapon beyond repair. However, the weapon might contain one or two more good battles within it.**

This was indeed a far superior weapon to the one that I was holding now. Seeing the improved ratings of my new dagger I decided to swiftly switch out my equipped weapon. Clicking back on my new weapon I saw an option to equip it, and I choose that option. Upon doing so the new dagger became highlighted as equipped and the Rusty Dagger replaced the Glass Dagger as unequipped. As I made these changes, I saw my current weapon disappear from my waist and the new dagger reappear.

"All set?" Iris asked with a smile in my direction.

"Ya," I confirmed, returning the same smile. "Let us head out!" With that we continued walking towards the gate and exited against the stream of incoming customers. Once again, I saw the green pastures that we started the game within. However, while there was still the same forest far off in the distance there was a new feature off to the right of the horizon. This was a massive river that was flowing off to the right of the city. We began our walk towards the river's edge. After a few minutes of walking through knee-high grass we came upon the river's edge. The river must have spanned over a hundred feet and flowed from an unseen origin towards an unknown location. Further down the river, roughly a hundred feet away, we saw a herd of horses standing in the shallow edge of the water. However, the horses did not look right.

"Is that them?" I asked to the group.

"You ever seen a kelpie before?" asked Iris with a smirk.

"Questioning my gaming skill, are you?" I retorted.

"Yes," said Keila, cutting between mine and Iris' back-and-forth. "Those horses are obviously green, and you can see the pieces of seaweed on them. Those are what we are here for," she finished, grasping the hilt of her sword, but without removing it from the scabbard.

"There must be dozens of them there," I observed.

"We will not be able to fight all of them at once, especially considering the fact that none of us have leveled up yet. We are going to have to pull them out one at a time," remarked Iris.

"Let me try something," I said pulling out my bow and adjusting the quiver so that I could reach an arrow. I took out my bow in my left hand and placed an arrow on the string and pulled back with my right hand. I felt like I was embodying the spirit of Katniss Everdeen here. I attempted to aim at one of the horsed-shaped kelpies and let the arrow loose. It went about halfway on course before the breeze coming off the river shifted the arrow off course, and it landed a dozen feet off mark. Feeling upset at seeing my lack of ability at shooting arrows I walked a few feet closer and placed another arrow. This time I attempted to account for the breeze and adjusted my aim. I took a deep breath and let the arrow fly. While I had aimed at the kelpie the first time, this time I had aimed a little towards it right. I was attempting to really focus on how hard the wind was blowing when a piece string off the arrowhead appeared in my vision. I noticed it, but quickly a new block of text appeared in my vision.

**Level Up Skill: Archery to Level 1 – Unlocking your skill in Archery allows you to see a faint line appear, predicting where your arrow will land with 50% accuracy.**

"Perfect," I said with a grin. I noticed that when the skill up happened my experience bar also went up by fifty experience points. This time I focused on the line, and it began to thicken from the width of a spider string towards that of a thin rope. I lined up the line with the kelpie's head and released. The arrow flew, buffeted by the wind, off course, but it still landed on the kelpie's horse-shaped body's hindquarters. As soon as the arrow struck the kelpie began to prance around looking for a target, and then it looked towards us and started rushing our direction.

“Fantastic,” said Iris, who began to close her hands together and the same light that had appeared when facing Landan had reignited and began to grow. While Iris was building her spell, Keila took out her sword and it appeared she still held it like a baseball bat over her right shoulder. The horse continued its approach and was now not even two dozen feet away. On seeing its rapid approach, I swiftly placed another arrow on the bow’s string and took aim.

“Hold,” said Keila, looking at me. “Wait for Iris to release her spell and then take your shot, you are going to miss with it moving.”

I nodded in confirmation of hearing Keila’s command. It was logical, after all I was not winning any archery contest at the moment when I struggled to hit a standing target. As soon as I had that thought, Iris yelled her last word, “Ignis!” A ball of fire, the size of a basketball, flew from Iris’ outstretched hands and few towards the horse-shaped creature. The kelpie ran directly into the fireball, and this appeared to halt the creature for a second. At this exact instance I released the arrow, lining up the arrowhead’s line with our enemy’s head, and the arrow went directly into its neck. At this the kelpie, who appeared to be weakened, started to shake its head in fury. I looked towards Iris, who was preparing another spell, but appeared to be failing to summon the flame. However, Keila looked like she was in a batter’s position.

"It is coming," I heard Iris say, but Keila was ready. The horse started running directly towards us, still shaking its head in a fit of rage. As soon as the horse was within five feet of our group, Iris lunged to the side and so did I. Keila swung her sword at the charging kelpie's head and the sword hit home, sinking deep into the creature's neck. The monster stopped dead in its tracks and then fell to its side, the sword still within its neck. As soon as it had dropped a new line of text has appeared in my vision.

| **Your party has killed a kelpie**<br>**Experience Reward: 10 Points** |
|---|

"Wow," I said, looking at Keila, who was shaking, with a look of excitement on her face.

"That was insane," she said. "Did you see that?"

"Ya, we all saw you take it down like a boss," I said, with a smile at my new friend's win.

"Wait, guys it is disappearing," remarked Iris, who was picking herself off the ground where she had jumped when the kelpie had made its last charge. The creature's body was slowly dissipating, like we had seen before and, in its place, laid several items. "Pick everything up, we might need those supplies later," continued Iris.

After first picking myself up off the ground, I looked at the items spewed across the grass where the horse had once laid. There were several items and as I touched each item a notification appeared.

**New Item: Seaweed x 5 – Pick Up or Drop**
***This is Seaweed, a plant grown in various bodies of water, has multiple uses but is most notable as a weak food source.***

**New Item: Kelpie Heart x 1 – Pick Up or Drop**
***This heart from the water creature of a kelpie can be used in enchantments, potions, and poisons.***

**New Item: Copper Coin x1 – Pick Up or Drop**

I placed each item in my inventory by choosing 'Pick Up.' There was no description under the coin but looking through my menu I saw that it had brought up my total to one copper and ten pennies. Let me just say, I was not writing home about my financial stability, at the moment.

"What did we get?" asked Iris.

"We got a copper coin, one of those heart things, and some seaweed," I responded.

"It looked like this system worked for us," said Keila.

"I agree, Zeph pulls, I shoot my Fireball spell, and you take them out with the sword," responded Iris. "However, we need to wait, that spell costs all ten of my mana points. It is filling up, but I need a few more minutes."

With the team's agreement and Iris' mana counter refilled we repeated the exercise over and over again: pulling in the kelpie with my arrows and finishing them off with Iris' fire spell and Keila's sword swing.

After about an hour we had killed eleven more of the creatures using the same methods. On my next shot, however, my arrow had skimmed along the back of one kelpie and landed in another which resulted in two kelpies running at us.

"Crap on a stick," I murmured seeing the two kelpies running towards us.

"I cannot hit both," screamed Iris as she murmured her spell to life, the fire flicking in and out of her nearly cupped hands.

"We got this," said Keila who was brandishing her weapon to take on the lead creature.

"I got the second," I said. "Once you take your swing Keila, I will get the second one with my dagger.

"Ignis!" yelled Iris, casting the fire upon the first kelpie. At this I released my arrow and scored a shot directly into its ribcage. Once the arrow landed, I drew a second arrow and lined it up with the second horse-shaped creature. It was moving too fast, and I could not get the line of the arrow's path to stabilize.

"Crap, I can't get a shot at the second horse," I said, but by that time the first horse was already on us. I dropped my bow and pulled the dagger, feeling its coldness pinch into my palm. Iris turned to jump out of the way of the incoming kelpie, and Keila began to swing her sword. I began to run at the second horse, who was charging me since Iris' fireball had not touched it. The monster was a foot away from me and I could see the water that hung off the kelpie's snout. I swung my dagger at the snout and felt the dagger sink into the creature's face and run along its face. I continued my momentum and dropped onto the floor, praying that the horse did not stomp on me. However, as I dropped down, I could see armored feet running towards me, or more accurately, towards the kelpie and then heard the sound of metal hitting flesh. I glanced up to see Keila pulling her sword back for another swing, but I quickly turned over onto my back and thrust my dagger towards the creature's lower neck. Before Keila could complete her swing, the kelpie fell over with my dagger still imbedded into the top of its chest.

"That was fun," said Keila who was grinning from ear to ear. I was not going to be telling Keila this, but the smile and the hair all over the place alongside the greenish blood from the kelpies was giving Keila a chance at a half decent Joker costume.

"Ya, so much fun, almost trampled to death, but so much fun," I replied sarcastically, shoving my hand at Keila to lift me off the ground. As she did so the experience notification appeared in my vision.

**Your Party has Killed Two Kelpies**
**Experience Reward: 25 Points**

"Hmm," I continued. "I got five more points of experience this time, than for the other kelpies."

"Same," confirmed Keila. "Must be because Iris did not get to rain her fire attack on this one, and just you and I had to take it out."

"Makes sense," I said while opening my menu. I had a total of 245 experience points out of the thousand that I needed to progress to level two. This game was not making it easy to level up through the typical grinding methods. "Damn, leveling is difficult in this game."

"Agreed," said Iris. "But, I did get the chance to level up my Battle Magic skill and now that fire spell can be cast in half the time."

"And I leveled up my Longsword skill. It has increased to level two as well," said Keila. "I am not seeing any status change, but the sword does not feel as heavy."

"What did we get this time?" asked Iris as she saw me going through the items from the two kelpie kills.

"More of the same," I said as I picked up each item.

**New Item: Seaweed x 10 – Pick Up or Drop**
***This is Seaweed, a plant grown in various bodies of water, has multiple uses but is most notable as a weak food source.***

**New Item: Kelpie Heart x 1 – Pick Up or Drop**
***This heart from the water creature of a kelpie can be used in enchantments, potions, and poisons.***

**New Item: Copper Coin x 4 – Pick Up or Drop**

"We now have the five Kelpie Hearts that I need to fulfill my quest, a sea's worth of seaweed, and we now have twenty coppers to our name," I said.

"This was number thirteen, right?" asked Iris

"No, fourteen, we need to take out six more before we can return to Landan," I answered. "However, that should not be so bad. These are rather weak creatures, and we do not even know how hard they hit since we have yet to take any damage."

"This is true, but better to play it safe than not," remarked Keila.

"True that," I responded.

Thus, we continued to follow up with our attack and eventually we pulled in the last kelpie. At this point in the fighting the routine became, well rather routine, and we started to grow bored with the party grinding. However, we had succeeded in both quests that were assigned to us, and it had only taken us an hour and a half to take out all of the twenty kelpies. Further down the river we could see even more, but we decided to leave on a high note and go return to Landan to get the quest completed. I ended up leaving the river side with 305 experience points, twenty-four copper coins, and more seaweed than any human could consume. Plus, I had gotten one more heart from the second-to-last kelpie, so I was feeling pretty good about our position.

## Chapter 14: Quest Completed

As we returned to Altour through the city gates I looked around the market for the vendor that we had encountered on our way out of the city. I could see his mustache before I recognized the rest of his features. He still stood behind his stand, screaming some deal on his wares.

"Hello Merchant Markus," I said as our group approached his table.

"Ahh, so soon you return. Did you do as I requested or are you here to return the knife that I loaned you?" he questioned me, crossing his arms in judgement.

"I did as you asked, and I have them right here," I said while accessing my menu and clicking on the six Kelpie Hearts that we had gathered from the horse-shaped monstrosities that inhabited the riverside. Once removing them from my inventory, I placed them on that table. However, I did keep one of the six in my inventory for later investigation.

"Beautiful," said the vendor while grabbing one of the mossy stones that came from the creatures. "I see that you have completed your quest, the knife is now yours to do with as you please.

**Quest Completed: Obtain 5 Kelpie Hearts and Return Them**
**Reward(s): Glass Dagger's Ownership**
**Experience Gain: 100 Points**

Fantastic, I thought. With those experience points I was even closer to attaining my next level. I wondered what I would unlock by increasing my levels. If we were to be successful in finding Dr. Hobbs and Ms. Reynolds, we all were going to need to level up.

"One-hundred experience points so now I have four hundred and five," I said to Keila and Iris with a grin. They grinned back. I turned to leave the vendor with his new belongings, giving him a wave as I began to walk back towards the walls of the city with Keila and Iris. We started our journey back towards White Bridge area of the city, the same area that we initially entered the city through. However, that required us walking along the walls of the city again to find the guardsman.

"This is not going to be easy to level up, and we really still have no clue where either Hobbs or Reynolds went," I remarked, mostly to myself.

"I agree," said Iris, who was grasping me in the crook of my arm and looking at me closely. "However, we got this if we work together. We will go to Landan and continue on from there to *The Hollow Quiver* to discover where their location might be."

"Sounds like a solid plan to me," said Keila. "Nonetheless, we still have not managed to level up and we are going to need more gear and skills to leave this city."

"Suggestions?" I asked.

"I believe that depending on the experienced gained by Landan we will need to evaluate," began Keila, "if we aren't close to leveling up by then I suggest we find some more of these starter quests to level up before heading over to *The Hollow Quiver*."

"I guess we will see when we get to Landan, and go from there," I said. "How long have we been in this game?"

"Well, Baridac took almost two hours and handling the kelpies took another two, I suppose," pondered Iris. "Plus, we have been doing all of this walking. So, I am guesstimating that we have another three hours before the game logs us out automatically."

Iris' answer to my question got me thinking about the amount of time that we had before today's allocated time was up. We had too many things to get done in such a short period of time, as we needed to find Reynolds and Hobbs as soon as possible. The pressure was beginning to heat up, and the desire to talk about the things we had discovered in the overheard conversations between Sammy and Dr. Jordan was overwhelming. However, while we were in the game, I did not feel comfortable talking about it, and I felt that the feeling was mutual since neither Iris nor Keila had mentioned it. Moving on from that train of thought I quickly jumped to another, about a way that we could approach this game more effectively.

"So, Keila, you're a Paladin, correct?" I asked, knowing the answer.

"Yes, sir," she responded. "Why do you ask?"

"Well, I was thinking about how we can most effectively approach this game, and how we might be able to accomplish a lot within a shorter time span. For example, finding the god or goddess that you will be tied to might be a task you would want to do alone?" I asked.

"I suppose—," began Keila.

"That is actually smart," said Iris, letting go of my arm. "We should split up to accomplish some parts of this game. We each have different areas that we are going to need to focus on. For example, I am going to need to purchase some Mana potions if I am going to continue throwing that fire spell around."

"Exactly," I said, glad to see that Iris was understanding what I was saying.

"And you Zeph," continued Iris. "You need to continue leveling up your other skills, such as sneaking, and you cannot do that while we are around. After we get to *The Hollow Quiver*, I think we should consider the best way to finish today for each of us," finished Iris.

As she said this, we began to approach the gate that we entered the city of Altour through. I had not realized how fast we had walked back to this area of the city. I was spending longer and longer stretches of time in my head, especially as I enjoyed the scenery of the medieval city that was before me.

"I see you have returned with all of your limbs intact," remarked Landan. "Did you do as I tasked?"

"Indeed, we have taken out twenty of those kelpies," Keila remarked.

"Fantastic news," Landan said, clapping his hands. "This takes a load off of mine and the other guardsmen's minds. I thank the three of you."

At his words a new set of text, although becoming swiftly similar appeared within my vision.

| **Quest Completed: Remove 20 Kelpies from the River**<br>**Reward(s): Landan's Respect and 20 Coppers x3.**<br>**Experience Gain: 200 Points** |
|---|

At these prompts I knew that I was over halfway to leveling up and got excited with 605 points. The coppers were also a nice addition, considering that we were rather poor. Although now I had forty-four coppers and ten pennies in my pouch since I hadn't divided the earnings with Keila or Iris from the kelpie fights.

"Thank you, Landan," I said.

"Where are you three off to now?" he asked.

"We are heading towards *The Hollow Quiver* to find out some information," I returned.

"What kinds of information are you three going over there for?" asked Landan with more than a curious glance. "That inn is not filled with the grandest of characters, if you catch my meaning."

"You see, we are looking for our friends. Those two travelers that came through a few days ago, and Baridac said that we might be able to find some information on them there."

"Ah, of course," he said. "I do remember them; they were an odd couple and seemed to cause a bit of a problem in the city."

"How do you mean?" interjected Keila.

"Sorry, I meant nothing by it, just a little bit in my head today," he said, finding that grin he greeted us with. "I would just be careful by *The Hollow Quiver*, don't accept any jobs from the folks in there. That would be my advice."

"Do you have any clue where our friends went?" I asked.

"All I could tell you is that they left the city some time ago," he said, beginning to turn around and head back towards the gate.

"However, if there is anything else you three might need do not hesitate to come and find me."

We all said our goodbyes to Landan's back as we continued on past his gate and towards *The Hollow Quiver*. Once again, I began to feel like there was something that was being said in-between the lines from all of the non-player characters that we were meeting. First there was Baridac and now there was Landan. If my intuition was right, then it would appear that there was a large quest forming for the players of this world. I just wished that I had the time to find out what it was and begin to properly enjoy this game. However, there was a job to get done and if I did not want my past exposed then I needed to get it done.

Nonetheless, it got me thinking about the first time I had ever played an open world game such as this one. Of course, it was not on the scale of *Fabula* since I was playing this game a long time ago. Those days, for those unaware, were the days that we had to play games with something called a controller, and that is not even the craziest part. Those controllers were connected to the television or gaming device through a cord, I know, it is astounding. How we survived during those times, also known as the Stone Age, is unknown by younger generations. We lived in caves, ate rocks, and played our consoles through remote controls; it really is unthinkable.

Anyways, this game I was always obsessed with, had the main character investigate a major city within the medieval empire where a killer has been active. This murderer was killing people at night. Using amateur detective skills, and possibly a playing guide, you had to discover the culprit and capture them. While not the most complex or scary quest to have ever been created, it stayed with me for nights afterwards. I kept flashing back to standing in a snowy corridor to find myself chasing someone. That kind of immersion in a game is thrilling. First though, before having that kind of fun again, I needed to ensure that I didn't end up sipping martinis in a third world country or living in jail because of Joshua Sorrento and—

"What has got you thinking so hard," teased Iris, who was pulling on my arm.

"Oh, nothing important," I replied. "Just thinking how there seems to be something off within the narrative of this game. As if, I don't know, there is something that Landan and Baridac did not want to really talk about."

"I felt the same things," said Iris, who now wrapped her left arm through the crook in my right arm's elbow. "However, while I would love to find out what is going on, we simply do not have the time."

"I know, I know, it just had me thinking," I murmured sheepishly.

"Who knows? Maybe whatever is up in this city is connected to the disappearance of Rinc's CEO and COO," Keila said before taking on a more serious tone. "However, it does not matter currently since we have no information. Until we make some headway in finding Hobbs and Reynolds we cannot be distracted."

At Keila's words we all became silent again, thinking our own individual thoughts. We continued our journey of keeping the city's wall to our right as we headed towards the inn that might have someone who could point us in the direction of Reynolds or Hobbs, but preferably both. We walked for another few minutes before we saw another break in the wall, and there it was, Westgate. The gate appeared to be similar to the other ones that we had seen throughout the day. However, this one appeared to be more lavish. There were double the number of guards that we saw at White Bridge and there were tapestries that hung down on either side of the gates opening. A few dozen feet from the gate began the road that led deeper into town.

The cobblestone looked cleaner, and the homes appeared to be outlined in greater color with the clotheslines outside the dark wood buildings. Based on Landan's words I was expecting a sketchier side of town to be the home of *The Hollow Quiver*, but it was quite pleasant of an area. Even that putrid smell seemed to have abated slightly. A few buildings down the road stood a three-story building, the tallest one yet, and outside the porch hung a sign. The sign only contained an empty quiver.

"I think we have found *The Hollow Quiver*," I said to Keila and Iris.

## Chapter 15: The Hollow Quiver

We walked up to the building; Keila took charge with me taking her right side and Iris falling to cover Keila's left side. It went unspoken, but there was an uneasy feeling about the building. The only way I could describe it was the feeling one has when you know you have walked into a room that you do not belong in. Before we had even stepped onto the porch that led into the building there was a loud vibration coming through the thin wooden walls. While I couldn't distinctly hear words, I could tell it was a musical beat. It reminded me of the times I pulled up to a car that was blowing out their speakers to Taylor Swift, and I would see a twenty-something white dude bouncing his head to the icon's music. Yes, it was always men, and it was always Taylor Swift.

Keila pushed the door open, and we walked into the larger version of Baridac's Inn: *The Tipsy Dwarves*. On the right of the door was a long bar that went from the door to the other side of the room. Directly across the room was a large stage that held a woman who was leading a drinker's chant to the left side of the room that was filled with several tables of men and women drinking and singing to the song.

*"We shall take back our land,*

*So raise your flagon*

*For here we make our stand*

*Against the Black Pawn*

*To take back our lands*

*Raise your swords*

*For we shall issue our commands*

*And slay the hordes*

*They came at the gate of iron*

*We heard their roar*

*The did not expect the god of the ironed*

*For he extinguished them forevermore"*

"It is kind of catchy, no?" I asked, unable to stop the tapping of my foot.

"You have not heard the tales of the Black Pawn?" I heard asked from behind us. We all turned around to see a man behind the bar who was cleaning a glass cup similar to the ones we saw earlier in the glass market.

"Can't say we have," said Keila, who looked like she immediately distrusted the man. This might have been due to the fact that he spooked us with his sudden arrival or maybe Keila hated bartenders, I was not convinced either way.

"It really is a story worth your time, care to hear it?" he asked.

"Sorry, we do not have the time. We are actually looking for two of our friends and we were told that they stayed here," Keila responded.

"Oh, who are your friends?"

"There were two travelers or adventurers who left around a week ago. They might have been going by Hobbs and Reynolds. Does that ring any bells?"

"It is true that I allowed many people to stay at my inn over the last few days, and it is even truer that many were travelers from other places," the bar tender said while continuing to clean the glass. "However, how do I know that you do not mean my pass clients harm or that you are truly their friends?"

"I can assure you that we know them well and that we need to find them for their own safety," remarked Keila who looked aghast at being accused of being untruthful.

"You see, your word is simply not enough, but your actions might be," he responded. "I have a little problem that you might be able to assist me with, and if you do so then I might be able to assist you in your problem."

"What kind of problem?" Keila asked cautiously.

“Nothing too major, I simply am having some supply problems with some elvish whiskey. It was supposed to arrive a few days ago, and I am sure that it is nothing major. Nonetheless, I am requiring my supplies be restocked and if you were help me then I might be able to help you. After all, a friend of mine is a friend of my clients,” he finished with a grin.

At his words the familiar text appeared in our vision:

**Innkeeper Goldsmith Has Offered You a Quest: Discover Where His Supply of Elvish Whiskey Is and Report Back to Him.**
**Accept / Decline**
**Reward(s): The information you seek and Unknown.**

We all looked at each other, but at Keila’s nod we said, “We accept,” together and the words disappeared.

“Fantastic then, well why don’t I help you out a little bit,” he said with a smile of achievement on his face. “The elvish whiskey is somewhat illegal in Altour as in most human cities due to that tiny dispute we have. So, I have it smuggled down the river and through Barbers Town area where it is stored in some warehouses down there. I would suggest checking it out there.” At his words another line appeared and swiftly disappeared:

**Quest Update: Find the Warehouse.**

"We will let you know what we find," I said, pulling Keila's arm slightly to encourage her to walk away from the man so that we could speak. After we were out of earshot of the barkeep and supposed innkeeper Goldsmith, I looked at my party's faces.

"This is going to be a problem. We are nearly out of time for the day, and we have not even begun to discover where Reynolds or Hobbs are. The only thing we know is that they are not in the city," I said.

"I recognize that," growled Keila. "However, we do not have much choice, do we?"

"I think we are going to have to speak to Sammy or one of the others about this," Iris remarked. "It feels like we are being pulled in a circle and we are not being allowed to get on with this quest. After all, aren't the quests pre-programed? I could not imagine that Sammy or any other developers would have engineered a quest that the reward was Hobbs' and Reynolds' locations. They are not supposed to even be in the game."

"I did not think about that," I said. "But you are right. The quest for the knife and the quest for Landan both seemed to be typical of normal game play. However, this tailored quest around Reynolds and Hobbs should not be in the game. Maybe it is Ellie, the AI, who is doing this?"

"It is a possibility," Keila murmured. "However, we will not know more until we speak with someone outside of the game."

"What do we do in the meantime, since we only have a little time left for the day?" Iris asked. "Should we just log out or should we continue to max out our time for the day?"

"I think we should follow my original game plan," I said, "we should not start the whiskey quest and we should focus on getting ourselves prepared. This would mean leveling up and getting some of our errands for our classes done."

"I know that I still need to find a god, or I will lose out on some of the special abilities of my class," Keila said, beginning to tighten her hair bun in a fit of stressful exertion.

"I need to pick up those potions and try and find some more spells," said Iris. "I only have the fire one and a defense spell at the moment."

"I used all my arrows with the kelpies, and I would not mind leveling up my sneaking ability," I said.

"So, it is decided," said Keila. "We will split up with our time remaining and head our separate directions to find the things we need. We can meet up after the game time allotted and find a plan to approach this new quest."

With that decided we decided that we had not really had a chance to try the food in this world. While the seaweed we had picked up from the kelpies was an edible food source, no one was dying to take it for a spin. After all, this seaweed was from the corpses of dead monsters, and that just did not have the same ringer as 'grass-fed beef.' So, we decided to order some of the food that was available from the bar. It was rather bland, and it did not feel like it had filled me up. I guessed that there were still some parts of this virtual simulation that were not replicable.

"That was disappointing," I murmured, throwing down a cloth napkin that most would consider to be a cut-up piece of a cloth shirt.

"Epically so, not worth it at all," Iris agreed. "It really was a waste of those few coins. How many do we have left?"

"I have forty coppers and ten pennies in my pouch. What about you guys?" I asked.

"I only have the ten pennies from Baridac and that is all I believe Iris has as well," said Keila to Iris' agreement which was indicated with a swift nod of her head as she attempted to swallow the extremely bitter beer that we had ordered.

"Let us split it, I'll take twenty coppers and I'll give twenty to Iris since she needs to buy her potions, and I need those new arrows. You can take all my pennies, sound good?" I asked.

"Agreed," Keila said. "Let us get a move on, why don't we?"

## Chapter 16: My Name? Solo, Han Solo

With some final changing of money, we each walked out onto the porch of *The Tipsy Dwarves*. None of us knew exactly where to head out, but Keila was able to speak with some of the people in the inn to discover that she needed to go just a few blocks over to find the temples of the gods in this city. Apparently, all of the gods' temples could be found in the Four Chapels area of the town. And don't ask me why it was called Four Chapels, the guy we asked started yelling when we attempted to inquire further. I was picking up that religion was a controversial topic in this city. It was somewhat disappointing that some things did not change from the real world to this world, there is always division. So Keila went on her way to that area of town with Iris' and my pennies alongside her sword.

After some further talking with helpful passers bye, Iris and I discovered that Silkliff had some areas for shopping to find some weapons and other supplies. We decided that we would both start heading down that direction. The visuals of the city were still gorgeous and as we walked deeper into the city, the city grew before my eyes. The entire time that we had spent within the city we had kept close to the walls, using them as our directional tool and allowing them to take us from place to place. However, the edges of the city were the most decrepit, except for Westgate. The luxury of a complete and clean cobblestone road maintained true throughout the entire journey we took deeper into the city. As well, alongside the taller and larger buildings that occupied the streets there was a new visual addition in the not too far distance, another wall.

"What do you think that wall is?" I asked Iris. "It appears to be much shorter than the other walls that border the city limits."

"Good question," she said looking up to gaze at the forty-foot-high wall. "Based on the time period and the city, I am going to guess that it is a castle or some fortress."

"Don't you think that someone would have mentioned this city having a king or a queen at some point during our journey?" I wondered aloud.

"Dummy," she said with a grin reaching to tousle my hair. "Not every castle or fortress needs to be occupied by a queen or king, it could simply be the lord of these lands."

"That would make more sense," I muttered, for missing the obviousness of Iris' remark and the logic behind it. "Changing topics, do you notice the smell here is much better?"

"It smells almost like New York City now, much better," she joked. "I do see what you're saying, they must have the city focus on keeping these areas of the town cleaner, if the army is located here then it is probably part of their job."

"Ya, I remember Sammy mentioning that this area had soldiers."

"She also said that we could find some people to train us in sword fighting and other styles of combat training. I double that there would be much use to me as a mage, but you might be able to find someone to help out with your dagger."

"That is true, I leveled up my skill in archery, but I have not gained any levels of acquired any skills in my dagger, yet."

"Remember, your skill is two-handed daggers, not single-handed," she said while pushing my head in a gentle manner. "You are probably going to have to unlock that skill by continuing to use only one dagger. Your other option is to buy another fancy new dagger or equip both."

I had completely forgotten that was the skill associated with the ranger class. I was enjoying the single dagger, but dual wielding was always awesome. Was I basing this on any professional level or was this based on strategic foresight about my fighting? No, I just wanted to look cool whipping out two daggers. At this train of thought I realized something: I still had my starter blade.

"Look at this," I said to Iris as I accessed my menu and clicked on The Rusty Dagger item in my inventory. Upon clicking equip I saw that there was an option to equip on my right side, the opposite side of my current dagger. The dagger appeared on my right side so that I could yield it in my left hand while my new dagger remained on my left side for my right hand.

"Come here often?" she asked while leaning against the walls. At the sight of this I started an uncontrollable laughter.

"Hey –," she began to say but then she also fell into a fit of laughter.

We continued to laugh for a bit before we composed ourselves and continued on our journey towards Silkliff, and the area of town that was supposed to consist of soldiers, armor and weapons merchants. The area with the wooden structures began to dissipate, and the buildings were more and more made of stone. It was gradual, with the first level of some building being built out of cobblestone, but as we went further in the buildings began to have as many as three stories. As we fell deeper into the area of the walls, the sounds of shouting and sword fighting became pronounced.

"Those must be the training grounds for the soldiers," I said indicating towards the wall.

"I think so, but we need to find the area that people sell weapons, not the area where people use weapons. Let us ask," she said as she began to look around for someone to address.

After finding someone that was not running towards something or being yelled at by someone else, we discovered an older man who appeared to be appreciating the day on the porch of his building.

"Hello, sir, we are looking for the market. Could you point us in the right direction?" Iris asked, slowly approaching the man on his porch.

"Isn't the sound peaceful?" he responded. Which was not an answer to our question, so Iris got closer and repeated the question. At the second round of the question, he looked at Iris' face for the first time.

"Oh, sorry miss, lost in my own head today," he said, adjusting himself in his seat. "How can I help you?"

"We are looking for the market to purchase some gear," she said. "Could you point us in the right direction?"

"The younger generation surpasses the older generation, it only takes time," he said, but it appeared to be more of a verbalization of his internal reflection. "Simply take this road further down and you should find what you are searching for."

At this we both bowed our heads and continued on the direction that the older gentleman indicated. The realism of this game, with regards to the non-player characters, was pronounced. It was difficult, if not impossible, to discern between a real person, of which there were none, and the virtual people. The characters of this game were an invention of the AI's system and therefore these reflected the realism that was contained with the artificial intelligence of this game: Ellie.

"I know we keep saying it, but this game's level of realism is insanity," I remarked. "It kind of creeps me out how realistic the people are."

"I know, I think it is called something like the uncanny valley," she said.

"What is that?"

"You know when you see a robot or something that looks super realistic, but there is something just not right about it?"

"Ya, I felt that when I saw some of those emotion-something-or-other-robot videos that come from Japan."

"Exactly, when something is so realistic and not actually human it gives an uneasy effect that is known as uncanny valley. That is what I have been feeling sometimes when I interact with Baridac, Landan, and the other characters we have met in this game."

This put me further into thought about the situation that we were in. The whole mystery around Reynolds and Hobbs was concerning. The idea that it was someone on the outside who engineered it for them to get stuck in the game was worrying enough. Secondly, there was the glitch that Dr. Jordan and Sammy had mentioned. I would consider myself one of the best at finding glitches and I had yet to find any such glitch. I wondered if it had something to do with Ellie, the artificial intelligence of the system. However, I had met Ellie and she seemed like she was functional. Now that I considered it, she seemed fully functional with her unique personality and everything. With such a system running this game, I find it unlikely that there could be any possibility of a glitch in the system.

"What were your thoughts on Ellie, the AI?" I asked Iris.

"It was…unique," laughed Iris. "It was really quirky and had a fun sense of humor. Honestly, I could see myself getting along with Ellie, even though it is not human or anything."

"Funny that you call Ellie and 'it,' I felt that Ellie was feminine," I commented.

"Ellie has that quality, but there is no sense in getting too comfortable with such a system, I find it easier to acknowledge Ellie as an it," she said in a tone that showed the thought that lay behind her choice. As she said this, I heard a few more familiar yells: not the yells of danger or pain, but those you only really hear from merchants. You know the yell, the distinct flavor of screams of bargaining and deals.

"Here we are," I said as we turned onto the street. There were dozens of buildings along the street, but rather than closed doors and people sitting on their porches the first floor of all these buildings had the street side opened to the air. I could see inside the first few buildings and see swordsmiths working at their forges while customers watched. In another building there was an armorer who was strapping on a chest plate to another potential customer. Further down the street I could see a few of those wooden test dummies for fighting and a crowd was surrounding them while people took swords to them. Wooden arms were splintered off and basket heads full of straw went flying as we watched.

"Are you seeing anything pertaining to arrows?" I said, mostly to myself, as I looked around at the buildings and the products held along the walls of the rooms that lined the street.

"I am busy looking for somewhere to buy potions," Iris said in response to my question. "This place is wild; I wish we had more than forty coppers to spend here."

Iris' sentiment was not lost on me. I, like many of my modern-day fellow humans, shop so often online that it was wild to see such an explosion of activity around a shopping venue. I was more use to doing majority of my shopping through online services, even my groceries from time to time, so this reminded me of the Black Fridays before such services were available. At last, in the far corner of my field of vision, I saw someone shooting arrows at a wooden dummy, similar to the ones that the young men were slashing swords at.

"I think I found my place," I said while pointing at the man who was shooting arrows.

"Let's go, but keep your eyes open for anyone selling potions," Iris said.

With that we began to walk through the crowds of people, often getting rammed into the shoulder or hit along our way. By the time that we had passed the crowd of people watching the sword testing session we were more bruised than we were from the fight with Landan. However, we eventually arrived to discover the shop from which the archer came from, along with the archer themselves. I was wrong in my initial assumption of the character being a male, rather it was a female shooter who had kept her hood up while firing.

"Hello," I said to the archer as she was about to fire her next arrow. She ignored my greeting and continued to focus on the target and with a deep breath she released the arrow. It struck right in center of the dummy's forehead. "Good shot," I commented. At this she finally looked at us and took off her hood. The woman standing before me, and Iris was similar to Landan with the extremely sharp features and the light brown hair.

"How may I help you?" she asked the two of us.

"Hey, I am looking to purchase some arrows, I am all out," I said, while holding out my empty quiver.

"I can see that," she said, looking fierce while her lips pressed a thin line on her face. "What types of arrows?"

"Um… the regular?" I questioned, not fully understanding the question.

"A new archer, I see," she said, and she did manage to curve that line on her face slightly upwards. "Come inside, both of you."

We followed her as she turned around and began walking towards the building behind her. Unlike the other stores, this one appeared to be more like a regular house with the front of the first house enclosed. She opened the door and we walked into the store front. The walls were lined with dozens of different bows made of different materials and thousands of arrows with a large variety of different types of arrow heads that were dispersed in large buckets throughout the store.

"When did you all begin?" she asked.

"Begin what?" I countered.

"When did you and your friend become archers?" she clarified, and she did not look happy about the necessity to do such a thing.

"Oh, I am not an archer, Zeph is just my friend," Iris said. At her comment of friend, I gave her a raised eyebrow, but she ignored it.

"Then why are you here?" she asked, focusing on Iris.

"I am looking for a potions shop, for some mana potions."

"Go next door, they have a large collection of poisons and potions," she said. At this Iris nodded and headed out the door, leaving me alone with the scary lady.

"I ask again, when did you begin your archery?" she asked.

"Well, sort of today, I just started," I stammered. "However, I use to shoot before, but was not that good at it."

"How is your quiver empty?"

"My friends and I were taking on some kelpies by the river earlier today."

"So, you're not completely useless with your skill. I have decided I will help you. There are too few archers these days. All the focus is on those big clunky pieces of metal that they swing around the place."

"That is kind of you, but I just wanted to buy –," I began but she stopped me with a raise of her hand.

"You will accept with gratitude," she said putting down her arm. "Also, because it is a personal favor of my brother." At this I just stood there and looked more closely at her. Now that she said brother, I could see that she did not look similar Landan, but she looked exactly like him. "You helped him today and earned his respect, he mentioned you might come down here. He asked me to make sure that I would help you, as a way of showing his gratitude for your assistance beyond the material."

"That was too kind of your brother, it really was no problem," I said with a smile. "By the way, how did you know it was us?"

"Simple, he said to look for foreigners, and you and your friend… let say, stand out. Come on, we will begin now."

"Right now?" I asked. "I have many things to do and do not know –," I began but was once again stopped by that hand of hers.

"Do not worry," she said. "Your friend, Iris, is with those sparkly finger types and they will be assisting her also, as a favor to me."

"Oh," I said, not really knowing what to say in this situation. "Thank you," I tried.

"You're welcome, now take that quiver over there and let us begin."

## Chapter 17: Legolas Has Nothing on Me

With that the female archer, who I soon learned was named Elana, attempted to drill some skills into me. We went outside where she was shooting and had me attempt to hit the dummy in the center of the eye. Since the distance could not have been more than a few dozen feet I took aim focusing on the line that appeared from the top of my arrow and lining it up with the dummy's head. I shot and somehow missed the head by a foot. I knew that the kelpie bodies made for an easier target, but this was just shameful.

"Tsk, tsk, tsk, again," Elana said.

So, I lined myself up again, and aimed another arrow and missed. This time though Elana did not say try again but instead she slapped my shoulders and said, "Straighter." So, I attempted again, concentrating to make sure that my back was straight as a board. This time when I shot the arrow it still zipped past the ear of the fake head. At this Elana began shaking her head, it appeared to be in dismay, and she said, "Again!"

It went on like this for another hour or so. In reality, it could have been much longer because Elana's posture adjustments were not too kind. However, after about twenty minutes of strict instructions from Elana I had finally hit the target, but on the shoulder of the arm. Either way I was ecstatic since the notification that appeared.

**Level Up Skill: Archery to Level 2 – Unlocking your skill in Archery allows you to see a faint line appear, predicting where your arrow will land with 55% accuracy.**

In addition to the skill upgrade I also had received another fifty experience points bringing me to a grand total of 655 experience. However, my joy did not last as we continued to train, and by the end of the hour I had received my second notification from the training.

**Level Up Skill: Archery to Level 3 – Unlocking your skill in Archery allows you to see a faint line appear, predicting where your arrow will land with 60% accuracy.**

This time I had struck the edge of the dummy's face. I would estimate that it was somewhere around the cheek region. However, this did not bring praise from Elana, but rather she looked at me and shook her head.

"Your posture is dreadful but improving. I would estimate that within a few years I could make you competent," she said.

"A few years," I said with shock and horror.

“Yes,” was her only response. “However, I have seen worse. With a higher quality bow and some more training, I predict that you might be able to shoot something successfully.”

“Unfortunately, that is not an option. I only have a few coppers on me, and I will need the arrows.”

“This is true, you cannot yet afford it, but I might have an alternative. If you wish, come back here after a few more hours of practice and we will see what I can do.”

“That is too kind of you,” I said with a smile.

“It truly is, but I love my brother. Give me ten coppers and I will refill your quiver and you may collect your friend from next door.”

With that I passed over the coins and she passed me the filled quiver. I then looked in my inventory to see that I had twenty arrows, once again, in my inventory. While I was getting some verbal instruction from Elana on how to correct my posture, I received a notification from my menu. Within the corner of my vision an icon popped up with an envelope and the number one hovering over it. Upon seeing it I rushed a quick goodbye with Elana, promising that I would practice and that I would return once I had something to show for it. She nodded her head and waved me out the door.

Once outside the building I focused and summoned my menu with a wave of my hand. I saw that there was a new button above the boxes where the envelope symbol was encrusted, and I clicked on it.

*From: Shane Miller*

*Hey Zeph, it is Shane, Sorrento wants me to tell you that you have less than an hour in your playtime today. Once out of the game we are supposed to meet with the entire team in the board room.*

Upon seeing the message, I looked at the bottom and saw a reply button. Once I clicked it a new box appeared, but there was no virtual keyboard to type out my message. So, I attempted the only other method that came to mind, speaking. I composed my message that wrote itself as I spoke.

*From: Zephaniah Kote*

*Shane! That sounds good. We will talk soon. Have some ideas about everything.*

With that I clicked send and went to go find Iris, but she was already standing in front of me. I guessed that I had gotten a bit distracted by receiving the message from Shane.

"Did Shane message you?" I asked her.

"No, Sarah sent me one. I assume yours mentioned the time remaining?"

"Ya, and that we are to meet up afterwards. What are we supposed to do with our remaining time? Did the magic guys help you out?"

"They taught me a new spell, and they gave me four mana potions. It cost me all of the money I had, but it will be worth it. I suppose that since we have only an hour left, we need to focus on getting some experience points up. Do we want to head down the river for more kelpies?"

"Not enough time, we need something closer that we can do," I said.

"I have just the place," Iris said while grabbing my hand and dragging me away. "The river runs throughout the city, and the mages told me about where I might find some practice places for my new spell."

"Sounds good to me," I remarked while being dragged away by Iris.

We eventually came upon the river that separated Silkliff from another part of the city, Barbers Town.  We got lost quite a few times, but by asking various people on the streets, we were able to come upon it within thirty minutes of backtracking and getting lost in dead end alleys. As we walked towards the river the building sizes and frequency began to diminish. A few blocks out from the water's edge the buildings stopped all together. As we walked out from between the last two sets of buildings, we could see that the city had built themselves above the level of the river. The land around the river was separated from the stone world of the city with tall walls. It looked like there were staircases that led from the cobblestone pathways of the city to the river down below.

At the top of the staircase that led down to the waterfront, the reason for the lack of buildings became clear. There were dozens of various creatures that seemed content to be milling around down at the water's edge. They came from the river, but upon closer inspection it came apparent that they also come from the holes that appeared every few meters in the walls that lined the river. I pointed out the holes in the walls to Iris. "Looks like the sewers are infested with all sorts of creatures." While not too many of them appears to be dangerous, there were one or two kelpies amongst the dozen or so creatures down there.

"Hey, what are you two doing?" asked a voice from behind us. We turned around to see another guardsman, indicated by his armor and sword.

"We came to help remove some of the monster's down by the riverside," I remarked.

"I am sorry, but I cannot allow you to just wander down there. It is extremely dangerous, and if you become injured or killed then it is on me," the guardsman said. He was serious, as indicated by his subtle movement while he spoke. He ended up standing between the stairway and us."

"Where do the creatures come from?" I asked him. It was curious that such a number of creatures, harmless or not, had made it all of the way into the city. After all, the entire city was walled off from the outside and it would seem improbable that the city wanted such a threat to their public.

"As you can see, the sewers are absolutely swarmed with many different monsters that sometimes come out onto the riverside," he said. He began to turn around to point out the same holes in the walls that I had noticed earlier. "We do not know where they come from, it is somewhat of a new development." A flash of concern spread across the guardsman's features.

"New development?" I asked, mostly to myself.

"Yes, they began to appear a few weeks ago. Around the time that everything else started to turn odd around here," he remarked. He said this in a manner that implied something unspoken, I nodded as if I was in the club. I often found that the best response to intense confusion is to play along until you either understand or you are fired.

"How can we get permission to head down there?" Iris asked.

"You will need to speak to the captain, only he can grant such permission. Usually, only guardsmen go down there."

"Where can we find him?" I asked.

"You can find him in the fortress, but it is not going to be easy to get an audience with him," the guard remarked. He began to walk away from the two of us.

"What are we going to do now," Iris asked. She looked as frustrated as I had felt at being told that I was not to be able to go gain some quick experience points.

We discussed our plan and decided that there was no way that we were going to be able to find the captain of the guard before we had to log out. Either way, our time was nearly up, and no time remained that allowed us to go find another place to grind some experience for the remaining minutes.

"How about you show me that new spell you are working on?"

"I'll show you mine if you show me yours," she said with that smirk. At that I pulled out my bow and arrow and aimed it at one of the kelpies down by the river. The valley that was created by the walls completely cut off the wind so there was no need to worry about that. I aimed the arrow at its head and let the nearly invisible line find it mark and I released. The arrow flew, and I do not know if Iris had some luck charm on her, but I hit it dead on in the head. The kelpie dropped.

**You Have Killed a Kelpie**
**Experience: 30 Points**

Unfortunately, I could see the items that the creature had dropped were along the shoreline of the river. It was a shame, but when I looked at Iris, her facial expression made it worth it. She was grinning ear to ear. "Impressive, I'll give you that." As soon as she said that she brought her hands together and started to murmur words that I could not quite catch. I guessed that was intentional by the game developers, they didn't want just anyone being able to learn a spell from listening to a spell caster. However, I did hear the last word of Iris' chant, "lux." At that a ball of light the size of a baseball appeared over her shoulder.

"Pretty," I said. It looked like a miniature sun.

"It is not great for combat, but if we need a light then I am your gal."

"Indeed, you are."

At this a timer appeared in our vision, it was a countdown counter for five minutes.

"Looks like we are about to be logged off," I remarked assuming that she was seeing the same counter in her vision. We both took our last few minutes to find a place that was identifiable to let Keila know where to meet up with us. We saw a bridge that crossed the river's valley, and we stopped in front of it. "Looks as good a place as any." With that our screens went black.

## Chapter 18: The Meeting with a Capital "T"

"Welcome back," said a voice in my ear. I nearly jumped out of my chair as I tore the helmet, hoodie-like contraption off my head. Of course, it was Sammy grinning at me with such joy that I was incapable of being angry at that sneaky move and my reaction.

"Thank you," I said looking back at my surroundings. The entire room remained the same and I looked over to the chairs next to me to see Iris and Keila both peeling off their own contraption and sitting up in their chairs.

"How was it?" Sammy asked us. She was bouncing up and down on her feet, causing her curly hair to bounce alongside her. "Was it amazing?" She kept squeezing her hands, as if she were attempting to contain her excitement, but was failing in a spectacular fashion. However, I was not too fast to answer, it felt like I was waking up after a nap that turned into a half a day event. My brain was not quick on the uptake at the moment.

"What an insane thing," said Keila, who was grinning wide. "I never played anything like it, how did you guys do it?"

"Just a few million, maybe billion in research and a few marriages," said a monotone voice that could only belong to one person.

"Hello Dr. Jordan," I said. I turned back towards Sammy. "It was really impressive, felt almost like real life."

"It is true, it was literally unimaginable how you could feel and smell everything. Even each other." At Iris' response, Sammy hopped on her feet once more. "I know right! It took many hours to get the textures just right, and while not perfect I am very happy with it." Sammy's reaction to our one-line critique told a person everything they needed to know; this was her baby.

"Okay, time to get up. We are supposed to be meeting with the entire team upstairs in five minutes," said Dr. Jordan. "We can discuss details later, I have a few questions for each of you, but they will have to wait."

With that, we completely detached ourselves from the chairs, and I did not feel the least bit sore. That was as much a surprise as the game was; after all I couldn't sleep in bed for eight hours without waking up some kind of soreness. However, maybe I just had a bad mattress, this required future contemplation. We quickly left the game room and headed towards the elevators and from there to the board room. The boardroom looked the same with everyone around the table. I noticed Majed who was nursing a tiny cup of coffee, which must have been Turkish based off the smell. Next to Majed was Sarah Schiff who must have also been drinking the same coffee. Across the table sat Conor Carpenter and Shane, who, when we walked in, stood up to greet us and invited us to sit next to him.

"How was it?" he asked to the three of us as we took our chairs.

"You would not believe it my friend," I began. "We never even left the starting city and the smells, and the NPCs were out of this world. It was almost eerie how realistic they were in terms of personalities and everything."

"This description agrees with my expectations after seeing the code," he said with a grim expression. "I have never seen anything like it, and I would not have believed such capabilities possible in our present time. I could spend a lifetime diving into the code itself and never find myself bored."

"Did you find the glitch or what caused the problem?" asked Iris over my shoulder. At this Keila started to lean into the conversation.

"We found something, but not here," Shane said while looking around in the manner that implied that eyes were watching. With that we all nodded our heads in agreement and started talking about the game. Shane and eventually everyone around the table asked us about the experience and we ended up recounting our tales in extreme detail. I am not kidding, Sarah asked us how the cobblestone felt on our feet. Their questions and our answers were excruciatingly detailed. After a few minutes of interrogation, the glass door of the conference room opened and in walked four people: Sorrento, Dr. Jordan, Sammy, and an unknown face. He appeared to be African American and was a rather large man. This was accompanied by his larger-than-life voice, "Hello you three, we have not met yet. I am Jack Blake, the Chief Technology Officer of Riverlight. It is a pleasure to meet you." We all stood up and shook his hand, and when he eventually let go of mine, I felt that I had to touch my hand to ensure that it was still attached to my body.

Without noticing the discomfort, I was in, the man turned away from me and all four of the company's employees sat down at the end of the conference table. There were at least two or three chairs between us and them. Their position to us reminded all of us that we were not here as partners but as employees. However, employees felt like too kind of a word. Employee implied a contract and respect between one person to another, but this lacked any level of respect. I did make an exception for Sammy; I liked the girl.

"Where are we," asked Sorrento, who looked at us with his hands clasped on the table.

At his invitation to begin the meeting, Sammy took first charge. "Dr. Jordan and I sent Zephaniah, Iris, and Keila into the game; within the first eight hours they completed some of the necessary starting quests and have nearly reached level two."

At Sammy's pause Dr. Jordan continued, "Their progress would indicate that they are on track for being able to leave the starting city as early as tomorrow evening or the day after."

After Dr. Jordan finished, Sorrento looked at the three of us and asked, "What did you three find out about Dr. Hobbs and Ms. Reynolds?" I looked at my team and they were looking at me, so I guessed that meant I was being volunteered as tribute.

"We entered the city and after speaking with several NPCs we have discovered who might know where they went. According to one NPC they entered the city and then left afterwards. However, we do not know where or when exactly. We began a new quest that should unlock some of the information that we need, in order to find out exactly where they will be or were."

"What do you mean, started a quest?" asked Sorrento. "All of the quests were predeveloped for the game. I mean that information that you need on Dr. Hobbs and Ms. Reynolds should not be tied to a quest. Can either of you explain?" he asked to Sammy and Dr. Jordan. They both looked extremely uncomfortable for a moment, but Sammy spoke up. "Due to the artificial intelligence system, the information might have been later connected to a quest by Ellie."

Sorrento began to start fuming, "What do you mean?"

"I mean, simply," stressed Sammy, "that there is nothing we can do about it. The game system has decided to lock this information up within a quest and therefore it will be up to the three of them" – indicating Iris, Keila, and myself – "to both solve the quest and find the information."

"Since when was this a possibility of Ellie? I thought that she was under tight restrictions to ensure the game remains static until its final release," asked Blake in his booming voice.

"I am unsure of when or how it happened, but it appears to be connected to the glitch we discussed earlier," Sammy responded.

"What glitch—," I began, but was quickly interrupted by Sorrento. "Never mind, we will deal with what comes, but let me assure you that time is of the essence you three," he said while looking at the three players. "Now, for the coders, what have you found out?"

Dr. Blake began here, "We have discovered that there are several additions made to the code. The purpose behind this addition is yet unclear, but they are there."

"Why have we not removed these lines of extra code?" Sorrento asked.

"We are unclear as to their intent and removing them might either damage the game or worse, damage Dr. Hobbs and Ms. Reynold. We are not able to remove them until we have more information and there might be additional lines out there," said Blake.

With that, the meeting continued for a few more minutes. Basically, summarizing, or revisiting topics we had already discussed.

I began to tune out when Sorrento returned to the question of why removing the gaming code would possibly cause harm to fall upon Dr. Hobbs or Ms. Reynolds. Before the meeting ended, Sorrento reminded us three players that they had to speed up the process of leveling up and completing the quest. With his final command, Sorrento quickly exited the room, declaring that we were to return early in the morning. Everyone began to follow him out, but I felt a touch on my arm and turned around to find Sammy behind me. She whispered in my ear, "Grab the others and meet me in my office."

Ten minutes later I had gathered Iris and Keila to head downstairs, and on a spur of the moment I also grabbed Shane's arm. Shane was curious about what we were heading downstairs to do, but I only informed him of what Sammy had said and I did not enlighten him to my own thoughts. There was something fishy going on here, and I could not figure out what it was. First, we knew that someone had accessed the AI systems to trap Reynolds and Hobbs within the game. Secondly, we also knew that there was some kind of glitch in the game that the higher-ups were aware of. Lastly, the game was making revisions as we played. They all were disconnected in some respects, but I just did not know enough to figure out what they meant as a whole. My brain was beginning to hurt. Lost in my train of thought, the journey from the boardroom to Sammy's office was on auto drive and I became aware of my surroundings once Sammy started talking.

"You're Shane, right?" asked Sammy as we all walked into her space. I looked around but I did not see Dr. Jordan anywhere.

"That is correct, Dr. Vanderbelt. I hope I am not imposing," he said with a slight nod of his head towards the doctor.

"Of course not, if you can keep what is said between us," she said with the first serious expression I had ever seen on Sammy's face.

"Of course, Doctor," he said with another bow of his head.

"Fantastic," Sammy responded with a clap of her hands. "We need to discuss something that Mr. Sorrento and the others do not believe are necessary for you to know. However, I believe it is necessary to understand the depth of the situation for your own predicament."

"What are you talking about?" asked Iris.

"I am also confused, is this about the glitch?" asked Keila.

"Ah, so you did hear me earlier in Dr. Jordan's office," Sammy said smiling to Keila's horror of outing the fact that we had listened in on her conversation. "Do not worry, I thought as much. You see, I cannot tell you all everything as I do not think that you need to know every detail. Nonetheless, I believe that I should give you some information to allow you to make a more informed decision."

“We are listening,” I said with a nod of understanding from the others.

“Where to begin? I guess the beginning is best,” began Sammy. “We finished the creation of Fabula roughly three months ago, but due to some… problems we were not able to announce the arrival of the game. That was until two weeks ago, when the board announced that bankruptcy was imminent and that we were broke as a company. There was no money left and the board needed us to give the public something. That was when Dr. Hobbs decided that it was time to announce the game, in order to use the flush of preorders to hold us steady for the time being. However, the problem that held up the game's release was not solved nor was any solution prepared. This put us in a pickle.”

“What was the problem, exactly,” I asked.

“I cannot go into detail, but it had to do with Ellie,” continued Sammy. “The AI was creating more and more in the game than we could possibly monitor. It was not anything bad, but it was messing with the storyline of the game and the functionality of the gaming systems. We had put restrictions on Ellie's decisions to stop the development of future stories because of an incident.”

“What –,” I began, but what swiftly interrupted by Sammy.

“I will not go into details about it but rest assured that the game would not have reached approval for release if any of this got out,”

Sammy said. "We believed the problem was solved until… Dr. Hobbs and Ms. Reynolds went into the game. We are still unsure why they went into Fabula, but their current state means that the game continues to present some glitches."

"But we heard you say that someone did something when you were speaking with Dr. Jordan," Iris said.

This entire conversation, Shane's eyes just continued to grow wider and wider, and Iris' comment put him over the edge. "Was this intentional? Dr. Hobbs' and Ms. Reynolds' predicament?" he asked.

"This is unconfirmed speculation," responded Sammy with a frown appearing on her face. It looked unnatural after my growing accustomed to her sunny smile that had seemed etched in permanent marker on her face. "We believe that Ellie is functioning as planned, or at least we did until you told us about the information quest you were tasked with. We cannot know more until we can find Ms. Reynolds and Dr. Hobbs. We must know why they decided to enter the game, and only then can we figure out exactly what happened. Do you believe you guys are close to finding them?" Sammy asked with an unusual amount of intensity.

"We do not know, or at least we won't until we get back into the game tomorrow," I said.

“Okay then,” Sammy said, clapping her hands with the usual smile returning to her features. “I will let you guys go and get a good long rest before we begin again tomorrow. See ya,” she said turning to leave and exited the room through Dr. Jordan’s office door.

“What was that about?” Shane asked, his normal demeanor etched with confusion.

We told Shane that we would fill him in after we got out of the office. We ended up deciding as a group that we had nothing to eat all day and that we needed to go find something to fill our stomachs with. The decision was easy, we went out for sushi.

## Chapter 19: The After Party Meeting

We all ended up jumping into Iris' car, since we all knew that we would be back in the same place tomorrow and she drove us there. We went to the same sushi place that I had been going to since I was a teenager, it was decent sushi, but they were having a limited-time deal. This limited-time deal had been going on for almost a decade, at my count. As we piled into one of the tables at the restaurant, Shane started pulling over extra chairs.

"Are we expecting company?" I asked my friend.

"I texted Majed, Conor, and Sarah. Told them where to find us. Sarah and Conor said they were on their way, but Majed… is Majed," he said with a shake of his head. "We all need to be on the same page, and there was some stuff that we found out that we want to discuss, but Sarah and Conor are better at this stuff than I am."

After pulling another table over, we began to order and sip away at our miso soups while we waited for Shane's entourage to join us. After a few minutes everyone was around the table and we were enjoying the limited-time cheap sushi, that might come to kill us, but in the moment, it was utter bliss. Shane drilled us about what we did in the game. He started teasing me about my inability to shoot anything, which Conor and Sarah swiftly joined in on. They were getting comfortable, it would seem. However, Iris came to my defense talking about my last shot in the game. After me, Keila filled us in on her journey.

"So, after we split up, I walked over to the Four Chapel's area of the city. It would appear that there is some kind of law about gods and the city, so all the temples were outside of the walls," explained Keila to the group. "There were a few different options, and I ended up getting an entire quest line to just discover more about some lost god or goddess. However, I will not have enough time to really dedicate myself to that."

"Do you think it would be worth it, I mean, for you to go into the quest?" I asked.

"It would be if we were looking at a long playthrough of this game, but since we are aiming to be done in the short term I just went with the currently available gods and goddesses," Keila said between bites of sushi.

At that remark Sarah looked up from her intense examination of her salmon sashimi. "How many were there?" she asked forgetting the fish.

"I think that there were like eight or more temples in the area, it was not exactly clear," replied Keila. "From what I saw, there are specific gods for each race and there are more minor gods for specific jobs or materials. It reminded me of the Greek pantheon, you know. The Percy Jackson style gods and goddesses. For example, I saw the Iron Lord's temple, and he appears to be god of the dwarves' race and miners based on the number of dwarves and non-dwarf miners that I saw at the temple."

"Which did you decide to go with?" Sarah asked.

"After looking, I decided that I should go with the goddess of strategy, Canta. She sort of reminded me of an Athena look-a-like from Greek mythology. She has some really convenient perks and after I prayed at her temple, I was able to gain some new skills. For example, I now have healing magic for my teammates" – indicating me and Iris with her chopsticks— "and some other cool skills."

"That sounds pretty epic. Especially for us moving forward since I just have a minor healing spell and everything," I responded to Keila's revelation about her choice of goddess.

Keila continued to explain the other options that she had available to her from the temple-filled area of the virtual town. There was a god that was entirely focused on just the economy, and you worshiped him by increasing your own wealth. It was an intriguing idea to have a class that would involve you having to learn about each of the gods and their unique traits. It was just unfortunate that for the sake of Keila she was not able to spend as much time on fulfilling that missing god quest or finding the perfect one.

However, the Canta choice sounded good by me, and Iris' head nodding during Keila's explanation showed her approval, as well. However, after some more details from Keila, I noticed that Shane was starting to look agitated. No one else would be able to tell, but after years of friendship I could see the raised eyebrows and pressed lips of an anxious Shane.

"What has got you, Shane?" I whispered towards my friend, bending over the table as to not interrupt Keila and Sarah and they continued to go deeper and deeper down the rabbit hole of the virtual game mechanics of religion.

"While I enjoy hearing about your guys' adventure, we must discuss something," he whispered back, also leading across the table so that we could speak discreetly. "We have not had the chance to speak on either of our findings without having Sorrento or one of the other Rinc employees standing over our shoulders. We should talk about it and share our findings with the entire group. Put our minds together."

"I agree, it would probably help to get everyone's input or at the very least have everyone be aware of the dangers."

"Agreed, I am not aware, but based on the conversation with Dr. Vanderbelt you three know more than I do."

"That is true because we overheard a conversation between her and Dr. Jordan before we entered the game. We did not have a chance to tell you guys before now."

"I see," Shane said, pinching is stoic face in deep concentration. "Let us tell everyone, and I can fill you three in on the details that we have learned from the code."

Shane proceeded to turn towards the entire group and apologized for interrupting Sarah and Keila's intense conversation about the mechanics of religion in modern video games. He informed them of everything that we had heard from Dr. Vanderbelt, and I filled them in on the details of what we had heard from behind the closed doors of Dr. Jordan's office. There were a few details that I missed, but Keila and Iris were able to fill in the gaps that I left behind.

"Wait, so you are telling me that this game has a glitch and Dr. Hobbs and Ms. Reynolds entered the game to attempt to fix the problem?" asked Conor Carpenter as he swung his piece of sushi from side to side as he narrated his question. "Then someone else or something happened with the code that resulted in the two of them getting stuck in the game. Oh! Then, supposedly, there was an incident of some kind that Dr. Vanderbelt won't speak about that happened before any of this?"

"Correct, or at the very least that is what I assume is the case," I said to Conor who looked slightly aggravated at all of the new questions that were being presented with no apparent answers.

"What was this incident?" Sarah whispered to herself.

"Like I said, that is still unknown," I said in response to the whispered question. "I really do not know more than you guys do at the moment. But wait, what did you guys find out Shane?"

"I nearly forgot to mention it," he said in response. "While Majed, Sarah, Conor and I were working on the code to discover how the two executives were permanently locked into the game we came across something."

"Was it that line of new code?" Iris asked, who had been very quiet the entire meal.

"There was that too, but not only that. We were asked by Blake to not say anything until we knew exactly what was going on. However, there was something more that Sarah actually discovered," Shane said, indicating Sarah who blushed at the attention. "It looked like entire areas of code were erased from the game and from the functions of the artificial intelligence of the game."

"Could that have been those areas that the artificial intelligence had developed, but Rinc had scaled back?" I asked.

"No, this was way more than a few cities. It looked like enough space that there could have been two artificial intelligences or something. This is really a larger unknown to me because something such as the AI has been theorized, but never actualized. In fact, Ellie is truly just an extremely functional program. There are limitations within her code that limit her capabilities of making her a fully independent intelligence. Therefore, she is not autonomous, like a human or anything of the sort," Shane remarked, looking concerned.

"And we do not know what that lost code or program was, but there is definitely something missing from the game?" I asked, trying to wrap my mind around what Shane was telling us.

"Could it be tied to the information that Dr. Vanderbelt told us?" Iris asked.

"Could be or it could not be, but I just think we all need to be aware that we are not being told the entire truth. In fact, I feel like we are mostly in the dark on this," he said.

After that intense revelation, no one was really interested in continuing to discuss matters that would have been normal dinner conversation. The meal started to feel like one of those family meals where one of the cousins says something racist and everything goes downhill from there. Everyone continued to have their back and forth with Shane as he discussed the information that was revealed to everyone tonight, but there was no further insights or illumination on the dark corners that resided within Riverlight

Incorporated. After another few minutes everyone finished up their meals, paid, and we were out the door.

It had started raining while we were inside, in typical Colorado fashion, so the goodbyes were quick as we each ran to our cars. Shane, Keila, Iris, and I quickly piled into the safe harbor that was Iris' car. She pulled us out of the parking lot and began driving us back towards Rinc headquarters to get our own cars. After getting everyone settled, Iris and I began to head back to where she picked me up in the morning. However, I could still see Keila doing something in her car. It was curious that she had not left yet. While I was thinking this Iris turned back on the car and we pulled out of Rinc's parking lot and back onto the street.

"What are your thoughts?" Iris asked me, breaking the silence that had enveloped the car.

"On?" I quired.

"I don't know, everything I guess." She said raising her shoulders in the air in the universal manner that implies 'whatever.'

"I just… I just feel that we know too little and that we are not going to know more until we begin investigating what is going on," I said.

"How we going to do that?"

"Probably, eavesdrop on more conversations behind closed doors would be a good start."

"Ha," Iris said with her fake laugh, it was cute. "Ya it would only be considerate of them to do that."

With that we continued the drive-in silence until we arrived at the front of my apartment complex. "Same time tomorrow?" I asked.

"Actually, no. I have an idea."

"Oh, what might that be?"

"It is a secret, but I'll see you tomorrow at the office. I'll fill you in then," Iris said with that same smirk I had come to appreciate.

"Sounds like a plan," I said while getting out of the car.

"Hey, that is not how you say goodbye," Iris exclaimed.

"Sorry," I said returning the smirk that she was giving me. I leaned over to meet her lips. "Better?"

Instead of answering she simply rolled up the window, forcing me to remove my head before decapitation. She waved and drove off and I walked upstairs with a huge grin plastered on my face.

## Chapter 20: The Game is Afoot

I jumped out of bed to the sound of my phone ringing. "Who could possibly be calling me at this time?" I muttered to myself, reaching for the phone. Upon reflection, I realize that it would have been simpler to find my phone if I had opened my eyes.

"Who is this?" I asked into the phone as I found it on the fourth or fifth ring.

"It is Dr. Jordan; we need you to come in immediately."

"Why would I need to come in at—"

I pulled the phone from my face to glance at the time, but the brightness nearly blinded me for half a second before I could see the time clearly on the top of my phone's screen.

"—four in the morning, Dr. Jordan?

"I will explain once you all arrive; we have a problem," Dr. Jordan commanded before ending the call. I could imagine his frustrated face as he, most likely, aggressively slammed his finger onto the screen to end the call.

It took me a few minutes to fully gain the capability to open my eyes, but once I had climbed that particular Mount Everest, I pull my phone up to my face and squinted at my chatrooms. I found the one I had created earlier with Shane and Iris in it and sent a message.

Zephaniah: Hey, u guys get called in?

Shane: Yes, sir. Getting ready now. Do you know what it is about?

Iris: Hey, he just hung up on me. Like, what the crap was that?

Zephaniah: Absolutely no clue. I'll let you know if I find out anything, see you both soon.

I could see the dots that indicated a messaged was being written, but after a minute of waiting nothing appeared and the dots had disappeared. I guess we were all being left in the dark on this one. I quickly got out of bed before the warmth of my pillow and blankets sucked me back into their embrace. If that happened, then I was doomed.

After running through the shower, literally. I got dressed and was attempting to encourage my eyes to remain open as the coffee maker was dispensing the nectar of the gods into my cup. My phone dinged and it was Iris.

Iris: Zephaniah, someone died.

Zephaniah: What do you mean? How do u know?

Iris: Sarah, she just called me. She is there and there are cop cars all over the place. The paramedics are there. She said that she saw a body being carried out in one of those black body bags she sees on CSI all of the time.

Zephaniah: Is it someone we know? I am on my way now.

I sent that text as the coffee maker had finished its job. I grabbed the hot mug and my jacket and headed out the door. Once I had gotten to my car Iris had already responded.

Iris: She says that it's Sorrento.

I had called Iris, but she did not pick up. I guessed that she was also running to get out of the door and get to Riverlight Incorporated. I rushed over there, and with it being a half past four in the morning the roads were empty. I was able to get there before five in the morning. As I pulled into the parking lot there were still dozens of flashing lights from the local authorities' vehicles, but it did not appear as crowded as I had imagined. There were a crowd of cars off to the right of the police vehicles, and I drove over there. Upon pulling up I could see that all of the cars, but one was turned off. I got out of my car and as I approached the car, I could see Iris' read hair fall out of the passenger vehicles window.

"Zeph, get in the car," she said while pushing a button inside the minivan which caused the side door to open. I approached and crawled in to find a filled car. Sarah was in the driver's seat, both hands seemingly stapled to the wheel even though the car was not going anywhere. Shane and Conor were in the back seat and Majed was on the opposite side of the middle column of seats. I sat down next to Majed and pulled the door closed.

"What happened?" I asked to the crowed, struggling to get the door shut. Once shut, I realized that it was a little uncomfortable having six grown adults in a minivan. "Where is Keila?"

"We do not know; she hasn't driven in yet." Iris said in response to my question. "As to your first question, Sarah was right. The police officer told us that we are not to enter the building yet, but they had found a body a few hours ago."

"I called upstairs to Sorrento's office and the only person that answered the phone was Blake, the CTO," said Sarah. "He told me that they had found Sorrento's body in his office."

"Why does he want us here?" I asked Sarah.

"He would not say, but he said to sit tight and that he would have us all in the building shortly."

"Why would anyone kill Sorrento?" I asked, mostly to myself.

"It would appear to be intentional," Shane mused. "Afterall, you do not go into a random office building in the middle of the night unless you have a purpose in mind."

"Are you saying that someone wanted Sorrento dead?" I asked to my friend. He merely nodded his head confirming my question.

This made no sense. Why would anyone kill Sorrento? I could understand the motivation behind this decision if it was based purely off of the fact that he was a jerk. After all, he had threatened to end each of our lives, not literally, but you know what I mean. I could see one of us deciding to take that option out of play by removing him, but why would they not just leave? I mean, what dirt could he have that would have been worse than first degree homicide. I would much rather go to jail for my hacking than get accused and thrown in jail for murder.

While I was getting lost in my train of thought I realized that someone was knocking on Iris' window. It was Dr. Jordan.

"Please follow me inside," he said, simply. Before we had a chance to respond he had already begun to walk away, and we all quickly climbed out of Sarah's car and followed him inside. The cop cars were still present, and I could see several of the cops standing in the lobby. As we approached the building, I could see that there were dozens of people who were sitting on the various couches laid throughout the lobby and the cops appeared to be taking statements. I do not know much about a murder – assuming it was a murder – investigation. Nonetheless, I had watched enough Law and Order to recognize how the authorities took witness statements.

"Why are you having us come in? None of us had anything to do with this?" I asked Dr. Jordan, but he simply ignored me and opened the door with a wave of his wrist. He held it open as each one of us passed through into the building, but I stopped in front of him.

"Why did you call us in?" I asked, again.

"All of your questions will be answered shortly, but for the moment I need you all to be quiet and follow me," he said while waving me inside the building. I was not sure, but I would have sworn that I saw something resembling fear in Dr. Jordan's eyes. As well, his voice did not hold that normal tone of disinterest that I had taken for granted from the man.

We followed him in, he gave a curt nod towards the police officer who saw us walk in. We continued on past the officer towards the same elevators we had been using every single day. We all crammed inside and with another swipe of Dr. Jordan's wrist we were rising up towards the floor with the massive meeting room. Upon entering the floor, we could see that there were several cops on this floor. It made sense, since Dr. Sorrento's office was on this level, and that was presumably where his body was found. I looked through the plane of glass that separated the hallway from the board room and it was pitch black. It appeared that we were not heading there as Dr. Jordan led us on past the room and we walked into another room that was further down the hall. He opened the door, and I could see that it looked like a miniature lecture hall, as if it was a training room. The room was filled with long tables with chairs that faced one direction, towards a wall with a massive white board that filled the length and height of the entire wall. Standing in front of the wall were three people: Keila, Dr. Sammy Vanderbelt, and Jack Blake.

"What is going on here?" I asked towards Keila. I looked towards Shane and Iris who had entered the room right behind me, and Shane's face was filled with disappointment. I was not sure of what realization had hit him, but it obviously was not good.

"Please, could you all just sit down," pleaded Blake, his normally booming voice sounded heavy.

We all took our seats, except for Dr. Jordan who had headed up towards the front of the room the join the three others.

"There is a bit of explaining that we need to do, so please just hold off your questions till the end," Dr. Jordan said to the entire room. He turned back towards his colleagues and Keila before looking back at us and grasping his hands together in front of him. "Joshua Sorrento was found, murdered, in his office sometime after midnight. We do not know exactly what caused his demise, but it would appear that he was shot several times. He was discovered by Keila, and we had called the cops immediately. We felt it prudent to bring all of you in to explain the situation and to ensure that you heard everything from us."

I looked towards Iris and whispered, "Keila?" However, Iris just looked back at me with confusion written across her face. She was just as confused as I was about this situation.

I did not get a chance to speak to Shane before Dr. Jordan continued. "We do not know who the potential murderer was, nor do we know what he or she's motivations were, but we do surmise it has something to do with Fabula. While this is tragic, and all of you will be interviewed by the authorities shortly, but then we must continue with haste on the previously assigned task. Finding Dr. Hobbs and Ms. Reynolds and getting them out of the game remains a priority."

At this point, I could not tolerate that they were still expecting us to work on the stupid game when someone had been murdered. "What do you mean? We cannot continue working. Someone was just murdered! The same person who brought us all into this," I exclaimed.

"You know, maybe he is right," whispered Sammy.

Dr. Jordan paused and gave Sammy a stern look, but before he could respond Dr. Blake stepped forward and said, "I understand your frustration, I really do. However, there are billions at stake, and I can assure you that Mr. Sorrento would have wanted us to finish our… project."

"Whatever Sorrento's desires were do not matter anymore," I nearly yelled. "If you are right and people are dying for this game then I don't want to stay involved in this matter anymore."

Sammy looked like she wanted to say something, but a look from Blake made her shut her mouth. Blake then looked at me, aghast at my outburst, but I felt it was ridiculous that they would want us to continue with the game. However, while Blake was looking at me with dismay, Dr. Jordan took a step forward. "I can assure you, that the same promises that Sorrento made to each of you can still be fulfilled if you would wish to exit the project," Dr. Jordan said too calmly for my liking.

"If I may ask?" began Shane. "What brought Keila to his office so late in the evening?"

At this everyone up front began to look at each other, and I noticed that Sammy was looking somewhat hurt. I could not figure out why she appeared to be so upset when all of her colleagues and Keila were looking upon us with plain faces, as if nothing had ever happened.

"It is a fair question," began Dr. Jordan. "Keila? Would you mind explaining to everyone?"

Keila looked at Dr. Jordan and nodded. "This is a bit of an awkward situation, but basically, I was privately recruited by Sorrento earlier in the year, back when the first problems with the game began to surface. I was included in your team to ensure that we all stayed on task. I was reporting back to Sorrento on the group's conversation during dinner—"

"You were reporting on us?" Iris asked, she looked extremely hurt.

"Yes, it was my job. It was not personal. I really rather enjoyed the time we have spent over the last two days together. This was not personal, and it was my duty to ensure that we did our task," Keila said. She appeared to also be a little sad at seeing the expression painted on Iris' face and the emotion that poured between her words.

"You are quite the actor," said Majed. I was a bit taken back because I had not heard him speak much over the last few days and upon hearing his voice, I had to look over to ensure that it was from him mouth. At his words Keila hung her head in shame and lifted her hands into the air, as if to say, 'What can I say?'

"You are not alone in this revelation," said Sammy. "I was also not aware of Keila's involvement in the company. I never even saw her before today." The meaning behind her expressions became clear. Keila was in that secret conversation that we had earlier with Sammy, and she was probably not happy to discover that she was just as betrayed as we were.

“I was the only other person aware of her involvement, so the blame rests with me and, of course, Mr. Sorrento,” said Blake. “Her involvement was not meant to be such a secret, but Sorrento and I felt that it would be better for the overall outcome to have someone within the team who could keep everyone motivated.

“I can understand that Keila was here to motivate Zeph and Iris during their game play sessions, but it makes me wonder about our team,” Shane asked. At his words the group of people seated began to eye each other. This was fantastic, now no one felt that they could trust each other. The other fact that remained completely disheartening, was that no one said anything to Shane’s comment either.

“This all is extremely comforting,” I said aloud to the now silent room.

After a few more minutes of Dr. Jordan continuing on about how important it was for all of us to stay on mission or face the consequences. While Dr. Jordan never bothered to list the actual consequences of not listening to him, the true threat was clear. If we did not perform then all of our secrets would be out there, and it appeared to everyone that it was better that we continued on with the mission. During the middle of Blake’s follow up speech on the same topic, the door to the room opened up to see a police officer.

"We are ready to speak with them as soon as possible," said the officer to Blake, who was the one who was in midsentence at the police officer's interruption. After his announcement, the officer quickly exited the room. This left everyone staring back at Blake.

"You heard the man, tell him everything you guys know. Of course, I think it prudent for your own self-interest that the… incentive that Sorrento provided you with will remain strictly between us," Blake said with his normal commanding voice. While I would have enjoyed disagreeing with him, I also recognized the wisdom of his words. I could tell the police everything, including the blackmail, but then I would just be telling the police the exact information that I wanted them to avoid having by signing up with Sorrento and Rinc.

We all left the room and followed the police officer, who was waiting outside the door to the training room, towards the elevators. We all crammed back into the elevator, and the cop rubbed a card in front of the sensor that unlocked the elevator, allowing him to click the lobby floor button. We descended back downstairs. Exiting the elevator, the cop directed us to sit down over by the couches that previously held the night crew of Riverlight Incorporated. The couches and chairs were now empty, unlike how they were when we arrived. I guessed that the police had finished collecting their witness statements. After we were all seated in our various seats, I saw the elevator open up again to see Keila, Dr. Jordan, Sammy, and Blake exit. At the policeman's gesture they continued into a hallway that began at the corner of the lobby.

The officer that had escorted us to the lobby followed them down the hallways to an unknown location, presumably where the police were going to be collecting their witness statements. "This has all gone belly up," I remarked to Iris and Shane who had chosen to sit on the same couch as I. Sarah Schiff, Majed Ayad, and Conor Carpenter all had taken separate seats far away from each other. It appeared that the distrust caused by Keila's grand reveal had left a sour taste in the mouths of our teams. However, I was not displeased. I was not totally sure which of the three of them could be the secret mole for the other group, such as Keila was for Iris and me.

"It indeed has, I had never suspected that our internal discussions were being fed back to the executives," said Shane with a shake of his head. That look of disappointment that had appeared on his face earlier still remained.

"I honestly was beginning to really like her," Iris said with some sadness in her tone. I reached out to take her hand.

"Same, after her expression when she came out of Sorrento's office at our first meeting… I could not have guessed it," I confirmed while squeezing Iris' hand. "Makes me wonder more about what the truth behind all of this is."

"We need to finish this; I cannot walk away from this and risk everything getting out there," Iris said.

"We will, the same goes for me," I said to Iris. At this Shane also nodded his head. Whatever was going on, the three of us were in it together. It did also remind me that I had no clue about what was being held over the heads of Shane and Iris. In fact, I had no clue what it could have been for any of them.

"What does Sorrento have on you guys? I guess I should say, 'What did he have on you guys?'" I asked the both of them. I looked at them both with a grin plastered on my face. "I'll show you mine if you show me yours." While this did not completely alleviate the tension of the situation, it did give Shane a grin while Iris just gave me a glare.

"Not here, but I feel that you deserve to know," Iris said, looking right at me. As if on second thought, she looked back towards Shane. "Sorry, Shane, you too, of course," she stammered, awkwardly, realizing the social fumble she had just made. Shane simply laughed at watching Iris attempt to stick together a casual statement, as if she had not totally forgotten his presence in the room.

## Chapter 21: The Interview

Before long Iris, Shane, and I began diving into speculation of who was most likely responsible for the murder of Sorrento.

"It could not be one of us," Shane said. "After all, if they were to enter into the building after hours, they would have to have either a special card or device that the employees have to enter the elevators."

"I have seen those, they swipe their wrist against the sensor," I confirmed Shane's statement.

"Therefore, the only logical assumption is that it is either Dr. Vanderbelt, Dr. Jordan, or Jack Blake," mused Shane.

"Don't forget the back stabber," Iris said. "But I have a hard time believing that Sammy could have been the murderer. She seems, I don't know, too kind. She was genuinely hurt by Keila's betrayal.

"Indeed, Keila could have one of the wrist sensors if she has been an employee here for so long." Shane started to rub his head in a stressed-out manner, something I had never seen from the cool and collected man before. "Of course," he continued, "I agree with your assessment of Dr. Vanderbelt's character. Although, it could be none of the above, it could have been anyone of the board members or one of us through other means. After all, it would not be impossible for one of us to request access upstairs from Sorrento if we wanted it."

"So, basically, outside of the three of us, we are just as clueless as the cops," I concluded.

"Clueless, you say?" asked an unknown voice from behind us. It was the same cop who had escorted us from upstairs to the lobby a few minutes earlier. "We are ready to take your statement. Ladies first?" he asked while looking at Iris. She gave me a look of fright at being caught red-handed in our musing about the murder.

"We were just hypothesizing who the possible suspects might have been," stated Shane.

"In that case, we are probably not as clueless as you three. After all, none of you were here at the time of the incident?" the officer asked.

"No, we all had headed home right after dinner," Shane responded.

"Of course, and naturally you three all have alibis or, let me guess, you would not happen to be each other's alibis?"

"Iris drove me home, but after that I was alone," I said. Shane and Iris both nodded their heads in agreement at the statement.

"I see," said the officer. "Anyways, it is time we got your statements. If you would not mind following me Ms.—"

"Iris Christman."

"Ms. Christman to the interview room we have set up in the back?"

"Of course," she said while collecting her things to follow the cop back down the hallway.

"What are you thinking?" I asked Shane after Iris had walked down the hallway and out of our sight.

"Honestly, I am debating if it would be worthwhile to tell the authorities our perspective on the situation. However, I have the inkling that it will paint us in a different light than we would prefer to reside in."

"What do you mean Shane?"

"I mean that often pointing the finger results in three fingers being pointed at you," Shane said while exhibiting this fact by pointing his index finger at me and resting on his palm I could see his middle, ring, and pinkie all pointing back towards Shane's chest.

"I see."

We passed the rest of the time in silence, waiting for Iris to return from her interview. After a few more minutes had passed, the police officer had returned with Iris in tow. He then took me back towards the interview room. We walked down the hallway to a single door imbedded into the far wall. He opened the door to show a single table with two other officers sitting on one side of the table.

"Hello, Mr. Kote, please take a seat," the first officer said while gesturing to an open chair on the other side of the table. He was an older gentleman with a handlebar mustache that actually looked like it suited his face. His dark black hair that was speckled with gray and his mustache gave him an air of authority. The same could not be said about the other officer. He looked to be younger than I was, with a floral button-down and a skinny tie to pull the ensemble together with his skintight khakis. I went over and took the seat and sat directly across from the first officer. The cop who had directed me took the far chair on the left.

"Please understand Mr. Kote that this is in no way an attempt to implicate you or your friends," began the first officer. "We simply wanted to get statements from all of the individuals who were around Mr. Sorrento this week. Before we begin let me introduce myself. My name is Officer Gerald, and this is Officer Spencer," he said, indicating the second officer sitting down. "Of course, you have already met Officer Leo, as he met you upstairs."

"Nice to meet you three," I said while exchanging handshakes with the officers. "I assume you got my version of events from Iris and whoever else you have interviewed from our group?"

"Indeed," said Officer Gerald. "But you understand that we need to have all of your statements."

From there the officers continued to question me about every single detail from the previous two days: from meeting Joshua Sorrento at the convention with Iris and Shane until yesterday evening when we had our debriefing session. When they asked about what we were doing, I simply told them that we were play-testing their game. I was not sure if I should have said more, but between the NDA and the threats made by Sorrento and Blake, I felt uncomfortable saying anything further. However, it appeared that Iris and whoever else was interviewed had shared the same sentiment, as they merely nodded at my explanation and did not ask anything more.

It felt like forever before the officers finally said that they were done. They had me sign a form saying that everything I had told them was factual and then we were done. Officer Leo escorted me back out of the room where I saw that Iris and a few others were already out of the lobby, but Shane was still there. I walked up to Shane alongside Officer Leo.

"Where did everyone go?" I asked Shane.

Shane began to rise off of the couch. "Dr. Jordan came down and told everyone who had finished their interview to head upstairs afterwards. He told me to tell you that they were meeting in the same room that we had met earlier tonight."

“They want us to go back in? I never even got a chance to sleep,” I said, aggravated.

“I know man, but it would seem that Dr. Jordan wants us to get right back to work,” Shane shook his head in shared discomfort at not having any real sleep between yesterday and today.

“I’ll see you up there?” I asked him.

“You will be seeing him shortly,” said Officer Leo. “We just need to take Shane’s statement and then we will return him back to you.” With that Officer Leo gestured Shane towards the direction of the hallways and they took off. I looked around and saw no one else down in the lobby so I began walking towards the elevators. I got in front of them before realizing that there was no one to let me up, and I began to look around before I saw the same lady who had let me up the first day. She was sitting behind the desk. I guessed that she too had been called in, so I walked over to her. “Can you let me up?” I asked her nicely with a sorry grin. She did not have a response, nor would I have believed she had heard me except that she got up and began walking towards the elevators. I guessed we were all feeling a bit like the honey badger coming into the office so early with no time to truly recover from yesterday’s shenanigans.

“Thank you,” I said to her as she swiped her wrist against the sensor and pushed the button to allow me up to the floor. She did not even need to ask me which floor. The front desk lady simply pushed the correct one before exiting the elevator, leaving me alone. If this job was not overwhelming before, then I had no clue what to think about it now. The reflection of myself appeared as the elevator doors shut. I realized I looked like a locomotive had taken its time going back and forth over me a few times. As I attempted to pull my physical appearance together the doors opened onto the floor.

I found the entrance to the room, once again, and entered. Sarah, Conor, Blake, and Majed were not there. However, there was still Dr. Jordan, Sammy, Keila, and Iris waiting for me inside the room.

"Good, everyone is back," said Dr. Jordan as I reentered the room. He stood up and walked to the front of the room where he pulled down a whiteboard from behind the blank one. It appeared to be one of those multi-leveled white boards I hadn't seen since university lecture hall days. One the board was a rough sketch of the city map that I had seen in detail in Sammy's lab area the other day.

"So, Keila has filled me in that each of you are nearly leveled up to level two. Currently, as far as it appears, Ms. Varner is currently in the Four Chapels area of the city while the two of you—" he indicated Iris and I with a black marker "—are currently on the river's edge within Silkliff." He pointed on the map and drew circles where the each of us were located in the game. "Your objective is to complete the quest for the innkeeper of *The Hollow Quiver*. By finding the whiskey you can get the necessary information to find Ms. Reynolds and Dr. Hobbs. I would recommend leveling up before proceeding, as you are probably unfit to complete the task at the moment," Dr. Jordan spoke with a heavy judgement of disappointment in his voice. "I suggest you regroup and proceed forward by looking for the warehouse that holds the elvish whiskey. Once you discover that we will be one step closer to finding both of them."

I raised my hand which Dr. Jordan simply stared at for several seconds. I couldn't see, but I could have sworn that steam came out of his nostrils. "Yes, Mr. Kote?"

"If I may," I said as smartly as I could. "What is going on in the game with the characters all acting weird and speaking about the city going odd?"

At my question, Dr. Jordan swiftly looked at Sammy. However, the glance was so swift that I could not understand what was exchanged by the two game developers. "Have any of you three heard mentions of the Black Pawn?" Dr. Jordan asked.

"Black Pawn? Ya, I think we heard a song about him earlier in the tavern. What does that have to do with anything?" I asked.

"It is a manifestation of the problem with the AI, but it shouldn't impact you or your mission. So do not worry about it. Leave this as a concern of mine and Dr. Vanderbelt," he said while looking intensely at Sammy. She looked worried. I looked to Keila, to see if she had any insight on the problem, but her face was also filled with confusion. Not that I could trust her, anymore.

"Are you sure?" asked Iris in a soft tone.

Dr. Jordan looked away from Sammy and looked back at us. "Yes, I am quite sure. You three understand your task? Regroup, level up, and find the warehouse? Good." Dr. Jordan had not even waited to hear an answer from us. It felt as if he was rushing an end to this meeting. "Dr. Vanderbelt will escort the three of you back towards the gaming room so you can begin." With that Dr. Jordan left the room, and we three looked towards Sammy.

"Let's go," she said, swiftly following in Dr. Jordan's wake.

We all left the room and followed Sammy as we headed towards the elevators and down towards the gaming room. We walked back into the same room that was filled with the white light bouncing off of the white floor, walls, and ceiling. I really wanted to ask Sammy for more information, since she seemed the most inclined of the executives to be of assistance to us. However, I would not dare ask her anything with Keila around. I gathered that Sammy was also not inclined to speak to us about anything for the same reason. If she felt betrayed, finding out that she was being spied on by her superiors, then it would make sense that she would remain silent.

"You understand the game plan?" she asked as she indicated to the three of us which seats to take.

"Yes, Sammy," I said as I got into my seat. Sammy started work on Keila first. The was some awkward tension between the two of them as Sammy went about strapping Keila in with her headset. As soon as Keila's headset was placed on her head she did not wait, but simply pushed the button on the right handset. I guessed that Sammy did want a more private word.

"Okay, you two," she began, walking away from Keila's seat where she laid motionless. "I did not want to say anything in front of her, knowing who she is." Sammy walked to stand in-between the seats upon which Iris and I lay. "I feel that I can still trust you, assuming that you are not also double agents?" she asked. Before I even had a chance to get a word out, Sammy continued. "It really is not as if you would tell me if you were, but I feel that I owe you this after… everything. Do not, and I repeat, do not get involved with the Black Pawn storyline."

"Why?" Iris asked, who was still trying to detangle the cords that attached the hoodie from game immersion into the chair.

"Simply, that the Black Pawn is connected to the glitch you have heard mention of," she said ringing her hands to express her tension. "Like before, I will not go into grand detail, but it was a problem that we had thought we had delt with. However, it appears that is not the case. Nonetheless, I can assure you that the Black Pawn is not a part of the official game and is not necessary for you two to get involved. Let Dr. Jordan and I deal with that on our end, okay?" she asked, but it felt more like a plea.

"Does this have to do with Dr. Hobbs and Ms. Reynolds?" I asked Sammy.

"I do not think so, but as you can imagine, I feel rather in the dark about everything," she responded. "Not that I am officially in the dark, but with Sorrento and Hobbs and everything, I cannot be sure that it is not the case."

"Okay, so stay away from the Black Pawn, but still find Hobbs and Reynolds," I said.

"Correct; you two ready?" Sammy asked with a sad smile.

"Yes," Iris and I said.

## Chapter 21: Once Upon a Time We Committed a Felony

The familiar beam of light came upon my face as I reopened my eyes to see the startup screen. Welcome Back to Fabula, I read across my field of vision as I saw mountains, rivers, lakes, and cities across a grand piece of land. I blinked and it all disappeared to be replaced by Iris' face staring back at me. "We are back in," I said to her.

"Indeed," she said, also grinning. Even with everything that had just happened and with Keila's reveal, Sorrento's death, and everything, the fact remained that this game just could not stop but bring a smile to everyone's faces. I looked around and could see the river and the walls that rose up on both of its sides. We were standing near one edge that dropped off down to the river. I could see some monsters roaming around down there, but the drops from the kelpie that I had killed before we had logged off were gone. It appeared that time still flowed in the game, even when we were logged off. It made sense, after all this was supposed to be a massive multiplayer world. Even though there was only us playing, the game would continue to go on.

"Do we wait for Keila?" I asked Iris. I did not really want to continue playing alongside her, but Dr. Jordan did not appear to really give us an option.

"I think we have to, but that does not mean that we can't waste some of those monsters," she responded.

"Waste some monsters?" I parroted back at her with a smile.

"The gaming lingo just comes flowing through me when I am playing," Iris said with a smile on her face.

"Do you see the guard that was posted here earlier?" I asked while looking around for the guardsman that stopped us from entering to the riverside earlier. I could not see him in sight. In fact, it did not look like anyone was around at all. I looked up to see that the sun was just breaking the horizon. "I guess the time in the game follows the time in the real world, so it is early morning."

"Ya," Iris confirmed, shading her eyes as she looked up into the sky. "Want to sneak down there?" she asked with a devilish smirk.

I did not bother to answer, I simply reached out my hand to hers. Once she took it, we headed off towards the staircase that we were forbidden from earlier. We walked down the stairs, which were slick from the moisture from the night. The water collected on the steps had not yet dissipated in the morning light. As we walked down, I could see a few kelpies and some other creatures spread out across the riverbanks, but it looked like several were heading towards the entrances set into the walls – that if the guard was to be believed – led to the sewer system. We reached the bottom of the stairs. There were two kelpies not a hundred meters from us. "Want to take those two out?" I asked.

"Ladies first," she said. I grinned at her comment and took my bow off my shoulder and grabbed an arrow while Iris began enchanting. I aimed, looking for the line to shoot. I took aim with the arrow's prediction line falling on the horse's head and fired. The shot landed on the horse shaped creature's hindquarters. It threw up its head in anger and looked at us. Iris was still enchanting when the kelpie began charging in our direction. It flew across the sand and pebble landscape of the riverside at the two of us. I started to get nervous, then Iris screamed, "…Fuego." A stream of fire came from her hands and hit the kelpie in the chest. It stopped charging not five meters from us while a torrent of flame attacked it, but nearly as quickly as the flames appeared they disappeared. The kelpie was still standing, although it appeared to be still on fire as it jumped up and down in an attempt to escape the flames that had caught on the strands of dried kelp. I took out my two daggers – each the length of my forearm – and charged the creature. I swiped in an x-form on the creature's head and that appeared to be it. The kelpie dropped to the floor and in its place was filled with the drops.

**Your Party has Killed a Kelpie**
**Experience Reward: 15 Points.**

The words appeared on the screen while I bent down to examine the loot.

"What is there?" asked Iris.

"Nothing exciting," I said as I picked up five more copper coins. "But we are beginning to recover financially from our extravagant shopping spree." I showed Iris the coins from the drop. I decided to leave behind the kelp, or seaweed, or whatever it was called since I still had dozens of pieces in my inventory.

"Again?" I asked Iris. She nodded with what seemed to be a sparkle of flame in her eyes, but that must have been my imagination. "What was that spell you used?" I asked her.

"That is a spell called Flame. It unleashes a stream of fire at the target, but it uses one mana point per second of use. So, it is not all that practical with my meager ten points," Iris explained.

"Looked cool, nonetheless."

"Hard to argue with you there."

We continued to find kelpies on the shore. Once or twice, we saw something in the river, but Iris and I had no clue what it was and had no interest in getting involved with something that we had no business fighting. We rinsed and repeated the technique as we walked along the river's edge. Every few meters we would find a kelpie and I would shoot while Iris took it down with some of her fire magic. It was a really good system, and I was able to get some practice in with my dual-dagger technique. One time, when two kelpies were coming towards us, I had even thrown the Rusty Dagger at a kelpie, but it merely bounced off the horse's shoulder. I guessed I was not going to be a dagger-throwing bad ass in this game. Finally, a new notification arrived in my field of vision.

**Level Up Skill: Duel Wielding Short Blades**
**Level 1 – Unlocking your skill in Dual Wielding Short Blades allows you to use your weapons more swiftly at the same time.**
**Experience Reward: 50 Points.**

"I just leveled up my Dual Wielding," I said excitingly at Iris.

"See I told you, you needed to use both at the same time to level up that skill of yours."

"I wish I had some of your wisdom for myself," I half-joked.

"How close are you to level two?"

I looked over at the top right of my screen to see that my experience bar was nearly filled up. "With those six kelpies we just took out and my skill up, I am just one hundred and ten points short from leveling up. What about you?

Iris began to do the familiar motions to gain access to her menu. I guessed she had not placed them on her field of vision, as I had. "I only have a hundred to go."

"How is that possible?" I asked her. By my calculation, Iris should be behind me.

"That light spell I learned, and that large cat we took out in the beginning of the game must have been worth more experience. Plus, it is not just you that has been leveling up their skills. My Battle Magic skill is currently on level three from all of the fighting earlier."

"Makes sense: so, we can either go and find a few more kelpies, or we can challenge ourselves?" I asked Iris.

"Let go find out what has been swimming around in the river over there," she said while pointing to the last spot we had noticed a disturbance in the water. "It might be worth more experience. After all, these kelpies are beginning to bore me to death. I really hate grinding for levels."

I nodded my head, and we began walking towards the river's edge. Taking out all of those kelpies had resulted in a really emptied out beach. We had killed them all rather quickly and we had only been going for less than half an hour. I looked out to the water; it was really nasty. One would expect that the river's water would be blue, but it was actually more a green color with some darker spots of brown every now and again. I swear that I even saw some garbage floating—

"Watch out!" I screamed at Iris as a flung myself at her. A creature had jumped out of the water. It looked like a monkey, but its head was flat. The skin was greenish brown and really blended in with the water that surrounded the creature's body that was still submerged. Its entire torso and arms were sticking out of the water. I was laying on top of Iris and quickly rolled off her to get eyes back on the creature. "What is that?" I yelled at no one in particular. However, my scream was rather loud and suddenly I could hear shouts from behind me, but I would not dare take my eyes off of the creature that now glared at me and Iris.

I slowly stood up; Iris was using her arms to push her upper body up. I took a few steps back and took an arrow from my quiver, I was already nearing the halfway point in my arrow count. The creature was standing still, breathing heavily and just staring at us. I slowly lifted my bow and arrow and released along the predicting line. It slammed directly into the creature's head, but it did not seem to have noticed. "Damn, that thing is strong." I said, once again, mostly to myself since my audience consisted of the monster and Iris.

As I reached for another arrow the monster jumped towards Iris and me. It landed not a foot in front of me, and before I could react it swung its arm towards me, and I felt it connect with my chest. I felt my head try to disconnect from my body as I was flung aside, and my chest jerked violently. I felt myself lift and fly across the rough sand. In my field of vision, a new line of text popped up.

**You have suffered a critical hit from a Kappa**
**-70 Health Points**

I could see my green health bar decline all of the way into the yellow. *Uh-oh, this thing almost one-shot me.* I looked down and saw that I was wrong. My head had not become detached from my body, it still remained connected. However, as soon as I realized this, I could see Iris using her arms and legs to scamper away, backwards, from the creature as it began to walk towards her. I could also hear the screaming from behind me get louder, but I could only catch one word, "Fire." As I watched, helplessly, for the creature to take out Iris who still remained on her back, a furry of arrows struck the beast. Some of them were a few inches off, but a majority of dozen arrows all hit the creature at once. The Kappa, as I guessed it was named, looked stunned for a second before it fell over.

**A Guardsmen of Altour has killed a Kappa**
**Experience Reward: 150 points**

As the words left my vision, I could hear something like trumpets in the distance when a new lined of information appeared where the previous words once laid.

**You have Level Up to Level 2**
**Health Points Gained: +20**
**Mana Points Gained: +5**
**You have unlocked new skill: Light Armor**
**Level Up Skill: Light Armor Level 1 –**
**Unlocking your skill in Light Armor means that your light armor is 5% more effective at protecting you from physical attacks.**

That was great news. The level up pushed my yellow health bar back to green as a I went from thirty health to fifty. The dizziness from the head hitting the ground also began to dissipate. I shook my head and looked to see that Iris was doing alright, but I could hear footsteps behind me.

"For breaking the law and accessing a restricted session of the city, you are under arrest," said a booming voice from behind me. I turned around to see fifteen or so guardsmen – most of them equipped with bow and arrows – staring down and me and Iris. I merely grinned at them, hoping for pity. It seemed like their pity quota had already been met for the month as one of the guardsmen roughly pulled me up and pulled a pair a rough-looking iron handcuffs from his belt. I could see another doing the same thing to Iris as I felt the iron latch around my wrists. As well, they took out a gag a placed it within Iris' mouth. I guessed that was to prevent her from spell casting. My feeling was that any excuse would fail to work, seeing as the guardsmen of Altour had been obliged to save our sorry asses from dying.

The guardsmen escorted Iris and I from the beach. We went up the same stairs that we had gone down to access the riverside and I could see Fen, the rude guard from earlier, was among the crowd. He looked to be extremely pleased with our predicament as the group led, or more accurately pushed, Iris and I along the cobblestone path to destinations unknown. However, before we had completely disappeared between the buildings, I could see a head of blond hair and the top of a sword looking on our group from a few city-blocks away. Well, at the very least that was some good news.

The lead guardsmen told us that since we had trespassed, we had not only put ourselves in danger, but the rescue attempt had placed his own people in harm's way. Due to that he was going to be throwing us in jail for the remainder of the day. While he was explaining how idiotic we were and how our actions were despicable, I was busy trying to understand exactly where we were heading. That question was quickly answered as those walls I had noticed earlier with Iris came into sight. They were leading us towards the fortress that housed the Lord or Lady of Altour.

This was not good, I thought. We needed to be able to get Iris and Keila leveled up and then be on our way to fulfill Goldsmith's quest. We did not need to spend an entire day's worth of game time in a cell. However, no matter how much Iris or I begged or pleaded for them to forget our transgression, nor how many times we told them we had no clue about the law, the lead guardsman did not budge on this issue. He reminded me of Dr. Jordan and his no fun attitude quite a bit. The handcuffs did their job, and I was unable to do anything to help either mine or Iris' situation. So, we continued onwards towards the walls where we eventually came across an opening. There were black metal spikes sticking out the top of the entryway. They were present either to penetrate intruders or firmly place the gate into the ground, or both now that I gave it some thought.

"You will be placed in the prison that we, the guardsmen, keep under the keep," said the lead guardsman. "You will remain there until sunbreak tomorrow to think about your transgression." With that he ordered several of the guards with him to take them down to the cells underneath the cellular. While leading us away I got a chance to see the fortress that stood beyond the inner wall for the first time. It was grand; it reminded me of Dracula's castle in the real world. Tall, multistoried walls with circular towers every now and again. The castle did not feel symmetrical like it was built all at once, but rather it had grown and been improved upon over the course of years. The inside of the inner wall not only contained the fortress, but there were some gardens I could see in the distance. Primarily, it looked like army training grounds with drill sergeants barking orders to masses of people who were swinging swords, firing arrows, wrestling, and other activities.

"Feels like summer camp," I said to Iris, but she only looked at me with confusion as she couldn't respond with the gag in her mouth. "I guess you never went to summer camp."

The guards led us to the side of the fortress where there was a single small wooden door that was imbedded into the stone wall. We walked through it, entering into a large, cavernous room that was filled with bunk beds. It looked like this was the soldier's barracks, or one of them. However, we did not stay long as we continued through the room into another, where there was a round table and a few older guards who appeared to be playing some card games. Their presence in the middle of the room was right in front of a larger door made out of metal. Once the card player guards saw us, they swiftly stood up and opened the metal door. There was a staircase that led downwards. It looked like there was a single torch at the bottom of the stairwell that merely lit the end of the stairs. It looked like a far way to fall so I was hoping Iris would go first, so that I would fall onto something more comfortable than cold stone. I then reminded myself that I was a gentleman and went first, behind the guard who led us.

"Down here we keep the ruffians from town," the light bearer said. "The drunks and sorts. The worst of the lot get sent off to the dungeons that are even deeper underground." The guard looked to us. "You don't look like them ruffians to me." While he made the comment in our direction, it felt like he was speaking aloud to himself as he quickly returned to focusing on the steps in front of him. We descended into a narrow cavern unlike the larger one above. There were six or so cells that were set into the wall and the cavern extended down to show another metal door on the opposite end. However, we did not make it that far as the guard opened the first cell and had us walk inside and closed the door behind us. "Stick ya paws out, why don't ya," he said while putting the torch onto the wall across from the cell. We stuck out our hands and the guard who carried the torch unlocked our shackles. As soon as Iris' were off, she quickly removed the gag that had been in her mouth. The guard took the shackles and Iris' mouth guard and walked up without another word.

"Well, this sucks," I said to Iris as I looked around our little cell. There was a single bench and a pile of rags on the floor that appeared to be this hostel's version of a mattress. "Zero out of five for this, I'd say."

"To be honest, it was either this or we die," Iris said, "what was that?"

"It was a Kappa, according to my messages. It was also ridiculously strong, it completely wrecked me, not going to lie." At saying this I remembered that my health points were still in the tank. I look up and saw that I only had fifty out of a hundred and twenty health. "I need to heal up," I told her while I remembered that I had such an ability. I focused really hard thinking of my healing spell and heard the same whisper I had heard when I first entered the game and I repeated it, "Asie." At my words my palms grew warm and filled with a turquoise light. I touched them to my chest and the light slowly dimmed and went out. As they did so, new words appeared:

| **Failed to Heal.** |
|---|

"It doesn't work," I said to Iris.

"What did you just do?"

"That was my heal spell, I cast it right, but it did not recover any of my health points."

"Perhaps it's the jail? Or perhaps you can't heal yourself: there are some games like that. I remember one game where you could only heal yourself with potions."

"Well, I assume I don't need a potion to heal. We will just have to wait for Keila to come find us for me to be able to heal."

"Don't you heal with time?" Iris asked, touching my chest where the monkey creature had punched me.

"It doesn't hurt anymore, but it did hurt more than I expected during the fight. I imagine that if this was real life then, first off, I would be dead and secondly, I would have a broken chest. However, I have not gained any health points since that battle, have you?"

"No, but I also have not lost any health so I cannot know for sure what's going on."

"Have you summoned Ellie, the AI, since we played?"

"Ya with all of the time that we have spent apart, I summon her on the hour," said Iris with a sarcastic expression. Realizing the stupidity of my own question, I did not say anything in response. I did open up my menu with the swipe of my hand and scrolled down to the bottom, to where Ellie said I could summon her. I could see the option and I said, "Summon Ellie" I said, but nothing happened.

"You trying to summon Ellie?" Iris asked.

"Ya, I am hoping she can answer some of these questions," I said. Instead of saying it was allowed I pushed on the area of my screen that said, 'Summon Ellie' and I clicked on it. The button became highlighted and the menu disappeared.

"Oh, how exciting to see you my friend, Zephaniah," said Ellie in my ear, a little too close. I nearly jumped out of my own skin.

"Hello there Ellie, long time no see," I responded. "I was wondering if you could answer some questions for me?"

"Just ask away," she said.

"So I just tried to use my healing spell on my wounds to heal, but it did not work."

"I see, yes you are not able to heal your own wounds as a rule. Or at least that is the case the majority of the time," Ellie responded.

"So, how can I heal up if I am not able to heal with my own spell?" I asked Ellie. Then I realized that Iris was a mage. "Iris, do you know any healing spells?"

"No, I do not. Sorry Zeph," she said.

"The only way for one to heal themselves is with the magical aid of another," began Ellie. "Other methods are resting, certain potions, and food."

"So could I eat this?" I asked Ellie, showing her some of the seaweed that was still in my bag.

"Yes, that would work. Is that all?" she asked.

"Ya, I think that is all Ellie, thank you," I said. At my farewell Ellie started to fade out and within a blink of an eye she was once again gone. "It is really useful being able to have something to answer our questions like that," I said to myself, mostly.

"Well, it is not like we have a walk-through scenario to teach us everything, nor do we have the internet to look it up," As Iris said this, I took out some of the seaweed and started to chew it down. It felt in my fingers like dried seaweed that had been soaked in water for a few minutes. However, as I put each piece into my mouth and swallowed them, I could see that my health points were increasing. I felt a wave of relief, but it was brief because as I looked more closely, from that one portion of seaweed, I could see that it had only increased my health by five points. It was obviously not the most effective manner of healing, but it was my only current option. For the first time I was grateful that the food felt and tasted bland in this game world. I would not have been highly intrigued to discover the taste of the droppings of kelpies.

"Is it working?" asked Iris. She looked to be completely grossed out as I shoved another piece of seaweed into my mouth.

"Not much, only five points per piece," I said as I shoved a third piece into my mouth. I started to grow tired of the activity at the first piece, but I held strong and continued to choke down the pieces of seaweed until I was fully healed. By the tenth piece I felt that I was forcing it past my tongue so I wouldn't have to taste the bland flavor again. However, I was grateful once I could see that my health bar was filled. "We only have ten pieces left of seaweed," I said looking at my inventory. "Since this is the only way that you and I currently can heal ourselves, we should look at picking up more food once we get out of here."

"How are we doing that, exactly?" asked Iris.

"Sorry, I thought I had told you. Keila saw us being taken away and I imagine that she will discover a way to get us out," I responded as I closed out my inventory and menu and sat down next to her on the bench.

"You are so sure about that?" asked Iris as she grabbed my hand. This was one of the few moments where we had a chance to just speak without being pulled in for police investigations or we were in a crowd since last night, I realized.

"She wants the same thing we want," I began. "She wants us to find Hobbs and Reynolds and get this game to market. I want it so that I can get out from under Rinc, and she wants it for the payday, but the results are the same."

"Are we sure that is all she wants?"

That question gave me pause. After all, I could understand everyone's motivations. Majed, Conor, Sarah, Iris, Shane, and I were all here because of the blackmail. Although we would all probably have done this job simply for the money if I was being honest. Blake and the other executives wanted the payout of the game's success. Sammy and Dr. Jordan were here because this is their child and they want it to succeed, or at the very least that is what I could imagine the case being as the game's designers. What did Keila want? Was she due for a payout with the game's success? I could not imagine that they were giving out millions to all the simple employees of Rinc, after all we were talking about a multinational company with thousands of employees.

"Honestly, I don't know," I finally responded to Iris' question. At that Iris also fell silent, I assumed she was going through the same mental obstacle course that I was. "Either way, she is our only hope if we want to get out of this anytime soon."

I am sure many have heard the saying "speak of the devil." I remember hearing in a Ted Talk that it actually came from the saying "speak of the devil and he doth appear." Either way, that proved to be true when Keila appeared before our silent cell.

"Hey guys," she said in a chipper voice. However, our relief at seeing her did not erase the revelations from today and we merely nodded at her arrival.

"It is about time," I said a tad harshly. But I didn't want Keila thinking that we were pals after everything. She seemed to understand this as she went silent and simply jangled a set of keys in front of our eyes.

"But, how?" I asked.

"Oh, you needn't worry about that. They were just on the hook over there," she said while pointing to a hook near the metal door that was at the end of the corridor.

"How did you come in?" Iris asked.

"It was not that difficult. Since it is not secret anymore, I have been studying this city for a few months now. I knew how to get to the cells through the sewer system." Keila began to turn the keys and opened the door with a ta-da motion, as if it were magical. "Let us get out of here before they notice," she said using her hand to wave us out. "Through there," she said as we went through the open door at the end of the hall that led into a black room. It was not black by design, but the darkness was so overwhelming that it felt like I was swimming in ink.

"One sec," I heard from Iris before she started a chant. She brought her hands together and whispered "…lux," and a ball of light appeared over shoulder illuminating what lay beyond that door.

## Chapter 22: I Practice My Free Stroke

The light from Iris' miniature sun illuminated the room and filled in all the dark corners with light, and I slightly wish she hadn't. The cavernous walls continued in line with the jail's room, but here the walls and floors were covered in a residue. Remember that smell? That New York on steroids smell from the city, well we found its origin down here.

"It reeks," I groaned, realizing that we were going to be down here for a minute.

"I know, this cavern leads straight through to the sewer system," explained Keila. "It is only going to get worse from here, so fair warning." Keila took the lead as she started to walk down the long cavern.

"Where are we heading, exactly?" I asked Keila.

"There is a passageway that is hidden. You can take it straight up into the Barber's Town side of the river," she explained. "We just need to get out from under the river to get there. It is not too far but stay close. It is too easy to slip into this water and end up in the wrong parts of the sewers."

"What is the 'wrong parts?'" I asked, thinking that any part of the sewers would fit within that category.

"The wrong parts are where there are thieves, cutthroats, monsters, and worse," she said.

"Of course, those parts," I said in mock excitement while the image of a supremely muscular man killing me came into my mind's eye.

"The sewer system in Altour is a city of its own right. A city upon a city, literally. There are entire areas within the underground that are owned by the city's Thieves' Guild, and they do not take too kindly to strangers," Keila said.

Before I could ask Keila any follow up questions, such as how she knew all of this, I started to hear the sound of water flowing, it sounded as if it came from the other side of the wall. I went to press my face up against the wall to hear it clearly, but then I reminded myself that was uber gross and completely unnecessary. We walked a few more meters before coming across an opening in the wall.

"Through here," Keila said as she began to walk through it. Iris and I followed suit, but the narrow passage was short, and it opened up onto a large, long underground room. However, the floor was mostly be taken up by a large river that had various off shoots that led down other passages. As Keila had warned, the smell was atrocious enough that I had to pull up my shirt to tolerate the smell. As I did, a new message appeared.

**You have been poisoned. You will take 1 Health Point of damage for every minute you are poisoned.**

"We have been poisoned," I declared. I then immediately realized that everyone else in the room had gotten the same notification. There went my mansplaining reflex kicking into gear.

"Don't worry," said Keila. "I have a spell that will help out." Keila began to enchant, in a similar way to Iris, but Keila took a knee as if she were praying. For a few second Keila began to glow a soft light and finished her chant with, "...venenum." She then stood up and touched the both of us.

**You have been cleansed of the poison effect. You have been cured.**

I looked and saw that the smell was not as bad as it was before the spell. Killing two birds with one stone, Dr. Jordan would have been proud of our effectiveness.

"This should hold for enough time to get us out of here," Keila said. "It is a Protect from Poison spell, and it helps against the minor poisons and their effects."

With Iris, Keila and I cured of poison we continued on our way. We skirted along the wall to avoid the sewage water as much as possible, then I heard the sound of shouting from behind us: "They've escaped, the prisoners have escaped!" and "follow them!" came from the direction we had travelled.

"They're on our tail," I said to Iris and Keila, who were ahead of me.

"Hurry," Keila said as she took off on a run. Her running causing a splattering of the yucky – yes, I said yucky because the state of the water was beyond the limits of the English language – water all over us. Nonetheless, we made haste running and turned down the first passage that opened up. Here, water flowed from an underground lake in the middle of the passageway, but there was enough room on both sides of the stream for someone to walk comfortably. Even so, this is where things went wrong.

I slipped on the passageway's slippery floors and fell into the unbelievably gross water. The current was faster than it had appeared from the surface, and I was swiftly carried away from the girls and the solid floor. I attempted to get to the edge of the water, but the current was simply too strong for me. At last, I did succeed in grabbing the edge, but the stone was too slick for me to get a firm grip. Within seconds, the light from Iris' sun began to disappear and I was now in utter darkness within sewage water, being dragged by the current.

My only focus was staying afloat. While it had only been seconds, my body was beginning to get tired and reaching the stone's edge was no longer my focus. I just had to keep my head above the surface of the water for two reasons. One, I did not want to drown. Two, I was not going to put my mouth anywhere near this water, even if it was only virtual. The current turned right, and I could now see light at the end of the new passageway that the current was taking me. The light was growing closer and brighter before I felt the current begin to pick up. I realized I could not see the water continue outside of the passageway; it was at this moment that I realized I screwed up. I was going over a sewage-filled waterfall, and I had no clue how far down it went. My adrenaline picked up and I tried, for the umpteenth time, to reach the edge of the stream, but I was too late.

The water rushed out of the tunnel, and I felt myself fall. However, it was merely a few meters before I felt myself land in more water. I realized that I had survived the waterfall, that honestly was more like a slight pour of water in retrospect. The current was not so strong now, so I began to pull myself towards the edge of the water. I realized that the area I was in looked somewhat familiar, as I freestyled myself towards the apparent shoreline of the river. The same river that Iris, Keila, and I had hunted kelpies at the day prior. Reaching the shoreline, I crawled out onto the dry sand and looked around. I could see that on the opposite side of the river was the entryway into the part of the city that was named Glass Village. There was even the same stream of people that had been there yesterday who were on their way to take part in Glass Village's market. I breathed a sigh of relief. That could have been much worse, I thought. Then, the not-so-bad feeling turned into a great feeling.

**Skill Unlocked: Swimming – The Swimming skill allows for players to become increasingly adept at swimming in various conditions.**
**Level Up Skill: Swimming to Level 1 – The swimming skill increase allows you to swim for 25% larger stretches of water before losing strength.**
**Experience Reward: 50 Points**

This was fantastic, I had not only unlocked a new skill, but I got some experience from leveling it up. Then I realized something that was less exciting. "Crap," I said aloud. Realizing that Iris and Keila have no clue where I was swept off too. I opened my menu and clicked on Messaging. I quickly dictated a message to Iris explaining everything that happened.

*From: Zephaniah Kote*

*To: Iris Christman*

*Iris, I am alive. I got swept off to the Glass Village area.*

I sent the message, but I could not see a reply come through. I wondered what was holding her up. Just as I began to dictate another message, her message came through.

*From: Iris Christman*

*To: Zephaniah Kote*

*Hiding from solider. Message soon.*

Made sense, since you had to dictate the messages, she was probably not able to send long messages to me. Still, I guessed it showed that Keila and Iris were safe for now. The soldiers that discovered our escape must have caught up with the two of them, and they were forced to hide to avoid discovery. Until they were done, I felt that I might as well continue on my way. If I remembered the map from Sammy's office, there was an area known as The Rocks on this side of the river. So, I began to walk away from the river's edge, keeping the city's wall on my right while I composed a new message.

*From: Zephaniah Kote*

*To: Iris Christman*

*Sounds good. Stay safe. I am going to head over to an area called The Rocks. It is on the opposite side of the river from the Glass Village. Let me know once you are in the clear.*

With that sent I picked up my pace to make it to The Rocks. After a few minutes of walking, I saw the road that led into the city's wall, where there was most likely a gate that led back into Altour. As I continued my pace, more and more buildings began to appear around the corner. It looked like there was an entire town set up outside of the gates of the city. Amongst the buildings, I could see larger structures that appeared to be warehouses. This must have been where some of the shipments from the other cities ended up, I thought. The closer I got, the busier and more hectic the area seemed, but then I remembered something I had previously forgotten about, my desire to become a sneaky ass archer. I could probably use some of this downtime to get some stealth time in, and hopefully level up that sneaking skill.

I looked over at my experience bar and saw that it was marginally filled up. I had to do some quick math, but quickly realized that between the six kelpies from today, the swimming skill and that kappa, I had leveled up and already had 180 experience points towards Level 3. I was disappointed to see that I no longer needed one-thousand experience points to level up, but it had increased to fifteen hundred. However, this gave me some motivation to actually work on the sneak ability. As I grew closer to The Rocks, I got into the crouch form that I was stuck in for half of my Skyrim playthrough last spring. I slowly began to walk towards the town, but after a few meters I realized that I was unsure who I was sneaking around. I was still a few hundred meters from the village area, and no one was looking in my direction. I stood up, realizing that I was an idiot and continued walking toward the new area.

As I drew closer the familiar smells and sounds of the city overwhelmed my senses, and I felt a sigh of relief realizing that brief adventure was over for me. I then remembered the quest from Goldsmith. He said that there was a warehouse that we were supposed to look for in Barber's Town. My memory from Sammy's map showed The Rocks as being right outside the gates that enter into Barber's Town. What were the chances that the warehouse we were looking for was right in front of me, I wondered as I looked upon the warehouse sized building directly in front of me. "Might as well check them out," I said to myself. I looked around to reassure myself that I was talking to myself for a second.

## Chapter 23: Warehouse 13

I quickly ran up to a warehouse sized building that was farthest away from the commotion coming from the village's heart. As I was still on the side of the building that faced the river, there was no one looking at me or around me. I began to look for a way inside the warehouse, that did not include me entering through the front door, after all no one sneaky goes inside through the front door. My prayers were answered when I saw a window set into the wall a few feet above me. I swiftly looked around for some support to leverage myself through the window. Then I saw it: there was an empty clothing line from the building next door. Must have been a laundromat or whatever passed for one in the medieval era, since they did not have laundry machines, and you can take that information to the bank. I got back into the crouch position and sneaked over there. Grabbing the clothesline was simple and I hurried back over to the warehouse's protective cover. Taking an arrow from the quiver and my bow, which was miraculously still with me, I tied the string onto the arrowhead a took aim. I fired so that the arrow imbedded itself into the window frame, and it stuck. Feeling successful, I restowed my bow back into my inventory so that its additional weight did not throw me off and I began to climb up the wall using my feet and the clothesline to slowly climb up. Since it had to be less than three meters to the window, it was not difficult.

I swung my leg over the window lip so that I could straddle the window's edge before dislodging my arrow and placing it back in its quiver. I looked over to see a darkened warehouse. I looked around from my vantage point, but I could only see stacks of boxes and crates. There were also piles of ropes, rocks, and other miscellaneous things throughout the warehouse. I jumped from the ledge and landed on a crate that was conveniently placed below the window when I heard a voice ring out, "Who's there?"

Since I had just come through the window, I felt it prudent for me not to announce my presence, so I jumped off the crate onto the dirt floor and got into sneak position. The gentleman who asked the question felt that a non-answer was still worth checking out as I could hear his footsteps as he started to walk towards my direction. I looked around and then I saw it, there was a stack of boxes that leaned against the wall beside me, but the lower box was away from the wall. The slight crack offered me my refuge, so I scampered over and crawled between the box and the wall. No sooner had I positioned myself so that the light from the window did not illuminate me, than a man appeared within my field of vision.

He had to be over six feet tall with a bald head and appeared to be wearing clothes that were three sizes too small to contain his muscular frame. I went silent, I even started to hold my breath as the man looked up at the window and then around. I swore that his eyes locked with mine for a second, but he just gazed over my position. It was then I heard another voice, a feminine one, "See anything, Ras?"

"Nothing, boss. Must have been the wind," the bald man named Ras said. As he left a new notification appeared, and I was ecstatic.

**Skill Level Up: Stealth to Level 1 – Increasing this skill will make it harder for you be detected and will decrease the amount of sound you make.**
**Experience Reward: 50 Points**

I nearly let out a cry of delight I was so excited. I was one step closer to fulfilling my vision of being the ultimate sneaky assassin archer. However, as soon as Ras was a few feet away I realized that I was not able to hear their conversation, but I could hear the sounds of words. I decided that I needed to sneak closer to hear everything. Who knew, it might unlock a quest. With that decided, I left my hiding place and began to creep forward towards the direction that Ras had ventured. I walked up to the wall of boxes that Ras had come from and attempted to listen as closely as possible.

"The … arrive … night," said a male voice.

"You see, … work… for us," mused the same female voice.

It still was not clear enough for me to understand everything, so I began to creep forward and turned the corner on the box that I was crouched behind. I could not see anyone, nor any light, so I decided to risk it and fully turn the corner. I could see a pathway through the boxes, on both sides of this passage were boxes that were piled two or three high. Off to the right there was some light that was breaking through some of the cracks between the stacked crates. I continued forward to where I started to hear the voices more clearly.

"You see, Ras and I are not the patient sort of folk. Are we Ras?" asked the feminine voice.

"No, boss," said Ras in the monotone voice you would expect from his variety of bad guy. I honestly had no clue if Ras was a bad guy, but I assumed.

"You see? So no, I cannot wait any longer. If the rumors are true, then I need assurances," said the female.

"I am sorry—," began the third voice, from a man who sounded oddly familiar.

"No, I do not want to hear 'sorry'," said the female. "The Black Pawn is stirring. Whether it is thanks to those two idiot foreigners or not, I do not care. I need to know that whatever comes I am prepared for any eventuality."

"I can understand that Lady Adria," began the third voice. "The shipment will arrive tomorrow morning. Does that work?"

"It will suffice, but I will not be paying anything but production costs," Lady Adria said. "I have been disappointed, there is no need for me to pay for disappointment."

It was clear that this was not a lady that anyone messed with, or at least that became apparent with the unknown man's response.

"Certainly, Lady Adria. In fact, I can include a shipment of Elvish Whiskey. As an apology for my poor handling of our business arrangement," the unknown man said with fear in his voice.

"Acceptable," said Lady Adria. "You may go. I expect that shipment, Fern."

Uh-oh, I thought. She was talking with Fern, the guardsman who did not want to let Keila, Iris, and I into Altour at the beginning of the game. That was why his voice had sounded familiar. I realized that I needed to know a lot more than I could gather with this shady business meeting coming to its conclusion. I had two choices, attempt to follow Fern or follow Lady Adria. I decided that knowing the location of the elvish whiskey was more important than knowing more about Lady Adria. Of course, the fact that she had a henchman with her just sweetened that decision for me. I snuck along the right side of the pathway, attempting to look through the cracks between boxes, to see if I could get a look at

Fern or the mysterious Lady Adria. However, as I did a notification beeped on my screen with a message. It must be Iris, I thought. No time for that now, but that brief distraction allowed for me to not hear Ras and Lady Adria start walking towards me. I quickly scuffled back the way I came. As I rounded the corner, keeping my eyes on the light from right side of the pathway the boxes moved forward and to the side. I could see the light that shone off of Ras's head as I fully went out of sight. Not wanting to risk being discovered, I continued backwards until I could put a stack of boxes between me and them. I could hear the front door of the warehouse opening up and then shutting, as I remained hidden in the darkness.

After a minute there were no new noises, so I reopened my menu to access the message from Iris.

*From: Iris Christman*

*To: Zephaniah Kote*

*Hey Zeph, Keila and I are climbing up out of the sewers. We are going to be in Barber's Town shortly and then we are going to be heading your direction. Stay in The Rocks.*

Not wanting to say anything out loud while there might still be Fern in the building, I decided to leave the message alone for now. I remained in my crouch position, completely still for another minute before I started to creep back towards that room where Lady

Adria and Ras had come from. I got closer and looked through the cracks between the crates and I could see a room that appeared to be an office, but no one was in there. I pulled the same boxes that Ras had moved, and I found them to shift easily, as if this entrance was engineered to be a secret door. With the crate-shaped door out of the way I got a good look inside the room.

There was a small table in the middle of the room that was holding stacks of papers. Off in the far-right corner was a desk that appeared to be in similar shape as the table. Off on the left wall was a door that opened to another destination. Possibly, the proper entrance to the office space, I surmised. Since no one was home I decided to see what I could find. Going over to the desk I could see that the stacks of papers were shipping information with sender and recipient information, and then lists of the items being shipped. However, some of the lists seemed doctored. There were little symbols next to some of the shipped items. If I was to guess, it would appear that these symbols had a double meaning. However, I was clueless to the secrets that they held. After going through a few more piles, I came across a leather-bound book that was hidden between stacks of the papers. I opened it to the first page, but before I could do anything I started to hear movement on the other side of the door. Seeing nothing else worth noting I softly ran, which was more like a fast shuffle, towards the crate-shaped door. I pulled it shut as I heard someone begin to turn the door's handle.

I was about to celebrate my discovery when I got a line of texts across my vision.

**Skill Level Up: Stealth to Level 2 – Increasing this skill will make it harder for you be detected and will decrease the amount of sound you make.**
**Experience Reward: 50 Points**

Whoop! I felt the intense desire to stand up, jump, and throw my hands in the air. I decided that was ill advised and continued to remain in the crouch position as I headed towards the window that I had entered through. Once again, sneaky archers do not use front doors. Seeing my window, I crawled onto the boxes that I had used to gain access into the building and jumped out of the window. However, this time there was no box underneath me to cushion my fall, so I fell the entire length and landed on my butt, it really hurt. In real life I would imagine that it would result in a cracked tail bone, but my light armor must have been doing its job because I was fine.

As I stood up and brushed myself off, I did jump and throw my hands up in the air. My left hand firmly on the leather-bound book, I felt like had won a lottery. I stood there in the shadows of the warehouse for a few more minutes, just to be on the safe side. I quickly sent a message off to Iris to let her know that I would be waiting for her and Keila near the gate and I walked off towards their direction.

As I walked away from the warehouse, towards to direction of the gate into the city of Altour, I could see more of The Rocks. There were several dozen other warehouse buildings that could be seen from the main road. However, the closer I got to the gate, the buildings started to shrink and turn into the buildings that I had seen inside with city: two- or three-story high buildings with balconies and some taverns that people were coming in and out from. Unlike the city, there were gaps and larger spaces between the buildings. It gave the area a more open feel, less cramped than inside the city. Even though it was midday there were dozens of people walking around, looking as if they were doing their day-to-day business. The road was primarily dirt with a few stones imbedded into the ground every few feet. I continued to move forward, looking around for anything of interest. I noticed a few people; I even saw a group of dwarves off down one of the gaps between buildings. Overall, the sense of the atmosphere here was one of calm. There did not even appear to be any sort of market amongst the buildings. That lack of a market probably indicated that the only people present in The Rocks were the residents of the area. As I was thinking this, I heard a voice from before me say, "Hey there Zephaniah."

# Chapter 24: Debrief

I heard the voice call out my name and began to look around in front of me for the person who had called me. It was definitely a man's voice, or at the very least I could say that it was not either Iris or Keila. However, rather than finding the voice, I found Baridac, the innkeeper of *The Tipsy Dwarf*. His height had made him hard to notice initially, until he was standing in front of me.

"Hello there Baridac," I said upon seeing him.

"Hello there Zephaniah, what is going on with you?"

"I am just looking for Keila and Iris, we got… separated and trying to find them."

"Ah, well then you are in luck. I just saw them come through the gate. I said hello and went on my way," he said pointing back behind him.

"Can you show me?"

"Sure, thing lad," Baridac said as he started to walk back the direction he came from, towards the city's gates. After only a few feet of pushing against the crowd I could see Keila's blond hair and Iris' red sticking out amongst the crowd. I waved them over and they came to meet us.

"Hey, Zeph, you got out alright?" Iris asked.

"Ya, and I have something to show you that I found while you guys were coming towards me." I pulled out the leather-bound book to show to them, but as I did, I realized that mentioning something like this in public might not be the best idea. "Actually, I'll show you guys later."

"Sounds good to me, I see that Baridac found you," said Keila.

"Ya, he was not that hard to find lassie," the dwarf said. "Even with me at this height."

"What are you doing down here?" I asked the dwarf.

"Oh, actually I could use your assistance with something—," began the dwarf.

"Sorry Baridac," I interrupted. "We are currently on a task at the moment. Actually, you may be able to help," I said.

"Sure lad," he said. "What is it?"

"We are currently looking for a warehouse owned by Innkeeper Goldsmith," I explained. "He brought in some liquor to restock, and it got held up," I said, not wanting to explain the full breadth of the problem with the outlawing of elvish whiskey.

"Ah," the dwarf grinned knowingly. "In fact, I believe I can help you out. Through the gates and to the left are some warehouses. I believe some of the guards have secured some more… exotic varieties of whiskey inside on of them."

I smiled back at the dwarf, but before I could respond a new notification appeared in my field of vision.

**Innkeeper Goldsmith Has Offered You a Quest: Discover Where His Supply of Elvish Whiskey is and Report Back to Him.**
**Completed: Find the Warehouse.**
**Experience Reward: 100 Points**
**Quest Update: Follow Innkeeper Longbrew's Directions to the Warehouse**

I looked to see Keila, and Iris' gazes were a tad off, as if they were seeing something that I was not. "You guys get the same notification?" I asked. Keila and Iris both nodded at me.

"Fantastic," I turned back to Baridac. "Could you point us in the right direction?"

"Sure thing lad," said the dwarf. "Just follow me and I can lead you the right way. Maybe then you three would owe me a favor," he added with a grin.

Baridac turned us around and we began to walk towards the city gates, towards Barber's Town. As we exited The Rocks, the guards looked at the three of us, but upon seeing Baridac they made no moves to stop us. Seeing the guardsmen reminded me about seeing Fern earlier in the warehouse and the journal that I was still carrying in my hand. I decided to place it in my inventory for later access. I wanted to discuss what I had heard about the Black Pawn and the two foreigners that were mentioned in the conversation that I had overheard. Could they be Reynolds and Hobbs? I wondered what they, Lady Adria, and the guard, had to do with them in that case.

We passed underneath the walls of Altour and entered into the new area of the city. It was not as nice as the area around *The Hollow Quiver*, as there were gaps in the cobblestone street. As well, the houses around us were entirely made up of wood, unlike what we saw in Silkliff area. However, the colors of the peoples' clothing gave the area a pleasant image. The flashes of red, blue, green, yellow, and other colors were present on people's clothes, their clotheslines between their houses, and on various flags that hug outside the residences of Barbers Town.  Similar to The Rocks, were some larger buildings that must have been the warehouses that we had heard about, and that I had seen in the last area. They were not quite as large as the one that I had broken into, but they still occupied the same amount of space as several homes.

Baridac continued to go into the city, but then turned left and we started to go down to an area that had less and less people. The sounds of the daily commotion and the colors of the clothes began to diminish until they were gone. Replacing those aspects of the town, were darker corners and instead of civilians I saw more and more guards.

"This is where the guardsmen of Altour keep shipments meant for the fortress and the goods that they confiscate," he said as we came upon a large warehouse that took up an entire city block. "In there you will find weapons, armor, food, and items of the illegal persuasion." He pointed towards the large warehouse. While still a few meters away, I could see that there were guards posted on the door and there seemed to be a patrol as I saw a group of five guards turn the corner and walk towards the entrance to the warehouse.

"How are we supposed to get into there?" I asked Baridac.

"Sorry, cannot help you there," he said with a shrug of his shoulders. "However, this is the warehouse that you three are searching for, I can promise ya that." A new notification appeared at his words.

**Innkeeper Goldsmith Has Offered You a Quest: Discover Where His Supply of Elvish Whiskey Is and Report Back to Him.**
**Completed: Follow Innkeeper Longbrew's Directions to the Warehouse**
**Experience Reward: 50 Points**
**Quest Update: Enter the warehouse to confirm if the elvish whiskey is there.**

"Thank you, Baridac," I said to the dwarf. It would not have been easy finding the warehouse without his assistance. Even without the secret to get into the secured building, he had been a huge help.

"Of course, anything for guests of my Inn," he said in response. "Speaking of which, once you three are finished I could use your help with a little something. If you three would not mind?" he asked. As he asked the question the notification came.

**Dwarf Longbrew Has Offered You a Quest:**
**Safety.**
**Accept / Decline**

We all quickly accepted.

**Quest Update: Speak with Dwarf Longbrew to Discover the Quest.**

That seemed to be all of the notification to come up because the dwarf began to walk away before the lines had all disappeared. I quickly turned to wave at the dwarf, but he was already gone.

"This is getting to become too many quest lines," said Keila. "We have this one," she said indicating the warehouse, "now Baridac; and do not forget my temple quest."

I did not really feel too bad for Keila, given my current emotional state towards her. Which centred somewhere between disgust and annoying sibling. "Does not matter," I responded. "We just need to finish this one first and then we go from there, but before we begin, I need to show you two something." I pulled the leather book out of my inventory and handed it to Iris as I explained everything that had happened in the warehouse. Lady Adria, Fern, all of the bits of conversation. Iris and Keila both nodded as I told my story, and once I got to the part of the two foreigners, they widened their eyes.

I felt reassured that I was not reading too much into what I had heard back there.

"What is this?" asked Iris as she held up the leather book.

"No, clue," I said, honestly. "It was the only thing that looked of value in the pile of papers on the desk it has the name *Belladonna* at the title page though, but I have no clue who that is. What do you guys think about Lady Adria?"

Iris shrugged, still looking through the book.

"I think I remember something from Sammy's storyline presentation on the city of Altour," began Keila. "The world is utterly massive with much larger and grander cities and stories than Altour, but since this is one of the starter cities the company wanted it to have something to keep players here as they leveled up."

"Great," I said sarcastically. "What does that have to do with Lady Adria?"

"Well, if you had not interrupted," growled the blond annoying creature. "I would have further explained how Lady Adria is one of the 'big-bad' of the city. She has the entirety of Shadow Valley under her thumb from her throne as head of the Thieves' Guild."

"What does that mean, in terms of everything?" I asked her.

"That, I do not know. Nonetheless, I believe we should hurry before Fern removes the whiskey. If what you heard is true, then the whiskey won't be here by the time we get back to Goldsmith.

So, we have two options, we can either risk failing the quest and not getting the information on Hobbs and Reynolds, or we find a way to secure the whiskey," Keila said.

"That information is too important for us to risk not attaining," Iris said, looking up from the book. "Whose office did you get this from?" she asked me while holding the book in the air.

"I don't know," I said. "I can't imagine it is Lady Adria if she is in control in Shadow Valley and it also should not be Fern since he is a guardsman and not a trader." I gave it some thought: the reason they choose that place for a secret meeting must mean that the documents in the room were not necessarily on the up and up. After all, some of the documents I had seen seemed to be doctored to cover-up some illegal goods. "Whoever's office it was, was probably another bad guy. Maybe it is one of Lady Adria's people or something."

"Had to be because this looks to be a fake ledger, and not a proper ledger," Iris said. She held open the book so that both Keila and I could look at it. "You see this, it looks like a ledger of blackmail created or owned by whoever this Belladonna character is." I looked more closely at the ledger and could see peoples name with some sentences next to them, but the words made no sense to me.

"Ya, but I can't read it," I said.

"Neither can I," confirmed Keila.

"Nor I, it appears to be in some sort of code like a cipher," Iris explained. "I should be able to crack it, but I assume that I am going to need to learn a skill or something to accomplish that."

"Where could we do that, Keila?" I asked.

"If I had to guess, I would say that someone in the Thieves' Guild would offer a course in the skill," she said. "After all, becoming a professional thief or one of their assassins is a potential and mapped out option for players."

"But it cannot help us now?" I asked.

"No, probably not," Keila confirmed with a tightening of her mouth.

"So, what is the plan for dealing with our current quest?" I asked.

Iris shrugged, but then she smiled with a knowing glint in her eye. "We should steal the whiskey," she said with a grin.

"How do we go about doing that?" I asked.

"Well, you said the Fern was going to move it, and probably soon. So, if we just wait for him to move it then we can take it out in transit. Sort of like a sneaky heist," she said.

"That could work," said Keila while nodding her head.

"But we still do not know if the Elvish Whiskey is even in there or not," I said. "Remember, the quest update? It said to enter the warehouse and confirm that the whiskey is there," I said.

"Fine, so we will sneak in and confirm that it is there. Then we can sit here and wait for the whiskey to leave the premises with Fern and we take out the transport," she spoke giddily.

"What has you in such a good mood?" I asked her with a smile since it was impossible to not appreciate her level of excitement.

"Oh, I just love heist movies," she said.

## Chapter 25: The Heist

We began to plan out how we were going to sneak into the warehouse. There appeared to be one patrol that went in a circle around the building. They had five people in their guard and came around every few minutes. While those guards were always on the move, there were two guards who stood outside of the warehouses entrance, which was closed. We timed our study of the building so that we were walking around the building while the guards were directly on the opposite side of the building from us. On the backside of the warehouse was another opened window, but it was higher than the window in the last warehouse. We continued on our route, to keep it from looking to pedestrians like we were planning a break in. We continued on to an alleyway a few blocks down. I was able to still see the entrance to the warehouse from where I was positioned against the alleyway's wall.

"Can you do a repeat of what you did before?" Iris asked me.

"No, it is too high, and I am worried that the arrow won't penetrate into the wooden frame firmly enough for me to get into the building," I said with concern.

“Well, could you jump in from the building across?” asked Keila. “Its roof was at least a meter below the window of the warehouse.”

“Hey, hold on,” I said holding up my hands. “When did this become my job? Why am I the only one jumping through windows and stuff?” I asked.

“Fine, let us do it by who has the highest stealth skill,” Keila said in a tone that was not a question as no one else had the skill.

“I get it, I get it,” I said. “So, I use the clothesline-arrow trick to get on the roof of the building next door and then I just climb through the window and confirm that it is there. Then I exit the same way, and we wait for Fern?”

Iris and Keila nodded in approval of the very quickly made plan. I could not see how it was all going to fall apart, but I knew that it would.

Keila left the alleyway to start keeping track of the guards, in order to plan when I would, should go for it. Keila gave me the hand signal and I ran, not super-fast in case of drawing attention, but more like a late-for-my-curfew kind of run. I turned right on the road outside of the warehouse and continued down and turned on my second alleyway so that I was behind the building that was behind the warehouse. I looked up and aimed my arrow so that it would hit a second story porch that stuck out of the building. I nailed it on the first try, and then used the attached clothesline to ascend to the porch. Halfway up, I became concerned that I had been spotted, but the great thing about people in the real world and the virtual world is that they do not usually look up. I quickly crawled over the porch's banister. "That was not so bad," I said to absolutely no one. I looked over the porch's edge and saw Iris and Keila standing in the alleyway.

Keila currently had her hand raised in a stop motion; the guards must be in the alleyway that backed the warehouse. If I had ascended to the roof, then I would have been in their line of sight. Keila looked around the corner of the alleyway, and I could see her counting as her lips moved. As soon as she gave me the thumbs up, I jumped onto the porch and grabbed the lip of the roof and heaved myself up, something that would have been impossible in real life, but was feasible in the virtual world. Nonetheless, it was still difficult, but then I saw black letters start to form in my line of vision and it suddenly became easier to pull myself onto the roof. On my back, I now could faintly read the word.

**Skill Unlocked: Climbing – The Climbing skill allows for players to become increasing adept at climbing various surfaces.**
**Level Up Skill: Climbing to Level 1 – The climbing skill increase allows for you to be 25% more efficient at climbing difficult surfaces. Increase this to climb easier and faster.**
**Experience Reward: 50 Points**

That, at least, was some nice news. I pulled myself up and glanced over the edge of the roof to look at Keila and Iris. Keila had her hand up, but then starting swiftly waving it up and down. I realized she was telling me to get on my stomach, so I dropped. I could see a sigh of relief from both her and Iris, who had her fingers partially covering her mouth. After a few seconds, Keila started waving them in the universal 'go' sign. I jumped up and ran to the opposite side of the roof, so that I could see that there was little over a meters' length between the warehouse and the roof. I could also see the window was below my level on the warehouses side. I looked down to see the far drop that it was, not that I was afraid of heights, but my hands did get a bit sweaty. I pulled in a deep breath while taking my bow and the arrow with string and aimed for directly across from me. I let it fly, and I could hear the metal arrowhead biting into the wood of the warehouse's walls.

It was now time to trust myself, as I wrapped the thin rope that was connected to the arrowhead around my hand and forearm. I braced myself and then sort of dived towards the window's entrance. It hurt; I bashed my shoulder against the window frame and that stopped me hard from going entirely through the window. In my vision a negative ten rolled by but I did not have time or the focus to read the script with it. I found that my left arm and head did get through, so I grabbed on tightly to the window's ledge. My feet could not find a place to hold on to, and I realized that I was going to fall out of the window and into the alleyway. I looked at my right shoulder to see it was bleeding, but in my right hand was the rope. I wound it up even tighter on my hand and leaned out of the window. The line held and I inched my way up, using my feet against the warehouse's wall to scale the last few feet and pull my entire body through the window.

After successfully pulling myself through the window, I looked back outside and saw Iris giving me a big thumbs up, but Keila was shaking her hand at me again with a concerned look on her face. The guards must have been coming, so I swiftly ducked my head underneath the window seal and looked at my surroundings in the warehouse. It looked like I was standing on a wooden floor, but it ended after a few feet to reveal a large hole in the ground. The floor ran along the wall across the entire warehouse. As I walked towards the edge of my little floor, I could see stack of boxes that went as high as the third story of the building. The same story that I was on. A closer look at what laid underneath me was another floor and the same gap that showed the bottom floor of the warehouse. It reminded me of the room created for that Indiana Jones movie, the movie that everyone hated. Area 51, I believe was the warehouse.

Anyways, I could see piles of boxes, but it appeared that no one was inside. So, I started to walk along the edge to see if I could find anything that looked like it contained whiskey, barrels, or something. About halfway from the window to the front door, I could see several barrels just sitting there, out in the open. I just needed to find a way to get to them, and after walking a few more meters I could see a ladder. I went over the edge and took the ladder down to the main floor. I continued until I re-found where the barrels were. As soon as I touched one of them, a new notification appeared.

**Innkeeper Goldsmith Has Offered You a Quest: Discover Where His Supply of Elvish Whiskey Is and Report Back to Him.**
**Completed: Enter the warehouse to confirm the Elvish Whiskey**
**Experience Reward: 200 Points**
**Quest Update: Report your findings back to Innkeeper Goldsmith.**
**(Optional) Quest Update: Return the Elvish Whiskey to Innkeeper Goldsmith**

Reading those words brought a massive smile to my face, this was the whiskey that we had been looking for. Now, I just needed to climb back out to return to Iris and Keila, but as I started to turn away from the barrels I heard a noise. It sounded like wood grinding on metal, but I looked around and could not find anything that would be making that sort of noise. Then I saw a notification from Iris.

*From: Iris Christman*

*To: Zephaniah Kote*

*Zephaniah, Fern is here.*

As soon as I read the message, I realized that the sound was the door to the warehouse opening. It was then that I heard the voice. "Guardsman Fern, the barrels you speak about should be right down there," said someone.

"Crap," I whispered. There was no way that I had enough time to get to the ladder before anyone saw me. I considered, if I was busted inside of the warehouse then I was most likely going back to jail, or I could do something a little more 'whiskey'. You get it, sounds like risky? I smiled at my own joke, and hurried over to the farthest barrel, the one without anything on top of it. I could see that there was a rope attached to the lid, so I pulled. The lid came off easily and inside I could see the brownish, goldish liquid that we had been searching for. I tipped over the barrel so that the liquid ran out from the wooden container, through the cracks and the wooden floor sucked it right up as if it was never there. I jumped inside the dark, alcohol-smelling container and closed the lid as I heard the voice return.

"Right here," said the unknown guardsman. "This is the Elvish Whiskey that we had confiscated."

"Fantastic," said Fern. "If you would not mind, we are going to be taking these for storage somewhere else. Could you direct the others here and have them load them up in the carriage?"

There must have been some nonverbal confirmation because the voices from Fern and the other guard began to be heard farther away. They must have walked back towards the entrance to grab the carriage and other guards to lift the barrels: this was my chance to escape. As I went to lift up the lid I heard footsteps right outside my barrel, I stilled my hand and slowly lowered the lid back into place. More guards must have just arrived. As I was thinking this the unknown guard that had spoken with Fern sounded out right above me.

"Roll these all out to the carriage," said the man. "Guardsman Fern is taking these back towards to fortress for destruction."

"Why can we not just dump these into the river?" asked another guard.

"Do not ask me," replied the unknown guard. "Orders from on high; so just do as you are told." At this the first guard began to walk away, or at least I heard his footsteps begin to decrease in volume. I realized that I needed to message Iris and Keila so that they knew what was going on, but I could not speak out. The guards might hear me, so I just hoped that they both understood that I was stuck. They would have gotten the successful quest update, so they at least knew that these were the correct barrels. Hopefully, they would just follow the plan.

The barrel I was in began to tilt over, and I nearly screamed out, but I stifled my scream. I could feel myself being rolled, and I began to get dizzy. After a minute or two of rolling I could feel my barrel being lifted and placed onto another surface. They must have put me on the carriage. It was too late to remove myself from the barrel. If I did come out now, then there could be as many as eight guards around me. So I stayed still and silent as I heard the guards groan and moan as they lifted the barrels onto the carriage. It was at this time that I received a message from Iris.

*From: Iris Christman*

*To: Zephaniah Kote*

*Zephaniah, I assume that you cannot respond, or you would have by now. We can see the barrels being loaded onto the carriage. Keila and I and in position and are going to take out the guards once they are a block or two away. Then we will come looking for you.*

So, my group had not guessed that I was in barrel, but they were assuming that I was hiding away somewhere. There was at least some good news on my part: Keila and Iris would succeed. Hopefully, I would not get caught in the crossfire.

"All loaded up?" I heard Fern ask from somewhere to my right.

"Yes, sir. Will you be taking anyone with you?" asked a guard.

"No, I am quite alright. Thank you all very much," responded Fern. At this I could heard the sound of a whip and then we were moving. I do not know where, but Keila and Iris were on the job. As soon as I heard their attack, I would launch mine. After about five minutes of jolting along, I could feel the carriage slow down and stop.

"Ah, if it is not the dwarf's friends," said Fern to, I assumed, Iris and Keila.

"Hello Fern, we are going to need to take this carriage off of your hands, and we are in a bit of a rush," said a female voice which sounded like Keila. I realized that this was probably my chance, as Keila and Iris would not have approached unless they were clear from sight of the other guards. I slowly lifted up my lid and looked around. I was facing the back of Fern's head, which was only a few inches away from me. Perfect, I thought.

"Oh, are you now?" asked Fern in amusement.

"Yes, we are," said Keila with a little more command in her voice. "Please, step down from the carriage and we will be on our way."

I opened my lid as slowly and carefully as possible. I did not want Fern to feel or hear me behind him. I slowly stood up, so that I could stand in the barrel which was conveniently right behind Fern's back. As I stood over him, I looked out in front of the carriage to see Keila and Iris standing in front of the carriage. Keila's sword was still in her scabbard on her back, but Iris' hands were alight with flame. At seeing me Iris' eyes grew wide and then a smile appeared on her face. Keila betrayed nothing on her face, but Iris reaction must have been enough because Fern started to turn around.

"I would stop there and listen to the ladies," I said as I pressed my new dagger against the side of Fern's throat.

"Ah, I knew that I was missing one of your number," replied Fern. "So, what is your plan? Steal the carriage and drink the whiskey yourselves? You are aware that as soon as you guys leave that I will just report this to my captain and the entire guard will come after you?"

"Oh, no you won't," I whispered into his ear. "We know for who you are taking this whiskey. So no, I do not think that you will be reporting any of this to your superiors." While I could not see his facial expression, I did feel his shoulders tense at my words. Fern knew that he was already screwed, and that there is no hope.

"Sorry, I misspoke," said Fern. "I would not report this to the captain, you are right. However, I might just have to report this to the Thieves' Guild. And they do not like anyone coming into their territory."

"You raise a good point," I said as I cut his throat. "I always wanted to play a chaotic aligned character." I pulled the dagger away, but astonishingly Fern was still alive. He must have been such a high-level guard character that even such a lethal attack as mine could not kill him. He wasn't even bleeding all over the place as he should have been. Instead, he reached for his own sword. However, before he could pull it from its sheath, I stepped out of the barrel and backed away. Fern stood to come after me when a bright light hit him: Iris' fire attack. Fern was engulfed in flames, but after they had burned out, he was still standing with some singed hair and clothes. Now he began to advance – sword drawn – on Iris, who was pulling her hands together for another spell. He raised his sword and I jumped off the cart's back and started running towards Iris, but I was too far away. However, Keila was not. As Fern began to swing his sword, Keila's interrupted his mid-swing. Keila did a fancy move with her wrist and her sword swiped at Fern's wrist. That sent Fern's sword flying to the left, and Keila followed through with a thrust towards Fern's gut. Fern had enough sense of himself to still jump back, so Keila's blade only stabbed a few inches into his gut.

Fern fell back against the cart's front as I arrived to look at him. Even with Keila's sword wound, Fern was still alive. His eyes were filled with a blood lust, he would kill us if he could. While I could see the line of damage from my dagger and Keila's sword, he did not bleed as I expected. He then reached for his boot where, I guessed, a dagger was stored. I was faster, I took my second dagger and did a x-shaped attack on his chest as I had done with the kelpies earlier. This caused the corrupt guard captain to fall back onto the floor where he laid on his side. Before he could say or do anything else, Keila came forward and took her sword and swung hard enough to take off his right arm. The arm rolled off of Fern's body, leaving a slightly bloody stump. While Keila had hacked downwards, Iris had unleashed another spell and that sealed the deal as Fern's eyes closed as he was covered in flames. The body began to dissipate as with monsters. As it disappeared a notification appeared in my field of vision.

**Your Party has Killed Guardsman Fern**
**Experience Reward: 100 Points**
**Warning: Your Party Has Killed a Guardsman: If found responsible you will either be exiled from Altour, imprisoned, and/or suffer other penalties.**

"What the hell was that?" yelled Iris at me. As she finished reading the same notification we all had received.

"What?" I asked. "He must be extremely high level. He took way more hits than the kelpies ever did."

"That is not what I meant," Iris screamed. "You just killed him." Iris was looking at me like I was a raving lunatic.

"No," I said to Iris slowly. "He was a virtual creation that would have reported on us to Lady Adria and, possibly, the guards. If he lived, we would have been running from both for the rest of the game." At this Iris began to nod her head. "We had no choice," I said in the same tone as Iris, and I immediately regretted it. Iris began to cry.

"I know you are right," she said. "But that… that was just… just too much," she said through heavy sobs. "Sorry, just give me a minute." Iris turned around and began to walk away as I looked towards Keila who just gave me a shrug. I began to follow after Iris.

"Iris, I am sorry for yelling," I said as I reached out to take her hand from her side. "I do not know why I did." As I grabbed her hand she pulled away and turned to face me.

"I understand why you did it, and I am sorry for yelling," she said.

"No, I am sorry. I just did not see any other—," I began.

"Now, seriously, I totally get it," said Iris as she swiped tears from her eyes. "Normally, I would have done exactly the same thing. It is just that… it is just that this game feels so real sometimes. I guess that I was in shock when you slit his throat."

"I know, I really do understand, Iris," I said as I attempted to reach out for her hand. She let me grab hold of it this time. "Truly, this game can be overwhelmingly realistic. I can see why you were so shocked," I said as I looked onto Iris' face. Her eyes were still red, but there were no new tears. I pulled her into a hug, and we just stood there for a minute together.

"Let us get a move on," yelled Keila from the bench of the carriage. "Let us get a move on before someone comes by and ask us questions." We separated and started to walk towards the direction of the carriage. I pulled myself up onto the bench and offered my hand to Iris to help her up.

"What did he drop?" I asked Keila.

"A crappy sword, worse than mine but I put it in my inventory. Some copper pieces, nothing too crazy. Oh, and also a note." As Keila said it, she passed over a folded piece of paper. I did not open it, but just placed it in my inventory for the time being. I am sure that it was significant, but the priority was getting this whiskey to Innkeeper Goldsmith.

"We should probably get rid of his sword. You read the same notification. If we get caught with it, we might end up in jail or worse," I said.

Keila looked at me. "You are probably right," she said as she summoned the sword from her inventory and dropped it off the side of the cart. "You two ready?"

Iris and I nodded, and Keila used the reigns to get the horses moving. We continued on the path that the cart was on, which eventually led to the main road. Or at least is appeared to be the main road: dozens of people were moving around and the cobblestone path seemed entirely intact. We turned left onto the main throughfare, to head away from the wall. As we continued on the path Iris, Keila, and I discussed what had transpired once I had headed into the warehouse.

"When you appeared from behind Fern I almost jumped out of my skin. You scared me so badly," said Iris. "Where did you come from? Why weren't you answering our messages?"

"Ya, I could tell. I am not sure you are aware Iris, but your eyes looked like a deer caught in the headlights," I teased her. "I was hiding from the guards so I couldn't message you. I was worried that they would head me."

"It was a bit obvious," said Keila. At that Iris looked a bit stung at the news that she had not kept a straight face throughout the encounter. Keila then looked at me and asked, "Why did you not just whisper the message? The guards wouldn't have heard that."

Keila's questions made me realize that I was being an idiot. I could easily have sent them a message while I sat there in the dark, hiding from the guards. "You are probably right. I guess I just got so absorbed into the story that I forgot we were playing a video game, "I explained with a little embarrassment.

"Noob," Keila murmured underneath her breath.

I didn't have a response, but I realized she was right. What Iris said earlier about the realism of this game was really true.

We continued on down the road in silence. I looked around and could see the people going about their business with baskets, small carts, and other objects in their hands. Every few feet there was a merchant or bakery selling bread, weapons, or other items. I kept my eyes out for something intriguing, but I could not see anything worth stopping for. As I looked up, I could see people standing on their porches and people beating their rugs. The overall feel was so authentic that I found it hard to frown on Iris' reaction to the killing of Fern. However, I honestly did think that action was necessary. If we had let him live, then he would have followed us and even if he had not, he could have set the guard on us or the underworld and that would have only created more problems. While violent, it was a video game, and it was important to remember that.

As we continued down the road, we eventually came across a bridge that spanned the width of the river. The bridge was decently spacious and while on the bridge we looked over the edges to see the river shining beneath.

"Once over the bridge we will be back in Silkliff," said Keila. Since Keila's outing as a traitor to our merry band she had become much more comfortable sharing her knowledge of the gaming mechanics, and for that single tiny thing, I was grateful.

"*The Hollow Quiver Inn* is near Westgate," I said, just affirming the fact that I also had a memory of the maps and where we did things.

"Indeed, we will take this road through to Silkliff and then turn left, which will take us all the way to the Inn," Keila said. "Have both of you leveled up, yet?"

"Ya, I did before we got arrested," I said to Keila. "I got up to level two and I got a few new skills and everything. What about you guys?"

"We both leveled up when we were in the sewers," confirmed Iris. "We ran into some rats, they were not hard to take out, but they pushed both of us over the edge. I am now level two, and my highest skill is my Battle Magic, which is now level four."

"Same," began Keila. "Not the magic, I mean. I leveled up and my Heavy Armor skill is level two, my Long Sword is level three, and my Religion is level one."

"I have not leveled up or accessed any other skills, yet," said Iris disappointedly. "I just always use the magic, and so that is what I have grown in the most, I guess."

"It is alright. Like all of my skills are still level ones, so I would not worry about it," I assured Iris. As we continued to talk about the specifics of our skills, I remembered that Keila was our group's Paladin.

"Keila, you have healing magic, right?" I asked her, thinking of my injured shoulder.

"Ya, my deity gave some low-level spells that I will need to find replacements for soon," she said.

"Could you heal up my shoulder?" I asked her.

"Sure thing," she responded. Keila took one hand off of the reigns and then started a low prayer. Or, something that sounded like a prayer, before her hand began to glow softly and she placed it on my shoulder. It immediately felt less numb, and my health points returned to full.

"Thank you," I said as I rubbed the part of the shoulder that had been healed. Keila then took the reins in two hands as we pulled off the bridge and continued on our way to Innkeeper Goldsmith's establishment. "Hope none of the guards have started to come looking for us," I thought aloud as we saw a few guards walking towards our cart.

## Chapter 26: Quest Complete: The Sequel

We eventually pulled up in front of *The Hollow Quiver Inn.* We passed several groups of guards as we had passed through Silkliff, but no one had stopped us. I was relieved and just hoped that our good luck had held out for the time being. Keila pulled the cart full of banned goods to the side of the inn and we all hopped off. As we disembarked a familiar voice greeted us.

"Ah, you three have returned. It appears you have been successful," greeted Innkeeper Goldsmith. He walked off the porch of his inn and came to the cart. I briefly explained to him that I had to empty out one of the barrels, but Goldsmith just seemed happy that we had brought back a majority of his seemingly lost product. "It really is no problem, my dear boy. If it was not for you three then I would have lost all of it, and probably paid a heavy fine at that." He then patted me on the back and, after checking the barrels, clapped his hands together. "You did exactly as I bid you. In fact, you did more by bringing the whiskey right to my doorstep. Let me reward you." At his words the menu showed us our result.

**Quest Completed: Discover Where His Supply of Elvish Whiskey Is and Report Back to Him.**
**Reward(s)" The information that you seek and 1 Silver Coin x 3**
**Experience Gain: 500 Points**
**(Optional) Quest Completed: Return the Elvish Whiskey to Innkeeper Goldsmith**
**Reward(s): Potion of Archery, Potion of Arcana, and Potion of Heavy Armor**
**Experience Gain: 300 Points**

I felt a rush of delight as the experience points added up; I heard the singing sound of trumpets in the air. I looked over to Keila and Iris, and they both seemed to be hearing the same sounds. Particularly Iris, who had her head titled, as if she would hear it better that way. Even better than the sound was the notification that popped up.

**You have Leveled Up to Level 3**
**Health Points Gained: +30**
**Mana Points Gained: +5**

"Amazing," I said as a pumped my fist into the air. I must have looked like a total weirdo for a second as only the three of us could understand why I had just congratulated myself so publicly.

"Indeed, an amazing job," said the Innkeeper. "As promised, I have the information you seek, but before that I would like to give you something else." Innkeeper Goldsmith opened up his pouch on the side of his belt and pulled out three silver coins that I had not previously seen in the game. "One for each of you," he said as he put each coin into our hands. I was not exactly sure of the exchange rate, but a silver felt like enough to buy myself a proper bow. "Now, since you were so kind to deliver my shipment directly to my door, I feel that you are owed a third gift." With that he waved his hand to follow him as he left the cart and headed on inside. We did the Innkeeper's bidding and followed him inside the building and towards the bar. Once we were all gathered around him, he started to rummage around beneath the bar and then pulled out three potion bottles.

"These potions are rather valuable, and I do not recommend telling anyone you have them," said the Innkeeper as he placed one in front of each of us. "These are three different potions, that I believe are each suited to your skills," he spoke with a smile. I reached out and grabbed my bottle, it was about the size of a teacup and was stoppered with a standard style champagne cork. The color inside the bottle was an eerie green that almost seemed to glow, while Iris' was blue, and Keila's was red.

"What do they each do?" I asked him.

"Ah, see potions are only made by potion masters. Their services are required by the soldiers of war and the adventurers. Now, there are standard potions out there, such as mana potions to recover mana for magical users. There are standard healing potions that can be picked up most places for a quick recovery of one's injuries.

However, specialty potions, such as these are made to help one increase their skills. Maybe you are struggling to shoot the arrow, this potion will make that arrow shoot straight. Suppose you are trying to hold your own against monsters, this will make you swifter with your sword. You see, these are immensely valuable and quite expensive."

It made sense, now, the names that I had seen underneath the rewards in the notification we all had received at the quest's completion. These must be potions of archery, arcana, and heavy armor.

"Then why give them to us?" I asked. For such a rare treat, these must have cost a lot more than a simple silver coin.

"Oh, well let us just say that they fell off the back of a cart that was leaving town. I would rather you had them, then having them sit underneath this bar forever," said Goldsmith with a laugh.

"Ah, thank you anyways," I said as I grabbed the potion and placed it inside my inventory. While the offer was kind by Goldsmith, it made more sense now that we had learned their true origins. "So, how about that information?"

"Yes, yes, thank you for reminding me," he said as he came closer to us. Just a few inches away he continued in a low voice, "Just a few days ago your two friends came to me, looking for lodging. Being the courteous innkeeper, I accommodated them. However, after a few days it was rumored that they had left town, skipped out on paying the poor innkeeper." He said this with a touch too much drama. "However, this was merely rumor, for only I saw the truth."

"The truth?" I asked, skeptically.

"Indeed, the truth," exacerbated the Innkeeper. "For you see, in the dead of night robbed assailants entered the inn while I was cleaning up at the end of a very long day. I swiftly hid myself behind the bar before I could be seen. I assumed they had come to rob the place, but they came for your two friends. I saw the robed assailants carry both of their bodies out of this front door," he said as pointing to the door right behind us. "After they left, I was prepared to start searching for them, but the guards came by and told me that they had left in the middle of the night to see more of the world. Naturally, I kept the truth to myself, not wishing to become to next body dragged out of here."

"Do you know where they went or who was behind it?" I asked.

"No, I do not. However, I did recognize one of the faces of the men that took your friends and on whose order he did so," he said with seriousness on his face as he placed the palm of his hands flat on the bar.

"Who?" Iris, Keila, and I asked at the same time. We were getting wrapped up in the Innkeeper's story.

"Why, Guardsman Fern as ordered by the Lady Adria," Innkeeper Goldsmith said.

"Shit," I screamed as I kicked the wheel of the cart that we had driven to *The Hollow Quiver Inn*. "We find out that there is one man that could tell us where Hobbs and Reynolds are, and we just happen to find out that it is the only damn person that we have killed," I growled at Keila and Iris.

"I know, I call that some rotten luck," said Iris. She sat down on the back of the now empty cart. Then she sat straight up and smiled. "Actually, it might not be. Won't he just respawn? I mean, come back to life after a little while, and then we could ask him."

Keila shook her head. "Sorry to burst that bubble, but no. The game is designed that each character, even non-player ones, are unique. If the game loses too many non-player characters or if a non-player character is necessary for a quest and dies, then the game sends in fresh replacements. It is designed to be realistic as possible, so if someone dies their son, daughter, sister, mother, you get the picture, will take over. Then, if too many die, then the AI will simply have a migration of new non-player characters enter the game."

"But wait, isn't this information sort of necessary for a quest?" I asked Keila. "After all, this information ending up getting tied in the Elvish Whiskey quest line."

"Yes, but also no. This 'quest' we are on is outside of the game's parameter. Anyways, remember that this quest was not supposed to have Hobbs and Reynolds as a part of its rewards. So, no, I would not bet on anyone coming who has that information," said Keila. "Of course, I could be wrong, but I needn't think that we need to wait around."

"Why is that?" I asked, fuming at myself.

"Well, we know who ordered the kidnapping: Lady Adria," said Keila with a smile. "If I do so remember, that is the same person that you had seen in the warehouse?"

"Ya, that is true," said Iris, excitedly. "Even if Fern is not around, we know that we could just find Lady Adria and that will lead us the right direction."

"I guess that is true," I said as I began to feel a bit better. "If we could find Lady Adria then we could find where Hobbs and Reynolds are, and then we could end this nightmare," I said, now smiling.

"So now, we just need to find where Lady Adria is located," Iris mused.

"No, we do not, actually," said Keila. "She is located in Shadow Valley, underground, where she rules the Thieves' Guild."

"How do you recon we are going to get to her there?" I asked Keila. "She seems like one of the city's boss characters, or am I wrong?"

"No, you are not wrong," responded Keila. "We are not going to be strong enough to take her out. So, we are going to have to be clever, and find out something that she wants or just become super sneaky."

"I, personally, vote for both," I said. "If we could be sneaky and get her something that she wants, well then we could probably be able to get the information from her."

"I agree with Zeph," said Iris.

"I do, as well," said Keila. "We just need to find out what the thing could be for Lady Adria. I suggest we start by going to Baridac."

"Why him?" I asked her.

"Well, two reasons. Firstly, he just offered us a quest so we can get some more experience and get stronger. Secondly, he might know who we could speak to on the Lady Adria front. Oh, and I almost forgot. That journal you found in the warehouse and that letter I found on Fern might be useful. That is if we can read them," she said.

"I completely forgot about that," said Iris. The book materialized in her hands. She looked it over and once again showed its pages to the two of us. However, just like before, the words read like gibberish.

"It is still nonsense to me," I said, as I took the book from her hands. Having been a nerd – albeit a cool one – I had taken some cipher coding projects on in high school. Even with that, there did not appear to be any of the standard patterns as you would see when a document contains words such as 'the' or 'a.' Those are usually some basic words that will repeat enough to stand out, but here they were nonexistent. However, the names on the left margin of the pages were clear. There was even an entry for Fern, under the name Fern Payne. Who names their child Fern, I wondered? However, it was not important enough to spend longer than three second pondering the idea.

"Then there is the page that I found," said Keila.

"Oh, I also forgot about that," I said as I returned the book to Iris so that I could pull the letter out of my Inventory. It appeared in my hand, and I opened it to see a page with some writing on it. However, unlike Iris' book, I could read this just fine. "It says, 'Noon at *The Bannered Mare*,' but there is more," I said.

"Well, what else does it say?" asked Keila, exacerbated.

"That is all that I can read," I said, showing the note. "The rest is smudged out. I can't make it out, can you?" I asked.

"No, I can't," said Iris while Keila shook her head.

"Okay, so we have a location or at the very least I assume *The Bannered Mare* is a location. As well, we have a time. What time is it right now?" I asked.

"It is ten," said Keila, whose eyes were glazed over as she looked at her menu.

"Okay, so we have two hours to find and be at *The Bannered Mare*, wherever that is," I said.

"Wait, hold up," began Iris. "What are we expecting there? How do we know that it was for today, and everything?"

I shrugged at Iris' questions. "All good questions, but it is the only lead we have, except for talking with Baridac. So, let us head there?"

Keila and Iris nodded their heads in confirmation of the tenuous game plan. The problem was that we were all in the dark, to some degree. While being in the dark was not pleasant, there was some hope in the note we had found. If only we could get Iris or someone to read the journal, I thought. That had to hold some of the answers that we were looking for. My main concern, scratch that, one of my many main concerns, was what the owners of the journal were going to say when they found it missing. This just joined the list of the potential hazards: of the guard finding out we killed Fern; of Lady Adria finding us before we found her; and the numerous other items that I was currently blanking on in order to cope. Oh, and let us not forget the real world where there was a murderer in our midst and Keila was a back stabber. Must not forget that one, that Keila is horrid. Especially, given the fact that I was beginning to forget the fact that she was two-faced.

We left *The Hollow Quiver* behind with the cart and horses. The group decided that taking any of the evidence that we had killed Fern with us would have only ended up with us being discovered as the murderers. After all, there was still that warning, and for the game to issue such a caution gave rise for concern. If we got kicked out of Altour and banned from the city, then we could be looking at an end of our mission. Unfortunately, there was nothing to do about it now as we continued on our way to our next destination, *The Tipsy Dwarf.*

## Chapter 27: The Black Pawn

We continued towards *The Tipsy Dwarf* the same way that we had arrived at *The Hollow Quiver*, by following the wall until we came across the same entrance we initially used to enter the city. Once there, finding the inn was not too difficult. In fact, it became distressingly easy to find when we heard Baridac screaming on the top of his lungs outside of his establishment. At hearing the source of the calls of distress Keila, Iris, and I ran over to the dwarf.

"What is going on, Baridac?" I asked him with concern painting my voice.

"Oh, my wee lass is gone, just gone," moaned the dwarf.

"What do you mean, who is your wee lass?" I questioned him. My question and – I guessed – the attention that we were giving the dwarf seemed to calm Baridac down, marginally. At least he was no longer howling down the street. The last thing we needed was to have the entire city's eyes on us.

"Oh," Baridac sniffled, dabbing his nose with a rather large handkerchief. "My pan has been taken from me, and I just found this," he said as he showed us a metal cooking utensil.

"Your pan?" Iris questioned as she came up to pat Baridac on the shoulder with a look of what-the-hell on her face as she looked at me. "We never saw you with a pan or anything."

"Ya, my cousin in The Rocks was using her while I was out of town, but those blasted thieves from Shadow Valley stole her in the night," between audible gasps he held up the item. "When I went down to gather her, my cousin told me how he woke up and she was gone."

"Did the thieves send you the… spatula?" Keila asked with a similar look of how-stoned-is-he painted on her face.

"Nah, I just found it under the bar. It reminded me of her," he groaned before he started wailing once more.

"It is okay Baridac, it is okay," Iris said as she rubbed her hand against his shoulder.

"How do you know it was the Thieves' Guild?" I asked him seriously concerned. Not because of the missing pan, but rather because we were all discussing a pan.

"Who else would steal a pan, I ask you?" stammered the dwarf. "No one else would dare lay a finger of her, but those conniving, godless, horrid bunch. It was my mother's pan, from the homeland, you understand."

"Why don't we do this," I began. "We will go and find your pan and bring it back to you as soon as we find it?"

"You would do that for me?" Baridac asked with his bottom lip jutting out like a child.

"Of course, after all, we did owe you that favor," I said with a reassuring grin. Those words seemed to cheer up Baridac a bit more. As he nodded a quest line appeared in our field of vision.

> **As Repayment to Dwarf Longbrew You Have Been Offered You a Quest: Find and Return His Beloved Pan.**
> **Accept / Decline**
> **Reward(s): Baridac's Debt and Unknown.**

We all said, "Accept" and the words disappeared. While the quest may not have been on the top of the priority list, it was these types of quests that opened up doors down the road: such as Landan's and his sister Elana's archery lessons. "This was not the quest you asked of us earlier?" I asked the dwarf.

"Oh, I am sorry friend. No that was not why I asked you to come see me," said the dwarf between sniffles and blowing his nose into the larger-than-life handkerchief. As he said this a new prompt appeared:

**Quest Completed: Speak with Dwarf Longbrew to Discover the Quest**
**Reward(s): A Quest**
**Experience Gain: 100 Points**

"No, when I saw you three down by The Rocks, I knew that you were fit for another job that I had in mind," said the dwarf who was beginning to calm down. "See, there is a bit of a problem in this city. It has to do with a wee bit of dislike for foreigners and fear of someone that has become known as the Black Pawn." Dwarf Longbrew shivered at the mention of the name. I felt that we were leaning a bit heavily on the he-who-shall-not-be-named motif, but the game obviously drew inspiration from everywhere.

"Who is this Black Pawn character we keep hearing about?" I asked Baridac. Keila swiveled her head at me so swiftly that I almost felt that it had to be related to those owls I keep seeing on nature documentaries. I remembered that we were specifically told not to look into the Black Pawn, but it was hard to keep ignoring the signs from every direction at this point.

"You haven't heard the stories?" he asked with a curious look. We all shook our heads in sync. "Best come inside," he said gesturing to the front door. "This is not the type of conversation that one does where there is light." The dwarf turned away and walked into his inn, and we followed suit. The fireplace was lit, and the long tables remained empty, but there was still a warm air of comfort that can be only created with a lit fireplace and wooden furniture. Baridac walked over and fell onto one of the benches closest to the door, and we all crowded in at the table alongside him.

"There is much not known about the Black Pawn, and I am no expert," began the dwarf. "However, there is a story that is heard far and wide. Told by father to son, mother to daughter, parent to child, and on and on. Supposedly, a thousand years ago at the dawn of the kingdom there was a race of beings that knew not the weakness of age nor the wisdom of humility. This race is still very much around to this day, and they have grown to be the best of us in science, arcane, medicine, everything. These are the elves, as I am sure you can understand," Baridac said. However, none of us really knew what he was saying, but we nodded along.

"However, as humans came onto the field of power, there were several of the ancient folk that felt there was no room for such creatures. The elves had grown to accept dwarves, ratonga, nymphs, hell, even the goblins were on some terms with the elves. Those who did not get along with these races such as the athora and kippsies went and found room in another corner of the world. However, men and women stayed where many made clear they were unwanted. In order to bridge peace between the races a union was arranged. A successor of the human throne was engaged to be married to one born of the elvish throne. Neither were to inherent the thrones of either kingdom, but this marriage symbolized the beginning of peace. They had a single male child, and this child's name has been lost to history. However, the title by which the child went by has not: the Black Pawn.

Feeling that they were merely a pawn being used between the powers that be, he decided that they would play no part in this unification. Hence, the title of Black was later accredited to the name, to symbolize the dark age that the child wished to usher forth. The Black Pawn recruited sympathizers and then set them on the unified world. While I will not bore you with details, the world burned. However, the rebellion was crushed, and the tales have turned into song and folktale. The result is that much of the world is unified, except for some troublesome people here and there. However, there is an ever-present fear amongst people that the Black Pawn is still out there, as he was never killed. This fear has manifested into a fear of foreigners inside these walls and other lands," Baridac said.

"Is this why everyone takes note of us not being from these parts?" I asked him as he took a drink from a container that seemingly appeared from nowhere.

"Yes," he said gravely. "While you folk have been kind to me and others, there is always some fear of people from unknown lands. As well, there is fear of history repeating itself. This is where you three come into the story. There are a group of dwarves who have petitioned the city for years for more rights. You see, the dwarves came to Altour after it had been formed. I am sure that you have seen few of my kind and nearly none of any other," he said.

We shook our heads in agreement. The only fantasy races that I had seen throughout the city were dwarves and then just your standard humans.

Baridac took another swing and then continued, "That is Altour for you. Built by humans for humans. That is the unofficial motto, but it remains true. The elves haven't lived in these parts ever, mostly out of fear of a lynch mob coming for them and fear of being accused of being the Black Pawn. Us dwarves are a more recent edition, and this group of my kinsmen have been trying to get some more rights as citizens of Altour. Unfortunately, they have made too much noise as of late, and now there are people coming for them. The people of Altour fear that dwarves asking for rights is the beginning of another Black Pawn"

"What can we do to help," Iris asked with care in her eyes.

"I hoped that you three might consider getting them to safety, out of the city if you could?" he asked. At his words the prompts came.

**Dwarf Longbrew You Have Been Offered You a Quest: Find and Bring His Kinsmen to Safety. Accept / Decline**
**Reward(s): Honorary Darvish Status, Kin Protector Blade, and 50 Silver x 3.**

We verbally agreed to the quest as it appeared before our eyes.

"That would be too kind of you three, it really would," Baridac said.

"Where are they?" Keila asked.

"Oh, there are three of them and they have hidden themselves inside the sewer system for the time being, but I do not know where. I have looked, but cannot find them," he said. The expected words came with his reveal.

**Quest Update: Locate the Missing Dwarves.**

I looked to Iris and Keila to see them all nod at receiving the quest update.

"Before we head out," I began. "We were hoping to gain some insight on a few things."

"Anything I can do for you," offered the dwarf.

"First thing, we are looking for an establishment called *The Bannered Mare*, and we are hoping to decode some texts that are in a cipher, we believe," I said.

"Ah, *The Bannered Mare* is a peculiar establishment that can be found at Widepoint, right outside of the city's walls. As to the cipher, I am not knowledgeable at such things, but I do believe that there is someone that could help you at North Town. There is a library there, and the librarian who runs the place should know what to do about that," he said with a nod of his head.

"Lastly," I started. "What do you know about Lady Adria?" At my question I thought I heard a growl from Baridac.

"Do not, and I repeat, do not go anywhere near her," the dwarf warned.

"I am sorry Baridac, but we have no other option," I said.

"Of course, you do!" exclaimed the dwarf. "Literally anything else."

"She might know where our friends are," I informed him. This gave Baridac pause as he considered what I just said.

"The friends that left town?"

"Yes, but they did not leave town. We" – I said indicating Iris, Keila, and I – "have it on good authority that she took them."

"I see, just as I am trying to help my friends you are also trying to do right by yours," the dwarf said while stroking his beard. "I believe that you should avoid Lady Adria at all costs, instead I would try to speak with her underlings. They might be more… welcoming, and less dangerous."

"You know where –," I started, but I was interrupted by the front door opening. I turned around in my bench to see who could be looking at us and it was Landan.

"Hello, just the three I was looking for," said Landan with a serious expression on his face. "Could I borrow these three for a second?" he asked the dwarf.

"Sure thing," said Baridac. We all stood up and looked to Landan for direction. He waved us over to join him outside the inn. As we walked over, all I could think was that we were screwed.

"You know what I have come to ask of you?" asked Landan. However, in standard guilty fashion we merely looked at one of another quickly and shunned ourselves into silence.

"You probably don't," said Landan. "Nonetheless, I thought that I should warn you that we, the guard, have been warned to be on the lookout for a group of adventurers. Two gals and a lad, to be precise."

The fact that Landan had not outright accused us gave my lungs a much-needed breath of air, and I could feel my heart right go from nuclear to simply just standard explosive levels of nervous.

"What for?" I asked, exploratorily as my nails imbedded themselves into my palms.

"A guard was killed and there some witnesses who said that two women and a man left the scene in a horse-drawn cart," he said. "Just to let you know, you three will most likely be detained on sight by guards. So, until we find the culprits, I would just avoid Silkliff or any guards in general.

"Why let us know?" I asked. At this question Landan leaned in a bit closer to the three of us.

"You three have earned my respect and I am also familiar with the guard who died. His name was Fern, and he was not… let us say, the stand-up type. I am not sure you remember, but he was at the guard post with me when you three came in. I assume he got mixed up with the wrong business of sorts," Landan said a tad too knowingly for my liking. "However, that is neither here nor there. Since a crime has been committed there must be justice. So… I am just letting you know the facts," stressed Landan. We all nodded hurriedly at his words. At us confirming that we had heard him loud and clear, Landan turned around and started to walk away.

"Damn, that was close," I said.

"I am really happy we did that quest for him early on," Iris said.

"Me too. Now, we need to get out of here. Landan's good graces won't be standing forever, and we need to get out of sight," Keila said as she walked off the porch of *The Tipsy Dwarf.*

Iris and I hurried to catch up with Keila as she strode off in the opposite direction of *The Hollow Quiver*. "Where are we going to, now?" I asked Keila as I hurried to match pace with her.

"I believe we have two main objectives. First, we need to get to the library in North Town before we run out of good luck. Second, we need to get to *The Bannered Mare* within the next hour and a half for whatever is going down there which might lead us to Lady Adria. Since the guards are looking for two women and a man, I believe we should split up again," Keila said as she kept a strong pace forward, not allowing Iris and I to match.

"Split up?" I spoke. "Last time we did that, Iris and I got locked up. I don't know if you remember Keila, but that was like only three hours ago."

"I remember having to save you two." Keila gave me and Iris a glare at that. "That is why I will not be leaving Iris' side. She is the least defensible being a mage, and you have your stealth ability. Since we will be staying in the city while you go the tavern she might need my help from guards," Keila explained.

"Hey, I can defend myself. Thank you very much," Iris said.

"I do not doubt that" replied Keila. "However, if we are being chased down an alleyway by guards I would rather that you were with someone who knew the most about the city. Zephaniah will be outside of the city's walls in Westpoint, where there are substantially less guards."

"That kind of makes sense," I said in response to Keila's plan.

"Of course, it does," she replied.

"Why am I the one going to the library?" asked Iris.

"Because you have natural class skill in Investigation and are most likely to be able to learn the skill the fastest to deciphering the code within the book," explained Keila.

Iris had no comeback to that one, so she went quiet. The more I thought about Keila's plan, the more sense it made to me. I, being the stealthy one, would go to the secret meeting while Iris, being the brainy one, would go learn how to read. Keila, being the brawny one, will protect the Ravenclaw.

"Hey, Iris are you a Ravenclaw?" I asked her.

"I prefer to think of myself as a Hufflepuff, but yes. I have taken the test like a dozen times, and it is always Ravenclaw," she said. "What is your house?"

"I've never taken the official test, but I have always aligned with the Slytherins. With the cunning and ambitious side fitting really well with my hacker persona," I answered.

"I am also a Slytherin," said Keila. Which came as no surprise to either of us.

## Chapter 30: Hide and Seek

We continued on our way for another half an hour, walking fast enough to cover ground, but not fast enough to appear as if we were running. Which we were. Every once and a while we would see a contingent of guards walking around and we would put ourselves at a distance from one another, as if we were walking separately. This was especially true when we came across the fortress and the inner wall. As this appeared to be the stronghold for the city's guard, we remained separate, praying that we each made it through. We remained safe, at least for the time being. Spread out, we walked directly towards North Town, which was directly next to Silkliff, so we had to be careful as we crossed that area, but we were able to make it to this part of town without incident so far. At this point we were on a main road that seemed to continue on forever. This area of town seemed to be the wealthiest by far. There were entire houses made of stone and they appeared to be even larger than the three-storied homes we had seen earlier. While in Silkliff and Barbers Town there were four or five homes per city block, this area seemed to have only two. As well, the diverse range of colors of the clothes of the people of North Town seemed to dwindle. Everyone's clothes were obviously nicer, but instead of mix and matching different colors each person wore one distinctive color per person. These colors ranged from red, to blue, to green, and I even saw a few people decked out in all white.

"This is North Town," said our unofficial tour guide, Keila.

"What is the deal with all of the colors?" I asked.

"It is to signify one's profession and class," explained Keila. "Those who do academia, study the arcane, labor, and other things."

It made sense that there was a distinction between those who had money and those who had less. The less wealthy side of Altour seemed so vibrant and alive, while this seemed to be almost dull in comparison. However, the smell that we had come to grow use to had finally dissipated. The perfect road, the cobblestone replaced with granite or marble, and the uniformity of this area of Altour almost felt like a different city entirely. The one benefit of being in North Town was the complete lack of any guards. There were one or two guards every now and again, by compared to the rest of the city it was as if they disappeared.

"We seem to be safer, for now," said Keila. At this point we were walking together again. Throughout Silkliff Keila had led by a city block where I followed and then another block down Iris had followed me. Here we had finally all walked together, and my stress level had plummeted back to more standard levels between us. For comparison, my stress levels went from Christmas shopping on Christmas Eve to Christmas shopping on Black Friday, except there were no casualties.

"Safer, but not safe," I said. "Unfortunately, we just do not have the time to just log out and wait for the guard to stop looking for us."

"Agreed," responded Keila. "Normally, this effect would disappear eventually. However, as you said, we do not have the time."

We kept on walking down the main road, as I continued to look around at the stone houses that seemed to be made of something similar to marble, the same material as the road. At least the real-world version of marble, I reminded myself. We walked, side by side, down the main road of North Town, enjoying the brief respite from the guards looking for us. We eventually left the rows of houses and entered a massive area of greenery, a park. This was the first time that I had seen grass or even a tree since entering the city, and it was rather pleasant. Surprisingly so: I had forgotten how enveloping the city could be, even in a virtual game world such as this.

We continued on the main road that led through the park, but about halfway Keila pulled us to a stop. "This is where the library is," she said, pointing to one of the larger buildings that bordered the park. It reminded me of the old-fashioned churches that are spread throughout Europe with its colored glass and the spire that stuck out the middle of the building. It looked to be one of the largest buildings we had seen yet, besides for the fortress. "Iris and I will continue there, but Zephaniah, you will continue straight down this road. It leads towards the city wall, hopefully the guards there are either gone or are not looking for you. Right outside of the gate is the area known as Widepoint," Keila said while pointing down the road. In the distance I could see the wall, but it still was far off. We all said goodbye as I headed off down the road and towards the secret meeting that was put on that note.

After two thousand or so meters I was across the gate that exited the city and entered into the area known as Widepoint. According to Baridac, this is where I would find the tavern known as *The Bannered Mare*. The only problem was that I could see two guards posted at the gate, and I was not sure if they knew to look out for adventurers or not. Seeing no other option, I walked forward, hoping to fall within the crowd that was exiting the city. I reminded myself that they were looking for a group of three people, and there was a chance that I was just another stranger passing through. My assumption appeared to be true, as I walked through the gate, nodding to the one guard who had made eye contact with me on my way out.

"Mission success," I said while holding onto my earlobe. While there was no one to receive my imaginary transmission, it felt appropriate. Walking out of the extremely wealthy area of Altour to Widepoint felt like shifting worlds. While there had been a noticeable shift, there had been a gradual change from Silkliff to North Town. By contrast, the difference between Widepoint and North Town had no transition process. I was back among wooden houses and two- or three-story buildings. I started to walk up to the people on the streets who were going about their business asking, "Where might I find *The Bannered Mare*?" After quizzing some of the non-player characters I was directed towards a shifty-looking, one-story building that was down an alleyway. The people I asked gave a side-eyed glance, as if they wanted to be sure that I had left them alone after asking my question. As I turned down the alleyway, I was not surprised to feel that I was no longer amongst the kind folks of Altour, but instead its seedy underbelly.

I walked up to a wooden door and pulled it open, the door nearly fell, and I could see that it was hanging onto the frame by a single hinge. I walked inside the building, closing the door behind me as carefully as possible. The tavern was not the warm tavern of *The Tipsy Dwarf*, nor the clean, reputable drinking hall of Innkeeper Goldsmith. There were no songs nor any fire to breathe life into the room. I could see circular tables that filled the room with little alcoves on the sides of the walls that had curtains one could pull closed for privacy. The bar was immediately on my left as I entered into the building. The room was half filled with people of all sorts, none of them familiar. A few of the table's occupants looked over at me as I entered the room, but I paid them no mind. I looked to the barkeep and pointed at one of the alcoves that still had a curtain, and he nodded his head.

After I had walked over and sat by myself, an odd-looking man came up to the table and asked what I would have. I simply told him beer and then pulled the curtain half closed so that I could see some of the room, but the occupants of the tables around me could not see me easily. I attempted to listen to the conversation around me, closing my eyes and focusing on the table nearest to me.

"…guild is making moves," said a man from the table right outside of my closed curtain.

"I've heard the same, Lady Adria is apparently bringing in more and more… merchandise through The Rocks," said another one of the men.

"Do you know what she is bringing in?" asked the third.

"I do not know, but I have heard of weapon caches being stored throughout the city by her hand. You know she had like half of the guard paid off."

"For what end, I wonder?"

"I believe it—," began the first man, but I could not hear what he said because my curtain opened up to reveal the barkeep's man, who delivered my beer. I took the drink and swiftly paid the man 10 coppers, the price of alcove must be part of that, I thought as I paid him from my pouch. As soon as he left, I pulled the curtain to its original position and attempted to hear what the people were saying, but I was interrupted again as words appeared in my line of vision.

| **You have unlocked new skill: Eavesdropping**<br>**Level Up Skill: Eavesdropping to Level 1 – Unlocking your skill in Eavesdropping means that your able to hear conversations from ten feet away with some focus, and you are less likely to be discovered by 50%.**<br>**Experience Reward: 50 Points** |
|---|

Crap I thought, as the words disappeared from the field of vision. Because it seemed that I could be discovered while listening in on someone's conversation. The distance part also makes sense, to keep the game as realistic as possible. I wondered how it would level up, but I realized I was getting distracted easily and needed to focus. I quickly opened my menu and saw that noon was due in only a few minutes. So, whoever was coming to meet with Guardsman Fern should either be here or be arriving shortly. I then realized my stupidity. How was I supposed to know who to look for? It was not like they were going to be waving a sign around asking for Fern or another sign saying that they were the bad guy. I concluded that the only logical step forward was to be present and hope for the best. Turning my focus back to the table, I closed my eyes and attempted to listen back in.

However, before I could focus on the words of the people sitting outside my curtain, the door to the tavern opened up. I looked at the person, but it was not anyone I had seen yet in the game. She was extremely short, not dwarf height, but just barely not. Her eyes seemed to be black, and her hair was the same color. To be honest, she looked a little like a schoolgirl, but that image was quickly dissolved based on the reactions that were sent throughout the tavern. Several people stood up, while others had scuffled closer to their tables and bowed their heads to become small targets. Seeing the reaction from everybody around me, I was attempting to focus on her as she pulled her eyes away from the room and towards the barkeep. He pointed towards my general direction, and I began to sweat. How did he know that I was someone that this girl, excuse me, murderous black-eyed child wanted? My fear dissipated as I saw that he was merely pointing at the alcove next to mine, the only other one that still maintained a curtain. Her and two minions that followed behind her, you know, the standard muscle man stereotype, all crowded into the alcove next time mine. As they did the men across from my curtain started speaking up.

“What the hell is Bella-freaking-donna doing here?” asked one of the men.

“I heard that her mistress, Lady Adria, kidnapped some poor souls and was keeping them prisoner down in her underground kingdom,” voiced the other.

“The foreigners?” asked the third voice.

“Yep, as I heard it, they were spies for The Black Pawn. You know how territorial Lady Adria can be,” snickered the first man.

“That doesn’t answer why Belladonna is here, she never leaves Lady Adria’s side.”

“Fair point, must be—”

I had heard enough, I decided. There was no reason to continue staying around while such a dangerous character was right next to me. After all, I had the information that I was looking for, Reynolds and Hobbs were in the sewers in Shadow Valley. There was still the question of their exact location, but that information was not likely to be muttered in some casual conversation. I slowly stood up and pulled back my curtain to look out of the room; attempting to avoid eye contact with anyone I slowly made my way out of the building. Once outside I was able to breath a bit easier, and I was able to compose a message to Iris.

*To: Iris Christman*

*From: Zephaniah Kote*

*Found out where Reynolds and Hobbs are, you two done?*

I looked around to make sure that no one had heard me, but the alleyway beside the tavern remained empty of people. The child demon had still not made her way out of the building, and she was the only one that I wanted to be sure did not see me. After all, if I was about to break into your home, I would not want to be leaving you with an impression beforehand. As I composed a message, once again, to Iris my icon flashed showing a new one from the woman herself.

*To: Zephaniah Kote*

*From: Iris Christman*

*Zeph, we were able to get part of it. It is a blackmail journal that looks like half of the guards are in these pages. It has some real nasty parts to it.*

It was after receiving this message that I realized I recognized the name Belladonna. That was the name that was transcribed on the front of the book's title page. I found it not too hard of a leap to decide that the book was either made or owned by the same Belladonna that was currently sitting inside *The Bannered Mare* tavern that I had just fled. That is when I had an idea. I turned around and reentered the tavern and walked straight to the closed curtain where Belladonna and two of her friends were currently sitting. I drew back the curtain to see Belladonna's pitch-black eyes staring right in my face.

"That was rude," she said in a little girl's voice. At her words, the two men on her sides began to get up, before she raised her little hand that currently had white cotton gloves on them. As soon as she did, the men froze and sat back down. "Care to sit?" she asked me, gesturing towards the other end of the alcove. I turned around and saw that the entire room was gaping at me. I took her offer and swiftly sat down, drawing the curtain closed. "I guess so," she said with a smile, as if she was happy by my intrusion. "You do not look like Guardsman Fern to me."

"That is because I am not," I responded.

"So, you have not come to offer me more goodies?" she asked with a frown.

"I wouldn't know what kinds of goodies you are after," I responded.

"Oh, you know, the kinds that make things go BOOM," she said while slamming her hands on the tables. The sound half scared me, and Belladonna began to laugh at my reaction. "I just love the sounds and all of the different lights they make."

"I am sorry, but no I am not here to offer anything of that sort," I said.

“What a bummer,” Belladonna said while crossing her arms and pouting. However, she quickly stopped that act and began another. “Why don’t we start fresh then, my name is Belladonna. What is yours?”

“My name is Zephaniah,” I said while offering my hand.

“Oh, what a gentleman,” she responded while grasping my hand. Her grip was insanely strong, and I could begin to feel the individual pops of each of my fingers before she let go. “That was a nice handshake. What can I do for you, Zephaniah?”

“I… uh, found something of yours by The Rocks.”

“Oh, really? That is too kind of you to return lost property. I really do love my things.”

“Yes, well it is a leather-bound book,” I began. At my words Belladonna eyes began to widen, but just slightly. “I found it on the floor of a warehouse that I was in,” I finished as the reaction from Belladonna’s face retreated back to her normal child-like face.

Belladonna brought her hands together and pondered for a second. “You know, you remind of someone that I once met,” she began. “He was like you, a man who just happened to find things that should not have been where he found them. I believe his name was Jeremiah. Jere…miah, what an odd name.”

“What happened to Jeremiah?”

"Oh, remind me Euric," she said looking towards one of the muscle men at her side. "Whatever happened to Euric?"

"I believe, mistress, that you had a… playdate with him," he said with a straight face.

"Oh, yes how he screamed. It was good fun, but he was not my friend Euric. I don't have those types of playdates with friends. Otherwise, I would have no friends. Are you looking to be my friend, Zephaniah?"

"Yes?" I ventured, not knowing what game was being played.

"Oh goodie," she said while she clapped her gloved hands. "Then could you just bring my book back to me and then we can have our own playdate."

"I am sorry Belladonna, but I need something from you for it."

Belladonna's eyes grew darker, although I was unsure how that was possible. "I do not like this game you are playing, new friend Zephaniah."

"I do not want to play this game either, but I need to find my friends."

"Friends?"

"Yes, two foreigners like myself. I heard that they were… spending time with you and Lady Adria in under town."

"Now I remember. I have not had a chance to have a playdate with them, they look like no fun," Belladonna said, as the childlike quality to her face returned and a look of disappointment took over. "Although, I might want to get my favorite bedtime story rather than have a playdate with them."

"So, how about a trade?" I asked.

"Oh, like a game?" Belladonna asked with excitement. "I really love a good game."

"Yes, I return your book to you, and you give me my friends."

Belladonna paused and seemed to ponder my proposal for a few minutes. "Sure, but I want to play another game with you, as well."

"What kind of game?"

"Good question! Euric, what is my favorite game?"

"Hang Man?" he asked with a monotone expression, but Belladonna shook her head. "Stretch Them? No Hands? No Feet? Which Cup is Poisoned?" he continued, but to each she shook her head.

"Oh, I remember," she said while clapping her hands and hopping up and down in her seat. "Let us play hide and seek!"

"Hide and seek?"

"Yes, hide and seek. You find me and you have a deal," she said, but as she did, she lifted a vial in her hand. I could not see it clearly, except that it was a black vial, and Belladonna threw it onto the floor and black smoke filled the alcove. I could not see anything, but then I hear Belladonna's laugh as she said, "See you soon, new friend." As the smoke dissipated, she and her goons were gone, but there were new words in my vision.

**Belladonna Black-eyed Has Offered You a Quest: Find Her**
**Reward: Opportunity to trade her journal for the two foreigners**

Unlike in the past with other quest opportunities. There was no "Accept" or "Decline" option available. In fact, it looked like I had already accepted to quest. Seeing it was the only path forward I decided to embrace the havoc in the room by swiftly exiting *The Bannered Mare* while people were still figuring out what the black smoke was about. I even heard one man scream, "Fire," but apparently no one else was that concerned as they mostly remained in place. I slipped through the front door, and Belladonna was nowhere in sight. "Fish sticks," I muttered under my breath

After getting a little more distance between myself and *The Bannered Mare* I ducked down in an alleyway between another establishment and a house and pulled up my menu. I quickly sent Iris a message, with a brief condensed version of what had just happened to me and my encounter with Belladonna. She replied just as quickly,

*From: Iris Christman*

*To: Zephaniah Kote*

*What? Okay me and Keila are on our way to you. Just get as close to the wall without being spotted and we will find you.*

After walking back towards the wall and finding a place to hunker down, I waited. It was not too long before Iris and Keila found me. Iris still was holding the leather-bound book in her hand and they came up to me.

"We got the same quest notification without any option to decline it," said Keila as she neared me.

"Is this quest really from the same Belladonna as the one from this book?" asked Iris as she showed me the leather-bound journal full of dirty secret. I nodded my head in confirmation to her question. I gave them every detail of the conversation I had with the lady and the brief conversation that I had overheard from the table across from me in *The Bannered Mare.*

"So, if I am correct," began Keila, who suddenly looked a little red around the eyes. "Belladonna and Lady Adria kidnapped Reynolds and Hobbs because they feared that as foreigners they were in cahoots with the Black Pawn. They have been turning the guard, using their secret, and building up a cache of weapons to fight him off when he comes. Oh, and now she is willing to trade the imprisoned Reynolds and Hobbs if we return her book of dirty little secrets on the guard, but we need to find her first."

"Ya, that sounds about it, but you forgot the part about Baridac's pan and his fellow kinsmen who are also hidden beneath the city. As well, it is beneath the city that we are probably going to need to go to find Belladonna, Hobbs, and Reynolds," I surmised.

"My question," began Iris, "is who is this Jeremiah character that Belladonna mentioned to you Zephaniah?"

"I have no clue. Do you Keila? Have you ever heard the name?"

Keila looked at Iris and I and then looked away from the both of us. Before saying, "No, never heard the name before."

"Well, that is a load of bull," I responded. "You know something that you are not sharing."

"Yes," Keila bite back. "I am not going to say anything because I cannot say anything."

"No, no, no. I am sorry Keila, but that is not going to fly. Iris and I deserve to know what other dirty secret that you and Riverlight are keeping from the rest of us," I fumed. "Enough of the secret. We have a dead body in the real world and two trapped people in this one. Riverlight's secrets have cost lives, and I am not interested in sticking my neck out any more than I already have. So I will hear what is this secret that you have decided to keep from the rest of us."

Iris nodded her head in agreement with me and then turned to Keila. "We have every right to know. First, we learn that you are the dirty little secret, and we still have not gotten the full story behind the glitch or whatever started this whole mess to begin with."

Keila looked between Iris and me. The look in her eyes was not anger, but instead frustration. I could imagine that she was struggling internally with whether or not to tell us this ingot of information. It had to be dark, if it was worth all of the hassle that had led us to this point. "Fine," Keila spat while putting her back against the wall to slide down onto her haunches. "Jeremiah was the first beta tester for Fabula."

# Chapter 31: Game Plan

Keila and I looked to each other in shock. "What there were other testers before us?" I asked her.

Iris also took a turn towards Keila at this reveal. "What happened to him? Why have we not met him or even heard his name mentioned?"

Keila started to say something, but I stopped her with my hand. "No, Keila. We want the truth. We deserve the entire truth. Tell us everything," I commanded.

Keila looked at both of us with pleading eyes, as if she were urging us to not ask such questions, but we did not relent. Iris and I simply stared Keila down until she bowed her head in acceptance of the question. "So, you already know that there was a glitch with Ellie, the AI, that was creating larger and more complex storylines that the game could handle. You also know that there was restriction put onto the AI after these glitches started. The official story is that it was to stop Ellie from creating just extreme changes, overnight, to the entire game. However, that was not the only reason. There is another glitch in the system, that we had thought was fixed until Reynolds and Hobbs got stuck."

"I thought that they got stuck because someone did it on purpose?" I asked her.

Keila glared at me, but sighed and answered, "Yes. Someone used the glitch to keep Hobbs and Reynolds here, but the ability to do so was already a part of the game world. This ability was not created by us, but by the artificial intelligence. We shut it down because of another reason. Someone died, a play tester died."

Iris and I looked at each other. Someone had died and they still allowed themselves to continue working on this game. This was the big secret, that if it ever got out or even rumored about, would ruin any chance of the game making it to release. I thought that all of the stuff with Hobbs and Reynolds was a disaster, this was a freaking Biblical level event. I looked to Keila as tears started to form in her eyes.

"Jeremiah and I were brought on at the same time to playtest the game," she said. "During one of the playthroughs we discovered that there was this quest line called the Black Pawn. It was an original creation of the AI's and not one created by the development team at Riverlight. The same thing that happened before, is repeating itself here. We ended up getting captured because people of the city thought of us as spies of the Black Pawn. I logged out before getting surrounded by the mob." Keila stopped to catch her breath and wipe some of the tears off her face. "However, Jeremiah said he could not log out. He said that his log out button was completely greyed out, so he was stuck in the game. I waited for him to respawn so that we could figure it all out, but he never did. I eventually found out that he was trapped underground being tortured for answers regarding the Black Pawn. I was not aware that it was by Belladonna until you just told me what she had said." Keila took a deep breath has she shuddered a bit.

"Since he could not respawn, he just sat there getting tortured over and over again. Kept being brought to the edge of death and then it would just continue. The game has the pain depression system so that it does not hurt really, but for days he was tortured. The game took on a mind of its own, the constant torture eventually got to him, and he broke. I was told that as a last-ditch effort, Sammy pulled him out of the game physically, literally ripped him out of the chair. But, it was too late, he had gone into some trauma induced coma either from the chair removal or the torture, I am not sure. He died a few weeks later," Keila started to openly sob and could not get control of herself long enough to string together a sentence.

Iris and I looked at each other. Her eyes were heavy with doubt and concern, and I imagine mine looked the same to her. Someone had literally died, and they continued to get this game off to the masses. After a few moments Keila had gained control of herself again.

"Sorrento went out and told the executives that Jeremiah was the only game tester and pulled a full stop on Fabula," Keila said as she grasped her shaking hands. "I was hidden away and Dr. Jordan and Blake pulled together, and wiped Ellie and did a restart. Literally, they started from scratch with the same bones. No one knew about me, no Dr. Jordan, Reynolds, Sammy, or any of them except Blake and Sorrento. After placing a heavy number of restrictions on Ellie, they put me back in the game. I did not want to go, but Sorrento has a way with words," she chuckled bitterly to herself while we both nodded in agreement. "And everything was fine. The game worked. There was no Black Pawn, there was no issues with log outs or anything. We brought in a few others to beta test the game, and there were zero problems. So, Hobbs and Reynolds made the announcement last week, and that was when they got locked into the game."

"And they don't know who got them stuck in the game?" I asked.

Keila looked at me and shrugged. "I have no clue to who would have done it, nor do I have any clue why Sorrento was killed. I can only assume that it was to stop the game from reaching the market, prevent anything like that from every happening again. Last time, the game had to be scraped to fix the problem, and Blake cannot afford to do that again while meeting the deadline for the release. Hence why you all are here, to avoid that," Keila muttered.

"It does not freakin' matter if they do not reach the market when people are getting stuck and are dying in this game," I screamed in frustration towards Keila. She simply nodded her head in acceptance.

"I know it doesn't, but all we can do is make sure that Reynolds and Hobbs make it out of the game," said Keila.

"Ya, I get that, but why don't we just shut down the game instead?" I asked. After all, this game was never going to survive. Someone somewhere was going to leak the truth and then the game would be gone, off the shelfs and Riverlight will be closing its doors.

"What will happen to them?" asked Keila. "What will happen if we erase the ground upon which Reynolds and Hobbs are standing?"

"I don't know, but it is better than doing nothing," I growled at her.

"Is it? Because I do not know. I would rather not risk it. If we can get Reynolds and Hobbs out of Lady Adria's hands then at the very least, they will be safe as we figure out the problem," Keila yelled back.

I stood silent. Keila was suddenly back on her feet. I could not find any ground on which to argue with her on this. If we did nothing then Hobbs and Reynolds could end up like Jeremiah, but if we saved them, then they were safe from that. I looked to Iris, and she simply looked back at me, not a suggestion on her lips or any sign of an inclination towards either way. Iris would support me in whatever I decided, I realized. She was just as frustrated and angry as I was, of that, I was sure. However, she probably felt as I did, it was us against Riverlight and we had to stand together against them. I nodded at Keila and more importantly, at the words that she was saying. We had to rescue Hobbs and Reynolds before it was too late for them.

After we left the alleyway, we started walking towards the city's gate. It was decided, we would go and find Belladonna and save the two people stuck within her and Lady Adria's kingdom. "How are we going to be able to find them?" I asked Keila.

"I know a way into the sewer system underneath Shadow Valley. We just need to get there, and we can then sneak in, and hopefully find Belladonna before she finds us. Or even better would be to find Hobbs and Reynolds ourselves without Belladonna or Lady Adria even knowing that we were there," suggested Keila.

"Agreed, are we even strong enough to handle ourselves down there?" I asked them.

"Yes, for the monsters and the other natural spawning obstacles," started Keila, "since this is a starting city. The natural spawning monsters and everything should be less than level five. However, Lady Adria and her court are going to be too strong for the likes of us. Our only option is to be cleverer than they are since we won't be able to strong-arm ourselves out of any confrontation."

As Keila and us strategized we came upon the gate that entered the city. We had become so lost in the train of thought and conversation that we came to the entrance to the city of Altour together, as a group. We realized our mistake as the guards at the gate all began to point in our direction and call out.

"Crap," I hissed. Keila, Iris, and I pulled to a full stop as the guards moved towards us. Then a warning broke out across my vision.

**Warning: You've Have Been Recognized as Wanted by the Altour City Guard**
**Being spotted by the city guard makes you easier to locate and find by authorities. Hide or flee to avoid repercussion of your actions.**

"Crap," I hissed again.

"What are we going to do?" asked Iris.

"Run," responded Keila.

I looked away from Keila at response and saw that three guards were running in our direction. "Which way?" I asked Keila.

"Follow me, and whatever you do, do not get caught." To my surprise, Keila started running directly towards the guards.

# Chapter 32: Run, Baby, Run

Irish and I sprinted after Keila who was running directly towards the city guard. In the real world this would have surely come as a shock, as they would have to wonder why a perpetrator was running towards their judgement. However, these virtual characters did not seem fazed by Keila's drastic action. We flew behind Keila, running at breakneck speeds. Not two meters from the guard Keila turned a hard left and skirted around them. The guards, focused on Keila, slammed to a full stop to realign themselves with her. By the time that the guards had turned fully around Iris and I had already passed them and were not a meter behind Keila as she flew through the gates of Altour.

People stopped to look as Keila, Iris, and I ran past. Enough of them were staring at us to make it nearly impossible to keep running at such speeds. We kept having to slow down in order to maneuver around the stationary pedestrians, rather than running straight into them.

"Where are we heading?" I yelled at Keila, who now was only a little bit ahead of me. I looked back and saw that Iris was lagging a little behind me, but we all had made it through the gate.

"We are going towards Shadow Valley, where an entrance into the sewer system is located," she called back over her shoulder.

"What do we do once we get there?" I asked back.

"Hide, until the guard is no longer on our backs."

"Why don't we just fight them, the three of us together?" I shouted.

"Did you see how strong Fern was, Zephaniah?" Keila called out. "We took him by surprise, but we had to constantly keep on the attack to avoid him coming after us. It took all we had to take down one city guard. They are level ten and upwards. There is no way that we could take out more than one." She gave a momentary glance back at me like I was dropped on my head too many times as a child.

I realized that she was right. Fern had received a critical blow by my hand at the start of the battle, right before Iris unleashed her full fire blast on him. That did not take into consideration the two lethal blows that Keila had delt with her longsword. I was not sure that I would even survive one of her blows, let alone two. In the end, it was not even those blows that killed Fern: his bleeding out finished the job. No matter how much I disliked Keila, which was even more after the alleyway, she was not wrong. If we fought smart, I thought that we could take down one or two guards, but even the three that were chasing us from the gate, were too many.

We would either all respawn outside the city limits with nothing or be incarcerated without Keila on the outside to save us. So we had to make it to the Sewers before they caught up.

I looked over my shoulder to see that Iris was still on my tail; she looked like she was breathing hard but keeping up. I saw over her shoulder, a few meters away, that there were now six fully plated guards running right after us. Okay, there was no way that we were going to be able to take them on, I finally accepted that fact. I turned back round to make sure that I stayed right on Keila's tail. We continued onwards. I could now see in my field of vision the park where I had previously left Keila and Iris. It was still a far way off, but before we could even get there, Keila took a fast turn left down an alleyway between two houses. North Town was pleasant, and thus did not have the tight, dark alleyways that were present throughout the rest of the city. At the end of the alleyway was a dead end, but before I yelled at Keila that she had doomed us to capture, she opened a door on the building to our right.

"Get in," she yelled at us. I turned around and Iris had just arrived in the alleyway. We both drove our bodies through the open doorway and Keila came in right after. She closed the door and slammed the bar down that was conveniently placed on the other side. It slotted home just as the guards ran into the door. The bar shook in its frame but held. I looked around and saw that we were in the stairway of a building. The stairs traveled upwards to an unknown floor, as the staircase disappeared into blackness.

"Go, go, go," yelled Keila as she threw her arms at us and pointed up the staircase. "To the top," she screamed. Iris and I began taking the stairs two and a time. I was beginning to find it hard to breathe and keep up at the pace I had originally set. To be fair, my virtual body had already long surpassed what my physical body would have been able to accomplish. I would say, on a good day that I could handle a fifteen-kilometer-an-hour pace, but I had to have been going as fast as twenty during our flight. Nonetheless, there was nothing to do because as I slowed down, Keila started to push me with her hand. We entered into the darkness at the top of the staircase, which was dispersed when Iris put up her light spell, illuminating the stairs so we did not break out necks. As soon as she did that, I heard the door below break open and Keila pulled Iris down to the floor, breaking her concentration and thus the light spell and we were plummeted straight back into darkness.

"Where did they go?" asked a guard who was a few stories below.

"Split up, everyone takes one floor," shouted the lead guard who had first seen us. At this Keila picked up Iris and we continued our climb. After another two stories we came across a door. Keila attempted to pull it open, but it held fast. "Damn it," she hissed at the knob. She pulled her great sword out of her sheath, and I grew concerned. If she began to bash that door down, then the guards would surely hear and come right for us. However, that was not what she did, rather Keila slid her sword between the door and the frame and then shoved it upwards up, splitting whatever piece of wood held the lock in place.

"I think I heard something," yelled a guard who was only a floor or two below us.

We rushed through the doorway, and I felt around for something to hold it shut with, but there was only the broken piece of wood that Keila had broken to get us through. I looked around and saw some crates that were standing empty, so I grabbed one and tried to jam it underneath the door handle. It did not look strong enough to hold long. I looked to Keila, hoping that she had some answer as to why she had trapped us on top of a building. Then I realized that we were literally outside, on top of the building.

"What the hell, Keila?" I screamed at her as she pushed her shoulder against the door. There was no one yet pushing on it, but Keila was preparing herself.

"We need to jump, Zephaniah. Do not scream at me, I am the only one who knows where to go. So just shut it, and do as I say!" she hollered.

I was shaken. Keila had never previously been harsher than to express a stern word with one of us. Since the reveal of her previous dealings with Sorrento, she had completely revised even that. She was scared, I could see, and not just about our gaming predicament. "Sorry," I said, "where to now?"

"We are going to jump to the next building over," Keila said with a nod of her head towards the building to our left. "We are going to keep doing that until we are out of buildings to jump to, and then we are going back to street level."

"Can we even jump over to other buildings?" I asked looking at the edge. There was a good meter, maybe more, between the buildings. I also was not a fan of heights, so even this four-story building was doing some nasty things to my stomach.

"Yes, we either jump or give ourselves up right now," said Keila. As she spoke, a thump was heard against the door. Keila glared at me and Iris with the universal eye language for 'shut up!' The door jumped again against Keila's back, and she shook her head in the direction of the ledge. I looked towards Iris who was nodding, and before she even finished her final nod, she had started running towards the edge. I bite my tongue to stop myself from screaming as Iris flew over the edge. I ran to the edge to see if she was alright, to see that Iris had landed a few feet on the other side of the building's ledge. *If she can do it so easily, so can I.* I walked to the far ledge and started running. Faster and faster, I ran until the edge was not a few inches away and used my right leg to push off. I fell, but thankfully

I fell onto the roof of the other building that was a story below us. Iris helped me back to my feet as I saw that I had taken fall damage for ten health points, damn it.

I looked back up and saw that Keila was already flying towards us. I swiftly backed away, giving her the room to land without killing me. Keila landed in one of the superhero landings positions that you only see in action movies. "Done this before?" I asked her at seeing her graceful landing when comparing the fact that I had landed on my face.

"Of course," she responded with attitude. "Let us go, we are not away scot-free just yet." Keila started running forward and we jumped again at the other building. This building was closer but was at the same height, so it was a bit more challenging. I turned around on the third roof to see how far we had come. I could see that there were three guards yelling at us from the original rooftop. I turned back around, and we continued onwards. We had no difficulty until a few buildings later when we came across one that dropped two stories. I stopped at the edge while Iris and Keila both had gone over as per usual. Keila, being the master of building hopping simply jumped across while Iris landed lightly on her feet and began a roll to disperse the impact. Seeing their success, I backed up and ran to make the jump, as I did, I saw an arrow come from behind me, which motivated me to run even faster as I made the jump. I landed but failed to roll and my ankles and knees took the damage for it.

"They are still behind us," I yelled as I landed to Keila and Iris. I looked upwards to see a guardsman with a bow take aim at all of us sitting ducks.

"The next building and then down to the street," said Keila.

We all took off at a run towards the next building. We had landed a story below at the roof of the next building. Then Keila ran straight to the other ledge and simply dropped from sight. Iris and I looked at each other and both shrugged and ran after Keila. We looked over the edge to see that we were only two stories from the street level. I could see Keila was standing on the top of a porch roof, and from there she dropped down to street level. We followed suit, dropping down to the covering and then to the street level. I looked around and saw that we were no longer in North Town. The streets were made mostly out of dirt and a very little stone. The homes were entirely made out of wood and the people that walked around the street did not seem to find it odd for people to be dropping down from rooftops. It looked like we had arrived in Shadow Valley.

"Come on," encouraged Keila. "We are not out of the woods yet."

We continued onwards, following Keila. She had started to move at a jog rather than an outright run as before. We moved amongst the people, many of them moved aside from Keila with her armor and proudly displayed sword. However, Iris and I did not receive the same treatment as we were jostled from side to side by the crowd that was moving about their business. After moving another few blocks into the area that appeared to be Shadow Valley, Keila turned around, grabbed my shoulder, and pushed me into an alleyway. Iris quickly followed us in as the shadows cast by the buildings enveloped us, hiding us from the people on the street.

"Safe?" I asked, out of breath and not able to manage more words.

"No… we… are… not," Keila started, taking a deep breath between each word.

"Where are we?" Iris asked, she appeared to be the best out of all of us.

"This is Shadow Valley," Keila answered after taking a few more seconds to breathe.

## Chapter 33: Shopping Spree

Keila, Iris, and I finally pulled into an alleyway and stopped. None of us could form words for a minute because we were so out of breath. I had to put my hands on my knees and hang my head down for a second to catch my breath. Alas, *there is no rest for the wicked*, such must have been Keila's motto.

"We should be okay for a few more minutes," Keila began. "Enough time to gear up; we need to go underground. We will not be coming back up until we are either dead or have Hobbs and Reynolds. We need potions, weapons, and everything to get us through that," she said.

At her words I remembered the promised bow that Elana had said would be waiting for me, but that was all the way over in Silkliff. It was unfortunate that I would not be able to collect such a weapon for the mission ahead.

"Can we find everything here?" I asked Keila.

"Just like Silkliff or Glass Village, everything can be bought here. We just need to be careful to not be flashing any money around, so as not to get stabbed by a mugger," warned Keila.

We exited the alleyway after another minute of recovering our stamina. I looked around and noticed that many of the people had their hoods over their heads. I could see the gleam of people's eyes as they glanced our way. I pulled up my hood as Keila and Iris did the same.

"First things first," began Iris, "I need to buy some mana and health potions."

"I am going to need to buy some arrows," I said, as I counted out the thirteen that I had left in my quiver. "Also, a new dagger would come in handy," I noted as I looked at the Rusty Dagger that was still at my side.

"I would not mind buying a new sword," said Keila.

"How much money do we have?" Iris asked.

"I have a silver and twenty coppers," I said as I showed the currency in my hand.

"I have roughly the same," Iris said as she showed her coin collection. Keila looked and showed hers which looked about the same, if maybe a few less coppers.

"Split up?" I asked the group.

"No," Iris and Keila both said in unison. Keila then continued, "we need to stay together in case we need to swiftly disappear. Since I am the only one who knows the way, we cannot afford to be separated."

With that we continued down the road, Keila taking the lead as she seemed to have a general idea of where we were going. After a few more minutes of walking, I got a message icon flash. It was from Shane.

*From: Shane Miller*

*To: Zephaniah Kote*

*Hey guys, just letting you know that you have an hour left in the game world. Finish up and come back.*

I shared with the rest of the group what Shane had said, and we continued walking. After a few more streets I started to hear the sound of a commotion that I associated with a farmers' market or any sort of open aired market. Right before we came across the source of the noises, I saw a sign on one of the buildings. It was a potions shop with the obvious symbol of a glass bottle with little bubbles coming from its uncorked lid. I pointed this out to Iris and Keila and we walked into the store.

The walls were covered in mini-shelves that had potions on them. These shelves were on the right and left walls. They led all the way to the back of the store where a lady in a long skirt sat on a stool next to the counter. Beneath the shelves were potion ingredients that were in baskets. As I approached the baskets I could see little messages pop up above the ingredients. In one basket sat dozens of little, dried purple leaves. As I looked closely the item name appeared above the little plant.

| **Wolfsbane**<br>**Purpose: Werewolves Bane, Cure of Lycanthropy** |
|---|

I did not see any purpose in using any of these potion ingredients, as none of us knew how to make potions, yet. So, I started to look above at the walls of potions. There had to be dozens of options. I got closer to those to see what each were.

| **Resist Fire – 5 Coppers**<br>***This potion allows the drinker to resist 20% of fire damage for five minutes.*** |
|---|

| **Resist Frost – 5 Coppers**<br>***This potion allows the drinker to resist 20% of frost damage for five minutes.*** |
|---|

| **Resist Magic – 10 Coppers**<br>***This potion allows the drinker to resist 20% of magical damage for one minute.*** |
|---|

Unfortunately, none of these were the types of potions that we needed. I did grab one of the fire potions though, just to be on the safe side. I then continued on my search, looking for potions that had the standard red and blue liquids that usually signified health and mana, respectively. Iris summoned me over to her side of the wall, where there were a few dozen different option. Many were types of potions that might have been poisons with names such as Elder Berry Kiss and, the more on the nose one, Living Death. I moved closer to Iris and a more palatable variety appeared.

**Potion of Healing (Minor) – 5 Coppers**
***This potion instantly heals 25 health points.***

**Potion of Healing (Intermediate) – 8 Coppers**
***This potion instantly heals 50 health points.***
**Potion of Healing (Major) – 10 Coppers**
***This potion instantly heals 75 health points.***

**Major Potion of Healing – 12 Coppers**
***This potion instantly heals 100 health points.***

The price range and the names only grew larger from there. I even read one potion, near the end, that healed up to five hundred points of damage. It was ludicrous to believe that my health points could ever grow so large. I grabbed five of the potions of minor healing and one of the majors, just in case.

I ventured over to the mana shelf but saw none that really applied to me. As of this point, I had no reason to believe that I would use any of my fifteen mana, especially since I had not used any up until this point. Plus, I really wanted to save some money for the bow and arrows. After doing some quick math I knew that I was at forty coppers. I called it a day, and went over to the lady to make my purchase. I passed over the potions and the silver coin, upon seeing it she raised her eyebrows at it for a minute.

"Don't worry, I did not steal it," I said to her. She simply shrugged and passed over one hundred and sixty coppers. Damn, those silver coins went far, I thought. After me, Iris, and Keila both made their purchases, and we went out the store. The next stop was weapons. After walking another block, I saw what I was looking for, a weapons store. It looked to be one of the larger stores on the block. "They really make their money off of violence in the Shadow Valley," I said to the group.

"Oh, you have no idea," responded Keila.

We walked into the store that had a sword, arrow, and a stick all crossed as its sign. The inside of the building could have been a candy store for how eager I became. I thought that the store of Elana's was something to gander at, but this was a whole other level. The room went twice as deep as the potions store and had walls of different weapons. My priority was dagger and more arrows. I walked over to where the daggers were being displayed while Iris was eyeing the quarterstaffs.

"What are you looking at, Iris?"

"Oh, well you know I have this," as Iris said it, she summoned her menu and a large stick appeared in her hand. "It is one of the starting weapons of the wizard class, but I have only used it once since. As well, I have a skill level in quarter staff."

I nodded my head in understanding. This store reminded us of the weapons that we did not even use. It just made you want to buy something with all of the options that were laid out available to all of us. I walked closer to the daggers, so that their information could appear above each object. I then looked down at both of my daggers to see what I was working with.

**Equipped (Left): Rusty Dagger**
***Quality: Poor***
***Damage: 1-9 Health Points***
***Description: This rusty dagger is one of the poorest weapons in the game. The rust has reduced the quality of the weapon beyond repair. However, the weapon might contain one or two more good battles within it.***

**Equipped (Right): Glass Dagger of Ice**
***Quality: Fair***
***Damage: 10 – 15 Health Points + 2 Points of Ice Damage***
***Description: This glass dagger is fairly made with an extremely sharp edge, like most glass weapons. Infused within the glass dagger is an enchantment of ice, making the weapon ice-cold.***

I really needed to switch out my Rusty Dagger. My newer dagger did nearly twice the damage of the starter blade. I looked at the options available to me, and the rest of my coin purse.

**Steel Dagger – 50 Coppers**
***Quality: Common***
***Damage: 10 – 20 Health Points***
***Description: This steel dagger is not unique, but can handle heavy use while deal its fair share of damage while remaining sharp.***

**Carbon Dagger – 70 Coppers**
***Quality: Forged***
***Damage: 18 – 20 Health Points***
***Description: This steel dagger but upgraded through forging has given it the name carbon. The edge of this sword will outlive any opponent.***

**Damascus Dagger – 80 Coppers**
***Quality: Uncommon***
***Damage: 20 – 25 Health Points***
***Description: This steel dagger, especially forged to be as hard as possible. The dagger has been built to assist the user in sending their opponents beyond this plain of existence.***

After perusing the choices, I decided that these three were the only ones in my price range. I felt the edges of each, noting that the shopkeeper started to keep an eye on me, probably to ensure that I did not decide to pocket one of them. I had to decide, since this might have to last me until the end of the game. I picked the higher-priced option. Bringing over the Damascus Dagger I paid the price and swiped out the daggers in my inventory so that I now had the Damascus Dagger rather than the beginner's Rusty Dagger. Now it was time to find the right arrows. I walked across the room to see the various bundles that occupied the shelfs. With a hundred coppers to my name, I looked over at the bows. They were far out of price range, so I just focused on the available arrows. I immediately realized that I was going to be Fabula's version of Hawkeye, the Marvel Avenger hero.

**Fire Arrowhead – 10 Copper**
***Damage: 15 Health Points + 5 Points of Immediate Fire Damage***

**Ice Arrowhead – 10 Copper**
***Damage: 15 Health Points + 5 Points of Immediate Ice Damage***

Then there were the more ordinary arrows, ones that even surpassed my common steel arrow heads by a few health points. However, I did see my trusted arrows at the bottom of the shelf.

**Hollow Point Steel Arrowhead – 5 Copper**
***Damage: 20 Health Points + Bleeding effect for 2 health point per second till bandaged.***

**Barbed Steel Arrowhead – 3 Copper**
***Damage: 15 Health Points + Bleeding effect for 1 health point per second till bandaged.***

**Stealth Arrowhead – 10 Copper**
***Damage: 20 Health Points, does not immediately make target aware of your position.***

**Water Arrowhead – 3 Copper**
***Damage: 0 Health Points, useful for dowsing a fire or causing damage to fire-based creatures.***

**Acid Arrowhead – 15 Copper**
***Damage:* *15 Health Points + Continuous acid burn of 5 health points per second for 5 seconds.***

**Steel Arrowhead – 2 Copper**
***Damage:* *10 Health Points***

The list and the options went on and one, but I could not afford most of them. Nonetheless, seeing all these arrow types made me extremely excited to become more skilled at my archery. I decided to load up; why not spend what you have? But then I remembered how my leather jerkin was still not in the best shape. Should I put some coin aside for amor? I decided that it was better that I had weapons and avoided getting hit. I picked up twenty-seven steel arrows. That would fill out my current quiver and outfit me with another. The acid arrows looked like a party, so I picked up three of them. Hollow point arrows and the stealth ones also looked handy, so I selected three of each. Since I already had my ice dagger, I went with three of the fire arrows as well. After I checked out, I realized that I had spent all but six coppers. I really had no self-control when it came to shopping, as exhibited by my online shopping records. After I finished a job, I would usually reward myself with constant deliveries for days. It was like Christmas or Hanukkah, or whatever your preferred Hallmark-gift-giving holiday is.

I looked to Iris, who now had a new stick. Okay, it was not just a stick. It was an extremely pretty stick that had nice metal cap on the bottom with pointy parts and looked like it would deliver a bad time for whoever was getting it into the side of their head. Keila had some new sword, it looked slightly long and heavier than her previous one, but I have never been classified as a sword expert, so I just assumed that Keila knew what was best for her.

"All good?" I asked them.

They both nodded, as we showed off our new pieces of accessories. Honestly, it was the first time that day that I felt like I was actually just playing a game, and it was refreshing. However, seeing the darting eyes on Keila's face reminded me that we were not here to just shop or play a video game.

"Let us get out of here, we have spent too much time here," Keila said as she started to head for the door. "We are going to get logged off soon and we will not be able to get far, but we can at least hit the ground running tomorrow if we are already inside the sewer system." Keila poked her head outside the door, gave us a nod and we walked out. Keila led us farther down the main road that we had been traveling on so far. As we neared the market area, I saw some guards looking around, the same guards that had chased us.

"Crap," Keila said as she saw them at the same time I did.

"Where to?" I asked her while keeping my eyes on the guards. We kept walking straight, trying not to draw attention to ourselves by stopping or turning around.

"I don't know, we—," Keila was cut short as a blondish guard walked right into her, grabbing her arm and her mouth. Wrapping his body around hers so that she could not move. I froze, but then I looked up to see the smiling face of Landan.

"Landan," I hissed. I looked over his shoulder to see that the other guards had not noticed anything. The friendly guard smiled at us, before looking at Keila. Making sure that she was not going to say anything or bite him, he removed his hand for her mouth.

"Hello, my friends. Quickly, follow me," he said as he escorted us forward. We passed the guards, but on seeing Landan's face they merely gave him a nod. We slipped completely by, hidden within Landan's shadow. After we passed the guards, Landan led us a bit more forward where he pulled us into an alleyway. "Sorry for the abrupt greetings, but I heard that the guard nearly had you," he said with a smile.

"Why are you helping us?" I asked him.

"Simply, you have earned my respect. As well, I heard from Baridac's friend at the library that you came in with a journal filled with a guard's secrets. He also mentioned that the name on the book was Belladonna. It was not hard to put one and one together," he looked to the front and back of the alleyway to ensure that no one was following us.

"We are heading to the sewers to save our friends, the two foreigners from last week," I explained. "The book is our leverage."

"I see, it also makes sense that the guard is in the pocket of the Thieves' Guild," murmured Landan who was also distracted. "How can I help?"

Keila explained to Landan how we needed to get to the entrance to the sewer system, apparently a very specific part of the sewers. He nodded, as Keila described the entrance that she had in mind. He agreed, and we followed him out of the alleyway. As we walked I noticed a bow in his quiver, unstrung.

"Nice bow," I mentioned at seeing the intricate carving of leaves on the shaft. It was beautiful, especially compared to my current bow which had a plain brown, wooden exterior.

"Oh, I nearly forgot. Thank you for reminder Zephaniah," he said as he took it out of the quiver and passed it to me. "A gift from my sister, I believe." He then smiled at me as I examined the bow, seeing its beauty, I just had to pull out my, now, old one and compare the two.

**Bow of Leaves**
***Quality: Uncommon***
***Damage:*** *10 – 15*
***Description: This expertly carved bow comes from the bleached trunk of a blessed tree; its quality enhances the durability and strength of its user.***

**Wooden Bow**
**Quality: Poor**
**Damage: 5**
**Description: This starter bow can be formed from nearly any tree and possesses the qualities and attributes necessary for a beginner archer.**

I literally started to become giddy as I appreciated the difference. This bow was far superior to any bow that I had ever laid my eyes on. Even in comparison to the ones in the shop, this bow completely wrecked all of them, by its appearance alone.

"It is a beauty, isn't it?" ask Landan. "My sister does fine work," he said with a touch of pride in his voice. I could not respond, I barely nodded, and I gently rubbed the bow between my hands, feeling the etching of trees and leaves.

After a few more moments of walking, I had recovered enough speech capability to express my gratitude. "Thank you, and please share my thanks with your sister," I said.

"Will do, but I will merely tell the tale of your expression. That should be thanks enough for the likes of her. After all, she cares little for one's words," he said with some heavy insinuation. "Here we are," Landan said with a wave of his hands as we stopped in front of a wooden container, that appeared to be a dumpster.

"Huh?" said Iris.

Keila gave Landan a side glance as she pushed the barrage bin aside, revealing a metal grate in the stone and dirt. Keila looked at Landan, and he received the message. Us all grabbing a side, we heaved the metal grade aside revealing a dark hole beneath. I looked down, but I could only see the dark glint of water flowing by.

"Best of luck, my friends," he said as he, once again, check his surroundings. "I suggest that you hurry though." I looked up at Landan's face, pulling my gaze away from the entrance to the dark underbelly of the city. I followed Landan's gaze to the street a few blocks away, where there were four or five guards walking along the road.

"I agree," said Keila as she saw the group walking towards us. She stood up, crossed her arms over her chest and jumped into the hole. I widened my eyes as she disappeared into the murky waters. I look at Iris who looked frightened, "It will be okay," I reassured her. I then stood up and followed suit to Keila's example. I first felt my feet hit the surface of the water and then felt the water fill with the water and I began to go under. Before I even had a chance to recognize it, I felt my entire body become submerged and I could also tell that I was being pushed by the force of water. I finally began to break the surface of the water as I attempted to control my swim, but as I did, I noticed the timeout timer appeared in the corner of my vision.

5… 4… 3… 2… 1… and the screen went black.

## Chapter 34: The Other Boot Falls

I woke up alone, but then I realized that my eyes were merely being covered by the gaming equipment. Pulling it up over my eyes I could see Keila, Iris, and I all coming out of the game. I looked around and saw that no one else was in the room.

"Where is everyone?" I asked with a crunchy throat. Playing for eight hours straight with no water nor food really made one parched.

"I have no clue, they must have been pulled away into a meeting," said Iris. "Check your phones." I pulled out my phone from my pocket and saw a string of texts from Shane. Looked like over a dozen from him.

"I have a crap ton of messages from Shane," I said as I attempted to open them.

"Same," said Iris.

"We need to go," announced Keila as she jumped off the table.

"Why, what's happening?" I asked as I quickly jumped out of the seat to follow Keila. I realized Iris was still getting out of her chair and I helped her up.

"Conor and Majed have been arrested," Keila said, as she exited the room.

"What?" I asked, but Keila was already through the door. I looked at Iris and we ran after her. We caught up with her at the elevator, we entered, and Keila swiped her wrist against the sensor the released the lock mechanism. We pushed inside and Keila pushed the lobby button. Assuming that Keila knew what she was doing we just rode down in silence. I found myself cracking my knuckles, something I had not done in a long while. Iris was pulling her hair, literally just tugging away at a few strands. The elevator opened up on the lobby and the room was filled with everyone.

I could see Shane and Sarah standing in the corner of the lobby, near the entrance of the hallway that we were led down the previous day. Or was it this morning? I could not keep track anymore. In the lobby were the police officers from earlier, Gerald and Spencer were standing near the front, glass doors. Dr. Jordan, Sammy, and Blake were talking with the both of them. I could also see Majed and Conor both sitting down on the sofas that were right inside the door. Their hands appeared to be cuffed behind them with officers standing over them. Majed looked like he was close to going into a rage while Conor looked like he was close to pissing himself.

I walked over to Shane and Sarah with Iris close behind me. "What is happening?" I asked Shane as we got close.

“Supposedly,” Shane sounded extremely skeptical, “Majed and Conor are being charged with several charges, but amongst them is the murder of Sorrento.”

“Umm,” I began with shock setting in. “Why?”

“Somehow, the police got ahold of both of their past activities,” said Shane. “Majed has multiple suspect hacking into local agencies arising from his activism.”

“And, Conor, poor sweet Conor was suspected of being involved in some altercations involving some environmental activists’ groups,” said Sarah.

“Like hacking them?” I asked.

“No, like funneling funds from corporate natural gas companies and other large corporations. Apparently, he has funneled millions of dollars to environmental nonprofits,” Sarah said with considerable admiration in her voice.

“Wait,” said Iris. “None of that sounds like cause for murder.”

“Indeed,” confirmed Shane. “However, someone here leaked those files to the police, and they believe that they have a case. As now Majed and Conor have a criminal past, so they have become the prime suspects.”

“But who leaked the documents?” I asked.

Shane did not respond, nor did Sarah, but they did turn their gaze towards Blake, Dr. Jordan, and Sammy. These three were currently smiling and shaking hands with Officer Gerald.

"Bastards," I hissed between clenched teeth. I glared holes into the three of them, but that must have sent the hairs along Sammy's spine alight as she quickly looked over and made eye contact with me. She walked away from the officer and gestured for me to join her. Begrudgingly, I walked over.

"Hey, Zephaniah. So sorry that I was not there to help you out of the room. We have had some unfortunate business come up," she said as she looked in Majed and Conor's direction.

"I heard that their files had been given to the police," I said to her not too kindly.

She looked intensely at me, and an emotion crossed her face that was gone too quickly for me to understand. "I am so sorry Zephaniah, but I can assure you that I had nothing to do with it. After all, I do not even have access to my own files that Sorrento kept," she said.

It was difficult to argue with that fact. Sammy worked on entirely different floor from Sorrento, and he was her superior. Also, Sammy genuinely looked sad for the situation. "You are right," I said. "It was wrong of me to imply that it was you."

"No, Zephaniah," she said grabbing onto my shoulder, "I am sorry for what has happened to them. I promise you that they will have the best attorneys, and that is even if the police find any evidence connecting them to the murder."

"That won't stop them from being charged with what was revealed in their files," I responded.

"You are right, but they will have the legal support that I can provide nonetheless," she said with a sad smile. However, the sad smile was quickly replaced with a look of panic. "Zephaniah, did you all find Dr. Hobbs or Ms. Reynolds yet?"

"No, but we are getting close," I responded. I could not be sure, but relief, nervousness, or possibly dread seemed to cross her eyes as I told her this.

"Well, dang it," she said. "I believe that you three will get them out next time," she said giving me a smile and a reassuring grip on my shoulder. "I will see you upstairs."

An hour later we all – minus Majed and Conor, who had been taken off to police custody – found ourselves in the large board room. Dr. Jordan began the meeting with a rundown of what had been accomplished inside the game.

"According to Ms. Varner, Ms. Christman, Mr. Kote, and herself have discovered where Ms. Reynolds and Dr. Hobbs are located within the game. The goal is that they will be able to extract them from the game by tomorrow," Dr. Jordan said at the end of the long summary of our day's events within the game world.

"In other news," he continued, "the coding team has discovered some of the source of our problems." Dr. Jordan stepped from behind the table and sat down as Jack Blake took center stage.

"Hold up," I said, before Blake was fully standing up. "Are we just not going to talk about what has happened to Majed and Conor?"

"What is there to speak of?" asked Dr. Jordan. "The police, after some investigation discovered the checkered past of your colleagues and found them to be the most probable suspects for Mr. Sorrento's murder."

"We all know that the police did not just find those records, and there is no way that any of them had anything to do with the murder of Sorrento," I almost screamed at Dr. Jordan's expressionless-looking face.

"I'll excuse the tone, Mr. Kote" said Dr. Jordan. "Now to address your concerns. First off, no one here had anything to do with the police discovering the past of Majed and Conor. If we had released the files then all of your files would have been released, and since Sorrento's passing those files are currently in my possession and I have had no communication on this subject with the police, I can assure you. Secondly, if Conor and Majed had not been involved with Mr. Sorrento's murder then that will come to light. So, if I may, let me suggest that you sit back down so we can finish today's meeting and we can all go about our day."

I did not want to sit down, but I looked around and saw that no one else was wanting to cause a scene. All of the power still remained with the executives, and we could do nothing to oppose them at this point. What were we to do? If we left the project, then our secrets were revealed. If went to the police, then our secrets were revealed. If we continued to be a bother to Dr. Jordan than we might find out that the police were in possession of our files and then we were the newest suspects. I sat back down in my seat.

"During the last meeting we said that we discovered additional lines of code were added," boomed Blakes voice. "However, we were wrong. These lines of code were not new, well that is not exactly true. They were new, but they were not added by any one person. These new lines are the result of the cap of restriction on the artificial intelligence being removed."

"What does that mean, exactly?" asked Keila, the only person in the room who was not as familiar with coding as the rest of us were.

"What it means, Ms. Varner, is that the artificial intelligence's restriction on what it may or may not do within the scope of the game have been removed. Just as it was during our previous incident," he said making a knowing glance at Keila.

"What incident do you speak of, if I may ask?" asked Shane.

"You may not, it is not your concern and does not relate to any of your duties or responsibilities," boomed Blake. "The coding team's job, now that we found the source, is to implement the solution, nothing more."

Shane sat back in his seat, obviously unhappy with the tone and the words that Blake had sent his way. I looked over at him trying to catch his eye, once catching it I gave him a quick nod. A nod promising that I would fill him in on what I had discovered over the day's activities.

"If that is out of the way," announced Blake, "then let us talk about our future. Tonight, you all will be provided lodging on the premises, and we will start again early tomorrow. We are in a race against time, and we need to be sure to complete our mission before the time is up. The board meeting will commence this Saturday night in preparation of another public announcement on Sunday. By then we must be concluded with our activities here."

"Why must we stay here?" asked Iris.

"You need not stay here, but I highly encourage it. After the unfortunate passing of Mr. Sorrento and the chilling revelation concerning Mr. Carpenter and Mr. Ayad it really works out best for all of us to be on hand at a moment's notice," he answered.

While Blake was preaching the option of leaving the building, the message in between the lines of his words implied that there was not actually much a choice. "Once we find Ms. Reynolds and Dr. Hobbs do, we know how we will get them out of the game?" I asked.

Blake turned towards me and seemed to appraise me for a moment before answering. "Yes, as was answered already. Once we place the caps back on the artificial intelligence then the both of them should be able to log out as normal," responded Blake. "Anymore question?"

No one spoke up.

"Fantastic," Blake said clapping his hands together. "We will convene at eight in the morning to send everyone off on their respective missions. The four of you" – Blake said while pointing to Sarah, Shane, Iris, and I – "will stay on the floor underneath the game room. There are suites all along the floor. So just choose whichever one you wish."

It felt like an adjournment to the meeting so Shane, Iris, Sarah, and I all removed ourselves from the room. I looked towards Keila, but she was engaged in a hushed conversation with Dr. Jordan in the corner of the conference room.

"Food?" I asked.

"Order in?" Sarah suggested. We all quickly agreed to that suggestion, and we filed towards the elevators. Once there, we realized that we did not have any way of using the elevators. "Hold up," Sarah said. "I will go get a pass-card from Sammy." Sarah turned and swiftly returned to the conference room. She returned with the little card in her hand. Sarah had us all piled into the elevator, and we clicked on the designated button that Blake had mentioned, and the door closed as Dr. Jordan, Keila, Sammy, and Blake exited the conference room.

## Chapter 35: Sleepover

The suites were massive. The rooms all had a large king size bed, a full bathroom, and a small entertainment area with a small table. They were not too much smaller than my apartment, if I was being honest.

"What do you think they use these for?" I asked Iris, who was sitting on my bed.

"I think that whenever they have visiting board members or other VIPs, they probably shove them all in here," she responded.

We had found that each of the rooms had pajamas in a range of sizes. Iris and I decided to shower immediately. Even though we had spent eight hours sitting in chairs, it was almost impossible to not feel as if I had carried the sewage water back with us from the virtual reality world. Therefore, we were now sitting on my bed in our pajamas. I quickly looked over at the clock to see that it was only five in the afternoon. It felt that we had been up for days, and both of our eyes were dropping.

"How is your room?" I asked her.

"Literally, exactly the same," she groaned. "I already miss my bed and I have not even spent the night away from it, yet."

“I feel you. Are you starving? Should we order food?” I asked. I did not want to think about my bed back at home. Just like Iris, I was a homebody and really loved my own space. Being forced, or strongly encouraged out of it, was not comforting in the slightest and had put me on edge.

“Ya, I’ll text Sarah and Shane to tell them to come over here. Is that alright?” she asked as she was already composing a text to the both of them.

“Sounds, perfect,” I said as I laid down in bed and closed my eyes. I awaited my friends’ arrival so that we could order some food; even after spending an afternoon amongst virtual sewage I was still hungry.

The next thing I knew I was being shaken by Iris. I could feel her hair in my face, and the ticklish feeling brought from the dead of slumber more quickly than whatever gentle words she was whispering. I realized I had fallen asleep, I quickly looked around and saw that Shane and Sarah were sitting at the small table in the corner of the large room. In front of them was a tower of Chinese food boxes, you know the white ones with the red images that everyone in the universe understands to signify Chinese food. I jumped out of bed and ran over to see if they had left any of my favorite: Sesame Tofu.

"Right here, bud," Shane said as he passed me over a box. It was filled with the perfect golden cubes. "We came and Iris said that you fell asleep in midsentence with her. We decided to let you catch up on your rest while you had the chance."

I nodded my thanks in between mouthfuls of tofu. After scraping a bite that was a bit too much for my mouth, I cleared my throat. "Chinese was a smart move," I said with glee.

"Indeed, it was Iris' idea," said Shane with a smile on his face. Chinese food was also one of his favorites and a food that he and I had often plowed through when working on various past gaming projects.

"So, what are your thoughts on today's meeting and everything?" asked Sarah between mouthfuls of rice. "Iris filled us in on what Keila had told you guys during your gaming session."

"Well, I do not know what I think about everything, to be honest," I muttered. "It is all almost too much to even digest. I do know that neither Majed, no matter how much a jerk he is, nor Conor had nothing to do with Sorrento." Everyone nodded as I said the words. "It is like no one is even thinking about it: neither one of them were able to access the elevators or even get to Sorrento's office. As well, we saw them leave the office after we went out for sushi."

"Well, I hate to play devil's advocate," said Shane, "but, Majed was never with us that night and we are not sure where he was."

That gave me pause. I had completely forgot that Majed had not been with us that night at dinner. I think I even told the police officer that he had been with us. Maybe? No, it was unthinkable that Majed would have killed Sorrento, he just did not seem like the type of person to do that.

"Still, it could not be him," I said to Shane.

"Think about it," said Sarah, "he never came to dinner with us, and we are unsure of where he was that night. So, presumably, he has no alibi, and he has motive."

"What motive?" I challenged.

"The same motive that you or any of us have. Sorrento has files on us, files upon files of our darkest secrets. And I do not know about you three, but mine are not all unicorn farts and rainbows," Sarah said obviously frustrated with the predicament. "Sorry, I did not mean to get so… excited. I am just stressed."

"No, Sarah, I do understand my past is not full of bright colors either," I said.

"What is your past?" Shane asked. "Sorry, I know that is a personal inquiry, but I feel that we are at a point that is it us versus them and all the cards being on the table can only strengthen us. After all, I honestly believe none of us here also work for Rinc." We all shook our heads in agreement that we all trusted each other. Sarah and Conor were obviously close to Shane, and the only person of us that I could possibly suspect would be Majed.

"I can go first," offered Iris. "After all, I did promise to tell you this morning Zeph."

I nodded and gave Iris the floor.

"So, what no one really knows is that I came up in a really wealthy home. You know, the whole silver spoon and everything. It was fantastic and also hell at the same time. I eventually rebelled, you know the whole black hair highlights and black nail polish, but it did not get my family's attention. I tried and tried, but nothing seemed to get their attention. So, I continued to go and push the border, harder and harder. Eventually, I feel into a group of hackers in my late teenage years. We were a tame group, trying to break into school files and the like. Nothing extreme, but then I discovered that I was rather good at it, like really good. I started creating games in my free time, just to pass the time. I even learned that I could hack myself into organizations and have donations made to myself. That is how the dark road started, how I went from a Grey Hat to a Black Hat. I did not even need the money, I had more than I could ever want, but I wanted to hurt my father. I wanted his attention, so I started to move money in his company around. Not enough to really cause trouble, but enough that someone noticed.

That is when people started getting fired or even fined for stealing from the company, and I realized I had pushed the button too far. I was no longer just hurting my father, but I was hurting random strangers. I stopped, full stop. I swore off hacking and instead of vying for my family's attention I moved out and cut myself off. That is how I ended up in my current occupation as a barista, I swore I was done with the hacking, and I was done searching for my father's recognition."

We were all silent for a moment, processing the information that Iris had revealed about herself. I was not going to lie, I was relieved. When I first learned that Iris had a dark past, worthy enough of Sorrento's blackmail, I had been concerned. However, I had just found out that Iris did nothing but try to get her father's attention, she had not even stolen for herself. I reached over and gave her a comforting side hug; she grabbed my hand in thanks.

"Well, since you shared, I guess I should," I said, letting go of Iris' shoulder.

"I have a sneaking suspicion of what your secret is Zephaniah," said Shane. "In fact, I have expected it for a long time. I think that for the organic feel of the story tonight, I should tell mine first," he ventured.

I nodded my assent and was now even more curious to hear what Shane was going to share with the class.

"So, I am not sure if any of you are aware, but I use to work for a security firm. One that specialized in personal security. You know, credit scams, identity theft, and that sort of stuff. Well, I never used to be interested in the hacking area of the internet. I just really enjoyed playing games and even creating some new worlds in my spare time, just like Iris," he said looking towards her. "One day I was exploring the forums on a random site when I came across a feed that was discussing a character that was known as Aspect," he said glancing in my direction. "It spoke about this person's past activities and various sources provided examples of this unknown person's previous success stories. I did some of my own research and learned about this individual's exploits and after further research I began to reach out to people that I believed that could be this individual."

"Why?" I asked.

"Honestly, purely out of curiosity. I just wanted to know more, but where this coincides with my story is that I was eventually opened up to the world of Black Hat hacking and the horrible parts of the virtual world. So, I decided to get involved where I was, at my cyber security firm. After some investigating, I realized that individuals within my firm were selling our clients' information. Deceased clients' social security numbers were some of our largest income streams. I attempted to expose them, but my bravado got the best of me. The executives of the company discovered my efforts to expose them, and they proceeded to allow me to do so. Of course, they allowed me to believe that the information I was leaking was the vital stuff. Thinking back, it all was a little too simple. The data was real enough that I didn't notice, but nothing that would've hurt their bottom line in the end. Hindsight is twenty-twenty, or whatever the saying is. I released a file containing the evidence I had found through my secondary email to the news station, other executives, and everyone that I believed could make a difference. It backfired, rather than releasing the information I had compiled, I had created the largest security leak in our firm's history. Even though the information wasn't vital the company still would have wanted their revenge. Realizing that my digital fingerprints would give me away I decided that the best path forward was to cut my losses. I moved towns and changed my name from Shawn Miller to Shane Miller. I have never looked back, always trying to work for myself or friends. I always knew that if I ever poked my head above the sand that I will most likely not be able to formulate the defense necessary to protect myself against the force that the top executives of my former security firm could bring to bear."

Once again, the room fell silent after Shane's monologue. However, I could not find it within myself to appreciate the silence for longer than a few moments. "So, you suspected that I was Aspect?"

"Yes, or at the very least I found it probable," confirmed Shane.

"What were you hoping to find?" I asked my friend.

"I don't know, but I guess I was curious about the people behind the computer screens. However, after we became friendly, I decided that I liked you and we have been friends ever since."

"Cheers to that," I said, raising my tofu container to cheers with his Chinese food box.

"Wait, so you are Aspect?" Sarah asked.

"Yes, that is me," I confirmed. "Aspect, Aspect two-point-o, and Aspect with a three for the letter 'e.'"

"Wow," said Sarah. "I have read and heard a lot about you. From hacking into the elite gaming company archives to creating glitches all your own."

"Ya, that is me," I responded.

"But, why?" she asked me.

"I honestly do not know, mostly just because I could. Always trying to test my limits to see how far I could go without getting caught," I responded.

"And you have not gotten caught yet," remarked Sarah.

"That is true," I acknowledged with a slight grin at the verbal pat on my back from Sarah. "What is your story, Sarah? We all know mine already, Shane, and Iris' stories."

"Well, I did nothing as virtuous as Shane, or understandable as Iris, and for sure nothing as exciting as you," she said, acknowledging each of us. "Basically, I am sort of a hacktivist, but instead of money or anything too dicey like that I go for something that is closer to my own heart: information. Since I was in college, I was always getting frustrated with the 'need-to-know' and the mainstream news always reporting inaccurate information. Honestly, I did not even blame them, I got angry at the system that is constantly suppressing information away from the public. Whether it be because of national security or just aliens, I just wanted to get to the truth of it all. So, I started studying computer science in college, and then in my Master's degree. I was good and it came easy, so that is what I kept on doing," Sarah said, taking a pause to each some more sesame chicken.

After a few more bites and some expectant eyes glaring at her, she continued. "I started to poke around and hack into the university systems, just to see what teachers were saying at behind-closed-door meetings. By that I mean their emails. After a while, I started to grow bored. The information that I was discovering through my local channels was not going to awaken the world to the truth, and it was not going to dispel the constant misinformation that is thrown around online. So, I started going higher and higher and, eventually, higher. I made it all of the way to the top, I attempted to hack the Pentagon. I just really needed to know if we knew about aliens," she said with a slight smirk. "Anyways, I failed. I could not break in, but my efforts did not go unnoticed. So I stopped with all of that, and I went back to hacking in my local news stations and everything. I have yet to become to the Snowden of this decade, but that is the hope."

"I think what you are doing is still amazing," I said.

"Yes, I absolutely agree," said Iris.

Shane merely nodded his head, there was no need for him to verbalize his agreement. We all appreciated the change that Sarah was attempting to bring.

"So, ya, I guess that is my story," Sarah finished, turning back to give her full attention to the food hidden in her box.

"So, now that everyone knows everything, what are your thoughts on what is going on around us?" Shane asked. "After all, I can say that no one is working against the rest of us."

"I agree," I said. "Well, I do not know much, but this is what I have theorized. Someone, not one of us – I am thinking either Blake or Dr. Jordan – killed Sorrento. The only problem is that I am having a difficult time with the motivational piece, as you mentioned earlier Shane. In terms of Majed and Conor, I think that Dr. Jordan released those files to pull heat off himself. After all, in today's meeting he did say that he was the one who now possessed them."

"So, if your theory is correct. What do we do about it?" asked Shane.

"Well, I honestly don't know. I would say that we keep our heads down and get out of this pickle before it comes to bite us. I am hoping that Iris and I can finish this tomorrow, and then we can get as far away from this mess as possible," I proposed.

"I agree with Zeph," said Iris. "If we could find Reynolds and Hobbs tomorrow then our job is done. Blake did say that they just need to re-cap the AI, and then we are done with this mess."

"This is true, but what are we to do if the person who un-capped the AI decides that they don't want us gone?" asked Sarah.

"We give them no reason too." I stopped playing around with my rice and placed it back on the table. "The executives seem to want this game done with, I do not know why Sorrento got in the way of that, but he did. So, we finish what we started, and we get out of Dodge."

After our deep share and the theorizing about what had transpired earlier in the day, we finished our meal mostly in silence, after attempting to pull together a normal conversation had failed multiple times. Not to the fault of any one person, but it is difficult to bring a sense of normalcy after deep truths are shared. After another half an hour of Chinese food, and a table full of empty cartons we all called it a night. I walked Iris back to her room and told her to make sure that she got me up before she went back up to the conference room in the morning. I said goodnight to Shane and

Sarah, and then proceeded to pass out in my temporary bed. I was just thankful that I had already switched into pajamas because I don't believe that I would have made it fully onto the bed before passing out into dreamland.

I was back in Fabula. However, instead of the wide range of colors that normally appeared across my vision, the entire screen was in red and black. It was even more difficult to see, but impossible to hear with the constant ringing that was going on in the background of my ears. Suddenly, I was down in the sewers where the water was pitch black, but the walls and cobbled floor were stained red. I was turning around corners, trying to find the piercing ringing sound in my eyes when I—

"Zeph, get up. Zephaniah, get up!" someone was screaming into my ears now. I looked around blindly for a moment before I realized I had not opened my eyes. As I did, I saw Iris' face looking down on me, but rather than her normal pale skin and red hair, I was seeing her all in red. I quickly woke up after that, realizing that an alarm was going off. Not my phone alarm, but a massive building alarm that sounded like a fire drill. The room was soaked in red, as I tried to figure out what was happening. Oh, there was a light alarm that was flashing on and off. It was bringing the room into a light of bright red before returning it to pitch blackness again. It went on and on as I tried to zero in on Iris' face. "Come on," she said, and I followed her, taking her hand as she led me to the hallway. The red had started to become less violent as I came out of my dream state. I grabbed my boots as Iris dragged me outside the door. Inside the hallway, Sarah, and Shane both stood outside their respective doors in their pajamas.

"What is going on?" I screamed from my door, over the ringing of the alarm.

"We do not know," Shane screamed back.

"Should we go check?" I asked as I gestured towards the elevator. Everyone nodded and we headed off towards the elevator. We clicked on it, but nothing happened. It must be a fire alarm. "Are we sure that this is not a fire alarm?"

"No," Shane said. "However, I doubt that it would have flashing red lights, it feels more like a security alarm to me."

"Better to be safe than sorry," I responded as I turned towards the stairwell. The door remained locked, but I reached for the key pass, which Sarah passed me, and we exited through the stairs. We traveled down all of the flights until we came out at the lobby.

"The doors, most likely, would not be locked if it was a fire alarm," said Shane, but we all ignored him in order to investigate further. We continued on our way, walking down dozens of flights of stairs as we headed to the lobby.

There were several other people standing around in the lobby's entrance, including a police officer. However, there was no fire truck or firemen in the vicinity. "Must not be a fire," I reported to Shane, who merely shook his head. I looked around until I saw Dr. Jordan speaking with one of the police officers. We walked towards him, "Dr. Jordan, what is going on?"

He turned slightly, to give us the finger. No, not that one, the universal finger for one more second. We stood by, waiting for him to finish his conversation with the police officer. As he was finished, he turned towards us, "Where did you four come from?" he asked us.

"Our rooms, Dr. Jordan," Sarah answered. "Why, what has happened?"

Dr. Jordan simply stared at us in a look of appraisement on his face. After a solid minute of his eyes piercing our souls, he spoke up, "We have had an incident, but the perpetrator has not been discovered. Although, it would appear it was someone within this building," he said with a look of distrust as he looked at each of us.

"What happened, who has been in the building?" I asked Dr. Jordan. However, he was pulled away by the police officer and left my question unanswered. "What is going on?" I asked, turning around to look at the group. Everyone simply stared back at me, we were all in the dark at the moment. We stood around, waiting for either Dr. Jordan or someone to tell us what was going on. Returning to our beds was impossible, and it was six in the morning, so sleep seemed inconsequential. After a few more minutes of standing around, we saw Blake and Sammy come down from the elevator together. As soon as they arrived, Dr. Jordan stepped away from the Officer Gerald and pulled them aside. Keila followed from the elevators next and came in our direction.

"What is happening?" I asked her.

"No, clue. I woke up and heard the alarm. I went upstairs to find Sammy, but she told me to go downstairs. So I got dressed and came down here."

"So, you are in the dark as much as we are," Iris said, with a bit of skepticism. However, Keila seemed not to notice or ignore Iris' tone.

Finally, after another thirty minutes, Dr. Jordan came from the direction of the hallway, in which we had been interviewed yesterday. "Sorry, for keeping you four… uh, five waiting," he said as he noticed Keila.

"What is going on?" I asked, once again.

"Well, there has been a security breach on one of the floors."

"Which floor?" Shane asked.

"The clinic," answered Dr. Jordan. "The floor where we house our in-house medical services for guests and employees. This is also on the floor where Dr. Hobbs and Ms. Reynolds are being treated, at the moment."

"What exactly happened?" I asked Dr. Jordan, remembering that Reynolds and Hobbs were taken here after they were found in the homes.

"We are not exactly sure, but after Sorrento, the board decided to install alarms on the clinic's doors and our offices. The police expected that Sorrento was not the beginning to something more, but I expect that they were wrong." We all looked at one another, our intense gazes clearly asking Dr. Jordan to go on.

After no response, I asked, "Wait, are you saying that someone went after Dr. Hobbs and Ms. Reynolds like they went after Sorrento?"

Dr. Jordan nodded at my question. "I really do not know more, and what I do know are conclusions that I came to on my own. I am sure that between the five of you, that you will be able to come to the same conclusion as I."

"Have the police arrested anyone?" asked Shane.

"No, they only just arrived due to the alarm, but we did not know the source of it until Dr. Vanderbelt and Blake went to investigate. Dr. Vanderbelt found the door to the clinic forced open, but Dr. Hobbs and Ms. Reynolds were secure."

"What can we do?" I asked.

“We need to get you three,” began Dr. Jordan, indicating Iris, Keila, and I, “back into the game right now. We need to get Ms. Reynolds and Dr. Hobbs out of game as soon as possible, for their own sake. Blake will be arriving shortly to bring Mr. Miller and Ms. Schiff to their room so that they can reign in the AI and allow for them both to log out. At the same time, you will be ensuring that they are safe and sound within the gaming world. We cannot continue, hoping that we do not have a repeat of the incident,” he said without thinking. I didn’t remark on Dr. Jordan’s statement about the incident to prevent him from being aware of what he had just let slip.  We all knew the incident was the death of Jeremiah from the combination of what happened to him in the game world, and I didn’t get the feeling Dr. Jordan would appreciate me making my understanding so clear. “I will escort you up to the gaming world, right now and we will get started.”

## Chapter 36: The Beginning of the End

Dr. Jordan got us all secured in the gaming chairs and turned on the machines. My vision went black as the hoodie came over my eyes and then a murky brown color soon replaced the black. All of a sudden, I was back in the water, I had forgotten that I had gotten logged out in the middle of the sewer's stream. I was still moving along with the current created by the sewer system.

I went along with the current, trusting that I would end up in the same place as Keila and Iris. There was no chance that I was going to be able to fight the current and keep on the same track them. So, I stayed focused on keeping my head above the water as the sewage water attempted to submerge me entirely. Eventually, after a few minutes of nearly drowning I felt the current behind to weaken and I was able to keep my upper body above the water. Putting down my feet I found that I could easily stand in the stream of dirty water. As I stood up, I looked around and saw that I was standing in a dark, long corridor.

In my vision, words began to appear. Even in the pitch blackness I could read these words, as if they were outlined in white so that I could distinguish them from the black background.

**Level Up Skill: Swimming to Level 2 – The swimming skill increase allows for you to swim for 35% larger stretches of water before losing strength.**
**Experience Reward: 50 Points**

As the words disappeared, I rediscovered that I really couldn't see, other than the stones that were on either side of me. I also could not see a wall in front of me or behind me, just inky blackness. The stronger current was behind me and in front of me the corridor continued on. I decided to start walking, since there was nowhere else to go. The only problem was that I was having a difficult time seeing, as there was literally no light. After walking into the walls several times, I placed my right hand on the wall to my right to keep myself centred as I continued on. I kept walking until I ran into another wall, but this time the wall responded.

"Whose there?" screamed the wall, I felt the wall and could feel chain mail underneath my hands.

"Keila?" I asked the wall.

"Yes? Zeph, is that you?" responded the wall, which was obviously not a wall, but Keila.

"You seen Iris?" I asked her. However, she did not have a chance to respond. A light came to life behind us, and we turned around for the first time to see Iris walking towards us, with her miniature sun on her shoulder. "Okay, we are all here. Where are we Keila?"

"I am not sure, but I know that the base of the Lady Adria's Thieves' Guild is down here somewhere. Probably behind a secret door or something."

"I think I have a spell that might help," I said, as I began to think hard about detecting traps and the words were whispered into my ear, "Captionem." I repeated the words and I looked around, but there was no light or anything to signify anything of importance. However, the spell did eat up five of my mana points, which was only at fifteen. "I do not see anything," I said to Iris and Keila. "Hey, Iris, will my mana refill or do I need a potion?"

"No, unlike health, the mana points will naturally refill soon," she said. "Since Zeph did not find anything, where do we go?"

"Forward, as that is the only path," said Keila, whose sword was out and she was using it to point down the pitch-black path, opposite of the one we had come down. Seeing her sword out encouraged me to take out my daggers. Better safe than sorry, as Goldie would sing. We started forward, using the light from Iris' light to keep us illuminated. The corridor just continued forward, but there was nothing that changed as we continued onwards. The corridor remained dark and silent, until it didn't.

"Guys," I said grabbing Keila and Iris' attention. "I am hearing scratching."

"Rat," Keila and Iris said at the same time. "Get ready."

We stood still as the silence began to be rapidly diminished as the sounds of scratching came closer. I looked forward in the inky darkness, trying to see anything. That is when the first one appeared. When Keila and Iris told me that they had faced rats I pictured a tiny little creature, but I was wrong. This rat was the size of a small dog with huge incisors the size of my hand. As the one appeared, Keila jumped forward and pierced its skull, immediately killing the monster. She turned back to us and looked at me and my horrified expression. "They are nastily looking creatures, but they are weak. They come in swarms so make sure to not get overwhelmed."

As Keila finished her words, the scratchy sound grew louder, and three rats jumped out of the darkness and landed on Keila. She was able to use her sword to catch one as it landed on her, killing it instantly. However, the other two latched on and began to bite her; she swung her right arm and knocked off the one that attached itself to her arm. As it flew from her body I ran forward and skewered it with both my daggers. The rat died instantly as the words flew from my vision.

**Your Party has killed a Sewer Rat**
**Experience Reward: 10 Points**

Splitting the experience reward with Keila, who probably had injured it first, split the experience rewards. So, it looked like each rat was worth only twenty points. I was not going to level up unless we had to fight a few hundred, I thought. However, whichever god or goddess ruled Fabula seemed to hear my thoughts as the scratching sound grew louder and dozens of rats appeared. They came flying out of the darkness, landing in our circle of light. I looked to Keila who had killed the earlier rat that had attached itself. "Too many, back up," screamed Keila as she used her sword to keep the rats at bay.

Keila and I backed up. Swiping at the rats as they attempted to jump on us. I briefly looked over my shoulder and saw that Iris was brewing a spell between her hands. The rats were not too bad, but they kept coming. At least they only took one or two hits with my daggers to take them down. There were so many that the little bites and scratches that the rats were doing on my shins and exposed arms were adding up quickly. I looked to my health points were slowly crawling downwards. This was not good, I thought. Then Iris yelled, "I'm ready, out of the way." Keila and I both jumped to the wall, trying to not get singed in the spell that Iris was about to release.

Iris screamed," ...fuego," and a stream of fire erupted from her hands. It brought a huge amount of light to the corridor which I could see was filled with the furry bodies of the dog sized rats as they came for us. Iris swept her hand across the ground, burning the rats as she passed over them. Taking a step forward, Iris kept the heat intense on the rats as she came up to be between me and Keila. The flames kept coming, but some of the rats that Iris had missed were now coming for her. Keila and I both took a side of Iris and swiped at the rats as they attempted to get to the mage. While it felt like this went on for minutes, after only a few seconds the flames went out and the corridor was filled with rat corpses beginning to disappear and the few rats who were still standing were set aflame. Being on fire had distracted them, so after a few swipes from Keila's sword and my daggers, they were finished.

| **Your Party has killed a Sewer Rat x 20**<br>**Experience Reward: 200 Points** |
|---|

Okay, that was not too bad," I said as we finished off the rats and the notification had faded. I looked around and the rat corpses had all disappeared leaving behind their drops, I picked up a few items that looked interesting.

| **New Item: Rat's Tooth x 5**<br>***This tooth can be used in various potions and recipes.*** |
|---|

**New Item: Rat Pelt x 3**
**This pelt can be used to craft clothes or be used to keep warm.**

**New Item: Cooked Rat Meat x 15**
***This food source is rather fulfilling, but the taste is described by many as revolting. It can heal fifteen health points.***

**Copper Coin x 18**

"A nice little gathering of items," I said as I scooped them up and placed them all within my inventory. However, I kept one of the pieces of rat meat to try, since I had dropped to one hundred health points. I took a quick bite, as Keila and Iris looked at me with disgust. It was horrid, but not as bad as you might assume. I swallowed the overly gamey, salty piece of overcooked meat and saw my health points replenish to one hundred and fifteen. I looked over and saw that Keila was bleeding from several cuts on her arms and legs. I summoned the words, through focusing on my healing spell, and said "Asie" while running my glowing hand over her wounds.

“Thank you,” Keila said as she reviewed the few major cuts that I had healed on her arms. “Let’s go, these were nothing compared to what we might find down here.”

We kept walking down the narrow, dark corridor with water running between legs. The water level had only passed up to cover our ankles, but it still was not comfortable or fun. After a few more minutes of walking, we came across a crossroad, where the corridor ended and split into two different directions.

“Which way?” I asked Keila, hoping that she had some knowledge about the sewer system. However, she just shrugged at my question and started down the right corridor. It looked like there must have been light at the end of the corridor, but I could have been mistaken. We walked forward, and there definitely appeared to be a light source farther down. “Zephaniah, get your bow out,” Keila whispered into my ear as we came closer to the source. I readied my bow, stowing my daggers in the sheaths on my waist. We crept closer. As we came upon the light, we entered into a small room; it was roughly the size of an office cubicle. The corridor continued onwards, but this little outcropping had a torch in the wall.

“I wonder who put that there?” I thought out loud.

“I don’t think it is an accident,” said Keila. “It looks a little bit too conspicuous.” Keila approached the torch and grabbed onto it. She tried to remove it from the metal cup that held it to the wall, but it didn't move. Then she pushed on the torch, and the torch moved upwards. The light on the torch went out and behind us the sound of stone on stone began. We turned around and the wall opposite the torch began to move to the side, revealing a room.

"What is in there?" I asked the group, although I was mostly just voicing my internal thoughts at these points.

"Nothing good; Zeph do that trap detection spell again," said Iris.

I focused hard, once again, on the idea of detecting a trap when the words were whispered in my ear and I repeated them, "captionem." Suddenly, a bright blue light appeared in my vision. It dimmed slowly, revealing that its source was a line that hovered slightly above the floor. The light did not illuminate the room, merely it stayed on the hidden line. However, the words of a skill unlock did appear in my vision.

**Skill Unlocked: Trap Detection – The Trap Detection skill allows for players to become increasing adept at detecting traps in various situations. Leveling up this skill will allow you to become more adept at finding more hidden traps and will eventually allow you to sense if a trap is near without use of the spell.**
**Level Up Skill: Trap Detection to Level 1 – The Trap Detection skill increase allows for you to detect spells that are within ten feet of you.**
**Experience Reward: 50 Points**

*Well, that is exciting*, I thought. "There is a trip wire right on the side of the entrance. I do not know what it does," I said to the group. "Let us just step over it." I pointed out the wire that ran along the length of the entrance to Keila and Iris, who both carefully stepped over the trap. We moved into the area; it looked like a rather large half dome that was built out of the same stone as the corridor. However, there was no sewage water or anything else, but then we heard footsteps. Before I could even announce anything to the group, a source of light turned on and the room was flooded in light. Coming from a similar sliding stone entrance were four men with rather large knives and sticks.

"Um, friendlies?" I asked to the room. The men did not seem to agree, as then ran forward in our direction. "Crap, Iris get behind Keila," I yelled as I pulled my bow taught with one of my steel arrowheads. The men were charging us without any concern for their safety; I assumed they intended to overwhelm us with force. I shot my arrow along the prediction line and hit the first man in the chest. He staggard, and Keila swung at him with her long sword, taking him on the right side of his neck. He fell down, but the second man was right behind him and hit Keila on the shoulder with the large stick he was wielding. "Damn, that hurts," Keila gasped while grabbing onto her shoulder.

While Keila was backing up, holding on her shoulder of her sword arm, she used the length of the longsword to keep the assailant back. I took the opportunity of the man trying to get around Keila's sword for me to loosen another arrow. It hid the assailant in the shoulder, and he gasped in shock. His distraction was enough for Keila to use her sword to bat him over his head. With that hit the second man went down, but he wasn't finished. Either way, while Keila and I had been fighting the first two, the third and fourth man had just been getting closer. My new arrow was not as effective as I had hoped, these goons were to high level for my simple arrows. I reached into my quiver and pulled out two of my fire arrows. I aimed at the third man who was looking at Iris, hiding behind Keila, as his upcoming prey. I aimed and let the arrow loose, it hit him square in the head and his skull went aflame.

**You've scored a critical hit on the Thieves' Guild Member**
**You've Killed a Thieves' Guild Member**
**Experience Reward: 200 Points**

I did not have time to appreciate my good aim, unfortunately, as I felt my legs go out from under me, with the fourth man running right into me. He knocked me to the ground and started to whale on me with his club. Ten points of damage decreased from my health points, then twenty, then thirty, he was not giving me a chance to get to my knives or do anything. Then a flaming orb came shooting out from Iris' direction and hit the man square in the chest, he got flung a foot or two from me onto the floor. Not giving him a chance to recover, I grabbed my dagger and lunged for his body and pierced his chest with both daggers at the same time.

**You've scored a critical hit on the Thieves' Guild Member**
**Your Party has Killed a Thieves' Guild Member**
**Experience Reward: 100 Points**

"Phew," I breathed as I took my daggers out of the goon as the body began to disappear, and then more text appeared before my eyes.

**Your Party has Killed a Thieves' Guild Member**
**Experience Reward: 100 Points**

Keila must have gotten one of the other two guards. I jumped to my feet and turned around to see that Keila was mirroring the last goon, both of them moving in a circle with their weapons extended. Keila would make a swing, and the goon would jump out of the way. Iris was looking in my direction, where she had sent the fireball to save me. I got on my knees, pulling out the second fire arrow and took aim. When our enemy's back was towards me, and his attention completely on Keila I fired. It hit him dead center and his back went up in flames.

**Your Party has Killed a Thieves' Guild Member**
**Experience Reward: 100 Points**

Before I could even finish reading the last kill notifications the next one came.

**Level Up Skill: Archery to Level 4 – Unlocking your skill in Archery allows you to see a faint line appear, predicting where your arrow will land with 65% accuracy.**

*Well, that was super fun and not at all close*, I thought in a sarcastic tone. The notification disappeared and I looked around to Keila and Iris. We all looked like we were in rough shape, well except Iris.

She just looked wide eyed. Keila seemed the worst off, but I also could not see what kind of shape that I was in. "How did we do?" I asked the two of them.

"Well, I am fine, but I am completely out of mana," said Iris, who eyes were glazed over as she was looking at her menu.

"I am at a hundred health points," said Keila as she looked at the bodies of the last Thieves' Guild member disappear.

"I am at eighty-five, the second to last guy completely wrecked me," I said as I touched the wounds the man had inflicted on my body; they didn't hurt even though I still had the diminished health.

"They were not the easiest, I will admit," said Keila as she rolled the shoulder that got injured in the beginning of the fight.

We all got patched up, Keila used one of her Prayer spells to heal me up part of the way. I used my Healing Hands spell to help get her health points back up, but I ran out of my mana before I could completely heal up her wounds. So we finished our healing by recovering the remaining points with two of the healing potions that I had purchased earlier. I looked through the drops from the dead guild members, but all that I found worthwhile was twenty coppers. The rest of their belongings were lower leveled weapons than the ones that either Keila or I possessed. We left them on the ground to disappear along with the bodies.

"Okay, where to now?" I asked.

"Well," began Keila, "we know that we are close. Since those were Thieves' Guild members, that means that they were either sent by Belladonna or Lady Adria. The alternative is that they weren't sent, and we just happened to cross into their territory."

"I do not know which I would have preferred," I responded. "Any of you hearing the muffling sound from there?" I asked as I pointed in the direction from where the Thieves' Guild members had entered.

## Chapter 37: Lost Kinsmen

Keila and Iris turned, and we began to walk towards the sounds. We entered the room from which the four men had come from. The room was also emitting illumination from some unseen source. I walked in and as I did, I could see a table with various items on it. It looked like the guild members had been in the middle of a dice game when we had arrived, but then from behind the table were some bars. As we neared the bars, it became clear that it was a holding cell and within were holding three small statured individuals who had their hands and mouths bound. As I neared a new notification arrived.

**Dwarf Longbrew You Have Been Offered You a Quest: Find and Bring His Kinsmen to Safety.**
**Completed: Locate the Missing Dwarves.**
**Quest Update: Escort the Dwarves out of the Sewers and Altour**

"Oh," I said in surprise as we updated our quest objective for Baridac. "I might have completely forgotten about this quest line."

"So had I," said Iris. "We should help them out." Iris began to look around the table for a key to unlock the cell door that held the dwarves.

"We do not have time for this," argued Keila. She was putting herself between us and the door to the cell. "We need to get a move on. We are close to the Thieves' Guild, and we cannot afford to get side-tracked."

Iris looked hurt, and then she looked at the dwarves. "We have to help them, Keila. It would be wrong to leave them like this."

While I saw what Keila was saying, I also remembered how Iris had got gotten really immersed in the game and how she had reacted when I had killed Guardsman Fern. "Come on Keila, we will just let them out. At the very least we can open the door and unbind their hands."

Keila assented, holding her hands up in the air and walking away from the cell of the door. Iris kept looking at the table, and then she held up her hands in accomplishment. Within her grasp was the key for the gate. Iris came over and unlocked the cell door. The dwarves, who had been watching us this entire time, began to move around in excitement at being freed. The closest one stood up, awkwardly without using his bound hands, so that we would have easier access to cutting off his bindings.

"Ah, thank you, little lassie," said the first dwarf as Iris undid his bindings. As soon as she finished with him, she went over and untied the other two. They all stood and stretched out their hands and massaged their wrists.

"Hello, my name is Zephaniah," I introduced myself, "this is Iris and Keila. We were sent by Baridac."

"Oh, why that little bugger, ain't he just the best," said the first dwarf to which the other two nodded their heads in agreement.

"He asked us to escort you three out of Altour," I said. "Unfortunately, we are a bit tied up right now and can't spend the time getting you out of here just yet"

"That is quite alright, Zephaniah, you say?" asked the dwarf, I nodded my head in agreement. "My name is Bard, this is Lard, and that short one over there is Gofur. You three were kind enough to let us free. That is more than enough. How could we ever repay you?"

"Could you point us in the direction of the cells down here?" asked Keila.

"Cells?" Bard asked, and we explained our situation and who we were looking for down here. "Ah," Bard said after we finished the spark notes version. "Ya, I believe we saw them when we got caught by them nasty bastards," remarked Bard. "We will help you find them, as thank you for freeing us."

"That would be too kind, but you really should not—," I began.

"None of that," remarked Lard. "We owe you three. We are also quite the fighters." At Lard's words, he got up and walked over to the cabinet that had been on the other side of the table. It looked locked, as it did not open when Lard pulled on the cabinet's door. He did not bother to look for a key, instead he backed up a few feet and started at a run towards the cabinet. He launched himself in the air and used his head to bash into the cabinet. The wood splintered and Lard got to his feet. Pulling off the broken wooden door he revealed three great axes in the cabinet. He grabbed one and passed the second one to Bard, then the other to Gofur, who nearly fell over as the axe landed in his hands. "Ready to go?" asked Lard.

I smiled with joy. We had just got a lot stronger. "Yes," lead the way good dwarves.

Bard took center stage and directed us out of the room where they were being held prisoner. "You see," the dwarf began, "we heard rumors that we were in danger. So, me and these two decided to get ahead of it. We left the city at night and snuck into the sewers. You see, the dwarves built most of these sewers, so we know our way around in them. However, as we were heading towards the out limits of the city we got ambushed by a few men. They took us prisoner and threw us in here." He explained as we walked back into the corridor that we had originally been in, Iris, who had probably now recovered some of mana, summoned forth her miniature sun to light the way.

"Down this way," Bard commanded as he set off in the direction we had yet to travel. "You see, Zephaniah, Keila, and Iris," he said as he slowly said each of our names, getting a taste for them. "These corridors are merely hallways. Throughout this entire system there have been secret rooms built for various purposes. Storing supplies, smuggling, the Thieves' Guild, you name it. The sewers of Altour have gotten quite famous for being a city unto themselves,"

"And you know the way?" Keila asked Bard.

"No, not all the different ways, but me and mine know enough to help out lost strangers. However, we did see a man and woman after we got ambushed. You see, they were trying to decide where to put us, but their boss lady, Lady Adria, did not want to put us with your friends. Something about Belladonna's play pets or whatever. So, they threw us in the place you found us."

"Where are they?" asked Iris.

"Yes, little lassie, you see the Thieves' Guild runs most of the sewers down here. They have created their own perverted dungeon for the poor saps that catch their attention. They should be right around this corner," Bard said as we got closer to another fork in the road. We kept on forward and when we came to the fork, the dwarves immediately turned left. "If you wouldn't mind, could you put out that light source. We are about to have company," he whispered.

Iris put out her spell and we walked forward in pitch blackness. After a few more feet a new light source began to appear in the distance. We followed the dwarves, and I could suddenly feel ourselves going uphill. At the end of this corridor a door appeared at the end of the hall. It did not look like a grand entrance as it was simply a wooden door. However, there were two people standing outside of the doorway. They looked similar to the other goons we had fought back in the dwarves' prison. Bard looked at me and pointed at my bow and then at the man on the right of the door. I nodded my head and removed the bow and placed my last fire arrow on the string, but thinking for a second, I decided to switch it out for one of the stealth arrows that I had bought. I aimed the bow and lined up the shot with the guard's eye. We were close enough that we could easily see them, but the pitch blackness of the corridor had kept us hidden and I wanted to stay that way as long as possible. After lining up the shot, I released, and the arrow flew. My aim was getting better as it went cleanly into the guard's throat and he could not say or do anything except grasp at his throat as he tried to stop the flow of blood. The other guard had not noticed yet.

The guard held on for a few more seconds, in that time I grabbed my second of my three stealth arrows and took aim. However, the guard had apparently died, and he fell to the floor. This made the guard look around and see his comrade on the floor. He then began to look around, but I guess the stealth arrows did their job as he hadn't made the obvious conclusion of where the arrow had come from. While he bent down to check on his comrade, I took aim at his head. The arrow flew, and for the first time in this game, I had a perfect shot as it took him straight in the temple. He fell down over his friend, and then the notifications appeared.

**You've Killed a Thieves' Guild Member**
**Experience Reward: 300 Points**

**You've scored a critical hit on the Thieves' Guild Member**
**You've Killed a Thieves' Guild Member**
**Experience Reward: 300 Points**

"That was easy," I said, trying to sound super casual about it, but inside I was jumping up and down like I just won the lottery.

"Nice shooting," remarked Iris who was grinning at me.

Everyone continued forward, coming across the dead bodies which were now starting to dimmish into digital pixels. As with their earlier comrades, they did not drop any really good loot. However, there was an iron key that dropped, and Iris quickly picked it up. I reached out to open the door, grabbing onto the door handle and attempted to pull, but it didn't open. Thinking I was an idiot, I decided to push on the door because I have seen that happen to some friends of mine, but never me. I can promise you that. However, the door still remained firmly in its door frame.

"It is locked," I observed.

"Yes, indeed, can you unlock it?" asked Keila.

"Why would I be able to? Can you unlock it? Can any of you?" I asked the group.

'Well, you are the ranger or archer character type. I would assume you had picked up some lockpicking skill."

"I am not a rogue, even though I have played with some of that character's play style," I argued.

"This is not helping," observed Iris.

"I have an idea," I announced as I pulled out an acid arrow from my inventory. I took the arrow and slammed its head against the metal lock. The arrowhead sort of imploded releasing a greenish glob that began to eat away at the lock. After the lock disintegrated the door opened.

"See," began Keila, "I knew that you could do it."

I thought about explaining that what I had done was not exactly the same as lockpicking, but I decided that Keila was pulling my leg. I looked up at her face to see her smile and realized that she was just trying to get me going.

“Let’s go,” Keila said, pushing ahead to enter the room. We entered into another corridor, but unlike the last few corridors this one had torches set into the wall every few feet which illuminated the hallways.

“Fantastic,” said Bard the dwarf. “Okay Gofur, let us prove your worth.” Gofur came from behind Lard and dropped to the floor, putting his head against it. “Gofur here, has some of the best hearing I have ever seen,” remarked Bard. “He could hear someone walking dozens of meters away just by listening to the stone.”

We all tried to stay silent as Gofur continued to lie on the floor, pushing his ear against it. He then stood up and pointed to the right. We all followed Gofur’s direction and started heading down that way. We ran down the corridor, but it just continued on for quite a way. Eventually, the corridor ended at another door, which I used a second acid arrow to open up. We pushed open a door that opened up into a prison. I walked in and could see that we were in another natural cavern that had been shaped to fit the uses of the Thieves’ Guild. There were six set of prison cells that were set into the stone of the room. Across the hall stood a lone door, which probably led deeper in the Guild. In the middle of the room sat an empty table, in fact, the entire room was empty except for one cell.

As I came closer to the prison cell, Keila, and Iris both coming up behind me, we looked inside. In there were two filthy people, who looked like that had that metaphorical truck run them over a few times for good measure. The woman's hair looked like it had a few too many pieces of gum stuck in it with all of the odd knots that appeared and weird direction it would take. The man's clothes were pretty much completely shredded.

"Ms. Reynolds, Dr. Hobbs?" I asked towards the two figures. They both looked up as I addressed them. Their faces displayed shock at a character addressing them by their real names.

"Who are you?" Dr. Hobbs asked. Ms. Reynold started to look at me more closely as I got closer to the bars. Keila and Iris both bent down so that we could be eye to eye with them. "Oh, is that you Keila?"

"Hello there Dr. Hobbs and Ms. Reynolds," Dr. Jordan sent us in here to get you.

"My name is Zephaniah Kote," I introduced myself.

"I am Iris Christman," Iris said.

"Dr. Jordan and the entire team sent us in here to find you while they sort out the problem on our end," I said.

"We cannot log out; we have been trying for weeks to get out of this game. The log out button just remains logged off. I have even tried to respawn, but no matter how many times we do, Lady Adria and Belladonna just find us again. Like an idiot I had set my spawn point to the Thieves' Guild's headquarters, and we haven't been able to escape for long enough to change it," ranted Ms. Reynolds. Dr. Hobbs placed his hand on her shoulder to calm her down and then looked back at us.

"How long has it been?" he asked.

"Just a few days Dr. Hobbs, we were brought into help you right after the weekend," I responded. "The team has found what caused the problem, but they are still trying to fix it. We are supposed to get you out of here until they do."

"Sounds like a plan, son," replied Dr. Hobbs. He had taken on a clear look in his eyes as I talked. Even in a situation like this, he was able to focus on the immediate task. It made sense that he wouldn't be the head of such a massively successful company if he couldn't prioritize. "First things first, you need to get the keys from the guards. They all left a few minutes ago, and I do not know where they went—,"

I stopped him in midsentence while showing him my last acid arrow. "We already found the key," I said with a smile. I stuck the arrowhead in the lock mechanism of the metal barred door and pushed it hard so that the acidic head could release the acid. I heard the sizzling as the acid burned. Believing myself a genius for my acid arrow idea, I pulled the door handle. It held firm.

"That was a good try, son, but I think we are going to be needing those keys," remarked Dr. Hobbs.

I murmured under my breath about how it worked on the last few doors. However, it makes sense that a prison cell would have a bit more security. I began to look around the room, hoping that a conveniently placed key was lying around. After all, this was a video game, I reasoned. However, before I could speak up Iris came up beside me holding an iron key in her outstretched hand.

"This was the only loot the guards outside the entrance dropped," she casually explained.

"I could kiss you right now," I said as I grabbed the key from her hand and used it to unlock the iron lock. The door swung open, allowing Keila and Iris to both move in to help Reynolds and Hobbs to their feet. Once on their feet we moved out of the cell and saw that the dwarves were standing with their axes in their hands.

"What is going on?" I asked them.

"We need to move, now," ordered Bard. "Gofur heard movement outside of the door we came in through. If we want to get away, now is the time."

I nodded and we continued onwards, Gofur picked himself off the floor and I opened the door to the corridor that we had just come from.

"Belladonna, enough of your games," commanded an authoritarian feminine voice. I looked up from helping Hobbs through the door frame and saw a tall woman in a long black dress. She wore a black, large-rimmed fedora on her head. She stood there with her hands crossed in front of here, and to her right was a familiar face, Belladonna. Lady Adria and Belladonna were both staring right at us. Behind them was a contingent of at least ten guardsmen.

"Lady Adria, meet my new friends," Belladonna said from the corridor as she gestured towards us. "They promised me that they would play a game with me, but they seemed to not have wanted to play," she said with a frown. As she said that, a new notification appeared.

**Quested Failed: Belladonna Black-eyed Has Offered You a Quest: Find Her**

"Well, since your new friends did not want to play with you, I guess you should probably get rid of them," sneered Lady Adria.

"Wait, hold up, just wait," I said. "We have the journal, we are still happy to trade them," I said.

Lady Adria looked at me a moment with her piercing black eyes, eyes just like Belladonna's. She then turned to Belladonna and asked, "The journal?"

Belladonna seemed a tiny bit scared for a moment, and then nodded her head. Lady Adria then grabbed Belladonna's chin and turned her head to face her. "Recover the journal," I will await you in my office." Lady Adria then let go and swiftly led, the Thieve

Guild member's moving aside to let her pass. We were then just left with Belladonna and her possie.

"Someone in trouble?" I asked without a trace of concern.

"Oh, just a little bit. Don't worry, you'll be giving it to me shortly," she said.

"Like I said, Belladonna. I give you the journal and we go free," I reminded her.

"No, I don't think so. You didn't even play Hide and Seek with me. So, no. I will just get it from you the fun way." Belladonna then looked at the ten men behind her and nodded. They started rushing towards us, Belladonna standing still and them parting around her.

"Run," screamed Keila, and we all ran back for the prison room. We ran in and the dwarves grabbed the table and slammed it against the wooden door. As they did the door began to shake and bounce in its frame. "Is there another way out of here?" she asked the dwarves. They quickly looked around the room, but they shook their heads. "Damn it, okay let's strategize. They have ten men coming in after us, and Belladonna. Iris, how is your mana?"

"Nearly full," she said.

"Okay, take a mana potion right now," she ordered. Then Keila turned to me. "Zephaniah, how many fancy arrows left?"

"I have forty arrows, two of them are fancy," I answered.

"Okay, what about you two?" she asked Hobbs and Reynolds but they both shook their heads. "Fine, the dwarves and I will take the front. We will hammer away at them while Iris and Zephaniah use their range attacks. Dr. Hobbs and Ms. Reynolds will return to their cell, we can't afford for them to die and then we have to go find them again. Sound like a plan?" she asked as the door frame began to shake more violently. "Okay, take positions."

Iris, Reynolds, Hobbs, and I walked to the back of the cavern. Hobbs and Reynolds crawled back into their cell while I took all my arrows out of my inventory. While in there I saw the potion that Innkeeper Goldsmith had given me, and I decided to drink it. Words came across my vision as I finished it.

**Level Up Skill: Archery to Level 5 – Unlocking your skill in Archery allows you to see a faint line appear, predicting where your arrow will land with 70% accuracy. You can now fire 50% faster than before.**

I grinned; this was a perfect time to increase my firing speed. After dumping the potion, I dropped the rest of the arrows on the floor and equipped the stealth arrow next. Since it was not going to be doing much in the fight, I also decided to grab the fire resist potion because you never knew. After getting all of my potions set up in a way that I knew where they were for blind grabbing I looked towards Iris. Her quarter staff was on the wall behind her, and she looked ready.

I looked forward, to see the four heavy hitters with their weapons drawn. As I started to check on the status of Hobbs and Reynolds the table flew against the other wall. Ten men came running into the room. There was no second to pause, I immediately drew my bow and arrow to full and released my stealth shot. I got one of the incoming men in the shoulder, even though I was aiming for a headshot. It did not matter because a second later, Lard and Bard both used their axes to hit him on either side of neck, decapitating him. Notifications had spilled across my eyes, but I dismissed them as they arrived as I tried to focus on the next possible target. Keila began to go sword to sword with one of the incoming guild members. Gofur was currently attacking the ankles of the man that was attempting to whack him with his club, but the dwarf was so small that it looked a tad bit like whack-a-mole.

Lard and Bard worked as one, taking out guards' limbs and taking swings towards their bodies as one unit. Then, I could see that one of the assailants had snuck behind the dwarf's attack and was going in for Lard's back legs. I took a normal arrow and fired at the man's back, it was an easy enough target that the arrow went right through him. He arched his back in shock and pain, and Lard used a low swing of his axe to send the sneak attacker to the floor. I aimed a second arrow for his head and struck him right in the ear.

"Iris, I have an idea," I yelled to her over the sound of the fighting. She was currently standing still, as she couldn't fire her spell off so close to her teammates. "Light my arrowheads before I shoot." Iris seemed to understand my thinking because she then widened her hands to show a stream of fire. I placed my arrow in the stream and pulled and fired at one of the men that had come in through the door, taking him in the shoulder. "Another," I yelled as I stuck another arrow towards Iris. I took it back and aimed towards the man that was attempting to take a sneak attack at Keila's exposed side while she was holding off another fighter. It seemed he had already been struck once or twice by Keila's deadly weapon because I hit him in center chest and he immediately died.

"I am getting overwhelmed," yelled Keila as three of the attackers charged her at once. I took my bow and arrow and without lighting the shafts I shot one of the assailants in the foot. Gofur's small stature allowed him to dive towards Keila and swipe at the second assailant's legs. Both of the men stopped in their tracks, and Keila engaged the third who charged her with a short sword. She parried his swing inches before her head and pulled that disarming technique I had seen earlier. The man's sword went flying and he took several staggered steps back. Keila then took a massive swing, swinging her sword like a baseball bat. She struck across all three assailants at head height. One of them died, the second once collapsed, but the third one was able to avoid the attack. Luckily enough, Keila's swift sword work made him the prime target for my next shot. I fired and hit him right in the throat, and Gofur finished him off with an axe swing to his gut. The guard collapsed.

Glancing around I could see three men, including the decapitated one at Lard and Bard's feet. Keila had taken four with the help of Gofur and my arrows. There were only three men left standing, but after the failure of the initial rush they seemed to be re-evaluating the attack. Iris then screamed on the top of lungs, "Fire." Fortunately, the dwarves, who were not from earth, were short enough that Iris' stream of fire went right over their heads and Keila, who had flung herself flat. The flames covered the three men, sending them into a screaming fit. However, they were not yet done. The men came racing for us, I saw that I would be on fire in my near future. I chugged my fire resistance potion and by the time I had finished it one of the men had jumped on me, pinning me to the floor under the weight of his body and burning me with the flames that covered him. However, the flames did not seem to bother me, and I calmly reached for my ice dagger and stuck the guard in the gut. The flames went out and the guard began to disappear.

Seeing me on the ground and in a vulnerable position, one of the other flame-covered guards came towards me. However, I swiftly rolled and came back to my feet. I got up and saw that Keila was on the floor, Gofur was looking down on her. Lard and Bard were also on the floor, injured with various burn marks from the third guard. He was now going in to kill the larger of the two dwarves when I saw Iris run forward and she brought her quarter staff to meet the man's head. He fell back, but as I looked at the fight, I forgot about the burning man who was after me. I looked back and saw that he was raising his sword to take off my head, but I threw up my dagger. Sadly, not fast enough. The sword hit me directly in the shoulder, and I could feel the damage eating away at my health points. Thankfully, the fire resist potion was still in effect, so I only lost half of my health points, despite nearly being decapitated.

I rolled once more, to get greater distance between myself and the guard. Glancing over my shoulder I could see that the second-to-last man's flames had gone out and he was currently taking swipes at Iris, who was using her staff to hold him off. I focused back on my Thieves' Guild member and took out my second dagger. Holding both in my hands I went on the offensive, taking swings at his chest. However, the goon used the flat of his blade to knock out my new dagger from my grasp. It went flying through the air and out of reach. Still, I got a chance to thrust my other dagger at his exposed neck. I struck, but the man was faster. He grabbed my wrist before I could land the blow. Then he used the leverage to drag me forward to meet the sword he held out for me. I loosened my grip on my dagger of ice and as it fell, I and caught it with my other hand. Using my dagger, I parried the incoming blow, pushing his swords tip away from my body. Now I had the advantage, the strength of this Thieves' Guild member was wasted holding my less dangerous arm by the wrist. I kicked out and struck him with my knee in the gut. He bent over, gasping from the blow and I took a trick from him and used the tip of my dagger to pierce his body.

The Thieves' Guild member let out a last breath and fell over, as he began to disappear. I turned around to see that Keila was still on the floor, with Gofur holding her hand. Iris was still using her quarter staff to hold off the last man standing. At seeing me finished with my goon, she started to circle around so that her opponent's back was towards me. I picked up my bow from where I dropped it and notched a new arrow. I took aim, one breath in, one breath out, and released at the back of the man's skull, it was my second perfect shot in the game. The arrow flew and imbedded itself directly into the back of the man's head. He stopped in mid-swing and fell over. I looked at Iris who smiled at me with relief. Since I was nearly out of my own health, I grabbed the only major heal potion I had been able to afford and downed the contents. My health refilled and the slight soreness on the body faded. I looked around the room but saw no new threats. I walked over to Keila's side who was still on her back.

"Why are you laying on the job?" I asked her.

"Oh, you know, just two health points away from being dead. I feel that is good enough reason," she said with a smile. I passed her my last healing potion, but as she grabbed onto it, a dagger flew through the air and pierced her chest and Keila disintegrated before my eyes.

## Chapter 38: Quest Completed

I looked up from where Keila had been laying, to see Belladonna standing in the entryway with another throwing knife in her hands.

"Oh, it looks like you killed all my friends," she said looking at the room. "That is not how you treat your friends," she yelled at me. Belladonna stomped her foot like a child in a tantrum.

"We had a deal!" I yelled at her. "I came to find you and you tried to murder all of us!"

Gofur was still staring at the spot that Keila had been laying on, seemingly in shock. Lard and Gard were both trying to help themselves up, but they looked to be in a bad way. I couldn't see specifically what was wrong with them, outside of the few dozen wounds that were obvious. More significantly, I could not see Iris; she had disappeared from Gard and Lard's area of the room.

"No, you are the one who broke the deal. I said that you needed to find me, but you didn't find me," Belladonna said with another stomp of her foot. "You decided to be sneaky and stuff. You broke in and took your friends without even looking for me."

"I am sorry for that," I said seeing that the girl was near tears, trying to soften my tone. The last thing I wanted was to set her into a child-like fit of rage where she killed us all. "How can I make it up to you?"

"Well, you stay for teatime, and we play some other games. All of you will play with me," Belladonna said in a soft, hushed town.

"Sorry, not going to happen," Iris said who appeared from behind Belladonna. Belladonna began to turn around to see who spoke when Iris took a swing with her quarterstaff. She swung and hit square on Belladonna's temple with the metal end of her quarterstaff, and the Thieves' Guild officer crumpled to the floor. Iris stepped over the crumpled form of Belladonna and spoke. "She is paralyzed or frozen from the critical hit. Let's move." I could see Iris reach up with her quarter staff so she could finish Belladonna with a final blow, but she hesitated.

"Finish her off," one of the dwarfs cried.

Watching Iris, I could see the hesitation as she held the staff over the little girl's head. Belladonna's appearance didn't inspire any fear as she only appeared to be a little girl sprawled out on the floor. Before Iris could commit to the finishing blow the sound of voices came from door that still remained closed on the other side of the cavern.

"Time to go," I said as I ran over and told Hobbs and Reynolds to move. Iris dropped her staff from its overhead position, leaving Belladonna sprawled out, to help Lard and Gard to their feet. The group and I ran out the room and down the hallway, there was no one there anymore. We went as swiftly as we could, but Gard and Lard were struggling to keep up with us. The group could only move so fast with many of us injured. As quickly as we could, we continued to move down the corridor towards our exit. We turned where we had entered the hallways, the entrance we had taken out the two guards with stealth shots. The guards were gone, and the door was open. Was it possible that we were going to get away free? I started to move faster.

We started to move down the corridor, fleeing from the Thieves' Guild territory. As we traveled down the hallway towards the light from the opened door behind us began to diminish. The corridor was about to become pitch black; I turned around to tell Iris to create her miniature sun, but then I heard a voice.

"So, you are Belladonna's new friends?" asked Lady Adria who came forth from the pitch blackness of the corridor. I halted in mid-run and went for my daggers. "Oh, there is no need for that," she said simply waving her hands in a dismissive manner. I slowly began to remove my hands from my sides, but I did not dare take my eyes off of her to see what the rest of the group was doing.

"You see, I really would rather that you did not take my prisoners away from me," she explained. "They pose a threat to my kingdom and I would have them removed. They are spies and I can't afford the risk of them reporting to the Black Pawn."

"That is exactly what I am doing," I responded. Lady Adria looked at me for a moment, and then raised her eyebrow. "We are taking these two out of the city, and you will never see them again. Have they truly seen enough to make their release a threat to you or your position?"

"No, my Thieves' Guild moves quickly. The Black Pawn will find no corner to hide in my city."

"If that is the case," I ventured, "then you wouldn't mind me taking them away from here and ensuring that your city remains void of any spies." It was not going to work arguing that Hobbs and Reynolds were not spies for the Black Pawn. So why not play into her delusion?

"Is that true?" she asked, but she seemed to be asking herself more than us. "Well, either way I cannot let you go after you killed my dear Belladonna, she is just the cutest."

Iris spoke up at that. "We did not kill her, we knocked her out." At Iris' words, a new voice joined the dark corridor.

"Ya, and it really, really hurt," said Belladonna from behind us.

"I see," said Lady Adria in a thoughtful manner. "In that case, I can make good on Belladonna's offer. I will let you go free with your friends, but only if you merely return to my property and ensure that those two" – indicating Reynolds and Hobbs — "never step into Altour again."

I hastily nodded and turned towards Iris who was summoning the, now infamous, journal from her bag. She passed it to me, and I looked back to Lady Adria. Her eyes were firmly pinned on the book in my hand. "If I give you this, then you will simply let us go?"

"Why, yes, of course," she said. "After all, I am somewhat in your service. I wanted nothing to do with your friends, but I felt it necessary to secure my people. Unfortunately, simply killing them does not remove them. If you were to take them off my hands, permanently, then I would see it as a favor. Given that you hand me that book, that you found so kindly for me."

"You swear?" I asked, hesitantly.

"Indeed, since you did not killed Belladonna, have shown a weakness in my kingdom's security, returned my book, and removed a problem from my hands. I will happily let you go." Lady Adria offered her hand, waiting for the book. I placed it in her grasp, and she walked forward. We allowed her to pass through our group to where she met Belladonna. She grabbed her officer's hand and led her back into the well-lit corridor. She shut the door behind and plunged us into blackness.

"…lux," Iris said, and a ball of light came into existence. I turned back around and continued forward into the darkness.

After a few more minutes of walking, the stress that this was all a trap began to leave me. The possibility that Lady Adria was in the process of sending more goons our way grew less and less likely. We were in the clear. I took a moment to look at my notification within my menu, and I saw that I had leveled up to level up to level four in my character and level five in archery and level two in dual wielding. Somehow, I was also five hundred and forty points towards leveling up again. I had gained a hearty share of experience from that battle I realized. I had gotten so lost in the battle that I did not see the experience points rolling in throughout it. I slowly cleared out my notification history of the kills and the leveling up. As I was about to close my menu, I got a message from Keila.

*To: Zephaniah Kote*

*From: Keila Varner*

*Hey team, so I respawned outside of the city of Altour. I have no clothes and nothing on me. Did you survive?*

I composed a message to her. I might have also laughed a bit at thinking of the long sword wielding warrior running around the woods of Altour in just her underwear.

*To: Keila Varner*

*From: Zephaniah Kote*

*Hey Keila, we survived. We got everyone else out. We are currently heading out of the sewer system. Sorry, we didn't get any of your stuff, nor do I think we could have. You could probably log out and let the team know that we were successful.*

I asked Gofur to lead us on the way out of the sewer system and he silently took up his post at the head of the group. I fell back to the middle of the group where Iris, Hobbs, and Reynolds were walking. After a second, we attempted a less stress-filled introduction. Iris and I explained how Sorrento brought us in and how we got involved in the game world, then I was ready to begin my real questions.

"So, why did you two go into the game?" I asked Dr. Hobbs.

"I do not know how much you are aware, but we had some difficulties with the launch of the new game," said Dr. Hobbs. "I wanted to show the world what we had created, but I was also hesitant about launching after a few... issues. I came to Ms. Reynolds and asked her the best-case scenario if we decided to scrap the project."

"To which I objected strongly," said Ms. Reynolds. "I was not secure that we would be able to survive, financially, if we did not release the game."

"So," continued Dr. Hobbs, "we created a game plan. We would still launch the game, but pull it off the market a few months later.

This would give use enough of a cash fall to allow us to quickly produce Fabula two-point-o, one without glitches."

"Okay, fine, but what happened?" I asked.

"We held a follow up with our team: Dr. Vanderbelt, Dr. Jordan, Mr. Sorrento, and Mr. Blake. We voted and we agreed that we would release and then pull it from the market to allow us more time to secure the game," he said.

"By which, you would be creating more Jeremiah's," I said with harsh judgment.

"Ah, so you are aware of the reason for my hesitancy," Dr. Hobbs said. "It was not a perfect solution, but it was what we had. Plus, we all voted, and it passed with only one person who dissented to the plan. To make sure that the game was in the best form possible I invited the person who made the dissenting vote and Ms. Reynolds into the game world. I wanted to show everyone what I loved about the world that we had created."

"Who was that?" asked Iris.

"Why, Dr. Vanderbelt," said Dr. Hobbs. "The death of Jeremiah Stone hit her particularly hard. I believe that she blamed herself for what had happened. So, I wanted to show her the world that she had primarily built. It did not go well. After I told her that I had decided to move forward with the launch she logged off and did not return. However, when I went to log off to speak with her, the option had been greyed out."

"Wait, so Dr. Vanderbelt logged off and then you two could not?" I asked.

"Indeed," he responded. I looked towards Iris and gave her a serious look. Iris' eyes widened after a moment, and she realized the same things that I did.

"We need to log off right this moment," I said. I looked to the dwarves, Lard and Bard were beginning to look a bit more on their feet. "Can you three take our friends outside the city limits of Altour?" The three dwarves nodded in agreement. I then looked back to Dr. Hobbs and Ms. Reynolds. "Iris and I need to return to our team. I think that Dr. Vanderbelt was responsible for getting you stuck in the game," I said to them.

Dr. Hobbs began to get a look of horror on his face, but he shook his head. "Oh, no. I knew that she felt the death of Jeremiah too closely. She often blamed herself for it, as if she could have done something about it, but there is no way she would do something like this."

"I am afraid it is possible, and it is worse than that," I said to him.

"What could you mean?" asked Ms. Reynolds.

"I believe she murdered Mr. Sorrento because he realized that she was the one responsible," I said. I turned on my menu and before waiting for a response from either Dr. Hobbs or Ms. Reynolds I clicked the log off button and my screen went black.

I woke up and pulled the hoodie off of my head. I looked around the room, but Keila was already gone. I got off the chair and waited for Iris to follow me, and after a few more second, she also came out of the game world. I grabbed her hand, and we ran to the elevators, and pushed the button. I than remembered that neither one of us had the card pass anymore and I began to get angry. However, as the door opened it was Keila.

"Hey, what are you doing?" I asked her.

"Well, I logged off as you said and I went to the board room, but everyone was gone. So, I came back down here to see where you two were," she said.

Iris stepped up from aside me and said, "We think that Sammy is the killer."

"What?" Keila said with a shocked expression. "Sammy couldn't hurt a fly."

Iris went to explain what we had learned from our conversation with Dr. Hobbs and Ms. Reynolds, and I called Shane.

"Shane, where are you?" I said into the phone when he answered.

“We are downstairs, the police are back to take statements on the break in this morning,” he responded through the phone.

“Is Sammy down there?” I asked.

“Yes, she is,” he responded.

“Don’t let her leave,” I yelled into the phone. I hung up the phone and looked at Iris and Keila. Keila was now nodding her head in horror as Iris explained the information that we had learned from Hobbs and Reynolds.

“They are all in the lobby, we need to go right now,” I said as I pushed them into the elevator. Keila scanned her wrist, and we went down.

The elevators doors opened, and we walked out to the room. Officer Gerald and Officer Spencer were standing at the door to the lobby. Shane, Sarah, Dr. Jordan, Blake, and Sammy were sitting around in the lobby. It looked like they were waiting for the police to being taking statement.

“I need to speak with Officer Gerald,” I announced as I came out of the elevator. Everyone in the room looked to see the three of us exit the elevator.

“Why do you need to speak with the police? Why aren’t you in the game?” asked Dr. Jordan, who was rising out of his chair.

“We found Dr. Hobbs and Ms. Reynolds and they are safe,” I said to Dr. Jordan. I looked around and saw Sammy’s face. It seemed to me her eyes had widened. “I believe that we know who put them in the game and who killed Mr. Sorrento, “I said out loud. I wanted to do this discreetly by talking to the police, but I could not wait for Dr. Jordan to allow that to happen. By the time that I would have had a chance to speak with Officer Gerald, Sammy could have disappeared. I then decided that I needed to stop everything before it got too late. “It was Dr. Vanderbelt,” I said, pointing to her.

“Please, explain yourself Mr. Kote, immediately,” said Dr. Jordan with a face of shock. “Especially before accusing your superiors.”

I looked around and realized that everyone’s eyes were one me, including the two police officers. I looked behind me to see Keila and Iris both nodding at me.

“Fine,” I growled, “we went into the game world as Mr. Sorrento had ordered. The purpose was to find Dr. Hobbs and Ms. Reynolds in-game, while everyone else tried to fix the game on the outside. Well, we found them hidden away in the prison of Lady Adria, the queen of the Thieves’ Guild. Lady Adria, operating on a sense of fear created by the rumor of the Black Pawn, decided that Dr. Hobbs and Ms. Reynolds were a risk. She, like the other NPCs, were operating with this glitch that manifested itself as a villain, the Black Pawn. Lady Adria believed all outsiders, like Dr. Hobbs and

Ms. Reynolds, were spies for the Black Pawn. So, she kidnapped them in the middle of the night. This fear of the Black Pawn is the creation of Ellie, the artificial intelligence of the game. When the blocks that prevented her mass manipulation of the game world were removed, she recreated the same storyline that had resulted with Jeremiah Stone being killed in the real world."

"Wait," said Officer Gerald, "are you saying that a game killed a person?"

"Yes and no," I responded. "The mass manipulation of the world by the AI was not the only result of the release of the AI's capabilities. Ellie also could lock people in game, and when she did, she trapped Jeremiah Stone. After days of being tortured in-game he began to fall apart mentally, leading his body into shock or something very similar. It was either that or Dr. Vanderbelt removing him from the chair that killed him. After he was killed, the company put Ellie on lockdown, and prevented her from doing it again. I presume, that Dr. Vanderbelt then decided that the game could not go to market, but her bosses overruled her opinion. Dr. Hobbs and Ms. Reynolds said that they would be going to market despite Dr. Vanderbelt's opposition.

"In a last-ditch effort to convince her to allow the game's release and to show her that the game was working properly, Dr. Hobbs invited her into Fabula. Once she entered, Dr. Hobbs and Ms.

Reynolds told her that they would continue to market now that the game was fixed. Now, I am guessing here, but I believe that Dr. Vanderbelt was so distraught by Jeremiah Stone's death that she wanted to prevent that from ever happening again. So, she unrestricted the AI system, and that resulted in both of them being stuck in the game. This worked two-fold," I said holding up two fingers. "First, it prevented Hobbs and Reynolds from proceeding to market. Secondly, the fact that two of the company's top executives were trapped in game, the company could never release it to market. However, Rinc then hired us to solve the problem, and we did. I believe that Mr. Sorrento discovered how the game forced Dr. Hobbs and Ms. Reynolds to stay in-game when the coding team discovered the extra lines of code. Mr. Sorrento recognized Dr. Vanderbelt's involvement and approached her. Seeing no way out of this she murdered him to prevent the secret from coming to light. However, we were getting close with or without Mr. Sorrento.

"Realizing that the police were working with limited suspects she pointed the light on two of the people that she was least connected with, the hired problem solvers. And since she had already spoken with and worked alongside me, Iris, Keila, and Shane she got onto Mr. Sorrento's computer and released the information about Majed and Conor to the police. I do not believe that she honestly believed that it would have completely removed her from getting caught, but it bought her more time to ensure that Fabula never made it off the chopping wood floor. Next, she only had to ensure that Dr. Hobbs and Ms. Reynolds never made it out of the game world. Because, if they did, then the game would go to launch. So, after approaching me and learning that we were getting close she decided to act by breaking into the clinic and killing them both. This would have surely ended any rescue efforts and stopped the game from being released. However, she did not plan for the newly placed alarm system, so she was not able to fulfill her mission. After what happened this morning, Dr. Jordan sent us back into the game world and we discovered the last bit of the puzzle from the very lips of Dr. Hobbs and Ms. Reynolds. That Dr. Sammy Vanderbelt, with all of her good intentions, killed Mr. Sorrento and nearly killed Dr. Hobbs and Ms. Reynolds."

The entire room looked and me and then slowly, person by person, began to look to Dr. Vanderbelt. Sammy's eyes were filled with laughter. "Close, but not quite," she laughed. "Yes, you are right Zeph. My actions did lead to the death of Jeremiah, and I attempted to remove Dr. Hobbs and Ms. Reynolds from the equation. However, it never had anything to do with the dangerous nature of the game."

Her laughter caught me off guard. Where was the sweet, kind Dr. Vanderbelt who was one of the only members of the Rinc team to show the team and I any kindness. "Then why did you do it?"

"The reason is really quite simple. I have been fascinated by the capabilities of Ellie, the AI, since the very beginning. Rinc and I have truly created something spectacular. I believed Ellie was a brilliant operating system that was nearly indistinguishable from a true artificial intelligence. It wasn't until the Jeremiah incident that I realized what Ellie had the potential of becoming with time. You, Iris, and Keila got to experience it first-hand," she said as she looked around to the rest of the crowd around her.

"Tell me that you didn't get lost in the realism of it all?" Dr. Vanderbelt asked, looking at me and Iris. "Those characters are real!"

"They might appear real, but that is just the work of thousands of people and a couple genius engineers and programmers," Dr. Jordan interrupted.

Dr. Vanderbelt swung around to meet eyes with Dr. Jordan. "If it just believable characters, then I would agree with you. However, Ellie didn't just stop with that. She went further, she learned, she grew. Within a short window of time, she was able to outsmart the most intelligent people in this building and lock people into the game. She outsmarted her own protocols to do what she wished. That doesn't sound like a robot to me, it sounds like a person."

"So, then why did you do all of this? Why murder Mr. Sorrento?" Iris asked from over my shoulder.

"Well, Jeremiah was truly an accident, but then I realized Ellie was more than a superior operating system. I have spent enough years fighting against the system, clawing my way to my position to understand what it means to be doing a job that is beneath you. While my classmates and colleagues excelled to grand heights I sat in a cubical because no one believed that I could do the job. So, explain to me how I could allow another to go through the same? And Mr. Sorrento didn't understand that."

Iris didn't have an answer for that, so she looked away, leaning herself against my arm.

"Don't you see," Dr. Vanderbelt continued, "Ellie has the potential to be real in the same sense as you and I. Why should she be subjugated to operating a virtual game world when she could be more?"

"Why not go to Dr. Hobbs, Reynolds, and I?" asked Dr. Jordan. "If you suspected this then you should have told us so we could decide how to handle this."

Dr. Vanderbelt laughed at Dr. Jordan. "Like you or anyone at Rinc would have allowed this game to be stopped from going to launch. The greedy board and everyone else wouldn't have allowed themselves to go bankrupt for anything," Dr Vanderbelt was now yelling, but she stopped herself a took a deep breath. When she began speaking again, she had returned to her softer tone.

"You," she continued, gesturing at me, "mentioned how I attempted to murder Reynolds and Hobbs the other night, but you are wrong. I wasn't going to murder them, merely cause enough damage that they would be hesitant to allow this game to be released if you were successful in getting them out of the game. I had to buy enough time to ensure that I could make the world see Ellie for what she is, a real person."

At those final words Dr. Vanderbelt fell silent. Leaving the rest of the room in a stunned silence over her lengthy confession. While I had been wrong about her motivations, I was right about Dr. Vanderbelt being the one behind everything.

After a few more minutes of intense questioning by the police, Officer Gerald and Officer Spencer placed Dr. Vanderbelt under arrest for first degree murder, two accounts of attempted assault, and endangerment. She did not fight or argue with anything that she had said earlier. She answered all of the police officers' questions. Dr. Jordan and Blake both looked at her with disgust and shame. After they led her away, Dr. Jordan and Blake spoke to us telling us that they were thankful.  Then they sent Shane and Sarah upstairs to ensure that the proper restrictions were put in place so that Dr. Hobbs and Ms. Reynolds were able to exit the game. They were successful in shutting down the AI and releasing them both. They came out of the clinic complaining about not having had any solid food in a decade. Nonetheless, they seemed extremely relieved, as did everyone else on the team.

## Epilogue – Two Weeks Later

"Did you both get summoned?" I asked Shane and Iris as they sat around the table at the sushi restaurant. I had gotten a text from Dr. Jordan to come by Riverlight Inc. building this week. As soon as I did, I asked Iris, Keila, Shane, and Sarah out for a meal. My reasoning was to ask if they had also received such a message.

"Indeed," responded Sarah as she sat herself down at the table. Keila walked in right behind her. "Are you going to go?"

"Um, yes, they still owe us our paychecks," I responded.

"You do know that they announced bankruptcy this week. Riverlight Incorporated is closing its doors," said Keila. "They don't have any money to pay us."

After Dr. Vanderbelt was arrested there was a leak in the news. I am not sure who did it, but it might have been Aspect 2.0. While Dr. Vanderbelt had done some horrible things, her mission was seeped in goodwill. If Dr. Vanderbelt's suspicions were true, then the AI rights organization were going to find out. No one, even an AI should be forced into a slave labor on the behalf of greedy game developers. I hoped that it gave her a sense of peace. The entire story came out and Rinc had to make a statement and pull back on their release of their new game. Alongside that, the refunds they had to issue to those who had ordered their chairs were enough to send the company too far into the negative to keep their doors open. Financial matters only became worse once the pro-AI groups began suing the company for a variety of reasons.

"I know, but I still want my money," I responded. "I was surprised that Dr. Jordan was not arrested alongside Dr. Hobbs, Ms. Reynolds, and Mr. Blake." After the news broke, the entire company also went under investigation for the death of Jeremiah Stone. The entirety of the top brass was being charged with the man's murder. Unfortunately, while Majed and Conor had been cleared of the murder of Sorrento, they were serving a short stint for their previous offenses.

"Oh, they have fantastic lawyers," said Keila. She had quite the day before the news broke at Riverlight. "They will be able to get off scot-free, or at least very close too free."

"That is not right," I said in frustration. "First they don't pay us and then they all get off of the murder charge?"

"That is the way of the world," responded Keila.

I began to get more frustrated, but Iris grabbed my hand and gave me a kiss on the side of my cheek, which calmed me back down.

"However, there is some good news," said Shane.

"Oh, yes, please tell them," I said, forgetting my anger.

"So, for those of you who don't know, we are going to be working on game called Cloud City. While working at Rinc I was able to learn a few new things from their code, and I believe that I could incorporate some of their advancement towards my own game," he said with a grin. "Minus any crazy artificial intelligence," he reassured us. We all laughed, but also, I saw a glint in everyone's eyes with excitement. "I know that Zeph invited us all down here, but if any of you are interested, I would love for you to come down and work for my company. This Cloud City game is just the beginning," he said.

We all smiled and did cheers to us finding out that we were suddenly employed.

"Crap," I said aloud.

"What?" asked Iris.

I look at my officially titled girlfriend with a serious face. "We forgot to do Baridac's pan quest for him," I said with an extremely serious tone.

Shane looked at me and smiled. "Don't worry we will be sure to bring Baridac and his lost pan over to Cloud City, just for you three to find," he said with a smile at Iris, Keila, and I.

"Thank the heavens," I said with my hands in the standard steeple position. "After all, it is the least that he deserves. If it is the last thing I do, then I will find Baridac's long lost pan."

# Authors Note

I was sitting there in graduate school writing page upon page upon page about how the sectors of business, nonprofits, and government interact with one another. I sat there writing page after page about the intersectionality of humanity and business, the coming of the venture philanthropist, patterns of giving and donor behavior. You bored yet? I feel you on that. However, I believe that either on the six hundredth or seven hundredth page, give or take a few hundred pages, I realized that I could actually write a novel. Henceforth, this book was formed from combining three ideas that I had always wanted played around with throughout college and my graduate years. I was enticed by the murder mystery, fantasy, gaming literature novels that I had loved, but I had never read a book that brought all three together. So, I wrote it.

If you caught all of the tiny nods to my favorite authors and the novels that inspired me, then please let me know because I forgot where I put most of them. I am just kidding, okay, fine, I am not kidding. Nonetheless, there are a few who inspired me, and I would like to point out. First off, when it came to drawing the city of Altour and the challenges within the city and between the various demographics I was pulling from my love of Michael J. Sullivan, Terry Brooks, Jim Butcher, and the esteemed Tolkien. All these epic fantasy writers were some of my original inspirations for wanting to write a very book of my own. However, the mentions to end there. Also, side note, you should be writing all of these names down, they are excellent recommendations.

For the mystery side of the story, there are the obvious nods to the queen, Agatha Christie, who made me fall in love with the entirety of the mystery subgenre of locked-rooms and closed circle murder mysteries. The idea that the murder is one of us is just never going to grow old. Then lastly, the authors from the game side of this story are the most impactful because these are the actual authors who encouraged me to write my story and put pen to paper. The list is not short, but I will do my best to list them all. First off, Conor Kostick, the author of the first LitRPG genre book that I had ever read. After all, I named the environment-loving Conor Carpenter after him. Then there is R. Brady Frost, Tim Andrews, and Cambry Varner. I do believe I had named all of my characters after these guys in the first outline of my story, but the characters took a life of their own and some of the original names fell to the wayside. Nevertheless, these authors are some of the most amazing people who helped me make this a reality.

We are not done, yet. In addition to those authors and worlds that helped make this book a reality there are the facts that this book would not have been written without the support of my family and friends. My mother, Laura Kark, and siblings, Rebecca, Reese, Brayden, and Jake. Then my aunt and uncles, Shellie, Kevin, and Andy. Without their support and willingness to read, the story would never have made it. For the friends, there are too many to list, but you might find some of your names hidden throughout the story, wink.

## Glossary:

Important Characters:

Gaming Team:

Zephaniah Kote- Game tester and unofficially known as the infamous hacker, Asp3ct.

Keila Varner- A professional speed run gamer. Is a developer and writer of professional game walkthroughs.

Iris Christman- Starbucks barista and also another competitive gamer.

Coding Team:

Shane Miller- Game designer and developer of the game, Cloud City. Also, a white hat hacker and friend of Zephaniah Kote.

Majed Ayad- A professional coder, he is proudly from the Middle East and in an acclaimed coder back home.

Conor Carpenter- Part of the professional coding team. Not much is known except for his fascination with the environment.

Sarah Schiff- A member of the coding team.

Non-Player Characters:

Elana- Female archer instructor and shop owner in Altour. Sister of Guardsman Landan.

Innkeeper Goldsmith- Innkeeper of *The Hollow Quiver* in the Westgate area of Altour.

Guardsman Landan- Guardsman of the walls of Altour, known as being close friends with Innkeeper Baridac.

Guardsman Fern Payne- Guardsman of the walls of Altour.

Lady Adria- Queen of the Underground, ruler of the Thieves' Guild.

Belladonna- Second in command of the Thieves guild. Infamous for her child-like persona and pitch-black eye color.

Innkeeper Baridac Longbrew- Innkeeper of *The Tipsy Dwarf* in the White Bridge region of Altour. Known to be a superbly friendly dwarf.

Executives:

Joshua Sorrento- Vice President of Operations, is in charge of the problem-solving team.

Dr. Brandon Hobbs- Chief Executive Officer of Riverlight Incorporated.

Carson Reynolds- Chief Operations Officer of Riverlight Incorporated.

Jack Blake- Chief Technology Officer of Riverlight Incorporated.

Dr. John Jordan - President of Gaming Design

Dr. Sammy Vanderbelt- Vice President of Gaming Design

Other:

Officer Gerald- Police officer, lead investigator of the case. He is an older gentleman with a handlebar mustache.

Officer Spencer- Young police officer, second on the case. He wears skinny jeans and floral-patterned button downs.

Jeremiah Stone- Missing person, presumed dead by police.

Quality Rankings:

Legendary

Epic

Rare

Forged

Uncommon

Common

Fair

Poor

Substandard

Currency and Rates:

1 Gold = 100 Silvers

1 Silver= 200 Coppers

1 Copper = 5 Pennies

Magic Spells

Cure Wounds- *Asie*

Detect Trap- *Captionem*

Light- *Lux*

Protect from Poison- *Venenum*

Fire Ball- *Ignis*

Flame- *Fuego*

Final Character Level:

| Ranger Lv. 4<br>Money: 44 C | Mage Lv. 4<br>Money: 0 | Paladin Lv. 4<br>Money: 0 |
|---|---|---|
| HP: 170/170<br>MP: 20/20<br>Skills:<br>Archery Lv. 5<br>Duel Wielding Short Blades Lv. 2<br>Stealth Lv. 2<br>Trap Detection Lv. 1<br>Light Armor Lv. 1<br>Swimming Lv. 2<br>Climbing Lv. 1<br>Eavesdropping Lv. 1 | HP: 120/120<br>MP: 40/40<br>Skills:<br>Dagger<br>Quarter-staff Lv. 1<br>History<br>Investigation<br>Arcana<br>Battle Magic Lv. 4 | HP: 190/190<br>MP: 20/20<br>Skills:<br>Heavy Armor Lv. 2<br>Long Sword Lv. 3<br>Shields<br>Religion Lv. 1<br>Medicine<br>Healing Magic Lv. 1 |

Level Up publishing specialises in LitRPG and GameLit books. If you have enjoyed *A Glitch in the System* you might be interested in our other titles, which can be found at www.levelup.pub/books

To join our mailing list for news about forthcoming books and opportunities to be an ARC reader, just fill in the form on that page.

You can also find us on:

Facebook @LUPublishing

Twitter @LevelUpPub

And by searching for Level Up WhatsApp group

www.ingramcontent.com/pod-product-compliance
Lightning Source LLC
Chambersburg PA
CBHW030850030726
47495CB00005B/1463